PRAISE FOR
HEATHER TUCKER'S

# The Clay Girl

"It is the voice of the characters, the kindness of strangers, and the ingenuity and determination of our protagonist against terrible forces that make this story sing."—*San Francisco Chronicle*

"Tucker's rare gift of showing us beauty, hope, and humour amid profound trauma make *The Clay Girl* an extraordinary debut novel."
—*Toronto Star*

"A beautifully written story of strength and resilience, leading to ultimate victory over seemingly impossible challenges. This novel is full of those take-away-your-breath lines, the ones you want to write down and keep in your pocket for when you need them."
—AMERICAN BOOKSELLERS ASSOCIATION

"In Ari Appleton, Heather Tucker has created an unforgettable little girl whose resilience in the face of heartbreaking circumstances is remarkable. *The Clay Girl* tackles a difficult subject with tenderness, empathy, and unflinching honesty."—LYNNE KUTSUKAKE, AUTHOR OF *The Translation of Love*

# CRACKED POTS

# CRACKED POTS

*Heather Tucker*

*a misFit book*

Published by ECW Press
665 Gerrard Street East
Toronto, Ontario, Canada M4M 1Y2
416-694-3348 / info@ecwpress.com

Editor for the press: Michael Holmes / a misFit book

M I S F I T  Cover design: Michel Vrana

This is a work of fiction. Names, characters, places, and incidents either are the product of the author's imagination or are used fictitiously, and any resemblance to actual persons, living or dead, business establishments, events, or locales is entirely coincidental.

LIBRARY AND ARCHIVES CANADA CATALOGUING IN PUBLICATION

Title: Cracked pots : a novel / Heather Tucker.
Names: Tucker, Heather, 1954- author.
Description: "A misFit book".

Identifiers: Canadiana (print) 20210210389
Canadiana (ebook) 20210210397

ISBN 978-1-77041-599-7 (softcover)
ISBN 978-1-77305-812-2 (EPUB)
ISBN 978-1-77305-813-9 (PDF)
ISBN 978-1-77305-814-6 (Kindle)

Classification: LCC PS8639.U324 C73 2021 | DDC C813/.6—dc23

We acknowledge the support of the Canada Council for the Arts. *Nous remercions le Conseil des arts du Canada de son soutien.* This book is funded in part by the Government of Canada. *Ce livre est financé en partie par le gouvernement du Canada.* We acknowledge the support of the Ontario Arts Council (OAC), an agency of the Government of Ontario, which last year funded 1,965 individual artists and 1,152 organizations in 197 communities across Ontario for a total of $51.9 million. We also acknowledge the support of the Government of Ontario through the Ontario Book Publishing Tax Credit, and through Ontario Creates.

ONTARIO CREATES

ONTARIO ARTS COUNCIL
CONSEIL DES ARTS DE L'ONTARIO
an Ontario government agency
un organisme du gouvernement de l'Ontario

Canada Council   Conseil des arts
for the Arts      du Canada

Canadä

PRINTED AND BOUND IN CANADA

PRINTING: MARQUIS  5  4  3  2  1

*For my sister, Susanne Rayner,*
*the gold filling the cracks in this world.*

ONE

The train slows. Mechanical wizardry, air and friction working together, is bringing this massive locomotive to a precise stop. Mikey tells me this. At eight years old, he loves the physics involved. Me? I just wonder how I'll move my one hundred and twenty-six pounds of cells through the warped space and time ahead.

I know where I am without clearing the window; still, I wipe away the condensation. The familiar landmark comes into view. When I was eight, "JOHN 3:16" was painted in big letters on the barn's roof. Now, at sixteen, just rusty holes and a faint "OH 6" remain. My *Oh shit* point on each journey back to Toronto. It's here when I feel most stretched in two, pulled east, back to my aunts, to clay, to Jake—and forced west, to chaos, to waste, to—

*Aaron.*

*Bloody hell, Jasper, don't start stirring this up again.*

Outside, a girl races the train, hair flying like a charm of finches. Her hand lifts and—pop-pop-poppity-pop!

Mikey's head snaps from the pillow. "What's that?"

"Just a kid throwing firecrackers."

"Where are we?"

*Eight hundred miles and four long months from Cape Breton.* "Quebec."

The passenger car is hot as soup. Mikey tucks up, stretching a worn undershirt over summer-scraped legs. He studies my swollen cheek. "Does it hurt?"

"Really bad."

"I heard Missus Butters tell Huey that the rockslide was an omen."

Neck hairs startle up with the draft from doors opening. "You know the Missus is the Cove's tall tale spinner. She's always telling shivery stories. It was just the heavy rains and growing roots that caused it."

He scratches at a mosquito bite on his ankle. "Maybe so. Just seems off when water breaks rock. And, and . . . there was all that other stuff."

William, the train's steward, directs a roly-poly man our way. "Well, little miss, look what I've found." I'm years, and inches, past being little, but through all my rides, I can't recall a trip where William hasn't taken care of me.

The man is a doctor, conscripted from somewhere on the train. He plunks down, eyeing my cheek with half spectacles. "Good gracious. What happened here?"

Mikey says, "A rock dinged her."

"Now, who'd throw stones at such a pretty girl?" He opens his bag. "When'd this happen?"

"Friday."


Eyes open. Eyes closed. I see it. Birds rocketing from the ridge seconds before the sonic crack. Then a boulder, big as a bus, ripping away, cartwheeling into the ocean. Water, red with dirt, pluming. Rocks, stones, pebbles cascading, trickling, then—dead quiet. In the settling dust, I looked up. The path to the acres we named Moondance, gone. By a root, a young cedar swung like an acrobat. Atop the ridge, Jake stood, peering down, looking as terrified as me.

Weeks before, same night as men walked on the moon, Jake and I went all the way. Sleeping with a boy was still cosmic with newness, and there I was, in the rubble, sensing in three days, two nights, one morning, I'd be launched away.

Now, on the train heading further into Jakeless space, Mikey quavers, like the words are haunted. "And you know what?"

"What, son?"

"Our dog snatched Ari's shoe. Spinner ran circles before giving it back. Then, Ari met Huey walking a cranky foster. She took the baby so Huey could go off and take a pee and wouldn't you know it, a bear was blocking the path back. If not for all the holdups, Ari would've been right where it happened."

"So, instead, she caught a bit of shrapnel?"

"Yes." I bury a scream as the doctor digs.

"Quite the whale tale."

It is. The kind of yarn that will become a down-home legend, a ballad even. Mikey shrugs. "Maybe, but it's not a lie."

"Here's the trouble." A granite shard, smaller than the tip of an eyelash, is in his tweezers. Disinfecting stings, but the agony is gone—poof. He gives me a tiny tube. "Dab of this and it should settle right down."

William leans over the plush seat. "Imagine that: a beagle, a babe, and a bear kept you from being squashed. There's big magic in that."

"You see good ahead, William?"

"Truth?"

I lengthen my spine. "Give it to me straight."

"Dark roads to come." Into a small leather pouch, William drops ten pennies, then tosses it to me. "But fret not, 'cause one by one, I'll collect these and when the last coin drops, you'll be home."

"In the Cove, right?"

"On my whiskers, day'll come when this walrus and your

3

seahorse will dance along that shore, and you'll know that it's your own solid legs that carried you there."

Mikey asks, "Me too, William?"

"Sure as sure. But I suspect you'll travel back on a wing, laddie." He tips his hat and moves along.

Across the aisle, a lady, sleek as an eel, tucks her skirt away from the disruption that always surrounds me.

Mikey asks, "Hey, how'd William know Spinner's a beagle?"

"Aunties M&N say he's got second sight."

"Because he's walrus kin?"

"It's as good an answer as any."

"That doctor was a penguin."

"Right. My cheek does feel cooler."

"If I died, would my dragonfly die too?"

"Yeah, Kira would be gone, gone, gone. Inner animals are like those cleaner fish who live because other creatures need someone to eat their fungus."

"They're symbolic."

"Symbiotic."

"If I died, you could stay in Pleasant Cove."

"Nah. The Dick would just go after my sisters to force me back."

"You're just saying that so I don't feel like the worm that hooked you."

Mikey is indeed the millstone dragging me back, but he's guilt-weighted enough without me adding to it. "Think about it, bro. When you go fishing with Jake, does the bait have any say in what happens?" I pat down his sea-urchin hair. "The Dick's not letting me off his hook before all Len's money comes to me. Why'd you think he got hitched to my mum this summer?" Mikey's dad, Richard Irwin, aka the Dick, is husband number three, giving me an Oreo of dads, two complete shits, with soft, sweet Len Zajac in the middle. If Len had known the trouble his money would cause me, he'd have burned every dollar. "Um, while we're talking

4

Dickshit, think we better keep this whole animal friend thing hush-hush."

"So he can't comet you to the loony bin?"

"Commit. Yeah. And maybe keep under wraps that the Missus taught you to knit."

"Jacques Plante's a knitter and a goalie."

"The Dick thinks Plante's a sissy for wearing a mask."

"I hate hockey."

What Mikey hates is the boozy fury when the home team loses. "Worry less, bro. We'll come up with a lie that gets us out of crapdom on game nights."

"How come those Commandments say we shouldn't lie?"

"Because Moses never walked through our wilderness. Just imagine life in Toronto without Sabina helping us."

"It'd be awful, but why even think it?"

"Lies got Len and his family out of Poland. Sabina was the best liar in the resistance, helped the good guys win the war. It's just story-weaving and we're going to spin one that gets us out of crapdom for good."

"If Pops died, we could both live in Pleasant Cove."

"We'll get back. Jasper says so."

"Has Jasper always been with you?"

"Since the moment Huey and Jake found me bundled on the shore."

"Is he really real or pretend?"

"All I know is Jasper gets me started and stopped like the magic that gets this train where it's supposed to be."

"I never told anyone about my dragonfly, not 'til you." Mikey blots a bead of blood from my cheek before dabbing on a pearl of ointment. "How come everyone doesn't have a talking animal?"

"They do. Most just stop listening."

Mikey offers me his pillow and starts a round of our favourite game, Death to Dick by Alphabet. He singsongs, "Arsenic

5

applesauce. Bowling ball bomb. Cyanide cookies. Dynamite doughnuts. Electric eels. Fire-ant fog . . . Here's a new one, ground-glass gingersnaps."

"With our luck he'd just shit chandeliers and clog the toilet." There's pulsing under me as the train picks up speed, like Celtic drums. I relax into it, closing my eyes to eel lady's disapproval of Mikey in raggedy hand-me-downs, plotting murder, and of me in quote-scribbled jeans, talking crazy.

"Hemlock hamburgers. Icepick injections. Killer kangaroos."

The window's frame creates snapshots as the train pulls into Union Station. Aaron West. Expected. Mr. Ellis. Unexpected. Officer O'Toole. Disturbing. Mikey looks from the platform to me. "Maybe Pops was in a shootout slaughter." It's the most hopeful he's sounded since leaving Pleasant Cove.

I stuff down fear and pick up our gear: Mikey's small duffle, my carryall, and the sixteen years of Appleton baggage that weights me everywhere.

Before my foot leaves the step, O'Toole snags my arm and my summer of peace and love dissolves.

TWO

Without a hello, Aaron untethers Mikey's hand from mine. In a funeral hush, he says, "Come with me, buddy."

Inhale knots with exhale as I ready for news of an Appleton apocalypse.

Mr. Ellis, frantic, desperate, asks, "Ari, have you heard anything from Natasha Koshkin?"

"Natasha? From school? No. Why?"

"She's missing."

"No way."

"You hear from her this summer?"

"Um, couple of letters."

"Anything concerning in them?"

"No."

"Shit. Shit." Mr. Ellis is my teacher, mentor, and the most grounded person I know. Right now, he resembles a turtle flipped feet up. "Okay. I'm heading back to the Koshkin's. Police want you at the station."

O'Toole manhandles me to a cruiser. He opens the front door, seizing my braid as I make for the back. "Sit where you're told."

"Fuzz off."

"Get uppity with me and I'll have you over the hood."

O'Toole is the Dick's best bud. Never have I met anyone more enamoured with his penis, and I've known a few. "You want me to tell the Chief there's a mole in his ranks and how I happen to know it's on your pecker?"

He surrenders. Drives me to headquarters.

The Dick is manning the front desk. Sleeves rolled up. Phone held to his ear by his jowly cheek. With a finger flick he commands me over. "Listen up. This has the ears of the top brass. It's my ticket to detective." He sucks pastrami from his teeth. "Don't you go messing this up for me."

*Welcome home, Hariet.*

The station is jittery. I'm not surprised to see Ellis's other half, my art teacher, Mina Burn, helping. She sidesteps desks to reach me. "Ari, can you believe this?"

7

"No. What happened?"

"Natasha's family went to the Ex on Friday. She asked to take in the midway with friends. Promised her dad she'd meet them at the Shell Tower at four, but never showed."

"Natasha never messes up."

"No, she doesn't. They've questioned everyone. No one had plans with her."

"Why am I here?"

"We've been going over her diaries. You"—she hushes into my ear—"and Jasper are mentioned a lot. They'll ask. Imagine up a plausible explanation."

In Pleasant Cove, I'm Ari, clay-conjuring, fey girl, whispering to sea spirits. In Toronto, I'm crazy Hariet, talking to the voices in her head.

"Miss Appleton." A man in a rumpled suit lifts a folder, waves me to a room, eyes narrowing at my inflamed cheek. "You been in a fight?"

"No, sir. Just a mishap."

"Hmph. I'm Detective Halpern. Sit." The walls are the concentrated-urine colour of the unflushed toilet on the train. Smudges and bits of tape remain where papers have been ripped away. "So, where's it you've been?"

"Nova Scotia. I spend summers with my aunts, making pottery."

"Rough work?"

My hands are a wreck: chapped skin and fresh nicks layer over scars, from years of war—with fosters, with Mum, with myself. "Wood carving. Chisels are tricky."

He leans across the table. Palms flat. Eyes fixed. "Level with me here. She just running?"

I meet his gaze. "No way. Not Natasha."

"Drugs?"

"Never."

He lights a cigarette. "You tellin' me there's a kid coming out of the sixties without testing the waters?"

"Wasn't her thing."

"Is it yours?"

My head shake is more a wobble than definitive.

"Tell me about your friendship."

"Walked together after school to collect our brothers. Shared books. We'd hang at my aunt's boutique making stuff while our brothers played."

"Stuff?"

"Tie-dye, purses, junk like that."

"She date?"

"Don't think she was allowed."

"Crushes?"

"Ringo. Elvis. Micky Dolenz."

"Who?"

"Drummer for the Monkees."

He peruses a coffee-ringed file. "In her diary she mentions someone named Chase?"

"He's my friend, from my old school. He and Nat were on the mayor's youth council."

"You know where we can reach him?"

"California. He got a scholarship to UCLA."

"How about an Aaron West?"

"Natasha mentioned him?"

He reads from a red leather journal, tiny key suspended from a chain. "Aaron West is dreamier than Brando."

"Natasha met him at a student art show. He came to see my painting."

"And you know him how?"

I weigh the depth and width of the truth and give the top inch. "He was my teacher in grade eight. I had this, um, family thing and couldn't keep my dog, so his parents took him for me. Mr. West is one of those Big Brother guys for my stepbrother, Mikey."

"You're Irwin's kid, aren't you?"

"My mum's been with him a few years."

"Mike's his kid, no? What's he needing a Big Brother for?"

Shadows, real and imagined, move on the flip side of the mirror. "He helps because Mikey's mom's messed up. Natasha only met Aaron the one time."

"Sure about that? I'd say she had a major crush."

"Pretty sure. Besides, he was in Kenya all summer."

"And do you have a boyfriend?"

"Yes."

"This Jasper?"

"Ah, no, Jake."

"The fiddler?"

"Yes. How——?"

"Mentions him too."

"Did Nat write she wanted someone like Jasper?"

"Something like."

"It's not about a boy."

"What then?"

"Um, well, she asked how I could draw like I do. We were studying the Greek muses in history. I said I had a muse named Jasper. She wished she had one too."

"He's not a real person?"

"Just the name I give to my imagination."

I feel a kick. *Just. Just?*

*Shut it.*

"So, are all these J's pretend?"

"All?"

His eyes slide up, then back to an entry. "I'd give anything to be Ari. With all the J's, it's like she's living *Little Women* for real." That anyone, for a second, would want my crap-full life leaves me mute. "Well?"

"Um, I have five sisters: Jennah, June, Jacquie, Jory, and Jillianne. Nat just thought having sisters would be nice."

"And you're . . . Harriet?"

"Yeah." I sigh. "And misspelled with just one R."

"Tell me, would ya, why all these crushes on boys connected with you?" He blows smoke over my head. "And why's your name coming up with every person I question? 'Ask Hariet.' 'Ari might know something.' 'Have you talked to that Appleton girl?' Huh?"

*Because I'm trouble, from trouble.* "Don't know. We weren't that close."

"Come on. Your name's on every other page of her diary."

"She thought my life was, I don't know, interesting."

"And hers was a bore?"

"No, sir. Ordered."

"Would she have gone for a walk on the wild side?"

"Can't picture Natasha stepping outside the lines, ever."

"So, good girl. No drugs. No boys. Nothin'." He paces like a penned lion. "You know anything about a guy she met in High Park?"

"She mentioned him in a letter. Bobbie something."

"Story. Bobbie Story. Know where we can find him?"

"No idea."

"Gimme something here." His "gimme" has a punch.

"Um, Nat wrote he was dreamier than Troy Donahue. She compared people to stars. So maybe sandy hair and gray eyes?"

"Would she just talk to some strange guy?"

"She'd talk to anyone, especially if it was about a book."

"Not following."

"He asked if she wanted to go to Arrakis. It's from the book she was reading. She'd dig that."

"What book?"

"*Dune*."

Mina knocks and opens the door. "Sandwich cart's here. What can I get you?"

"Corned beef."

Mina asks, "Ari?"

"Where's Mikey?"

"Aaron took him to Sabina's."

"Can you call and see how he is? And tell her I need a few dozen peanut butter sandwiches, heavy on the jam."

"Will do."

Halpern leans against the mirror. "Explain."

"Mikey's best buds with Nat's brother. He'll be worried."

"No, what's with the picnic?"

"When we finish here, I'll go to the Village. Kids hanging in doorways hear things. Food's currency."

"We've combed every inch of Yorkville."

"No offence, sir, but cops would have better luck combing a Rastafarian's hair than the Village."

"And you'll have luck because . . . ?"

"I wait tables at the Riverboat and my sister runs the outreach at the church. People know us."

Mina arrives with sandwiches and Halpern asks, "You teach art, right?"

"Yes."

"Sketch guy's on holiday. You think you could give me something that'd look more like she did on Friday than her school pic?"

"Ari could, better than me."

"That right?"

"I could try."

"Right then." He flips his notebook closed. "Things arranged for tomorrow's search?"

12

Mina says, "Staff are at your disposal. Busses will be at the ready."

"I'll have uniforms at the school by eight to brief everyone."

"I loaned her that book."

"What's that, kid?"

"*Dune*. The book she was reading." Burnt coffee collides with the smoke-clogged air. I ask Mina, "Did you talk to Sabina?"

"Mikey can stay as long as needed and her kitchen's mobilized."

Halpern says, "Leave it 'til morning."

"No disrespect, sir, but only thing standing in the Village in the morning are the lamp posts."

Mina says, "Ellis is picking up the sandwiches. We'll go along."

"Anything else you can think of, Ari?" he asks.

"She collected buttons."

"Buttons?"

I sigh. "Sewing buttons. She liked them because they held things together."

THREE

Yorkville is worn out. Dropped-out humanity clusters on steps and doorways. They talk to us for the food, a few because they remember Mina and Ellis as teachers who gave a shit. Or maybe they warm to us because they're a little hopeful that somebody is looking for someone.

We run out of sandwiches without a crumb in return. Ellis asks, "Where to? Sabina's?"

"Let's try the drop-in."

The church is crammed with tripped-out kids. My sister Jory hops, steps, and jigs over bodies when she sees me. She's prettier than that model, Twiggy. More ink has been added over the summer, but mercifully the butterfly around her eye remains the only tattoo on her face. She snaps me into a hug. "Cheese 'n' Christ on a cracker, look who's back."

Sister number four is as substantial as a licorice rope, but here in the Village, she's Jory of Arc, fighting the Sixties War. I hold tight and ask, "You hear anything about the girl that went missing from the Ex?"

"Just trash."

"Like what?"

"Ah . . . her dad's a Russian spy and she's being held 'til he gives up secrets."

"But Mr. Koshkin makes candy."

"These kids don't know where *they* are let alone anyone else. Come on. Best thing we can do is get the elders praying."

"Um, I'll leave you to get God in the loop. You know where Edjo might be hanging?"

"Mynah Bird, maybe?"

I lighten my pocket of travelling cash, knowing Jory will turn it into bread for her flock and maybe a little holy smoke for herself.

She stuffs it in her jeans. "Rock it for Jesus, sis."

We descend, stepping over wasted souls on the stairs. "I love my sister, but the God stuff makes my teeth scratch."

Mina says, "Well then, Aaron's new friend's going to give you hives."

"What? A girlfriend?"

"Nurse he met in Kenya. Very, um, zealous."

"She came back with him? Like with him, with him?" I

shouldn't care, not when I love Jake, but Aaron is . . . *What is he, Jasper?*

*Our ocean when we're stuck in Toronto.*

"She's finishing her degree at U of T."

Ellis says, "She's a real Mother Teresa."

"You forgetting I have a mother Theresa? No prize there."

The street is electric. I follow the current toward a tangle of Harleys and spot the leader of the pack. Edjo reeks of weed, leather, and fried chicken as he mauls me in a hug. "Ari-mi-amigo, where you been?"

"Paradise."

"You find that sister of yours?"

"Only in my dreams. Listen, the girl that went missing from the CNE. You hear anything?"

"Nada." He pulls hard on a joint. "You know her?"

"Yeah. From school."

"I'll ask around."

"Appreciated." I inhale his exhale before returning to Ellis.

"Ari, how is it you're cozy with a Vagabond?"

"He and June had a thing back in the day. She's like a melanoma. Once she's under your skin, you can't shake her."

Ellis's hand lands soft on my shoulder. "How long's it been?"

"Five years. June may've disappeared but at least she left clues. How could someone like Natasha vanish without cosmic trumpets sounding?"

"There were a couple of sightings on the midway, but that's it."

The last night of the summer of '69 has the Village jumping with freshmen and bikers, greasers and junk-sick runaways. *Where have all the flower children gone, Jasper?*

Mina says, "There's always chatter at the Riverboat."

I measure the line snaking up the stairs of the coffee house. "Let's go around back."

When I open the door, Crystal has a tray on her left hand, three mugs looped in the fingers of her right, sweat soaking her blouse, and a told-you-so smile. "Ha. Knew you wouldn't let Mikey come back alone. Now, help, please. I'm on my own here. We're outta glasses. Get to it. Plate up the strudel and keep it coming."

I tie back my storm of hair. Rummage through my inventory of tie-dye in the storage room and find a clean tank.

Wobbly legged, tray loaded with water, I enter the packed house, thick with smoke, music—and life. The tray empties before making it down a single row. A regular says, "Hey, Ari. Nice headlights."

My boobs are a B-minus at best, but they always plump a little after a summer of hearty East Coast fare. "Charming as ever, Lewis." I drape my cleavage with a red-checked towel before bending over. "You hear anything about the girl who went missing?"

"Zilch. She's from your school, eh?"

"Yeah. Same grade as me."

"Put them boots up as a reward and I'll find something to deliver."

I'm wearing Len's steel-toed work boots, now painted with the finesse of a Dutch master and the funk of Kandinsky. They fit in a relative way, my feet are proportionate to my length, which is to say, significant. And Len's feet were small in proportion to his goodness. It's astonishing really that his feet were able to support his kindness. "Lewis, you find some intel and I'll paint anything you want."

"Anything?"

"Yep. Just know I use a hot needle to etch in the design."

A preppy guy in the adjoining booth says. "Excuse me. Ari, is it?"

"Not yet, but I'm working on it."

"Pardon?"

Lewis says, "The name Ari. She's growing into it. She's a bit . . ." Finger circles temple, indicating my lunacy. "Dad's a pig."

The preppy asks, "He's a cop?"

Lewis oinks as the guy reads my face, line by undefined line, zeroing in on my fat cheek. "Do I know you from somewhere, Almost-Ari?"

"I'm unthinkable, therefore unknowable."

"Intriguing. Could I trouble you for another coffee?"

When I return to the kitchen, Mina says, "You're looking a little chartreuse. Sit. I'll water the herd."

I nab a stool and take over slapping sandwiches together. Crystal flies in, barking, "Three ham, two salami, six cheese."

"The guy behind Lewis ordered a coffee."

Crystal hoists up a loaded tray. "Good luck to him."

Hours pass. The crowd ebbs and swells. I'm up to my elbows in soapy water, asleep on my feet, dreaming about the nest, my attic escape, just a hop, skip, and climb down the alley. There, I'll find silence, a featherbed, the plush dog Aaron gave me . . . I sense a shadow in the doorway. I blink, trying to place the man in a fedora. "Detective Halpern?"

"Just checking in. Anything?"

"Just crap like her dad's a spy."

"Heard that one. Your teachers go?"

"Yeah. They needed sleep."

"Let's go. I'm seeing you home."

"No. I'll just crash here."

"I'm not losing another kid. Not on my watch."

"But there're hours 'til closing."

"You weren't scheduled to work in the first place and that sketch is priority one. Move it."

As I'm escorted out, music and conversations hush, draft dodgers turn to the walls, ragers against the establishment raise a glass.

17

Halpern drives me to crapdom and pulls in behind the Dick's sedan, waiting as I walk the plank.

*What kind of shit detective delivers a kid to the most perilous place on Earth?*

*Who could imagine life behind these walls, Jasper?*

A hip thrust opens the peeling door. Smoke and rotting lives hit like a beached tuna nine days dead. To my left, TV light fluoresces off two months of unfolded laundry mounded on the sofa. Odds are O'Toole is snoring under the pile. Rod Serling says, "A frightening tale for the more imaginative among us, next week on *The Twilight Zone*." The tinny do-do-do-do–do-do-do-do of the closing credits creeps through the dark house.

*Let's just split.*

*The Missus says to march straight at the hardest thing to be done and box it square on d'ears.*

*Christ, you're annoying.* I can't face locating Mum in this cesspit, so I head to the second hardest, a kitchen left in the hands of grievously inept humans. My boots fight against the sticky linoleum. Light averse creatures dive for cover when I flip the switch. *Hoooly shit.* The counter is a heaped jumble of crusted dishes, bottles, wrappers, half-empty tins. I poke at a plaid slipper atop a plate. *What the . . . ?*

*That skat is from a—*

*Mouse. A really big mouse.* I hear a creak on the steps. Waking the Dick is as risky as stepping on a grizzly's ingrown toenail. I turn, praying he'll have on underwear, boxers, not tighties. "Todd?"

"Alls I can say is thanks bejesus it's you and not a rat."

A summer in the company of socialized humans has Mikey's brother Todd in PJ pants and a T-shirt. He's still a mountain of an eighteen-year-old, but it's solid heft. "Thought you were in Rockton."

"Job's done for now." His face forever holds the expectation of a hopeful infant. "Figured Mikey might need me. Where'd you stash him?"

"Sabina's."

"Good plan. Ease him back into this shit hole."

Dick Irwin has four offspring. From his first wife: Ricky, the soldier boy. I once loved him like any fourteen-year-old would fall for the knight who takes a punch for her. And Ronnie, aka Devil Girl. Then there's Todd, from another mother and same age as Ronnie (let it be said again, the Dick is a big dick). And eight-year-old Mikey, son of flighty, drug-stuck Laura.

When I first arrived in crapdom, Todd was set to become the fabric that covered the chair in front of the TV. Now he's a veterinary assistant and what he lacks in appearance he makes up for in chivalry.

He says, "You believe this mess? Don't know where to start."

"Bleach. Barrels of bleach."

"Not gonna help this." He opens the door to the back porch and flicks on the light. Two months of putrefying garbage surpasses the windowsills.

"Oh . . . help me, Rhonda."

"Gotta clean this out ASAP." He tilts a box with a broomstick, uncovering a rat the size of the Dick's boot, belly up, legs stiff, whiskers singed. "Likely electrocuted itself."

"Good news is it's dead?"

"You can be damn sure it has family."

"We can't bring Mikey back here."

"Ah, he's an Irwin. He's tougher than he looks."

"I'm not worried about his mettle. He'll just drive us squirrelly insisting on a funeral for every creature we execute."

It's two a.m. before the Everest of dishes is down to several molehills and five crusted pots. Todd says, "Let's leave these to soak."

"You working tomorrow?"

"No. I was gonna help with the search." He steps on a bag, detonating the reek of rotten banana. "But this needs sorting before the place goes up in flames."

We nimble-foot over junk piled in the hallway and crap littering the stairs. "Why didn't you stay in Rockton, really?"

"Honestly? Couldn't see Mikey here on his own and never in a million years did I think you'd be stupid enough to come back." A whiff of summer sneakers escapes as he opens the door to the boys' room.

"Can you get your room ready for him?" I ask.

"Washer's broken."

"Figures."

"I could haul a load to the laundromat in the wagon."

"That'd take a month of Sundays. I'll ask Aaron for loan of his jeep."

I head to the bathroom and there is Mum, duchess of crapdom, slumped against the throne. When I left eight weeks ago, she was puking in the toilet. Now she has the frayed pink bathmat bunched under her head, an oozy cold sore on the corner of her mouth, and—*alas*, a pulse in her neck.

I wipe the seat and pee. Usually I can pinpoint what magic carpet has her flying. When stoned, she's easy. Angry when piss-drunk. Jittery on uppers. Messy on downers, and sick, sick, sick when she mixes the shit. It's hard to reconcile the once fierce, razor-witted woman with this deflated pile of skin.

Her eyes roll open. "Jilli?"

"No. It's Ari."

"Oh, Elsie, I have the fuel. The few. Th-th-the flu."

She's paper-light to hoist up. "Come get to bed."

Their room smells like farts and looks like a Goodwill dumpster. The Dick graces the bed, gape-mouthed, stained undershirt, tighty-whities splayed. As I load Mum in, the Dick rolls over and

20

sort of loves her up. The treasure here? Knowing what I could become if I don't pay attention.

When trapped in crapdom, I'm forced to sleep in a corner of Devil Girl's satanic cave. Ronnie is starkers, leg hanging over the edge of her bed like an albino python. Some pimply faced boy is passed out on my cot.

Backing out, I spear my foot on one of her pitchfork earrings, collapsing back onto debris. "Does no one in this bloody house ever pick up their shit!"

The boy on my cot belches, the sulphury stink hits like a bomb.

Ronnie lifts her head. "Hey, bitchface. You're back."

"Yeah, let the good times roll."

"Hey, you hear about that Natasha chick?"

"Some. What's the street buzz?"

"Scuttle is them sideshow freaks at the Ex snatched her. That monkey boy gives me the heebie-jeebies." She returns to the pillow like a stoned sloth.

A train ride away, there is a windowed room in a stone cottage. Sea treasures, books, and photos line the shelves. My pillows smell of lavender and the sheets of a summer clothesline. I close the door and head down to my only sanctuary here, Mikey's fort in the mouldy cellar. It's a metal shipping container, six feet long, four feet high, and three wide. There's an air mattress on the bottom and a flashlight on a hook. A treasured Zajac featherbed explodes like an over-ready dandelion as I rip it from its plastic cocoon. I spread the comforter under and pull it over me knowing that where I am is safer and warmer than wherever Natasha is.

*Can a house fall like a rock cliff, Jasper?*
*Rats chewing wires could do it.*
*Ashes, ashes, let it all fall down.*

## FOUR

The fort has a delicious way of warming. I stretch like a content-ed pup, soaking in the quiet as light fans through the mesh vents. My eyes stay closed, remembering Jake's muscled goodness, long and naked, beside me.

*Police sketch. Borrow jeep. Laundry. Groceries. Rat traps. Disinfect crapdom. Check on Mikey. School?*

*For frig's sake. Can you not give me ten minutes?*

*Don't say I didn't warn you when the Dick has you clipping toe-nails he hasn't been able to reach for two months.*

Without risking a pee, I'm out the door, running the twelve blocks to the Village. I zip down the alley, take the zigzag of steps two at a time, unlock the deadbolt, and skit into my attic nest. The air is stale with summer heat, cinnamon, linseed oil, and weed. I crack the windows and a hint of autumn floats in. Sister number three, Jacquie, owns the building. She made this hiding place for me before escaping to Poland. In the chaos of my world, it is Nirvana—divine ground, bliss. I collapse into my feathery chair and survey the totems suspended in the window. *Tell me we're not adding another absence to our collection, Jasper.*

Only silence. Not even a squeak from the floors beneath or the street outside.

I resist the lure of sleep, and shower. The pipes cough, sput-ter, water running rust, orange, peach, then clear. Aunt Mary's detangling shampoo smells of Pleasant Cove berries and strips the cigarette stench from my hair.

Len's old flannel shirt hangs on the back of the door. His scent has long been washed out, but the remembrance of his arm on my shoulder remains as I slip it on. The nest is always well stocked with non-perishables. Something Len's cousin Sabina learned in the war. I lighten my tea with powdered milk; fill a plate with nuts, seeds, and sugary oat bars; tuck on my chair; and start the sketch.

*Maybe she fell in the water.*

*When did Natasha ever step near the edge?*

*Sometimes we don't see the edge.*

*Or it just breaks away.*

My pencil blends her school picture with the "last seen" description: chestnut hair ponytailed, not quaffed like this photo. Pedal pushers, tie-dyed tank, fringed bag. From her painted Keds to the beaded thong securing her ponytail, she's branded by Ari art. *Crap, Jasper, you think this rotten Appleton tainted her?*

*Doing crafts can't spoil anything. Besides, you're not that important. If you went missing, they'd just wonder what took so long.*

*Yeah.* I rummage through my pencil crayons.

*Xerox it before you colour it.*

*See, that's why I talk to you. Seahorses have a practicality about them that the Almighty patently lacks.*

I tie up Len's boots and step into the day. *Tap your heels three times and remember you're the wizard behind your destiny.*

*Deep, Jasper.*


While Jarvis CI's student body searches the lakeshore, Mina and I tuck-up to a makeshift worktable at the police station. Mina flags diary entries while I colour copies of the sketch. She studies my face, like an art lover might gander at a Picasso. "I'm used to you leaving here with bruises, but not coming back with a doozie like that. What happened?"

"Rock talk."

"Say what?"

I recount the rock fall. "According to Missus Butters, the earth was sending me a message."

"Which was?"

"It's time for me to be picking up my own rocks and putting them where they belong."

"You do that more than any other kid I've taught."

"Not really, if not for my sisters, my aunts, the Zajac tribe, you, Ellis, Aaron, I'd be a directionless pile of rubble." I recall the blade of sun cutting through the dust cloud. "The Missus said one day I'll pick up a heavy, heavy thing and it will feel light and it will be light and I'll know that every cell in me is set right."

"That's lovely."

"She said it's my aria, my song-poem."

"Your story too, it seems. A split rock's a good metaphor for your double life."

"Pure schizo, eh? East and west hemisph*Ari*."

Mina closes Nat's diary and picks up a green pencil. "Tell me about your summer."

"What can I say? Mikey rose like a phoenix."

"And you?"

"A man walked on the moon." A smile feels wrong under present circumstances, but one emerges remembering starry nights, a summer house, and two aunties giving Jake and me space to discover the rightness of things. "All I can say is it's a good thing you took me to that clinic and got me on the pill."

"So, poetry? Soixante-neuf, sweet sixty-nine, summer lovin' with a fiddler fine."

"Mina. I'm shocked."

"I may be decades past sixteen, but oh, I remember first love." She fans her neck. "Well, Jake and you'll manage. Don't see how Mikey would've handled Nat's disappearance on top of the mess in that house."

Detective Halpern comes flying through, jacket half on. "Found her purse near the Redpath refinery. Perry, radio ahead.

24

Clear civilians from the scene. Get Norman in with the dogs. I want every available man on the scene, pronto."

Unlike my backpack, which involves an extensive rummage to find whatever I'm looking for, Natasha's purse was an organizational masterpiece: Band-Aids, tissues, sewing kit, manicure set, treats, always treats.

"Don't give up hope, Ari."

I meet Mina's huge eyes. "Give me one plausible hope."

"I can't think the worst. I just can't." She moves conversation from worst to bad. "How's your mum?"

"A void. Devoid. All six of her girls could vanish and the only thing she'd notice is a shortage of pockets to pick." The auburn of Natasha's hair is warm, like her, and I colour more pictures. "How can someone oblivious to time, place, and person find their way home from a bar and Natasha's lost out there?"

"Don't know, kiddo." Mina chins to the door and I turn.

No matter how much I love Jake, Aaron West makes my stomach do a double back flip. We're an odd equation. He's almost ten years older, but I have sixteen years of shadowlife on him. His positives take away from my negatives and the order in his life is drawn to the bedlam of mine. Every Sunday we meet at the lake for an update on my dog, Zodiac, and a charting of our stars. There's a solid chalk line between us that we never cross—well, maybe it gets smudged from time to time but in a supportive, not slutty, way.

We collide in a hug. "Geez, I'm glad you're back. Didn't have a chance to even say hi yesterday. Any word?"

I pull away. "They found her purse."

"That good or ominous?"

"Natasha separated from her purse is a bird plucked of feathers. It doesn't happen naturally."

"Is Detective Halpern here?"

"Just left."

"I'll leave this at the desk then." He clips together papers. "Cadets and scouts from Scarborough to Port Hope, parents and senior students from Oakridge, Birchmount, and Porter are at the ready for tomorrow's search. And Salvation Army's providing lunch."

"How'd you pull all this together in a day?"

"Had help." He turns and—*Oh. My. Goddess.* "Ari, this is Linda."

"So nice to meet you, Ari." Her extended hand is like a dish soap model's. Mine? A lizard with eczema.

Now, I know I'm a head-turner, even with this bruised face. All the Appletons are. With the J's, it's their sunshine hair and forget-me-not eyes. For me, it's my party of curls and the ocean in my eyes, gray nearing violet. Len's mother, Babcia, says I've the ethereal kiss of the netherworld about me, but this girl has the brush strokes of heaven. Huge green eyes, silky cape of indigo hair, peachy cheeks on translucent skin, and lips that turn the tongue to memories of candyfloss. Next to her, I'm a Komodo dragon with a tragic perm. I straighten. "May reason have mercy on your soul, Aaron West."

His smile accentuates his singular dimple. "I assure you my soul is safe."

Linda says, "Please know I'm praying for your friend."

"And has Jehovah gotten back to you with any intel?"

"Matthew 10:30."

"Good to know the Almighty's numbered the hairs on Nat's head, now if He could let us know the location of those follicles, that would be divine."

"You know scripture?"

"Oh, I love fiction."

Aaron puts a lid on my spite. "So, how can we help?"

"Could I borrow the jeep for a couple of hours tomorrow?"

"Sure."

I savour Linda's flush of surprise at Aaron so easily loaning me his sacred wheels. "And let Sabina know I'll get Mikey as soon as crapdom is habitable."

"She said she'd keep him."

"It's a hike and a half to get him to school from her place."

Linda says, "He was pretty upset when we left him last night."

I quash the urge to tell her to back her petite perfection out of our messes. "Yeah, leaving the Cove for crapdom is horror enough without adding this."

Aaron looks straight in my eyes, at home with my chaos. "Could we connect on Sunday? Catch up?"

Linda takes ownership of his arm. "That'd be so nice."

"Our bench. Regular time." I back away. "Bring pictures of my dog."

FIVE

Several cops sort items from the morning's search onto tables: socks, toys, hats, flip-flops, sunglasses, nappies, a scarf so diaphanous I imagine it peeling away from wet sand like sunburned skin. Detritus of picnic outings and moonlit romps. An officer uses a pencil to lift a pair of panties. "Her mother thought she'd be wearing underthings with a day written on them."

It's astonishing how many people leave their underpants behind, from big bloomers to lacy bits. "Can't imagine Natasha wearing Wednesday on a Friday," I say.

"What's that?"

"They come in a set, a pair for every day of the week. Wednesday panties on Friday would be breaking the rules." I survey the flotsam spread out in the cavernous space. "Wendy will have a better eye for something that might be Nat's."

The officer says, "She's just getting an update. Be along any minute."

I ask, "Any news?"

"Just the purse. Seems nothing's missing. Dogs are quiet." He looks at me. "That's a good sign she's not there."

"And the rosy side of that would be?"

Light and Natasha's best friend, Wendy, flood in with the opening of the door. "Oh, Ari. Can you believe this?" She's a knot of despair, snagging me in a hug. "We have to find her."

Words turn to stretched noise as the person behind her comes into focus. The preppy guy from the Riverboat cocks his head and says, "This is weird. We met the other night."

"Oh? I . . . I don't remember you."

"The Riverboat?"

Knowing what boys like him want from Appleton tarts, my head shake is a definitive no.

"Explains why I never got my coffee." He smiles, soul-winning like a pastor. "I'm Byron Silver."

Wendy says, "Byron's doing a placement here. From McGill."

"Wouldn't Montreal police be a lot closer?" I ask.

"My dad knows a guy upstairs. Supposed to be working on reform programs for teen offenders, but right now help is needed logging all this stuff."

Wendy asks, "Are you studying social work, Byron? That's what I'm going into."

"Haven't made up my mind. I'll likely follow my dad into medicine. He's just taken the post as head of orthopedics at the children's hospital here."

Wendy says, "Ari's from Montreal."

"Really? Whereabouts?"

"More places than I can remember. Too many to forget."

"Maybe we're related. Are you frog or les rosbifs?"

"Lioneagle, with a little seahorse on the side."

"Interesting lineage."

"Remains to be seen." I grab my pack and head over to the officer. "I put out some lines in the Village. I'm going to see if I caught anything."

I head toward Yorkville, quickening with the weird shift in light. The sky is sharply divided, black and postcard blue. Raindrops, big as pennies ping the cement. Chances are good the door to the Riverboat will be open for cleaning after a long weekend. Using it as a throughway to my nest always feels like a Narnian closet to a safer world. I jump down the steps and the handle turns. I sprint through, ignoring voices calling, "Ari?"

"Ari."

"Ari!"

Before my eyes adjust to the dim interior, I'm out the back, racing the rain down the alley, up the stairs, and in the door. A thunder-smash echoes the click of the lock.

As I smooth my jitters, knock-knock-knocking, more insistent than the rain pelting the window, rattles the door. "Ari. It's Mina. Open up before lightning strikes these metal steps."

*Oh, frig. Frig. Frig. Frig.* She pours in as I open the door. "You . . . you can't be here."

"The way you ran through, we thought there was trouble."

"Why're you at the Riverboat?"

"Only time I could steal away without Ellis knowing. Bernie's helping me with a fiftieth birthday surprise." She pulls her soaked blouse from her skin. "Just needed to check you're all right. Didn't expect the skies to split."

"This really is terrible." I fetch a towel and bulky sweater. "You can't know about this place."

She changes behind the ancient apothecary chest, used for paints and crafty clutter. Then circles my nest, absorbing spines of books, batiks on the windows, origami suspended from the rafters, my gallery of sketches. "Are you squatting?"

"Right." Air snits through my nose. "Someone like me must be stealing space."

"Oh, get over your doubting self. You know I'd cheer any kid that created a secret like this."

"It's my escape from gravity."

"You need it. The Dick and company are dead weights." She fills and plugs in the kettle. "This place reminds me of the 'shell' Ellis has constructed in our basement." She helps herself to a raspberry paczki as she examines the totems hanging in my window. "Oh, I love this."

"They're my presents and absences."

She examines the brass button, a monkey with rhinestone eyes.

"That's my latest addition."

"Is it a present or an absence?"

"Don't know. Found it in a thrift store in Halifax. Natasha wrote she was planning a big sweet sixteen party. It's her present."

"She does love the Monkees. She went to their concert just last week. Her dad said that he was so nervous at her going, he waited in the parking lot 'til it was over. It's so awful what they're going through."

"An absence is bigger in a family like theirs. Nat's mom knew down to her underwear what she was wearing." I look past the totems to quick-silver rain. "If an Appleton went missing, Mum wouldn't even be able to get our names straight."

"Nature of addiction to kill brain cells."

"I tell you, Mina, a head of cabbage has more insight. Even when she had firing neurons, she still never saw me."

"It can feel that way sometimes."

"When I was just weeks old, she left me on the shore as the tide was coming in. My grandma said it was on purpose, because I was another bloody girl. More likely, she put me down, got distracted, and forgot she had me." Each word hangs like jagged glass, best left untouched.

"I remember the day you landed in my class, you had on the most exquisite embroidered blouse."

"You remember what I had on?" She nods and I smile. "Babcia made that for my birthday." I finger five totems. "These are my sisters. They've always kept me safe."

"From your dad?"

"Mum mostly. I wasn't old enough for my dad's tastes. He checked out before totally screwing me." I set a circle of bone into a spin. "The ocean gave me this bit. The hole in the centre seemed like a good metaphor for Vincent Appleton." I journey over my helpers from A to Z, aunties to Zajacs. Two stone turtles clack like Newton's cradle. "This pair are you and Ellis."

"Oh, Ellis and his tortoise muse, Rochester. The pair of you are so much alike."

"Do you think we're crazy?"

She cradles her tea in a fat pottery mug. "Delightfully so. And in the thirty-plus years I've been with Ellis, that turtle in his head has guided us to adventures more extraordinary than I ever could've imagined."

"Ellis is the only being I've ever known that really seems to get this thing I have with Jasper."

Mina's smile is warm and sweet like Sabina's pastry. "I know the one seahorse in the centre is Jasper. The other one?"

"Jake's Jewel."

"Should've known. Rain's stopped. I gotta split." She places her mug in the sink and winks a promise. "I won't tell another soul about this place, but can I tell Ellis?"

31

"Yeah."

"Thanks. He'll appreciate knowing you have a shell to shelter in."

After she leaves, the silence is big. I want Jake. I want an ocean walk with M&N. I need to sit at the wheel and turn pots. I should go to Sabina's and give her a break from Mikey and Mikey a break from his worries. I rummage my shelves for some weed.

Enough is stashed for a float, a spin, a peaceful drift and a night without dreams.

SIX

As we approach police headquarters, suited men hurtle toward me, hurling questions. "You a friend of the missing girl?"

"Any developments?"

"Your name?"

"Is it true—?"

Ellis snaps, as turtle spirits do. "Back off." He holds the heavy door open for me. "They're like a squabble of gulls fighting for scraps at the Koshkins."

"Her parents must be going crazy."

"They're just shattered. Um, Nat's aunt asked if you could walk Alex and Joey to school starting Monday."

"Ugh, school."

"Listen. There's an independent study package at Jarvis. Go grab one and just tuck somewhere peaceful after you see them safe inside."

"I can skip classes?"

"Don't seahorses fare better sheltering from rough seas?"

"No question."

"And you don't need to be here now. There're enough volunteers to help sift through everything."

"Just came to get the Dick to sign Mikey's school forms. Peace out."

As I pass the clot of Natasha's friends pawing through the jetsam gathered on the searches, the student dick, Byron Silver, quick-steps over. "Hey, Almost-Ari. You here to help?"

"Can't. Have to go murder some rats."

"Heard you were imaginative."

"Stop hearing about me."

"Whoa. I'm just trying to get to know everyone."

"I'm no one worth knowing."

"Maybe I'm someone you should know."

"I'm usually the affable sort, Mr. Silver, but presently I'm in turtle retreat mode."

"What?"

"I'm shellbound and unreachable."

"Nothing I like better than a challenge."

"No challenge here. Just a foregone illusion."

"Pardon? Wait."

"Vermin wait for no man." I move toward the sound of the Dick's grunting, get the requisite signatures, then head crapward in Aaron's pristine black jeep.

I pull up behind a rusty Ford pick-up. A dozen cartons are stacked in the back. As I haul in supplies, Todd calls from the boys' room. "Ari? Come see." He's standing on a chair, sliding curtains onto a rod. There's a marine-themed comforter on Todd's bed. "Check out Mikey's tent."

I pull back the flap. His camp cot is draped with a matching quilt. "What the heck?"

33

"Your sister dropped off gear ·for Mikey. Said she'd just redone Dean's room and thought we'd like his old stuff. I pitched all the closet junk. Sealed every hole. This room's vermin free."

"Think I could fit in the closet?"

"In a pinch." He places a pillow on his bed. "My boss gave me loan of a truck."

"Good. No way can I haul garbage in Aaron's jeep."

"Let's get 'er done."

I load ratnip—cereal, chips, bread, saltines—into a metal cooler. Todd considers the large cage housing a mountain of bird shit belonging to the Dick's dead parrot, Cunt. "Do we dare take that to the dump?"

"It's a sacred memorial, Todd." I fasten the cooler's latch. "Gotta pick our battles."

"Right. Suit up." We step into coveralls, masks, caps and don industrial gloves. Todd checks the traps. "Score! We caught a mother."

"Mother?"

"She's got teats."

"So, babies?"

"Yep." It lands with a nauseating thud as he shovels it, trap and all, into a carton. A Kewpie doll, newspapers, rags, cigarette packs, motor oil, jumbled fishing line, and half-empty cans overfill the box.

Lifting a raggedy towel disturbs a nest. Baby rats scurry like fingers snapped from a hand. "Holy fucking son of a seacook!"

Todd laughs at my shuddery two-step as he shovels up hundreds of candy bar wrappers. "He must've had a call out to Rowntree's."

"He and O'Toole steal more than the thieves, don't they?"

"Their bonus for serving and protecting."

I unearth the contents of a pink bag: folded nappies, rattle, and a baby bottle fermenting with old milk. "What the hell?"

"Bastard likely thought he scored a purse."

34

I shiver at any police scenario involving a mom not noticing the absence of a diaper bag.

Two hours and twenty cartons later, Todd says, "Dump closes at four. Let's set more traps and finish up Saturday."

I step out of the tainted gear. "We've blown over fifty bucks cleaning up Dick shit today."

"Still a million times better than what those Koshkin folks are going through."

"Truth, bro."

## SEVEN

The dismissal bell has rung, but the schoolyard is empty of kids. I join the clump of parents at the door as teachers verify ownership. Miss Temple pats Mikey's head. "He's been quiet as a mouse."

I forgo discussing how noisy rodents can be and we head crapward. Mikey asks, "Who's at home?"

"Always a crapshoot, kid."

"Will you stay in my tent tonight?"

"Sure. I love camping in the great indoors."

"Do I hafta go to my mom's tomorrow?"

"We'll take her some groceries. Just say 'red apples' if you don't want to stay. Sabina said you're welcome there."

"Where'll you be?"

"Work. I'll crash in the Village after."

We amble along like two discarded bags left to the wind.

Removing the cot increases floorspace, but I'd like to meet the tiny people that declared this a three-man tent. Like a teaspoon to a tablespoon, Mikey nests against me. "Ari?"

"Mmm."

"That Linda said Jesus will fix everything. Could He?"

"The Missus says in her whole long life, no mythic being ever showed up with a toolbox, so she learned to fix things by her own two hands."

"What if it can't be fixed?"

"Then I guess you make what you can from the broken bits."

"Like Huey does with scrapped boats, eh?"


I wake, thinking about how little space Mikey and I take up in this house compared to an absence occupying a whole city.

Downstairs, O'Toole is asleep on the couch. Snake, an amicable gangster associate, is gape-mouthed on the chair. The cooler's top is on the floor. The counter is a clutter of Frosted Flakes, pizza crusts, beer bottles, spills, scum, and scat.

Mikey wanders in, wetting his hair at the kitchen sink. "Um, your mum's really going at it upstairs."

*I swear, Jasper, I'm going to exterminate her.*

*Ohhh, let's spray her with Raid.* I rummage in the closet for a pair of mittens, fish Benadryl out of the cupboard, and grab duct tape.

Mum is in the bathroom, manically scratching at her arms. "Oh, Jen-jin-jinny. Get this b-be-bee-beee off."

The bottle says take two pills, so I give her four, then force her hands into the mittens, securing them with the tape. I empty my little tube of ointment on the raw patches plaguing her arms. "Go back to bed and stop bloody scratching your skin off."

"Oh, that tinkles."

It's just seven fifteen when Mikey and I head off for the day. We stop at the variety, buying Fritos and chocolate milk for lunches. "Does your mum have lice?"

"No, imaginary bugs."

"Her inside animal itches her?"

"It's allergic to whatever shit she took."

He sighs. "Seems more like a year since Pleasant Cove."

"Does, doesn't it." Just one week ago today, I woke tangled in Jake's lanky limbs, lazily coming to the day as boats remained in the harbour. Half the cove gathered at Skyfish to weather the storm. The aunties' barn is huge. Ground floor is a shop for selling our creations. Behind is a windowed workroom. Upstairs is the gallery, one large open space, a place for parties and where neighbours sell wares during high season. Same day as Natasha disappeared, there was laughter, baked treats, and brewed drinks. Kids, stir-crazy from a week of heavy rain, played tag. Women knitted, quilted, gabbed. Men fiddled, mended nets, played checkers.

We reach school and I hand-lick Mikey's scarecrow hair. "Wash your face after breakfast club."

"Don't talk to strangers, okay."

"I'm a lioneagle on high alert." I watch until his small self struggles through the heavy doors.

People move with intention, stepping around the one-hundred-and-seven-pound absence. I turn a corner, cutting across the construction site. No hard-hatted men whistle. They're too busy righting an overturned backhoe. Posters cover the temporary hoarding: "Summerset Plaza, Opening Fall 1970." "Metropolitan Church Bazaar, Oct. 18th." "Toronto Rock and Roll Revival, Sept. 13th." "HAVE YOU SEEN THIS GIRL? Natasha Koshkin, Missing August 29th."

*Where am I supposed to be, Jasper?*

*East or nest.*

*Let's fly.*

After school, Mikey shops, choosing soup, bread, peanut butter, jam, and Sanka to take to his mom. "You think she'll like my present?"

"It'll brighten up her place and basement apartments are always cold."

"Don't tell her I knit it."

"Okay, but she'd find it all the warmer to snuggle under if she knew."

"Mikey. Mikey!" Laura is outside her building, jumping and waving, like a mom should after a summer away from her kid. Mikey drops his bags and runs into a hug. "Oh, baby, I missed, missed, missed you." Kisses land in bunches. "Let's go to the diner and you can tell me all about your adventures."

"Ari, too?"

Laura is thirty-four, but the Dick has a way of aging women in dog years. Her ashy hair is savagely permed. Face creased from decades of smoking and her wrinkle-free polyester pants look like the ones my grandma wore. She fast-talks, making it hard to sort if she's on uppers or just excited. "Well, let me set out the situation. Haven't had a minute to clean up or get anything ready. Got me a job at that new Becker's. Have the early shift tomorrow."

I see Mikey settle, like dust after clapping chalk brushes. There will be burgers and fries, storytelling, ending with a weekend at Sabina's.

EIGHT

Monday morning, Natasha's aunt releases Alex and Joey to my

care. They are like balled armadillos as I shepherd them to school. By day's end, they are a little less armoured. Joey takes hold of Mikey's hand. Alex, pale as fog, adheres to me and whispers, "Ari?"

"Mm-hmm."

"Mikey said, he said your sister disappeared."

"She just decided she wanted to live somewhere else."

"Do you think Natty wants to live somewhere else?"

"No, I don't."

"Then-th-then . . ." He fights with every muscle in his bird-thin body not to cry.

"Whenever I don't know what to do with my sister hole, I fill it with imaginings of her doing things she loved, like on her bike, hair snapping like a yellow flag. When I was small, June would give me rides in her carrier."

"Once Natty gave our cousin's pug a ride in hers."

"That's a treasure to put in the missing space."

There are reporters, but none pounce from vehicles when we approach Nat's house, though I hear camera clicks, capturing the sag of the boys' shoulders as they walk the path. Their aunt opens the door. "Was all okay?"

"They were very brave," I say.

Alex asks, "Where's Mama?"

"The doctor gave her something so she can sleep. Your papa is out looking very hard for our Natasha."

Mikey sounds like a veteran of two wars as we retreat down the drive. "They're not the kind that are made for this, are they."

The unspoken words being, we are.

A stack of beer returns on crapdom's porch do little to hide the peeling scabs of paint. Broken panes on the door are patched with cardboard. Scrub weeds and a disassembled Harley grace the grassless lawn. To my mortification, the dick-in-training, Byron Silver, is knocking on our door. He turns as Mikey nimble-foots over the broken step. "Ari? Hi."

39

"What the hell do you want?"

"Woah. Detective Irwin needed a copy of all the data I've compiled, pronto. Just dropping it off as ordered."

The door opens and there is Mum, wearing spiky shoes and silver lamé pants, so tight her legs look like knitting needles. Since my return, it's the first I've seen her vertical. By her upness, I'm guessing she scored some speed. "You see it?" she says.

"See what?"

"My ri—" She stops mid-word. "Vincent? You're back?" She turns. "I'll purse my kettle."

"Pardon?" Byron looks at me. "Who's Vincent?"

"Dead dad numero uno. Her brain's fried."

"Oh. Hey, *Easy Rider*'s showing at the Roxy. You wan—"

"No."

As the Dick steps onto the porch, I contort through an entrance obstructed by cases of Quaker Oats. *Any thoughts on this caper, Jasper?*

*Cereal murder?*

Mikey pops up from behind the sofa with Mum's ring pinched between his fingers. "Found it."

Mum trills like a hopped-up loon. "Ohhh-ohhh."

The Dick re-enters with an accordion file under his arm. "That thing cost a fortune and you're throwing it around."

"It just threw off."

"You lose it and I'll ring your fuckin' neck."

As appealing as that scenario is, I rummage an Elastoplast from the kitchen drawer and take Mum's wedding ring from Mikey, noting the inscription as I turn the plaster around the band: "Edna and Hank, forever."

*Pawn shop?*

*Corpse.*

*Yeah, more likely.* "Here, Edna."

"I'm meetin' with an old cop buddy. He's gonna have a look at these, see if anything pops. See Mikey gets his homework done."

"Ten four."

*He really loves this Dick Tracying, eh.*

*Like a hog snuffing truffles.*

Even with an empty sink and folded laundry, the craphouse is a smoke-fouled cesspit. I check the traps on the back porch. *Holy shit, Jasper, we caught a viper?*

*No, Ari, that'd be a tail.*

## NINE

Aaron pushes fries in my direction. "Please, eat something."

"Linda isn't going to get all preachy on me, is she?"

"Most likely."

"I don't get this, Aaron."

"She's the only girl I've ever met with an adventurous spirit."

"But your modes of travel are completely different."

"Just give her a chance."

"Do you have any idea how long it took Mikey to settle after she insisted he give his heart to Jesus? A dragonfly already occupies that real estate."

"Did you know she worked in Calcutta last summer?"

"No argument she's remarkable, but you're such different animals."

"We're just friends." He smiles over my shoulder and it's clear that both his heads are lobotomized.

Linda's entrance is an event. I half expect bluebirds to follow. "Sorry I'm late. We're so busy planning for the festival this weekend."

"At Varsity Stadium?"

She nods.

"I'm working it too. Amazing lineup, eh. Rumour is Lennon might show."

"Wouldn't know. Campus Crusade will be there for the lineup of lost souls." She slides in close to Aaron—very close. "After all, what music is there without Jesus?"

"Pretty much how I feel about Jasper."

"Jasper? Thought your boyfriend was Jake."

*For frig sake, Jasper, stop poking your snout in. You'll get us committed.* "Jasper's my um . . . guru."

"Guru?"

"What? The Beatles have Maharishi Yogi."

"The only true way is—"

Aaron snaps the conversation in a safer direction. "So, you found this place okay?"

"Traffic was crazy. All the way along Queen Street I was praying, 'Please, let there be a parking spot.' Before I could say, 'Amen,' one opened up right out front." Her eyelashes catch her bangs. "Isn't God good?"

I shovel in fries to weight my tongue. Words slide over the grease. "He's a real peach arranging a parking spot for you."

Jasper pinches. *Be nice.*

*Shut up.*

"All things we ask for in prayer, believing, we receive." Her head tilts with the weight of sincerity. Her eyes are as green as a spring leaf. "His care for us is that great."

"So, how about soup?" Aaron chirps.

"So, *He* finds *you* a parking spot but not a tortured family's precious daughter?"

"Or grilled cheese?"

"His ways are mysterious."

"He's a monster if He does one and not the other."

"Ari, please."

I look at Aaron's pained face and stand. "Sorry. I'm just not fit to be around decent, God-fearing humans."

TEN

It's just past noon and the Toronto Rock and Roll Revival is indeed rocking. Bernie, my boss from the Riverboat, checks backstage. "Ari, refill the snack table. Fold more shirts. Carl, take a load to the main gate."

I mound a table with Fritos, soda, and doughnuts, then sort another carton of shirts into neat piles. Outside, Chuck Berry has the crowd reelin' and rockin'. Inside, Jim Morrison, yes Jim Morrison, listens to the music and . . . eyes me? He edges closer and says, "Cool boots."

"Thanks." I fold up my jitters with the extra-large shirts.

His knees crack as he bends to take a closer gander. "Where'd you get 'em?"

"Ah . . ." *Act like I'm uber cool, Jasper.* "Um, the corridor between heaven and hell."

"That in San Francisco?"

"No. At the intersection of missing and joy."

"Deep."

Bernie talks to Morrison like he's a regular mortal. "Ari

painted them." He leans forward, for my ears only. "Keep him sober and I'll owe you the moon."

"What am I? AA?"

"Uh, *A*ri *A*ppleton? Step up."

Morrison pockets his hands. "You from here?"

"No. Far as I can figure I'm just a bit of carbon that fell into the Atlantic."

"Righteous." He turns to the buzz that ramps to a roar from the crowd outside. "Sounds like Jesus Christ has arrived. Never thought Lennon would show."

"If you're the rock god, does that make him your son?"

He takes in my face. Fingers a serpentine of my hair. "What say we get it on?"

He's not the first rocker to want in my pants. My years at the Riverboat have taught me that guys go for girls with miles of hair, and creative souls go for anything that keeps the music riffing after the gig is over. He's no longer the work of art on his album cover, but he's not as full of himself as I've heard. He's kind of sad, a muted blue, like a robin's egg.

"The day might come when I kick myself for not banging boots with you, but I gotta pass."

"Serious?"

"We're both too off-key."

"*Do* my boots, then." He sits on a large crate. "An eagle."

"Don't have my supplies." I recognize the haunt of a person looking for a bottle to escape into. "But I could feather up your jeans."

The supply box holds a motherlode of markers. I sit on a small crate and he settles his boot on my thigh. A keeper of propriety scuttles over. "Ah, Mr. Morrison? Perhaps you'd be more comfortable—"

"The lady's doodling and Bo Diddley's up. Get me a Jack and a beer."

44

"Hang on, Carl. Mr. Morrison might prefer a burger and Coke?" I slip my hand up his pant leg to give the fabric purchase and look up. "Get tanked and I'll think you're my mum."

He nods Carl away. "So, girl with the hair, what's got you discordant?"

"Regular stuff: disappeared friend, missing sister, exile from my boyfriend, tailless rats infesting my house, parentals that're life forms lower than botulism. You know."

"Yeah, well, my dad started the Vietnam War."

"Well, that beats my dad's fuck-up. Thanks."

"Fact of life. Always someone more fucked up than you." He smiles, a closed mouth smile. "You like The Doors?"

"Depends on where they lead to."

"Where'd you want 'em to go?"

"Cape Breton, a swim with a seahorse, a potter's wheel . . ."

"Seahorse?"

"Yeah. With this one right here."

"What one?"

I look up. "Thought you musical geniuses could see sound in air, music in water."

"What're you on?"

I knock on the splintered wood under my bum. "A crate. What? You can't see that either?"

The eagle emerges, full flight, a wing tip curving up over his knee. He cranes to get a better look and our eyes connect. "Rad."

"I'm part eagle."

"Part?"

"Yeah. And part lion."

"And seahorse?"

"No, Jasper just rooms in me."

"You're one weird chick."

"Cracked as they come."

"So, animism girl. You like my music?"

45

I use the ballpoint to feather up the masterpiece and fine-tune the eye. "To a point. There's enough yelling in my world. When you get screechy, I tune you out. But there's poetry in you."

He offers his left leg as Little Richard takes the stage. "Draw a lion on this one."

Nearing midnight, I wander out, moving away from the frenetic crowd. I climb the bleachers behind the stage and sit. Fifteen days ago, a girl disappeared. Today, people dance, sing, get high, spread free love. *Natasha would've flipped at all these rockers.*

Ten rows down, a strawberry-haired lovely and a summer-tanned boy are makin' it on the skinny bench, concert lights fluorescing off his very white ass. *Jake's butt is untanned like that.* From my perch, I survey the roil of people out front. *I'm an ocean girl, Jasper. This isn't my scene.* I inhale deep, longing for a joint to lessen the ache of missing Jake, my sisters, aunties . . . my better life.

I drift. Maybe I sleep. The current rippling through the crowd tells me the Plastic Ono Band is setting up. The MC asks everyone to get matches and lighters ready to give the next act a big welcome. *Oh, there're so many ways this could go wrong.*

Nothing catches fire, except maybe a spark of serenity. Lights flicker by the hundreds, thousands, ten thousands, then they're gone and the crowd amps up. I head toward the exit.

"Ari. Wait!" Carl nimble-foots through the throng and hands me a pair of scuffed boots, "He said, ah, paint poetry on them?"

"Will do." I tuck them under my arm.

"Why's Morrison giving you his boots?"

"They need re-souling." I back away from the caterwauling coming from the stage and exit the stadium, running smack into Linda, like a pigeon-toed ostrich nosing up to an adorable kitten. Her Campus Crusade for Christ table is heaped with soda and cookies to lure the lost. "Hey, Linda. Any luck landing a fish?"

She looks up, wincing at Yoko's cat-caught-in-an-escalator screech. "That's demonic. Even you have to admit that."

Yoko's performance is a nail-on-chalkboard invasion into all that is holy about music, but of all the stellar notes filling the air today, her lament comes closest to expressing the scream in my gut. "Definitely not divine."

I move on to Aaron standing by a tree. "Hey, cowboy. Here to save a lost generation?"

He half smiles. "You're more found than me."

"Keep leaning on that tree. It knows exactly where it is and why."

Aaron one-dimple smiles. "You leaving?"

"Yeah. Gave peace a chance, but I'm not feeling it."

"I just came to pick up Linda. Wait and we'll give you a lift."

"Think your jeep's a one-woman vehicle."

"It's after midnight. You shouldn't be out alone."

"I never am."

"Tomorrow? Our bench?"

"Thought after being such a royal bitch with Linda you'd be done with me."

Moonlight plays on his cheek. "You spoke the very thoughts strangling me."

"Then I don't get it. You've battled all your life to escape a fundamentalist box. Now you're climbing back in?"

"I think of breaking every bone in my body to fit into Linda's box."

"Is there not a niggle in you where that sounds off?"

"Isn't that what love is? Being what the other person needs? Aren't you what Jake needs and vice versa?"

"Suppose. But I'm not broken in it, I'm mended."

"I don't know what to do. She's going with a mission to Biafra this summer and wants me to go."

"So, are you proposing?"

47

"What? Geez. No."

"Time zones and borders can be crossed but not moral boundaries. No religious organization is going to sanction a man and a maiden travelling together outside the bonds of holy matrimony."

"I'm so not ready for marriage."

"You'd be plenty ready if you met your match. Too bad Linda can't put away her 'shalt nots' so you could clear your heads. You'd think straighter that way."

"Geezus, Ari, you're impossible."

"Tell me something I don't know." I back away. "Tomorrow. Elevenish. Bring coffee."

As I cross the parking lot, O'Toole slithers up alongside. "Mmm, mmm, mm-hmmm, sweet tits. You want some cream?"

"Just fuzz the hell off."

He nabs my thumb, bending it toward my wrist. "I smell dope. That gives me cause to search."

I yowl, writhing like a defeated boa as he ups the pressure.

"Problem, Ari?" O'Toole backs off, piss-scared of the Harley rolling to a stop.

"Yeah, Edjo. This officer wants to haul my boobs *out* for interrogation."

"Just checking ID." O'Toole raises his hands, palms out, and backs away.

Edjo may be head grizzly with the Vagabonds, but he's always a teddy bear with me. "Thanks." I massage my thumb back into place.

He nods a *get on*. "Where to?"

"Riverboat." I hold tight, absorbing his sour stink. It's a short jaunt. I hop off and take in his wind-burned face. "There wasn't a whisper about Natasha today. How does a person just vanish?"

"Biggest clue, right there. I put word out, coast to coast, cross borders. No one's heard or seen nothing. You ask me, one lone dude snatched her. If nobody saw anything, then there was nothing special to remember."

"You think she's dead?"

"Or holed up somewhere." He revs the bike. "Take care, kid."

*Holed up*. Mum used to hole us up, for hours, sometimes days. When sisters were with me, it was okay. When it was just Jasper and me, we'd curl to nothing, my small finger connecting with the crack of light under the door. *Holed up is such an awful place to be.*

*Now, we're wholed up.*

*Christ, you're annoying.* I nip down a lane, along the alley, and slip into my nest. *All the unholy messes can wait.*

*Amen.*

ELEVEN

It's Monday after the concert that rocked Toronto. When I pick up the boys, Nat's mom is packing lunches. Her dad is propped at an awkward angle on the brocade sofa, having succumbed to sleep. Eating and sleeping, so ordinary and so overwhelming.

I watch the boys safe inside the school, then take the shortcut where the trees meet in an arch and druggies huddle in a clump. All I want is a dime bag, a ticket to hide from a school jittery with angst. Matt Talbot laughs like a happy monkey when he spots me. "Arrrriiiii. Way to go." He polishes my shoulder. "Let me *touch the babe* who lit Morrison's fire."

49

"What? Christ. No. We talked. That's it."

"Not what I heard."

I keep my cash and walk on. Crossing the field, I gather groupies like flies to a sticky strip. Popular is something I've never been. Occasionally, fans cheer my volleyball prowess. But my bumping into walls while reading or responding to Jasper externally rather than internally makes me an odd peg in a square school. Today, as I trudge through the hall, I'm hailed hero. You have to have walked in on your mother adulterating with every Tool, Dick, and Scary to know how awful this feels.

Cassie Young, queen of Jarvis, says, "Oh, Ari. I'd give anything to be you. What was Morrison like?"

"Mortal. We talked. That's it."

"Right." She finger-quotes, "'Talked.'"

The silence when I enter the office to sign in tells me everyone, from juniors to janitors, believe that I was getting a rock star's rocks off at the rock festival. The secretary fastens the pearl buttons on her sweater. "Dr. Cornish, the board's psychologist, is in guidance today. It's mandatory you make time to meet with her."

*Remember, Ari, "Do you hear voices?" is a trick question.*

*Radio silence is our best tact.*

*My snout is sealed.*

In French, my unmute button is pushed and I use merde and tabarnac in sentences requesting taunters to ferme the frick up, s'il vous plait.

In history, I tune out the teasing by moulding plasticine into the *Mayflower*. The teacher, Mr. Corbin, is new. The kind that has girls preening before class and hanging off his every word. He walks over to my desk, opens his hand, waiting for the lump to be surrendered. The thunk as it hits the wastebasket stings like the strap. Head down, my hair curtains my topsy-turvy note taking. Natasha's notes were always an ordered, underlined masterpiece.

And she never balked at my requests to borrow them for all the classes I missed.

The bell rings and I make for the door. As I leave, Mr. Corbin's contempt follows. "I hope this kind of disruption will not follow you to my next class, Miss Appleton."

"Hope so, too, sir."

*My* history has taught me that teachers either love me or wish they'd pursued more pleasing careers, like sewer maintenance or undertaking.

I duck into the art room, tuck into the supply closet, and scrape away dribbles on the rows of paint jars. Mina nearly drops a palette of paper when she comes in. "Ari, you scared the cerulean out of me."

"You hear what everyone's saying?"

"If I heard Ellis bedded Morrison, I'd be more inclined to believe it. I know how you feel about Jake."

"How one feels doesn't trump scum DNA." I tuck my giraff-ish legs against my chest. "Anyway, why is this even being talked about? I mean, caring about what I might've done, not what Natasha didn't get to do?"

"It's how we cope. Distraction is as necessary as reflection. You have a lunch?"

"Nat's mom gave me one."

"Eat it, then get to class."

I unwrap the sandwich, wondering if Natasha is hungry, and afraid that she isn't. I remain in the cupboard, unable to swallow a lunch that should've been Nat's. Like the physics I don't understand, time has stopped, but still it moves, to bells, signalling next period. It's as certain as disappointment and as unpredictable as joy.

On my way to English, I pass the trophy case. Inside is a picture of a young O'Toole, 1955 Athlete of the Year. Natasha thought him dreamier than Rock Hudson. Beside the case, there is a banner, filling with heart-ripping birthday messages for Nat. *If I disappeared, what would they write about me, Jasper?* I don't really have friends at this school, just tenuous strings. To Matt, I'm a customer. To the volleyball team, a point scorer. To Wendy, a project, a family in need of, for example, the horror of a Christmas hamper last year.

If I write the sentimental things I'm feeling, that Natasha was the one person who made me feel welcome here, I'll blubber.

Behind me, reflected in the glass, Sean gyrates on a pretend guitar, singing, "Come on, come on, touch me babe."

*I really need some grass.* I bypass guidance and exit through the gym doors.

There is a willow near Mikey's school. Under the beard of branches, I calm, letting my body sway with the yellowing leaves while I focus on worksheets and wait for the boys. *Hey, look, we found some grass.*

All the walk home, Joey collects bottle caps, Mikey explains structures, and Alex steps over cracks. I wait by the gate, watching them through the door, and see Mr. Koshkin bent over the workbench in the garage. His eyes look like they've taken a punch. His animal, a gentle retriever, looks like it's gone seventeen days without food. His head turns; disappointment, or more disgust, lines his face when he registers I'm not Natasha but an Appleton.

On return to crapdom, Mum is passed out on the chair. Todd's ball of rubber bands has been disassembled. Hundreds line her arms. Dozens circle her ankles. In her feisty days, Mum was a pernicious force of nature. Today, she spent precious hours putting elastics on her limbs.

I load crusty dishes into the sink, moving like a greyhound at Mikey's yelp. He's trapped again—under filthy sofa cushions and O'Toole's miserable ass. I spit, "Get the hell off him!"

O'Toole levers his weight into the sofa, laughing. "Who?

What? Just waitin' for my ride." Mikey struggles out, gasping. The torment continues with quick head smacks. "Not my fault I can't see him. Happens when you're smaller than a sparrow's dick."

"You should know, you pull one out of your pants at every piss." I remove a half-chewed Tootsie Roll from Mikey's hair while shepherding him toward the stairs.

O'Toole palms his crotch. "Bigger than a stallion, baby."

"Then why'd your wife file a missing penis report?"

Snake, the gangster, emerges from the cellar. "You just crack me up, cupcake." Knuckles crack as he approaches O'Toole. "And you, fucking lay off my little buddy or I'll crack you up but good. Capisce?" He winks at Mikey. "Us smart guys gotta stick together, eh, Einstein?"

From her chair, Mum emits a long, stuttering fart. A fitting amen to a shitty day.

TWELVE

Life moves around Nat's absence the way the tides flow and ebb over the fallen cliff-rock. At school, the basketball team rides a winning streak, girls nab dates for the upcoming Sadie Hawkins, and the student council sells tickets for a fundraiser for the Koshkins. Sabina's Boutique is decked for Christmas, and I spend sheltered hours in the workroom flourishing purses for holiday shoppers. At the Riverboat we celebrate Ellis's fiftieth, Gordie Lightfoot singing "Happy Birthday" while an unsung sweet sixteen decomposes like the fallen leaves.

Despite crapdom's chaos and debauchery, I have a harbour. Todd, bless his big fat heart, removed his closet door, tacked up a sheet, and crammed my cot mattress into the two-by-five space. The way the edges curl I feel like I'm in a lifeboat. My sister-house may be scattered but here, in Toronto, Todd, Aaron, and Ellis make a damn fine brother abode. And bonus, O'Toole's under-dealings have provided Mikey and me with a hedge of protective thugs.

November is overly mild and blue-skied. The boys chase paper planes across the field as I float on Jake's words. His last letter contained a calendar of days, thirty folded word-pictures to be opened one a day. Lovely gifts, like this one from last summer: *Close your eyes. We're on the marsh, in the dinghy, your body resting against mine. Late sun fires the rushes, silver, gold, pink . . . An egret, wings stretched, passes over, spots your toes, landing for a closer look. We bob with its weighting on the bow. Now, remember the windrush as she lifted off—*

"Whoa, Ari, did you see how far that went?" Alex smiles— almost.

"Spectacular."

No reporters wait for news these days, so we see Alex and Joey through their front gate. Joey asks, "Can we go swimming again with Mikey and Aaron tomorrow?"

"That's the plan." They walk the path to their limbo and we head crapward.

It's disorienting to smell anything other than decay upon opening crapdom's doors. Baking? Cookies?

Mum and her recliner are missing from the front room. The Dick and Snake are at the crap-covered dining table, a file, a heaped plate of cookies, and half-empty glasses of milk between them. The Dick says, "Unless, we get somethin' soon, Brass's shuttin' the whole thing down." I shudder at the Koshkins never knowing where Nat is. More, I tremble at the thought of the Dick without this distraction.

Snake says, "Gimmie that file. We gotta be missin' a nose on our face."

In the kitchen, O'Toole empties oatmeal into a hefty bag, while a thug reloads the containers with bagged weed and a covering of oats. Another amicable bandit named Pinto measures brown sugar into a bowl. "Afternoon, doll. Saw the recipe on the can, and"—he points his cigar to a mountain of cookies—"ta da. Try one. Good as grammaw's."

They are good. Crunchy and loaded with Chipits. He watches me chew while trying to digest the tableau in the backyard. Mum is in her chair, snuggled under the filthy car blanket, drinking rum from a bottle, staring at the garage window like her favourite show is on.

"Fuckin' cough of hers was driving all us right 'round the bend."

"Yeah. It's her gift."

I begin the massive clean-up while O'Toole places containers of Quaker Oats back into the carton, resealing it so it looks untouched.

It's long past nine before crapdom empties and Mikey settles. I'm tucked in my nook, jotting essay notes on the suffragettes, when Todd says, "Anyone bring your mum in?"

"Her blood's ninety proof. She won't freeze."

*Leaving her when you remember seems scummier than her forgetting you on the shore.*

I sigh as I clamber out. *When will you learn to keep your friggin' snout shut?*

## THIRTEEN

The thing about a mild November is you're lulled into forgetting that winter is coming. Monday, December 1st has me running to escape a stinging ice rain. Inside school, I down my hood and see twenty cops in the hall. Over the PA we're told to proceed to homeroom and wait.

Ellis is taking attendance when the principal knocks and hauls Wendy out.

When the door closes, Sean says, "Bet they found her."

Ellis pales, then distracts us with a story prompt. "Okay, finish this sentence: 'I walked into the kitchen and'—Sean, what say you?"

"Uh . . . Mom was peeling potatoes."

Responses down the row are an interesting sociological study: Mom was cleaning, cooking, ironing, mopping up dog barf. He reaches me, "Ari? 'Walked into the kitchen and—'"

"The mafia were baking cookies."

Sean says, "Sheesh, you're a freak."

Before Ellis can ask fiction or non-, the secretary comes on the PA, "Everyone, please proceed to first period."

In French, I drift out the window and see Wendy being escorted down the front walk and into her mom's car. *You remember Mum ever picking me up?*

*Duh, a million times by your neck-scruff.*

*Truth.*

Next morning, Wendy is absent. On the way to math, Sean says, "You live with a cop. You must know something."

Following the Dick's warning that I'm to keep my mouth shut until police decide what gets out, I say, "I don't. I swear."

"Heard they found her shoes."

"From who?" I ask.

"Matt heard it from Cassie."

The rumours are true. Yesterday, when the janitor went to bring in the Remembrance Day wreath, he found a one-of-a-kind pair of sneakers tied to it.

Last year, inspired by my canvas runners, Natasha and I flower-powered hers with psychedelic swirls and peace signs. Riding a creative high, she disassembled her weighty charm bracelet, fastening the varied tokens celebrating her life through the gromets. Tinkling heralded her every movement. Now, the cacophony of a thousand students can't cover the absent chime.

When I collect Mikey after school, his top lip is puffed. "Geez, what happened, bro?"

"Sitting on the monkey bars at lunch, just thinking, next thing I knew my lip was stuck."

"Oh, major bummer. What'd you do?"

"Mr. McGregor melted me off with tea from his thermos." He tucks his mitten in mine. "Can I tell you something? Secret?"

"Unload away, kid."

"They found Natasha's shoes."

"Who told you?"

"Alex. Before he went to his aunt's. I promised not to tell but, Ari, they found them at your school. She was wearing them when, you know. What does that mean?"

Shivers skitter up my arms. "Don't know."

"Can I go with you at Christmas?"

"It's your mom's week with you."

His boots are too thin, and snot bubbles from his nose. "What if . . . if she has the flu again?"

Nine weekends out of ten, Laura has been "coming down with something." "We'll sort it. There's Sabina's or maybe we'll just freight-hop home."

"Like hobos, eh." His cough has a barky edge. "Do I have any wool?"

"We'll get some at Woolworths. Gotta get more Buckley's. My mum's like a bloody flock of whooping coughers, eh?"

"I just pretend there's a colony of seals outside my tent."

Nearing crapdom, Ronnie is seen teetering down the snowy street in a bomber jacket, micro-mini, fishnets, and sandals. The house is tomb-quiet when we enter. Mum sits in her chair, glassy eyed and hell-hot. Her cough has transitioned to a strangled wheeze. Mikey says, "Should we get a taxi?"

The cold will send Mum into paroxysms, ending with a boot-full of phlegm in the backseat of a cab. And the lines between good thug/bad cop are so fuzzy that calling an ambulance to this house of thieves feels ill-advised. The keys to O'Toole's Camaro are right where he usually drops them when he rides with the Dick. "Grab a bucket while I stuff her into her coat."

The Camaro is flightier than the aunties' truck, but the gears are like butter to shift. I slip into a spot near emerg. Mikey says, "How'd you learn to drive?"

"Huey taught me." I lift the seat to let him out of the back. "Go nab that wheelchair by the door."

I know she's bad when the nurses move her to the head of the queue; still I endure two humiliating hours answering questions. It's going on eight when a merciful nurse bolsters my bicep. "You and your brother go on home now. We'll get her sorted."

Back at crapdom, thug cars are out front. Snake greets me as I drop the keys on the mountain of past-due mail. "Hey, cupcake. How's tricks?"

"Just dumped Mum at the General. Pneumonia."

"By ambulance?"

"No. Borrowed O'Toole's wheels."

He laughs from his belly. "Oh, you got balls."

Mikey says, "Don't tell, okay."

Snake winks a promise of secrecy. "So, some weird shit going down with those shoes, eh?"

Mikey worries. "It's supposed to be a secret."

"Where'd you hear it?" I ask.

"Oh, I got connections. Boys in blue. Fellas in red. Men in green."

"Police, Mounties, and army?"

"I'm a friendly guy."

Mikey says, "My brother Ricky's a soldier. He fixes the biggest trucks they got."

"You don't say."

Mikey looks at me, then backs up the stairs, "Um, no, don't say nothin'. It's supposed to be a secret."

"Okay, Einstein," Snake says. "So, cupcake, you're good at stories. What's your gut sayin' about the guy that made the drop?"

Snake's words are warm against the December draft seeping through crapdom's cracks. I wedge on the step, between a stack of *Penthouse* and foul bowling gear. "Natasha's charmed shoes on a memorial wreath seems kind of, I don't know, creative. Poetic almost."

"What's the buzz at school?"

"Haven't heard anything." Reality is, the voice in my head is so chattery, I've missed the twittering outside. "Why're you helping the Dick solve this?"

"I got nieces. Three beauties. It'd kill me if anything happened to them. Plus, can't hurt to have a detective in my pocket. Am I right?"

"Better than one in your hair."

"Brass was scaling back the investigation, then a clue falls from the sky. Halpern thinks the guy's cleaning house, but mark my words, he wants to play. You just wait and see."

"Oh." I stand. "Um, Snake? The army thing? Ricky's keeping it hush-hush so it's a big birthday surprise for his dad."

"Secret's safe with me."

"Appreciated."

*Secrets are about as safe as ice cream in a fat lady's fridge, eh, Ari.*

FOURTEEN

The following week, Jake's letter and hope of a Christmas train heading east float me up the steps to school . . . *I sit for hours on the foundation of our house, trying to figure how to build a windowed wall that will withstand a maritime blow. We have to build it so the ocean comes inside, don't you think . . .*

Once inside, my content disappears like the snow on my boots. Teachers are clustered, crying.

I turn, heading for the exit before the devastation of details hit. My history teacher leans cross-armed against the wall. "You're to go to homeroom, Miss Appleton."

"I can't, sir."

If I had to give contempt a colour, it'd be the tanned hue on Mr. Corbin's face. "What makes you think that you're above the rules?"

"I've no idea what borders me." I back away. "And, you know, sir, under this unholy mess is someone who wants to understand *her*story and what it means more than any kid on the planet."

A heavy sprint lands me in the nest. I call Todd, tell him he needs to get Mikey, then uncradle the phone.

I love silence, love the way light splinters through quiet and how Babcia's featherbed feels softer under my bum and the wall feels liquid at my back. In silence, the clutter of smells—cinnamon, camomile, soap—has a bigger space. I close my eyes and see a tiny seahorse turning off lights inside me, closing doors, softly like the aunties did at day's end when I was little.

Time moves in light-inches, from the bed, to the chair, to the counter. I light a joint, not because I'm sad or scared. The whining in my head, *No fair, no fair, no fair, I can't go home now*, is intolerable.

Len's sweater and my woolly socks are small comforts as I feel the ground I want to be on collapsing away under me. I lie down on the bed, grab hold of my stuffed Zodiac, and stare at night shadows on the wall.

Opal light and a soft rap surface me. "Ari? It's Mina."

I let her in and she does what women do, makes tea. For a long silence we perch at my counter. I sip an inch, inhale, exhale, ask, "Is it better knowing or not knowing?"

Mina sighs heavy. "Better or not, Natasha's end is known."

"For sure?"

"Police got a tip to check the ventilation access on the roof of an industrial building, just northwest of the CNE. They found a body."

Snake's words, "he wants to play," slither through the hollow in my chest. "What happens now?"

"Halpern asked me to bring you by the station."

"Why?"

"To identify a piece of clothing."

At the station Halpern asks me only one thing: to identify the remnants of a tie-dyed shirt.

"Is this the one you helped Natasha make?"

"It is."

"We shouldn't need you for anything else right now. Please no info to the press."

At the front desk, the Dick pushes his bulk to a stand. "This is tough, kid, really tough. We'll get the guy."

O'Toole moves down the corridor like a bad smell. Under his movie star looks is pure slime. "Oh, sweet thing, you need a hug?"

The Dick snaps, "Back off."

"What's your problem, Irwin? Just delivering photos from the lab." O'Toole opens a file, like a teacher shows a page to a class.

The Dick's hand spans it in a millisecond. "Just back the fuck off." He turns to me. "Theresa still at the General?"

"Yeah. Doc says it's a bad case."

"Keep Mikey with you for now. Don't want him at Laura's 'til you get the clear from me."

*Fuck Mikey. I just want to go home.*

Jasper twists on my shoulder. *Wait. Was the Dick being human?*

FIFTEEN

Jennah comes with me to the hospital. Mum's in and out of delirium. I just want to put a pillow over her face and be done, with her and everything here. Jennah, however, bats her forget-me-not blues at the doctor and wrangles Mum a stint in rehab after the pneumonia is tamed.

I brush down Mum's squirrel-nest hair and offer juice. She swallows, rasping, "You're a good girl, Junie."

"Oh, for fudge sake, Mum," Jennah says. "It's Ari. Your good girl is Ari." She snaps on elegant black gloves. "Come on, sis. We don't need any more shit." She insists me down the hall. "How is it that lovely Natasha's gone and that waste of skin goes on?"

"That's how Mr. Koshkin feels about me."

"If he thinks that"—she links arms with mine—"then he doesn't know you from Adam's Appleton."

"Do you know how long before they'll have a funeral?"

"Sooner than later. Wilf said there wasn't much that her body could tell the coroner."

I hope the blast of fresh air will settle my belly. It doesn't and I hurl onto winter-killed marigolds.

"Jesus, you're like June. Never knew when that girl was going to puke all over everything." Jennah sacrifices her hankie and I wipe my chin. "Wonder where June got herself to."

"Last sighting was Coombs, British Columbia. I often send postcards there, to June and Spring Appleton, but never hear anything."

"Hard to imagine June with a baby, eh." We reach Jennah's shiny red car. "You stopping to see Jillianne on your way east?"

"How can I go now?"

"Oh, sweetie, how can you not?"


Sunday, AD—after discovery—it's too cold to sit, so Aaron and I walk the shore. "I don't get the reasoning in a prayer vigil, do you?"

His head waggles his bewilderment. "Why'd you think I'm here, not there?"

"You know, if I'd stepped off the train and been told that Wilf had pummelled Jennah into the great beyond, or June had been found with a needle in her arm, or Mum knifed Jacquie, or Jory tripped out off the church steeple, or Jillianne had offed

63

herself, it would've seemed the natural order of shit. But this is the universe messing with good."

"I really hate that you think you, or your sisters, deserve awfulness."

"It's hard to shake free from the Appleton family tree." Mitten bumps glove as we amble along. "Not for a squabble, but for hope to grab on to. What's Linda's take on this?"

"She's really struggling. She had complete faith Nat was going to be found alive."

"Well, there's something. Maybe there'll be a philosophical realignment that will make the pair of you less of a cat and fish."

He stops sharp. "You see a cat in Linda?"

"A sleek panther." He steps off the boardwalk, footsteps cracking the crust of frozen sand as he moves toward the lake. I scurry to catch up. "Sorry, I didn't mean it as a negative. It's an exquisite animal. Don't be pissed. It's just a ridiculous game I play."

He kicks at the stones. Not a single one frees itself up for throwing. "Your take on people spooks me. I've never had an affinity for cats." He scans the lake, shiny as a dime. "Yet I'm like them in that I'm always clinging to a shore."

"Well, you're lucky then."

"How's that?"

"Most go a lifetime without ever cluing in that their anchor isn't chained to them; it's just something they're holding onto."

"And some don't get time enough to figure anything out." He exhales. Frosty breath swirls. "Life is so frighteningly fragile."

"Can I tell you something?"

"Anything."

"At the police station, O'Toole flashed a photograph."

"Of Natasha?"

"An almost skeleton, bent to fit in that small space. Her clothes seemed on. I want that to mean that she wasn't . . . you know . . ."

"Raped? It's horrible enough without."

"My sisters, my dad raped them. My dad. My friggin' dad."

Aaron's glove warms my cheek, gentle like, and I wonder at hands that crush a sweet girl's neck. Shiver at hands that steal my beautiful sisters' innocence. He says, "Seems a worse betrayal when it's the person who's supposed to care for you."

"My dad seemed the nicest person on Earth. He was funny, fun. Smart." Silver clouds release huge crystalline flakes. With my looking up, they gather on my lashes. "Whoever coaxed Nat onto that roof must've been a shimmery soul."

SIXTEEN

I shelter at Sabina's from the mourning world. I have quiet tasks, gift-wrapping purchases for the customers and refolding rummaged stock. *Tomorrow is Christmas Eve.*

*Don't remind me.* The mood on the eastbound train will be all ho-ho-ho with porters handing out candy canes to homebound passengers. Christmas morning, Pleasant Cove will open like a holiday card. Boxing Day, there'll be kitchen parties and Jake's fiddling would be a little saucy because he woke up beside me. *We could've gone, Jasper, if Nat's mom hadn't asked me to say something at the funeral.*

I look up to Ellis shadowing the doorway. "How're you doing?"

"Inert. Unreactive." I curl gold ribbon into festive tendrils.

His head bobs, heavy with grief. "That must be very unsettling."

"Yeah. When my dad died, Aunties M&N sat me at the wheel, set me turning clay to pots. With Len, an ocean of salt tears kept me afloat. When Grandma and Jory's baby passed, the sister-house sheltered me. When Uncle Iggy was murdered, all the words he gave me reanimated into poetry."

"Uncle Iggy?"

"Len's uncle. He put quotes on my lunch bag every day." I affix a shimmery bow to the gift box. "I'm just so tired and I want to go home."

"You should."

"But the funeral's on Saturday."

"About that, I know Mrs. Koshkin asked if you could speak on behalf of her classmates. Ah, her dad would prefer, Wendy. They've been friends since kindergarten."

I've likely delivered more funereal words than any other kid on the planet: for Grandma, Len, Iggy, my tiny nephew Jet; even Ermiline Guthrie, a former fosterer, asked me to eulogize Papa Guthrie when he passed. "It should be Wendy." I dig Natasha's eulogy from my pocket. "Give this to her. And can you tell Mikey I've gone to see my mum?"

"I'll give you a lift."

"No. I need some shell time."

I scurry out the front door, fly to my nest, fumbling with the lock, hand trembling at the injustice of a rotten Appleton living and Natasha gone.

The phone rings. Rings again. I let it, not wanting to hear anyone say, "It's not you." But some people do deserve to live more than others. That's a fact.

Seahorses revive in water. I shower, sliding to a sit, and let the steam soak in. *I never even wanted to do it.*

*Hey, Ari. We're free to go home now.*

*What about Mikey?*

66

*The Dick said to keep him with us. We could catch the overnight to Montreal.*

*Yeah, we could.*

When the phone rings again, I untangle my long limbs and answer dripping wet. "Hello?"

"Oh, good. I caught you. It's Mina. You still going to see your mum?"

"Why?"

"Mikey's cough is getting worse and his temp's sky high. Sabina can't leave the store. I'll swing by with him so he can get checked at emerg."

I hang up, pull on Len's shirt, and step onto the rusty landing. *Oh, friggin' damn them all to oblivion!* Wind whips under the flannel shirt and my hair freezes stiff. The frost-biting pain underfoot is . . . exquisite. It's not Jasper I hear, but Len. *Corka, go back inside and get dressed.*


Christmas Eve, Mikey's fevered body smooshes against me on the pull-out at Sabina's. All I want for Christmas is Jake's naked heat beside me and snow falling outside my cedar-scented room.

"Ari?"

"Hmm."

"Linda said God picks the most beautiful flowers for his garden."

"Heard that one when Len died."

Mikey's chest is tight, both from his cough and fear. "Couldn't He just grow his own?"

"That's a necessary wonder."

"How long 'til morning?"

"Soon."

"If I could give Alex a present, it'd be to sleep until summer and wake up in Pleasant Cove."

"You're very thoughtful."

"He shouldn't hear 'Happy Christmas.' No one should."

"Let's take some baking to Todd and help him with the dogs."

He flicks on the light. Gray shadows cloud his porcelain face. "If I could give you any present, it'd be to wake up beside Jake."

SEVENTEEN

After-echoes of the Jarvis choir disappear like sparks from a stirred fire. I'm in the last pew with Mikey between Aaron and me. The primal moans from Nat's mom and silent racking of her dad are gut-churning. I've stood at the end of joy many times. Of all the leavings, this feels the worst.

When Mikey sags forward, Aaron's hand opens on his boney back, moving further to bolster me with a gentle squeeze on my shoulder and there it remains, and my belly stirs, then other parts spark. *What kind of a girl thinks about sex at a funeral?*

*More than you'd think.*

After the amen, I push through the throng to the Dick, arriving at the same moment as the retiring chief of police. He shakes the Dick's hand like he means it. "Irwin, just want to thank you for your service. Hear you've been working 'round the clock."

"Just doing my duty, sir."

"You've earned yourself a holiday."

"No, sir. Not 'til we catch this bastard."

"Good man."

The Dick puffs like a swellfish as Chief Mackey retreats. "I'm gonna make detective over this," he says to me.

"What's the new chief like?"

"Adamson's tough. He's not going to namby-pamby about in the Village. Watch who you're talking to there. Don't want your associations coming back to bite me."

"Roger that." That he doesn't see the maze of bootlegged goods O'Toole has stacked floor to ceiling in crapdom as waiting to kick him in the arse is bewildering.

"Mikey at Laura's?"

"No, he's here. Um, she, ah, being in a damp apartment didn't seem wise with his cough."

"Right. Good. I'll be workin' 'round the clock. Keep him with you."

I'm adrift in the sea of mourners. Aaron touches my arm. "Going downstairs?"

"No. Mr. Koshkin doesn't need to see me breathing. Can you ask Linda to watch Mikey, then give me a lift to check on Laura? Haven't been able to get hold of her all week."

"Sure. I'll let Linda know."

"Pilfer some food for her?"

"Will do. Meet you at the jeep."

The universe is kicking up a bitter fuss. In slippery shoes, I sprint to Jennah's car, dive in, suit up for the arctic blast, and grab the precious hand-me-downs from her for Mikey.

When we connect at the jeep, Mikey is adhered to Aaron's side. "Please? I don't want to stay."

"Get in."

The streets are busy with people on the trail of a post-Christmas bargain. Aaron says, "Do you feel completely undone?"

"We all need some knitting time with the Missus. It's amazing what she stitches together from life's unravellings." I turn to

Mikey squashed in the jump seat. "There's warm gear in the bag. Suit up and wait here."

It's a long hard knock on Laura's door before she opens it a crack. "Hey, Laura. Mikey's worried about you."

She blinks me into focus. "I've got the bronchitis."

"You up for a hug?"

"Don't want Mikey catching anything." She clutches her housecoat to her throat. "Say, Ari, can you spare a tenner?"

"Sorry. Banks are closed." I give her the cake box heaped with sandwiches and squares, returning to the jeep with the Christmas tidings Mikey usually receives. "She's sick and doesn't want you to catch it."

He escapes into his second-hand toque.

Aaron asks, "Where to? Back to the church?"

"Sabin—ah . . . Union Station?"

"Is there a train?"

The schedule is etched in me. "Two seventeen." I count the cash in my wallet.

"You have enough?"

"I'm never without escape funds."

"Wise." He half smiles. "Even with travel, you'll have a few days there to regroup."

Jasper spins when I say, "Head east, Aaron West."

The dolphin in him leaps that someone can just go without writing a list. At the drop-off he loans me the Hudson's Bay blanket from over the seat and a bag of trail mix.

"You're such a boy scout. Come on, Mikey. We've a train to catch."

Slowly his dropped chin lifts. "Me? Me, too? I can come?"

"Just following the Dick's orders." His unbelieving hand slips into mine and we run away home.

It's the worst of rides. Snow delays, long and many. Flickering lights. Shivery drafts. It's the best of rides. We sleep, snug under the blanket, reality whited out like the world outside the window. William Walrus joins the run at Montreal. "Wondered what train I'd be finding you on. Late start's better than none."

Mikey says, "We had a funeral."

"Aye. A terrible thing."

"You know? Was it in the Montreal papers?" I ask.

"There isn't a run where I don't gather news from here to there." William opens his palm. "I'll be taking one of those pennies for this sorrow." I find the pouch, lighten it of a coin, feeling like I've mastered the first challenge in a treasure quest.

December 28th, just as the sun slips off the world, we make our way up the aunties' path with too much sadness between separations. Mary holds on. "Oh, m'girl. Come here. Take off your boots."

"Not before I go surprise Jake."

Mary eases up the hug, bolsters with a hand on each arm. "When you said you couldn't come, Jake went with Salt Wind to Charlottetown."

*What? No, no. Fuck.*

*Yep, no fuck.*

My scarf unwinds like a blood-soaked bandage of a girl with a lacerated heart.

Nia says, "Mikey, I can't wait another second for you to open your stocking."

"For me?"

His astonishment that someone would fill a stocking for him does me in. I collapse between M&N and watch Mikey, gobsmacked by a compass, fishing lures, a harmonica . . . Nia lifts my hand to the firelight. "This suits your hand." On my finger is her grandmother's ring, a black diamond, sided by blue diamonds. A gift to me after Len died.

"Wore it to the funeral to remind me that treasures are found in dark places."

71

"And that a crushing is needed for those treasures to form."

"Shush, Auntie." There's a fire, three dogs, moonlit snow falling outside, a clay-etched hand calming my stressed hair, and I don't believe I have the strength to ever go back to Toronto.

EIGHTEEN

First day back at school has a quiet to it, like sounds heard underwater. Teachers don't bother with questions, there are no answers, just facts: binomials are the sum or difference of two terms. *We are minus Natasha.* During mitosis, some organelles are divided between two daughter cells. *At any moment the earth can crack and swallow a daughter whole.* Magma is a complex high-temperature fluid. *It's winter, twelve below with a wind chill.*

The secretary comes on the PA. "This announcement is for Miss Burn's fourth period art. Please come dressed to go outside for class."

We carry out cartons of squirt bottles filled with paint. Mina motions to the banked side of the snow-covered field. "There's your canvas. Have at it."

Sean says, "What's the point? It'll just get trampled on."

"Everything's temporal, Sean. But for a moment it'll be beautiful."

I dig the energy and angry playfulness. I like the flight of colour across the sky and its collision with the snow. Turning, smiling, a shot of magenta hits my eye, lime green coats my tongue, a hail of squirts follow. When my vision clears, I'm alone.

Jennah's beautiful cast-off, the warmest shearling any sheep ever sacrificed its life for, looks like a Jackson Pollock.

*Ohhh, I love it.*

*Shut up.*

Throughout the remains of the morning, I piece together that my freak status has been lowered to pariah. My semester of solitary study has been judged as me just not giving a damn about Nat. Chitter is I saddled Wendy with Nat's eulogy, ditching the funeral so I could go fuck the fiddler. Cassie Young and the gaggle of girls following like imprinted geese, spit, "Slut." "Selfish bitch." "How can someone like her be so stuck up?"

I muzzle Jasper from screaming. *If you had a molecule of insight into the human condition, you'd see she's haplessly stuck down.*

Pain gathers behind my left eye. A jagged occlusion distorts Dr. Cornish, the school board's shrink, as she stops me on my way to hiding in the art cupboard. "Rap session at one thirty. I want to see you there, Hariet." Her face curdles at my splatteredness. "This childish display is . . . is . . . well, I really don't know what it is, but it won't help. Coming together will."

The shake of my head stirs the pain and I close my acrylic-coated lids. When I open my eyes, she is gone and the student dick, Byron Silver, is close, so close I smell peanuts on his breath.

"Looks like you could use a friend."

His cheeks flush as Jasper locks on his eyes, searching for his animal. Fox? Possum? Chameleon? "Right. I do. But it isn't you."

A scrub with plain soap, two Midol tablets from Mina, finagling some math help in lieu of the dreaded rap-session, eighty-three percent on my history exam, and last period with Ellis reassemble me, a little.

Bone-chilling fog covers the field as I head to Mikey's school. I'm down the hill before I clue in that Wendy is blathering beside me. "I'm not mad at you, Ari. The others just don't get why you weren't at any of the stuff for Nat."

*Well, were they waitin' in emerg? Working two jobs? At parent-teacher night for a Dick's kid? Or cooking spaghetti for the hood, the bad, and the ugly?*

"Doesn't seem possible, does it? That she's gone. Byron says it all needs time and talking."

"Why's he still here? Thought he went to McGill."

"Finished. He got accepted into med school. Can you believe it? Doesn't start 'til fall so he decided to volunteer after his placement ended." She links her arm through mine like I'm a geriatric in need of assistance. "He lost a brother last year, so he gets how awful this is."

"Oh, that's—"

"Isn't he dreamy? I know he's twenty-two, but isn't your Jake like really old?"

"Nineteen."

"So, you get it. Guys here are so juvenile." She snaps an icicle off a stop sign and licks it. "So, um, ah, so, with volleyball starting next week, um . . . How about I start walking the boys home? I mean Mikey, too. As spirit head, I can't have you missing practice. The team needs you."

"No, I—"

The boys launch through the school door as fast as kids in sub-zero gear can move. At the crossroads Wendy says, "I'll see Alex and Joey the rest of the way."

"But—"

"It's cool with their folks."

I look at Alex. He nods and says, "But we can still go swimming with Mikey."

I turn from Wendy's insistence, absorbing that Mr. Koshkin doesn't want "that Appleton girl" around his boys. *Don't be sad.*

*How is it, when for once an Appleton isn't the root of all this evil, the shit still lands on me?*

*Nia says shit makes good fertilizer. Must be why your hair's so thick.*

*Shut, shut up.* "Come on, Mikey."

His snow pants shweep-shweep-shweep as he catches up. He stabilizes himself with a grip on my pocket. "Do you think there's a world like Narnia after we die?"

"Doubt it."

"Wish there could be."

"Nia says creating something while we're breathing is the only certain thing we have."

"Why did someone stop Natasha from breathing?"

"Why did Jadis make it forever winter?"

"She was mean and bad. Will it always be winter now for Alex?"

"It will. But, you know, after Len died I discovered things like . . . hot chocolate is more spectacular on a blustery day than in sunny summer."

"And puppies at Todd's work are better when your house is full of grizzlies."

"Truth."

"I wonder why Jadis wasn't happy living in a forest with talking fauns."

"Good wonder to have, bro."

NINETEEN

When I was ten, Jake took me out on a frozen inlet. It looked solid but I felt the shifting and hurried, jelly-legged, back onto solid ground. Right now, I feel the cracking but can't sort which way is shore and which is open water.

Mum is home from rehab, steady and pinked up. She passes me in the hall, the ratty bathmat balled in her arms. "Oh, Elsie, I had a boy. Seven pounds nine ounces."

*Perfect, an infant and a half-wit toddler.*

All the walk to school, Mikey clings to me like a fretful squid. "I think Aaron's sad."

"Me, too."

"Why?"

"Linda's a land animal and Aaron's dolphin needs the ocean. They're both just coming to terms with the reality that together they make a catfish."

We wait on the corner for his hook-up with Wendy, jumping foot to foot to ward off frostbite. His Christmas cough lingers. I hold a hankie to his nose. He lifts his face. Honks hard. "Did you know seahorses can look forward with one eye and backwards with the other?"

"I didn't."

"Do that, okay."

"I'll be extra watchful."

He trudges away to connect with Wendy. I cut across the vacant lot. For years, the Packham & Son Haulage truck has been in this spot. I climb into the cab figuring math is less incongruent when I'm de-edged. I light a joint. From my perch, I see Byron Silver round the corner, dressed like a posh Londoner in a peacoat, Doc Martens, and Beatles cap. Cassie Young approaches from the other side. She's extraordinarily pretty, like Elizabeth Taylor. As they quickstep toward an embrace, a mangy coyote with a winter-coated rabbit in its mouth darts across their path. They both scream.

Byron jimmies the lock on the office trailer, bowing in a grand gesture as he holds open the door.

*Poor Wendy.*

*So, Jasper, if a doctor spawned Byron, what hope is there for me?*

*We are not the scum of our parts.*

*Your math, I like.*

TWENTY

Tuesday morning, Mikey shrugs into his backpack. "You coming to watch me get my swim badge tonight?"

"Barring mayhem, I'll be there."

"Did you know dragonflies are born in the water?"

"Cool."

The entire day my water spirit flounders in a school of venomous fish. I don't bite at the Ari-is-a-selfish-slut bait. I do, however, attack at the volleyball season opener, smashing and spiking to a quick trouncing of Malvern C.I.

Now I have three glorious hours before going to cheer Mikey. As I head to my nest, the cold is the waking kind that lets a body know it has fingers, nose, and toes. Poetry sparks along my stride, D.H. Lawrence, "Song of a Man Who Has Come Through."

*In your case, woman coming through.*

*"A fine wind is blowing the new direction of time."* Images swirl as I navigate over patchy ice. *A winged gift. Jasper, we'll yield to the fine wind that takes us through the chaos of the world. An exquisite chisel driven by invisible blows.*

*"The rock will split, we shall come at the wonder."*

*Oh, I love that line.*

A man passes and the cloying stench of Old Spice splinters in the frigid air. A ghost whispers, *There's Daddy's good girl.* Looking back, I pick up my pace.

"Hi, Almost-Ari?"

I spin around, stopping an inch from Byron's smile.

"Just the girl I'm looking for."

I slip past him.

He follows. "Hold on." I dart. He weaves. "I was in the Caymans over Christmas. Brought you something."

"No thanks." I try to shake him in the crowd.

His grip on my bag stops me short. "It's just a kitschy souvenir." His hand opens. On his palm is a clear plastic case. Inside, on a bed of cotton is a tiny seahorse, a real desiccated seahorse.

"Oh, no. No, no, no, no." I snap away, run-walking through the pedestrian horde. He's on my heels like a sheep-herding dog.

He nabs my braid. "Wait up. Didn't mean to upset you. Wendy said you loved seahorses." There's an unplaceable familiarity to the tilt of his head. "Listen, there's something you should know."

"Let go of my hair."

"It's important. About your sister." His gloved hand winches up my braid. "Police found something at that church. Come on, you need to see this."

Hariet would comply in a blink. The Ari in me roars, "Just leave me the fuck alone!" With all my force, I reclaim my braid. Like the collapse after a tug-of-war, he tumbles backwards, over banked snow. A car rounding the corner connects—with his head.

"Oh, God." I scramble, catching him as he staggers up before we both topple down. "Oh, oh, oh, oh, no, no, no, no, no."

Someone wads a hat over the bloody mess and forces my hand on it. "Put pressure on. Keep him still. You, there, in the blue. Go to the bakery. Call for an ambulance. Now. Move it!"

A man, terror-full, says, "He fell right in front of me. Did you see? You saw? You saw?"

"Stand back. Everyone back!" A badge flashes. A coat falls over Byron. His pupils eclipse pale iris. Lips form, "Our Father," then still. I continue the prayer for him hoping the Lord will deliver him from this Ari evil.

Minutes waiting for an ambulance are interminable until helpers whisk him away. My body is ice, my legs frozen. Someone unfolds me like decomposing cardboard. "Are you hurt? Miss?"

The helping woman says, "She's in shock. Get her out of the cold."

A blanket weights my shoulders. "Did you see what happened, ma'am?"

"Not sure what I saw. I was behind them along Wellesley. For the length of the block it seemed like she was trying to get away. Then it, it looked like he grabbed her and she—" I fall like spring melt off Skyfish roof when the lady says, "Pushed him?"

I surface in the back of a cruiser. The lady is holding me together through the scream of sirens.

"Ari, you're at the hospital. Do you know what day it is?"

I know I'm on a plastic chair. I know Jasper is spinning. I know I will never be warm again.

There's a commotion outside the cubicle. Halpern's voice rips through the curtain. "What the bloody hell happened? You were supposed to pick her up."

"It went down in like ten seconds, sir." Ten seconds. One second, for that matter, is all it takes to break a life beyond fixing.

"Can I take her to the station?"

*We're going to prison, Jasper.*

"Doc says she took a nasty whack."

"They locate Byron's folks yet?"

"No, sir."

"Get Irwin here." Halpern scrapes the curtain along its track. "Ah, Jesus fuck."

"I'm so sorry. I—"

"Stop. No details until Irwin gets here. You know how we can get in touch with this kid's parents?"

"No."

Unknown minutes later, Halpern prods my gray matter while the Dick sits, pretending to be paternal. "Okay, kid, what happened?"

Thoughts and words are a jumbled mess as I try to explain what I don't myself understand. "He grabbed my braid and I . . ."

"You pushed him?"

"I made him fall."

"Ah, bloody Christ. His dad's a doctor, where?"

"Um . . . the children's hospital? Is he okay?"

"Critical. Are you keeping anything from me, Ari?"

"If I am, I don't know that I am."

"Okay. Sit tight. Irwin, you're on for another shift."

"Yes, sir." Halpern leaves and the Dick hisses through clenched teeth. "You stupid fucking cunt. A doctor's kid. Friend of the brass. You've never been anything but trouble. Now, everything I've worked for is down the crapper." He grinds his thumb into the dressing on my head and the pain feels— necessary.


When Len died, every waking was a relearning that he was gone. Today, before I open my eyes, I know Hariet Appleton has done the worst thing a human can do. I puke on the clean sheets in Mina's guest room. She scrambles from her slumber on the chair. "I'm supposed to get you back to hospital if you start vomiting."

"No." My head has taken enough whacks to know it's my

belly, not my brain, causing the upchucking. I sit up, hair dripping bile. "What's going to happen to Mikey when I go to jail?"

"You're not going to jail."

"Jillianne got two years for what she did. This is a million times worse."

"Her crime was bodily harm committed during a robbery. There was no intent in what happened yesterday."

"Yes, there was." I catch my aching head. "Look how wrecked Nat's parents are. Byron's parents . . . Wendy told me they already lost a son."

"Oh, Jesus. When?"

"I don—" I bolt to the bathroom.

When Nia's friend, lawyer Sam Lukeman, arrives with Halpern, I'm certain Byron's dead and I'm headed for Attica, which would be fair after what I've done.

"Is he . . . ?"

Halpern says, "It's not good. I won't lie, doesn't look good. Still can't locate his parents. No doctor at the childrens hospital, or any of them that fits. No hits from McGill for a Byron Silver."

"Wendy doesn't know them?"

"Never went to his house."

"Cassie?"

"Never met his folks."

"Doesn't someone at the police know his dad?"

"Apparently, Fitzpatrick wrote his placement recommendation. He died in August. Lung cancer."

"I can't believe I did this."

"That nurse and my guy at the scene say he was at you."

"Your guy at the scene?"

"Had a dozen cops out looking for you."

"Because of Jory?"

"What? Your sister? No. That *Dune* book you loaned Natasha landed on my desk yesterday morning."

"Like *the* book?"

"You print Ari Zajac inside the cover?"

I nod.

"Listen, you're on lockdown 'til we get a handle on this."

TWENTY-ONE

Mikey tells me when a dolphin is wounded, other dolphins circle underneath, lifting it to the surface where it can catch a breath. Mary and Nia arrive at Sabina's. All the J's, except June, come. Even Jacquie flies from Poland with my niece, Arielle.

Girls who push boys into a coma don't deserve all this fuss. Girls like me don't deserve workrooms with paint, a bed with soft sheets, and windows to snow falling in moonlight.

Everyone pushes food in my direction, gentles my stressed hair, and steps around my silence. Even Aunt Nia, who has always set me hunting for the treasures found in dark places, fluffs cotton around me.

Ellis brings Chinese takeout. Mina brings homework, shaking her head at my face. "That's a fine mess." I'm a spectacular bruiser, always have been. The goose egg on my head is down, but a purple fright has leaked around my eye.

"Did they find anyone who knows him?"

"They're tracking leads in Montreal," Ellis says. "His story appears to be complete fiction."

"I used to make up stories all the time about who I was, who my parents were. Kids do that because their real life is shit." I split an egg roll and what I saw of Byron's head, before the lady sacrificed her hat, floods back and I hurl in the sink.

Now I'm like my mum, retching, retching, retching in the toilet. A hand gentles my back and I hear Jillianne's small sure voice. "I won't tell you that it ever goes away, but you'll stand up and take a step away from it, then another."

"He's going to die and it's my fault."

Jacquie forces water into me. Jory promises that the whole mess is in His hands. Jennah braids my hair. Her words, a seeming non sequitur, are most soothing. "Did you know Grandpa Trembley helped build Union Station? I always look up when I walk through, marvelling at how they did that brickwork." She leans into my ear. "It's in us sisters to build something spectacular."

Jennah and Jacquie have always been my mother-sisters, but Jillianne's secret is what I need. Four years ago, she robbed an old lady, near kicked her into the great beyond. Today, I watch her from the steps dancing with Arielle. She cranks music to the point that the windows vibrate and they move like tambourine ribbons lifted by a wind. The music ends and she sits close beside me. "We are Ari and Anne."

"I've never felt more like a misspelled Hariet."

"You may've had the name dumped on you, but you have the power to change it."

"It's not that easy." I whine.

"Sure it is. I'm now legally Anne Trembley. Listen, just start with this, when the shame and fear come crashing in, get up and move, turn up the music and dance." She takes my hand, slipping a small packet into it. "We're better away from the shit, I know that, but this reset me."

"What is it?"

"Doctors have white pills for the pain, but it can't reach the metaphysical ache in people like us. You're the clay girl. It's a gift from the earth."


Saturday morning, O'Toole strides into Sabina's Boutique and takes me to police headquarters. That he doesn't mess with me means terrible news is about to be delivered—either that or I look less appealing than shit on a shoe. I've been eating less than sleeping, and when I do sleep, I'm like the bird who rests half its brain at a time, so it can watch for danger. The bruise is now a muddy puddle on my cheek. My hair has given up the will to curl and is an electrified stress from crown to butt. Len's lanky cardigan is a futile remedy for the cold that has settled in my core.

In a room with leather chairs, Halpern, Ellis, and Mina sit at an oak table. Halpern says, "Come in, Ari."

"He's dead, isn't he?"

"Passed away this morning. Your teachers are here to help with the sorting to come. Sit. Please." He lights a cigarette. "So, the young man known as Byron Silver is one Billy Smith. Born at the Misericordia Home, March 9, 1949."

"In Montreal?"

"Yes. Adopted by Olive and William Smith. They were farmers. Father died in an accident shortly after. The mother remarried some relation quick to save the farm. The guy was bad news. You know the drill, booze, money trouble. He was in and out of the system for years."

*He was a throwaway like us, Ari.*

"He's been holed up over on Palmerston with a senile old lady. Convinced her that he was her great-nephew. Been helping himself to her bank account. And"—he pours water into a paper cup—"it seems Billy Smith, aka Byron Silver, is the Bobbie Story Natasha met in High Park."

84

"What?"

Halpern fans pages of a steno pad. "We found a whole box of shit like this."

My heart skips at the tangential words and doodled pictures filling the pad. *They're just like mine, Jasper.*

*Indeed they are, Ari Zajac, aka Hariet Appleton.*

*Shu—*

"Ari!" Ellis's voice cuts through a graying haze. His hand cups my head as I turn liquid and spill to the floor.

Chewing gum stuck to the underside of the table comes into focus.

"How's the perspective?" Mina kneels over me with a cool cloth. "Sit up slowly. Lean against the wall." I comply as she uncaps a Coke. "Here. Get your blood sugar up."

Halpern rolls a chair close. I try to absorb his words, hearing only "smart troubled kid" and "wild imagination." He tamps my eruption of hair. "You know, Ari, there was nothing pointing to him 'til we got our hand on these notebooks. Seemed the nicest guy you'd ever meet."

"Who were his birth parents?"

"No one who plays into this."

"Of course they do."


After an eight-year absence, my dad is in a dream. Images stick like a web as I surface: my dad painting a high fence with my braid, my sisters sitting on overturned buckets, their golden braids half-red and drying like neglected brushes. A neighbour peering from her yard says, "Your daddy's the nicest man I ever met." Night has a way of magnifying fear. Jasper lists: *Troubled family. Wild imagination. Non-linear note writer. Is that genetic?*

There's a ball-defying hitch to the Dick's pants as he enters the boutique, doors he vowed never to darken after the store landed on the Zajac side of Len's will. He snorts. "Halpern wants to make sure you're clear that the only thing getting out to the press is you don't know nothin' about nothin'. Got it?"

"Yes, sir."

"Christ, when this hits the papers of how he played us, heads are gonna roll. There goes detective."

"Spin it."

Spittle shoots through his thin lips. "Yeah, right."

I channel a pitiful Walter Cronkite imitation: "By gut, grit, and tenacity, crack investigators working 'round the clock zero in on the suspect, keeping him right where they could watch him until a solid case was built. To protect the public, he was under twenty-four-hour surveillance. City saved cost and family spared trauma of trial . . . Blather like that."

He whips out a pencil and pad. "Write that down."

"Can Mikey and I keep hiding out here? Jennah finagled an aide for Mum."

He wags the little pad in a victory wave. "Just 'til things blow over."


Ellis sits with me long past midnight as I paint quotes on totes in hopes that Iggy's words will settle me some. "Can I talk to you, seahorse to turtle?"

"Rochester's all ears."

"The thing I remember most about my dad are his made-up adventure stories. Is that where *my* story-weaving comes from?"

"That and your life happenings."

"Byron was a story inventor. And he, he shared my hodgy-podgy writing quirk."

"Not sure what you're getting at."

"You know Jacquie had a baby by my dad. He's out there. Who knows with who or where he landed. My niece, Arielle, could meet him one day, never knowing they're half siblings."

"You're suggesting your dad sired Byron?"

"He screwed my sisters. Why not other pretty young girls? Byron's last words were 'our father.' Maybe it wasn't a prayer but confession."

"Did Byron look like your dad?"

"Jennah burned all Daddy's pictures. But I think he might've."

"Your dad in the army?"

"Yes."

"They'll have a photo on file. Put this worry to bed. Chances are a million to one, but I'll look into it so you can at least get this horror from your head."

"Is there any way you can find out his mother's name?"

"It's in Halpern's file."

"How'd you know that?"

"You know Mina, always getting the perspective on things."

TWENTY-TWO

Mikey tells me that most of a dragonfly's head is an eye. They see just about everything. What Mikey sees is that I can't sleep. Late at night, my door opens and he perches on my bed, comfy against a pillow. He knits, without light. There's something calming about the tick, tick of the needles as he chitters out wisdom far beyond his years. "Did you know that there're cracks in the arctic ice where whales can surface for breath? Without them they'd suffocate." A few hours of sleep follow as he settles at my back, like a forcefield against nightmares.

Mornings, I head downstairs to the windowless workroom. I should study for a science test and write a history paper but *my biology nag, nag, nags. Byron's age puts him between Jillianne and Jory. Daddy always wanted a boy.*

I pick up my paintbrush, stilling my imagination with painting quote totes for the boutique. My head lifts to Linda tapping on the open door. "Sabina said I could come down. You mind?"

"Are you here to blather about my redeemability?"

"No. I want to apologize." She lights on a stool. "That remark I made about the parking spot. It was so arrogant to say it when your friend was missing."

"Don't sweat it. Your faith is your faith and I can be a bitch."

"I think you're irreverently wise. I get why Aaron treasures his connection to you."

"And you, I believe, are reverently kind. I get why Aaron's heart and mind melt."

"Did he tell you we broke up?"

"Yeah."

"What'd he say?"

"Just that he's not ready to talk about it."

"I couldn't find the words to tell him why I . . . he just needs to know what's at the bottom of the ocean. His constant questions made me feel like I was drowning and my faith was suffocating to him." She looks at me with big cat eyes. "Tell me you'll take care of him."

"He takes care of me."

"Maybe so, but you connect with him on a spiritual plane that I never could." She glides like silk from the stool to the door. "Um, would it offend you if I said I'll remember you in my prayers?"

"Any cosmic forces for good are welcome to have a go at me."

No sooner does the panther leave then Ellis stands at the door, his turtle muse postured like a trench-coated sleuth. "Before I give you anything, what will it prove if you find out Billy Smith was fathered by your dad?"

"Was he?"

"Don't know, but what if he was? What will you twist that into meaning?"

"That Appletons are rotten at their core?"

"If that's where you're headed, then you better damn well be ready to declare each one of your beautiful sisters as bad seeds."

"I've always been odd one out, five golden delicious and one wormy, brown, barrel spoiler. I heard all the time, 'The J's are Trembley. Hariet is Appleton.'"

"You are Ari Zajac."

"And who is she? I don't know how else to be in a body that caused death without peeling off my skin and seeing what's inside."

He hands me an envelope. "Let me, or Mina, do this with you."

TWENTY-THREE

For six years, the Village has been a scene that fit the unfittable girl, the sister-searching girl, the tie-dye artsy girl. Now, Friday night at the Riverboat, I'm the freak who killed the boy who killed the girl.

After closing, I dry a rack of cups. My boss pokes his head into the kitchen. "I'm heading out. Finish off the strudel while it's fresh and grab a sandwich."

"I'll eat."

"Promise?"

"Yeah. Night, Bernie."

I navigate the dark alley to my nest. *Do I want to know if this boy is an Appleton, Jasper?*

*Huey says you can't fix a boat until it's stripped down and the rotten bits scraped out.*

*Rubber Soul* plays while I eat strudel and reread Jake's sappy letters. Mid–sweet sentiment I drift to sleep.

*Sisssster.* Byron's hiss in my ear catapults me from bed like a python just snaked up my back. When morning leaks in like quicksilver, I unfold from the chair. My skin feels tight despite having dropped seven pounds. *Where does that go? Are particles of me floating in the atmosphere?*

*Making their way back to the ocean.*

The shower can't reach the crawl under my skin. I layer clothes against the numbing ache in me: Len's shirt, Jake's sweater, Mikey's hand-knit socks. I search my shelves for weed, none. In the lining of my backpack is Jillianne's parting gift, the wax-paper fold of crushed shrooms. "Go confidently into this, little sis. It reset me to me. To *me*, without Daddy in me." I've gone on a few acid trips with Jory, taken one all by myself. Hated every second of the chaos and distortion.

*Reset.*

A broken bone is reset. A watch. A timer. *Who can reset DNA?*

I'm flabbergasted when I feel Jasper spinning. He's the goody two-shoes in this pairing.

*I'm a goody one-tail. Shhhh-rooms. Let's go there.*

I'm not the first person to mix this shit in Riverboat lemonade.

I down it fast before really considering if I'm prepared for take-off. I land in my downy chair, blurry around the edges.

*We're good. Nothing bad can come in the nest.*

*What if the bad's in me, Jasper?*

As my chair shifts from solid floor to a boat on water, I wish I could reset time. Wish I'd just put on the kettle and picked up my book. My eyelid judders and my toes cramp. Terror seeps, like oil, through the floorboards. Everything I know, I no longer know. What is solid, defined . . . blurs, morphs. My stuffed Zodiac twitches like a foraging rat. My cells feel pulled outward, like static-charged hair. Panic, big panic rises with it.

Music, guitar, quiet, a Bach sonata slips over my head, my arms, like honey spilling over the floor. The window opens and all my presents and absences clap their tiny sounds against the glass. *Oh . . . look at the colours.*

A white shell unspirals into pearly hues. Red plates split into big red, poppy-rose-cherry-pomegranate red. Blue glass fractures light. Green vibrates. An orange pulses, opens, smiles. A prism splinters into rainbows. Len's iridescent pot transmutes into scarlet, fuchsia, emerald, turquoise, amethyst . . . There's no fear of it falling as it spins. *It's empty. Fill it. You fill it.*

Fans of colour trail the movement of my hand. Air is silver and fluid, puddling on my palm before slipping through my fingers. The ocean licks at my toes, pulls me under. I breathe. My eyes close as sun through leaded glass paints me in sunset-coloured waves.

I wake to the smell of spring. My cheek rests on my braided rug and I see legs, many sturdy legs holding chairs, the table, bed, bookshelf, coat rack, my easel . . . and I see Jasper marooned on his back.

*My tail was a viper swallowing me. Never, ever listen to me again if I suggest a trip.*

I find my land legs, drink water, pee, brush my teeth, braid my hair, make French toast, eat apple slices with sharp cheddar. Sitting at the counter, I notice the changed places of several totems. Mum's and Daddy's are outside hanging from the window bars. *Do you remember doing that?*

*No. We could've gone tits over tail off the fire escape.*

*Should I leave them outside?*

*For now. Maybe forever.*

*I saw Len. He said that my life was an empty pot for me to fill.* I notice my stuffed dog atop the fridge and a scrawling apology stuck to the door. *There is a sorry in me shaped like a star. A room heavy with stars. For brother, sister rats, especially you without a tail.*

*What's up with that?*

Remembering is not like a disappearing dream. It's as clear and fragmented as the prism suspended in my window. *You can't murder as many rodents as we have without there being a day of reckoning.*

*Let's not ever do this again.*

*Agreed. Think it's in our best interest that we not squander any brain cells.* A toilet flushes somewhere below and water whooshes inside the walls. Sounds transmute into a visual crack. Hidden things: wires, pipes, vents become seen, luminescent, and alive. I blink away the after-tremor. Blink again, opening to quiet, calm shadows. *Jasper?*

*Mm-hmm.*

*Where'd the fear go? I can't remember a time when I've felt its absence like this.*

*Out the window. Just don't go filling up that space with guilt.*

*Oh, that's still there. Like a festering boil.*

## TWENTY-FOUR

My old teacher, Belle Standish, comes to the boutique looking for a dress. She buys two and asks, "And do you have a quote to add to the bargain?"

Considering how she sheltered me through many a storm, a little buoyancy is only fair. "Um . . . 'The wound is the place where light enters you.'"

"Rumi. Excellent choice. It's so mild out. Fancy walking with me a bit?" She chitters about her plans for March break, then asks, "How are you, really?"

"Fragmented."

"I'm here for you. Don't ever forget that." She stumbles around reluctant words. "Ari, I don't want to take away from your support, but, as Aaron's mentor and as his friend, I feel it necessary to say something."

"What've I done now?"

"Do you remember seeing Mr. Thornton the day of that boy's accident?"

George Thornton was my science teacher. He was on the accusing side when years ago improperness between Aaron and me was suggested by a clutch of bitchy girls. "No."

"He was at St. Mike's with his wife. She was in emerg with gallstones. He saw you brought in with blood, blood all over your, your lap. Shortly after, he saw Aaron rushing in."

"Aaron wasn't there."

"You didn't see him. He went when he got news of everything."

My feet feel booted in concrete as I step, step, step.

"Next day at school, Thornton worded things in a way that could leave people thinking you might've had a, a miscarriage."

93

"But, it was in all the papers what happened."

"I tried to set things straight, but gossip takes on a life. He added tidbits about Linda breaking up with Aaron. How often he sees you two together. All innuendo, but—people talk and some thrive on hurting people and George Thornton wants nothing more than to see Aaron fall flat."

"Why?"

"Jealousy. Inherent sourness." She squeezes my hand without a trace of meanness. "Ari, this is a dangerous game when it comes to Aaron's career. He's such a gifted teacher. Once he finishes his master's, he's going to skyrocket up the ladder, but not if these kind of rumours keep arising."

"We're just friends. You were my teacher. Ellis and Mina are my teachers. You're all like my family."

"I'm a woman and Mina and Ellis are a couple. It's different for a single man."

I'm ironing stock when Aaron brings Mikey back. I keep my back turned as he talks. "Did Mikey tell you my uncle's springing for a trip to Mexico?"

I nod.

"I fly out Thursday night, so I'll see you after the break. Ari? You okay?"

"The train for okay left weeks ago."

He navigates around to take in my face.

I turn a cuff and press, focusing on the steam puffing from the iron. "Remember when you said I was more worth than trouble?"

"Yeah."

"Nice sentiment. But nothing could be farther from the truth. I'm toxic waste. Please just stay away from me."

"Belle share Thornton's trash with you?"

"I'm not messing up your job. We have to stop pretending what we have is okay."

He folds his arms. Relaxes against the wall. "Mess it up. I don't care."

"That's not true."

"It's truer than I can say."

My head wobbles, no.

"When my dad went overseas, my mom was pregnant with me."

"Still don't get Amish going to war."

"Mennonite, and Dad was a medic. The point here is Mom said she knew I was a boy and I'd be my dad's legacy if anything happened. All my life I was AJ, Aaron Junior, and there was never any discussion about the path my life would take. All I dreamt about was joining the coast guard or merchant marines." His head cocks, asking for my eyes. "If you decide to end us because it's what you need, okay, but don't you dare do it to protect a dream that isn't even mine."

"What is your dream?"

"Not sure. Stretching beyond travelling and immersing myself in another culture gets my cells racing." His smile is splashy and big. "And until I figure it out, watching Thornton make an ass of himself is entertaining."

"No, he's a ferret. And his wife's a badger. I can't imagine what domestic life is like for them."

He holds my eyes with his. "I don't care what it's like for them. Just tell me we're okay."

"I can't. Not until I sort out the terror that I'm Typhoid Ari contaminating everything I touch."


I have a lie ready, but the Dick signs a border-crossing letter without asking for a single detail and Mikey joins the Zajacs on a

March break trek to Myrtle Beach. If I go to the nest, I'll drown in sleep. At the craphouse, occupants pose an eeny-meeny-miny of snares. If I hurry, I can catch the overnight train to Montreal. Without preparation, I make for Union Station.

As night settles in, so does the cold. I tent my legs up under my skirt, pull my arms into my sweater, and sleep the sleep of the perpetually rattled. Five thirty-five a.m., we pull into Central Station. It's too early to contact anyone, so I sit on the hard benches and wait for something to open.

At seven thirty, I scan food options, from Twinkies to toast, settling on tea and a toothbrush. At nine thirty, I navigate my way to an address in Griffintown. That I move with fluidity through the streets, the smells, the language seals the knowing that you never leave where you've come from. I climb the stairs to the apartment over the corner store and knock. "Bonjour. Hello?"

A voice, close to the other side of the door, asks, "Who is it?"

"Um, Ari Appleton. I'm looking for Pauline O'Leary."

"What for?"

"I just need to ask if she knew a man named Vincent Appleton."

"Never heard of him."

I slide my father's army picture under the door. "Could you look please?"

"Never seen him before."

"Are you sure? It's really important."

She opens the door a crack and measures me up. "This about that boy?"

"Yes. How—"

"Police've been here. Please go. This has nothing to do with me."

"I just need to know if it has something to do with me. With my father."

"What're you on about?"

"It's complicated. He looked like my dad."

The chain slides off and the door opens. "You knew him?"

"Sort of."

I've grown to expect craphouse squalor when it comes to our kind of people. This flat is tranquil yet homey. "I haven't been Pauline O'Leary for fourteen years. How'd you get this address?"

"I . . . I stole a look at a file. No one else knows and I swear I won't bother you again. I just need to find out who . . . if . . ."

"Come, sit. I admit I've a few questions of my own." She's petite, neat, and doe-eyed, like Audrey Hepburn, like . . . Jillianne. I turn from her weighted eyes. Framed prints and photographs fill the space above the chintz sofa. Durer's *Parrot in Three Positions* in a small gilt frame catches my eye. She says, "It's all about perspective, isn't it."

"You sound like my art teacher."

"They said this boy was good at drawing."

"Apparently. Are you artistic?"

"Just an admirer. I'm a bookkeeper."

"Byr—he was really smart."

"You were friends?"

"Not really. I'm just trying to unravel the mess so I can make sense of it."

"Don't know what help I can be." My height and disorder feel absurd as I follow her into the kitchen. It's bright and cluttered. An old pine sideboard is crammed with jars. Herb pots line the sill. Depression glass vases—amber, teal, and pink—are filled with pennies. "Like I told the police. Got pregnant when I was fifteen. My parents sent me off to that home. Didn't even know it was a boy until the police came." She puts on the kettle and warms a Brown Betty teapot like Grandma always did. "So, what's this about your father?"

"I grew up around here. He resembled what I remember of my dad."

"And you think what?"

"My dad liked beautiful girls and he was kinda messed up."

"I had a summer romance with a sixteen-year-old camper from Maine."

Despite my shortcomings in math, I know my dad was nearing forty the year Byron was born. "Are . . . ?"

"Am I sure? Without a hair of doubt, Charlie Turning was the father. He never knew."

"What was he like?"

"Just a sweet boy who loved horses as much as me."

The space expands. Evidence of a family comes into focus: photos on the fridge, a calendar on the wall, a Pooh cookie jar that says, "My mummy is sweet as hunny." "You have kids?"

"Two girls, thirteen and eleven. They're with my husband at the family sugarbush for the March break." I feel myself shrinking from five-foot-ten to eight years old. "Come sit down."

"I'm sorry I barged into your life like this."

"It's okay. Maybe a little welcomed. I haven't been able to sleep since the police came. Who do you talk to about a thing like this?" She pours tea. "Did this boy hurt you?"

"I hurt him."

"Oh, you—police told me what happened. Did you know the girl they say he . . . he . . . ?"

"Yes."

She picks up the photo of my father. "He looked like this?"
"Kinda."

She studies the handsome man in uniform. "I see my nose. Charlie's smile. God, what did we create?"

"He seemed special in a lot of ways, really creative."

"And without conscience."

I spin what I know to the light side. "The old lady he lived with said he was very kind to her. From what I've gathered, he lost his temper and made a terrible mistake."

Her exhale is heavier than lead. "Thank you. That helps."

"Do you know the people who adopted him?"

"The nuns just said he'd gone to a wonderful family." She absently sips the cooling tea. "If I'd known, I would've found a way to take him. It's odd saying 'him.' All these years I imagined a girl, with a princess room, her own horse, beach holidays. My older sister tried to arrange an abortion for me, but my mom knew before I did that I was pregnant. She was so devout, she wouldn't let that happen. She believed every life was a gift." Delicate fingers rake through her cropped hair. "And now this. How do I say sorry? Make this right?"

My brain tangles in the paradox, the crapshoot that makes us, us. "My aunt says all energy, positive and negative, makes art, if we let it."

"Maybe I'll go help my in-laws make some maple sugar leaves for the shop. It'd be better than trying to add things up."

"I can tell you for sure that Natasha would appreciate you doing that." Pain blooms behind my right eye and a worm wiggles in my peripheral vision. "I should be going." I stand and she walks me to the door, shrugging a sigh as bewildered as mine.

The stairs down to the street are narrow and the light at the bottom is sharp. *She's just a regular human, Jasper.*

*Clay, we're all just clay.*

*But I can't turn sense of it.*

*Let's make nonsense then. I want Mary's Cornish pasties, feather pillows, and . . . Jake.*

I plunk on the planter outside Pauline O'Leary's building. *Just let me get this head calmed and we'll go.*

"You know where a guy can get a decent cup of coffee around here?"

Neck hairs shiver up as I lift my eyes to Ellis limned in sunlight. "Oh, for pity sake. Aren't you supposed to be skittering down an Alp somewhere?"

"Would be, but Mary called your aunt to check that you'd arrived safe. Dolores said you were going to Myrtle Beach with Sabina. So, Mary got in touch with Mina, they talked, and here I am."

"Didn't mean to worry anyone. I was just trying to carve out some time to sort stuff out where no one was fretting over me."

His grip is solid as he encourages me to stand. "Where's your coat?"

"Made a mad dash for the train without thinking things through. How'd you know I was here?"

"We knew you'd go looking sooner than later. Mary and Mina put two and two together."

"Sorry for wrecking your holiday."

He opens the door of his station wagon. "Find anything that helped?"

"Definitely yes and absolutely no."

There is a lovely weight to the vehicle as he settles behind the wheel. "Where to? Jillianne's?"

Curling up and sleeping next to Jake is all I know to do. "Just drop me at the train."

He digs a wrapped sandwich from a paper bag, insists it into my hand. "How about keeping me company to Quebec City? You can catch the train from there."

"Don't trouble yourself." I force down tiny bites. "I'm fine."

"It'll be a long cold week if I don't come back with all the details."

"The short of it is Vincent Appleton didn't father Byron-Billy-Bob or whoever the feck he is—was."

As the miles pass the long of the story is told and my head-ache eases.

"You must be relieved."

"For as long as I can remember, I've believed evil was con-fined to the Vincent-Theresa vortex. That lady was just a regular human, who had a romp with a boy and obeyed her mom."

He eases his foot from the gas. "Look around."

Fingers of light reach though the mash of silvery clouds. Fields ebb and flow like a great white ocean. A horse runs as a playful yearling darts and weaves alongside. A truck unloads metal for a new barn roof. The air, still wintery cool, is laced with spring. I inhale. Ellis smells like soap and flannel. "Do you think evil is a choice or a cellular thing?"

"I suspect people have certain predilections and life events shape them."

"I've always imagined Jacquie's baby out in this world, being wanted and loved, growing into a great yellow bear like Jacquie. Now I'm afraid my dad's genes have leaked into the world."

"Only thing you have any control over is what's here in front of you."

"But I'm scared of what's in me."

"You're nothing like that BS."

"Oh, come on. I make up stories. My head wiring is freakish and I tell you I could bash O'Toole's brains to pulp when he tor-tures Mikey."

"Defence of a child and strangling someone over not getting what you want are two different equations, even if the results are the same."

"How do I figure out the result of me without being able to add up my mum or dad?"

"You can't unravel another person, or account for all the vari-ables. From what I remember from my psych classes, it's more likely all the trauma after he was adopted that royally messed up Byron."

"Do you believe in God?"

"Why do you ask?"

"Well, the birth family honoured God. The nuns found him a nice family. Then the dad takes a header off a horse? If God sees the little sparrow fall, could He not see a honking Clydesdale heading off course? Especially after all the people involved tried so hard to be good?" I help myself to a cookie. "My dad's enrapturement with the divine makes all the God stuff devilish to me."

"Our earthly father is most often how we view a heavenly one."

"I've no shortage of persons providing heavenly perspectives. Are your parents as good as you?"

"My parents are flawed, lovely, horrid, kind, distant, embracing people. And please don't beatify me."

"To me, you are saint and saviour."

"Ari, I'm as cracked as the rest of humankind."

He catches the shake of my head.

"Take the war. Your dad enlisted, didn't he."

"Yeah."

He sacrifices the last cookie. "Me? I waited 'til I was called up, then manoeuvred myself into a position of safety. While my buddies were dying on the front, I was tucked behind a desk translating documents. I'm just your run of the mill, self-centred bastard."

"That's hard to see from where I'm sitting."

"Surely you've had a peek from where Mina sits."

"She's nuts about you, sir."

"For decades, every time she was full of hope for a baby, half of me was ecstatic, the other half was whining, 'There goes trekking through India. So much for writing a novel . . .' Then she'd get her period and I'd be filled with such grief that I could barely get out of bed."

"How'd you learn to move?"

"Turtles are painfully honest guides. Rochester would whack me with his shell like a frying pan across the head and tell me to get over myself."

"That Dr. Cornish says hearing voices is a symptom of schizophrenia."

"Oh, Ari, you didn't talk to her about Jasper, did you?"

"I may be crazy, but I'm not stupid. No way I'm leaving a paper trail that the Dick can use against me in a committal when I turn eighteen. Half of Jarvis likely told her I was nuts."

"Who on this planet is normal? No one, that's who."

"It does scare me. I mean, I hear Jasper's chitter so clearly."

"That's how I hear Rochester. Worry about scrambled voices in your head. That clear singular voice arising from our core is the sanest we ever hear. Most shut it up, drown it out, edit it down, twist it into lies, or are deaf to it altogether, but if we listen, it guides us through this wondrous, terrible life." He half turns to the quiet smile on my face. "What's Jasper whispering right now?"

"That I'm more linked to you than my dad. To Mina than my mum."

"We call you our clay girl."

"Jasper tells me I'll be at your sides when you set off on your adventure into the sky." He squeezes my hand and my thoughts drift for a peaceful long while. "Um, sir, I'd never criticize an English teacher fluent in French but that sign said Quebec City."

"No train until tomorrow morning, but there's a station a hop, skip, and ski jump from where we're staying. I've a hankering to see how a seahorse fares on skis."

"Oh, you and I both know something wicked will that way come." I squash Jasper's excited little flips. "Besides, one doesn't take on a Himalaya in workboots and a peasant skirt. And it's March break. I'm certain there's no room in the inn."

"We have a cabin and gear can be rented."

Mina sweet-talks a sturdy Nordic type into loaning me her back-up ensemble. I look like an inflated roll of five-flavour Life Savers. I should be perched atop a variety store. Instead, I'm high in the Laurentians soaking in the vistas of sugared trees and frothed-up clouds floating above the St. Lawrence. "Just leave me up here."

Ellis lowers his goggles. "You'll love it."

"Think I need more lessons on the kitty hill."

"It's called a bunny hill."

"Not when you're a scaredy cat."

"Stomach tight. Keep your knees bent."

Gravity pulls me along. The spray from Mina and Ellis catches the sun, filling the atmosphere with jewels. The "gentle" slope becomes less genial and I need rabbit, not bunny, skills. I tuck and suck, unsteadiness lessening as I settle into a groove that is as close to flying as I could ever imagine. Ten-year-olds whiz past. Mina is no doubt at the bottom. Ellis is fathoms ahead, but I am soaring. What a poetic name, the Beginner Hill.

Where the trail opens, merging with others, the snow turns to glass. My ski hits a bump, sending me helter-skeltering down the hill.

"Ari?" Ellis skies over to me. "You good?"

"I'm changing my name."

"Pardon?"

"Ari Joy Zajac."

Mina smiles down. "Transformational run?"

"Spectacular."

Ellis fusses. "Can you stand?"

"Think I left a chunk of my ass up there." I ratchet up. Stretch out the dents. *Bloody suit should come with a warning: material turns lioneagles into greased Bambis.*

Mina asks, "Ready to go again?"

"Noooo, no, no. You go Jean-Claude Killy your day away. I'll be by the fire."

Before sunrise, Ellis drives me to the train. On the platform I say, "Thank you, for all of this. Skiing was kind of . . ."

"Fun?"

"Um, more poetic. I'm composing an ooohhhh-de to my gluteus maximus right now."

He smiles and snugs a "borrowed" granny-square throw from the cabin around my shoulders. "What were you thinking leaving home dressed like this?"

"I wasn't."

"You sure you have enough money?"

I tuck my ticket in my bra. "I'm good."

The train wheezes into the dark station. "I'll call Mary and let her know what train you're on."

"No. I'm not having her navigate midnight roads to meet the train. I'll have no trouble making my own way."

"Of that I've no doubt. See you back here. Sunday at nine."

"I've already imposed too much."

"We're heading back then anyway. Don't you want an extra day with Jake?"

"So, Sunday. Nine sharp."

I haul my aching self up the steps, past sleepy passengers, and make my way to a seat.

"Excuse me. You dropped these."

I turn as a man hands me one mitten and a tube of ChapStick. "Thanks." I check my purse and see only the floor of the train. *Shit, Jasper. I've come apart at the seams.* My reflection in the window scares the beans out of me. The hat Mina nabbed from the lost and found is a hand-knit, purple-pink-lime creation with a pom-pom near big as my head. *We have no book, no pencils . . .* I tuck up my legs and nest in the jumbled colours of the throw. *My wallet with my library card, my licence, and pictures of Zodiac. Oh, Jasper, the penny pouch from William is gone.*

The window is cool against my cheek and the new day is a smudge of pink on the horizon. Pewter light seeps in through closed lids. My breathing syncs to the cha-cha-cha, cha-cha-cha of the train. I float as the miles move under me.

A cloud eclipses the sun, and from the shadows, Byron snares my hair. His smile opens to a maw, swallowing me whole. *Come with me. You need to see this—*

A hand pulls me to the surface. "Miss. Miss. Wake up. You're having a bad dream."

I suck in air, whacking my head on the window as I fight like a netted trout.

"I'll get you a cup of tea, miss."

I sense thirty pairs of eyes on me and turn to the window. My reflected hair resembles a poodle après electric shock. I force the disgrace back under the hat and receive a cup of tea without looking up. "Thank you. Sorry about the fuss."

"No trouble, little miss." William Walrus's voice cuts through my shame. "Been waiting for you."

My eyes meet his. "You have?"

"I need this." He taps my forehead with a quick flick and, like a magician conjures a quarter from a child's ear, a lump of coal is in his hand. "The clan of walrus are sorry for the burden of it."

"Pardon?"

"We walrus always know what's what, but on land we're not a folk that can easily do what needs doing. It's not your fault. It wasn't your doing. I swear on my whiskers."

"You know—you know what happened?"

"I'll be collecting a penny for it."

"Oh, I . . . I . . ."

"It'll turn up when you're willing to release the weight of it."

"How can I?"

"Because it wasn't your doing. Just the universe using a brave seahorse to set things right." He blows into his hand, opening it

106

to a shiny piece of quartz veined with gold. "Finding the treasure in this is how we're made whole. Old William knows."

"How, but, what?"

"Kintsugi."

"Pardon?"

"You're a potter." He opens my palm, pens a word, and places the pretty rock in my hand. "Find out."

A lady places the blanket on the seat beside me. "Sometimes I have horrid spider terrors."

I look at her well-lived face. "Did I make a lot of noise?"

"Not to worry. There's nothing like turning the skin inside out to get the old ticker going."

"Oh, good grief."

I really have to pee, but straightening my stiff frame will be another spectacle. I set the tea under the seat, focus on the lavatory door, and rachet myself up. The pom-pom on the hat brushes the ceiling and I feel like a giant weed.

*Jasper, I need a comb.*

*We are combless but not without teeth.*

As I exit the loo, every eye skits up, then darts down. Even empty seats look embarrassed for me. There are hours before I switch trains and can escape this nightmare. I inhale. "Mes amis. Fellow travellers. Je suis désolé. My apologies for the irreverent caterwauling. I will try, with all my might, to remain awake for the rest of our journey together. I lost my book so if anyone has one, preferably sans murder and mayhem, that I could borrow it would be greatly appreciated. And five bucks to anyone willing to sell me a brush. Merci and mercy."

My plea yields three books: *Murder on the Orient Express*, *The Taming of Nurse Conway*, and a childhood favourite, *On the Banks of Plum Creek*, the latter being the hands-down winner. A wide-toothed pink comb is offered for free.

Keeping my weary cells animated from sunrise to sunset edges

107

me precariously close to collapse. In preparation for changing trains, I wash, wrestle my detangled hair into a braid, return books, gather my remaining belongings, while adding up the remaining journey—two hours between trains. Barring cows on the tracks, four to Sydney. And if I'm lucky and hook up with a ride, an hour or so to Pleasant Cove, or all night in the train station if I don't.

*Jasper, what if Jake's been lured away by an angelfish?*

*Fiddlers do attract groupers.*

*Don't think I could survive that coming apart.*

The seat back accepts the heaviness of my head, but the worrying-weight remains. William walks through the car. "Truro, next stop. Next stop, Truro."

"You on the Saturday overnight to Montreal, William?"

"Depends on what the walrus clan hears needs doing. Sweet dreams 'til then."

Maritime cold skitters in with the opening of the doors and—after seven soul-murdering months—I catch the warmth of Jake's gentle smile. Without touching a step I'm in his arms.

"I've got you, love. I've got you."

The platform empties and I'm still clinging like a koala to the last eucalyptus on Earth.

"Let's get you warm."

I gather him—coat, hair, flesh—closer, closer more. "Don't let go." The air stirs as the train pulls out. Hope floats as silence fills the space it occupied.

"Here, put this on." He navigates me into Nia's parka.

"I told Ellis not to call."

His arm remains firm as he moves me along. "He found your wallet and stuff on the floor of his car and was worried." He opens the door to the aunties' truck.

I hop up, nabbing his coat before he can escape. His lips are the best thing I've known. The neediness in my kiss draws him in

108

after me, grabbing the handle and locking the door in one blind movement. He slides in as I perch on his lap. Waiting is not a concept that exists on this frigid March night. The single light in the parking lot makes the fogged windows luminesce. We kiss, and kiss, then kiss better and longer and sweeter. I tug, unbuckle, unzip, and bring him next to me under my hoisted skirt.

"Miss Appleton, where're your knickers?"

"Zajac. Ari Joy Zajac." The salt on his neck stings my lips. "In my hat."

His hands unearth the skin at my waist. "Your hat?"

"I washed them on the train and they were too damp to put back on. If you'd met me in Sydney, I'd have been a proper lady."

He soft bites my ear. "Oh, geezus, I'm glad I met you here."

It's not our first romp in the aunties' truck, but this time I'm transported to a place where everything is forgotten. Urgency rockets me into a burst of stars and a spiralling back to Earth. I hold fast as our breathing calms.

I'd fall asleep for a long deep while if my ass wasn't cramping. Before moving apart, I take in his good face. "Tell me there's another long slow forgetting when we get home."

"I'm yours for the rest of the week."

"I'll believe that when I live it, Jake Tupper." I dismount like a wounded flounder. "Where's the nourishment?"

"What makes you think there is any?"

I mimic Mary, "Now, take this and make sure you get some decent food into her. She was down to skin and dust last time we saw her."

Jake zips, buttons, buckles, and opens the door; he nabs the small blue cooler from the back and hoists it in. "Mary says sandwich before cookies."

A whole cookie is already in my mouth. "Don't tell."

"Buoy yourself with as much sugar as you need." He slides in and starts the truck.

"Thank you for coming to get me. I was down to my never-lasting nerve."

"You want to talk about it?"

"Later. You know M&N are going to be poking at the horror to see what gems can be excavated." I pick at a savoury bun. "Talk to me about anything good that's washed up on our shore."

"Found our boat. A forty-five-foot Cape Islander. The owner thought it was ready for junking, but Huey says she's got fine bones. I'm afraid working on it has kinda slowed things on the house."

"No matter. If the house isn't ready when we are, we'll sleep in the boat. What will she be called?"

"She'll tell us when time comes."

I swallow hard against the ache for the ones that will never again chart dreams. "How're Huey and the Missus?"

"Went to Halifax to see a specialist about her arthritis. Would've thought she'd been on a holiday. Talked for days about a lunch out and a movie after."

"Who watched the fosters?"

"Sadie came and lent a hand. Wasn't much that needed doing. They're all in school except for Kylie and Carter."

"How many fosters do you figure they've had?"

"Hundred, more maybe."

"They ever send any back?"

"Most just went home after a parent's stint in prison or rehab. There were a few they couldn't manage. Had to think of the safety of the others. Danny was set to be sent back for setting fires, but when the leukemia was diagnosed, they just couldn't."

I know it was Jake that wouldn't have it. Jake who watched over Danny night and day. "You want your own kids, Jake?"

"Whoa, thought you were leaving the tough talk."

"Just need to open the box a little on this."

"Do you want kids?"

"Oh, sure, throw it back because you're too chicken to say what might not be my answer."

"Right, I am. So, do you?"

"Whenever I see Jennah with her kids or Jacquie with Arielle, I think, yeah, us Appletons have potential and I want a tribe. But after this mess, worrying my dad was—"

"But he wasn't."

"Did Ellis spill the whole drama?"

"Mina knows how much Mary worries. She calls regular with updates."

"You gotta wonder why the universe didn't give Mina and Ellis a quiverful of kids." I search his profile trying to read his take on things. "Is it okay with you that I don't know?"

"Right now, just gathering up some throwaways seems right."

I pour lukewarm tea into the thermos lid. "Did you know male seahorses are the ones who give birth?"

"Aye. We can do things different from the rest of the world. We'll figure it as we go."

"What if the world went to war? Would you go?"

"To protect you, I would."

"Would you go to Vietnam?"

"No, I wouldn't." Jake is usually so non-definitive that his emphatic no has a spectacular safeness to it. He'd die for me, but he wouldn't kill.

"Sing me home." I settle my weary self by his side and he sings one of his made-up songs that he spins for the kids. Seahorses float on hum-diddle-dee-heys, while starfish weave through lay-lura-lura-oh-lay-lura-lie. Now and then, his cheek connects with my head-top, spilling his niceness through my hair.

The familiar music of tires on gravel tells my half-asleep self that I'm home. It's long past midnight, but the aunties spring through the yellow door and gather me up.

Longings in me queue like thirsty children at a water fountain. I want dog kisses. Given. I want hugs without questions. Received. The rest of my wishes are filled one by two. An Epsom soak in the claw-footed tub. Jake's fiddle tunes slipping into the bathroom along with the fragrance of wood smoke. My flannel robe against soap-sweet skin. My cobalt-blue mug filled with honey-camomile tea. Aunt Mary's scones, warm and buttered. A tucking beneath sundried sheets and a hand opening on my cheek telling me, "You're our girl and nothing that happened was ever your fault." Jake, standing quiet as M&N head to bed. A moonlit glimpse of his nakedness before he slips under the sheets, snugging chest to back until the distant foghorn guides me to rare dreamless sleep.

Late morning sun splashes branch patterns across the feather-bed. The dogs scratch at the door and Jake nabs me before I can move. "Please, not yet."

"Have to pee. Keep my spot warm." I stretch like a charley-horsed giraffe, slip on my ratty robe, and limp toward a glorious week at home.

M&N are head-to-head over the kitchen island. Mary looks up, offering a weak smile. Nia gnaws her cheek from the inside.

"What's wrong?"

"We didn't want to say anything last night, but Ari, that awful bruise."

"What bruise?"

Nia sighs. "Don't. This is upsetting enough."

I go into the bathroom and take a gander at my arse in the full-length mirror. "Holy guacamole." My right butt cheek looks like a child's painting of squashed avocados. I return to the kitchen. "Sorry I scared you. I fell skiing."

"No one hit you?"

"Yeah, a mountain."

"You're not eating right." Mary slams the cupboard door. "There's no way you should bruise like that."

"I landed on a ridge of ice and torpedoed down washboarded snow." Mary comes at me with a dose of castor oil. I open and shudder it down. "Life in crapdom has been shit-free sailing. The only thing the Dick has hit me with is bad breath."

Jake emerges, dressed in low jeans and disappointment. Mary wags her egg flipper at him. "Did you see her rear end?"

"Uh . . ." He looks to me for the right answer. "No?"

I catch the faint outline of a K on my hand. "Shoot."

He tugs his T-shirt over his head. "Uh . . . maybe?"

I pull out a stool and gingerly sit. "William Walrus told me about something. Kissgui? Or kisugi?"

"Kintsugi?" Mary asks.

"Yeah. What is it?"

She plunks a lumberjack's breakfast in front of me, drags a chair to the shelf, and retrieves a graceful red bowl, veined with gold. "It's the Japanese art of mending broken pottery by using gold to fill the cracks." She turns it in her hand. "Making damaged, broken things more valuable than perfect ones."

"Did you make that?"

"I did."

"Can the technique be applied to people?"

"Kintsugi in any medium requires patience and an artist at peace." Mary heaps a plate for Jake. "Get a few bites down, then we'll walk and talk."


Helping with chores is what I should be doing, instead I circle atop the stone wall, trying to step over past fears to future hopes. The foundation for Jake's and my house is laid. It will be a big house for big dreams.

Huey emerges from the treeline like a great oak found its legs. "Hey, dolly." He bear-hugs me off the wall. "Can we walks for a bit? There's something I thinks has to be known, just betweens us."

"Jake said the Missus went for tests. Please don't tell me she's sick."

"Everyone's right fine." We follow the trail down to the shore. "It's a long ago happening about our boy lost to the sea."

"Sadie told me he drowned."

"He did and what needs knowing is this: it was me who lost him."

"You?"

Huey's head nods heavy. "I was full up on the drink. Details don't matter none, the core of it is I wasn't watchin'. I knows some of the weight in your belly right now."

"Is there ever real peace after?"

"I say there can be, but it's a slippery bugger to get a hold of."

"How did you?"

"Just kept moving in hopes of it."

"Jillianne kinda said the same thing."

His right hand sits light on my left shoulder. "And in the moving, I just keeps meetin' all these throwaways." We stop, taking in the size of the ocean. "The crack in me's always there, but it's crammed full with these kids."

Kintsugi.


Whales make music. Familiar like flutes, but singularly unlike anything known. Skyfish has a call, heard most clearly in midnight hours, it's earth music, clay notes, with the power to lure me from a sleepy tangle with Jake to the gallery.

I poke the coals in the wood stove. Kindling catches and I add a log. I choose a bowl from the rack, salt-glazed, cream and black, put it in a bag, lift and drop. I have glue, likely not the right glue for this, but putting something back together feels necessary, urgent.

I'm sorting pieces when Mary pads in, wearing flannel bottoms and a woolly sweater. "Not glue. Flour paste."

"That'll hold it?"

"With some lacquer mixed in."

"Is the gold added to the paste?"

"No. Several finicky steps before we get to that."

We reassemble, without introspection, retrospection, or extrospection. We just puzzle broken bits together. Mary's hair is more a cascade of waves than spirals, nose dusted with freckles. In this pale light she looks more like twenty-eight than forty-eight.

Long past sunrise, Jake and Nia arrive with coffee and muffins, looking delightfully miffed at our shenanigans. Jake assesses the pieced-together pot. "You, girl, are in charge of placing the stone for our fireplace."

"It's going in the centre, floor to ceiling, opening both to the kitchen and the great room."

"How's that safe with kids runnin' around?" Jake scolds more than asks.

"Hmm. You're right. How about we just don't put up any walls inside."

He sits at the bench, sketching what could be. I let go of what was—a little.

TWENTY-FIVE

I try to keep hold of my Pleasant Cove Zen but it slips away like maritime fog. Not even Jennah's designer hand-me-down, a Mondrian-inspired minidress, can cover the Appleton taint. In my absence, rumours have ulcerated over and around facts re-leased by the police. Stories like Byron was framed to cover up murder by a cop's daughter.

I leave school before the dismissal bell stops echoing in the halls. Would've stayed for volleyball. Smashing would be therapeutic, but teammates followed Cassie into her festering anger. When Coach Palmer found xeroxed pictures of me taped to every ball with the caption, "Smash her. Spike her," she called the season a loss.

I cross the field, passing Matt's empty spot on the path. Since I'm Mikey-free for a few hours, my intent is to find Edjo, make a purchase, then zone out in the nest. Before my resolve syncs with my spirit, I find myself approaching the building where Natasha was strangled and stuffed. I stop short, absorbing that the un-kempt man sitting on the saltbox out front is Mr. Koshkin.

He looks up, eyes narrowing. "You," spitting from his mouth like he's expelling rancid meat. "Do not expect a thank-you."

"Pardon?"

"Killing that animal was justice owed me, the only thing that could bring me peace."

I plunk on the concrete, back against a splintery pole. "Trust me, there's no peacefulness in what follows. Besides, you have to take your beef up with the walrus clan."

"What?"

"Apparently when murder on land is afoot, their flippers don't work so well so they get up to mischief with girls like me."

"Natasha said you were . . ."

"Weird? Crazy?"

"Magical was the word she chose." All his softness has dis-appeared into acute edges and needled whiskers. "What is it you want?"

"Not sure. Jasper pushed me here."

"She told me, too, about this Jasper."

"She was so open to delight and possibility, wasn't she?"

"Why are you here?"

I shrug. "To blow this awful place up? To tell Natasha that school completely sucks without her?"

"Life is unbearable without her." His eyes slip from my face, to hand, to boot before settling on a desiccated worm. "Being with her is all I want."

"Major bummer for Alex and Joey."

"Perhaps they'd be better off without my blackness surrounding them."

"Not for a minute."

"What do you know of any of this?"

"My father offed himself."

His head lifts. "Natasha said your father died of a heart attack."

"That was Len, my step papa. My DNA dad blew his head off."

"He . . . Why?"

"A universe of reasons that all boiled down to one reality: he was a selfish coward."

"Better he is dead then."

"For him, yeah. For his girls? We were left knowing he didn't care enough about us to even try to fix the awful mess he'd made."

"Some messes cannot be fixed. This will never go. This pain will never go."

"My Uncle Iggy said it never gets smaller, you just get more muscled in carrying it."

"And what does he know of any of this?"

"He lost his two boys, both his legs, and his wife during the war. He stuck around thinking one day a kid like me might need him."

"I am of no use like that. When . . ." His head sags. "When the boys laugh, I want to crush it out of them."

117

"I felt like that after Len died. Music, joy, a spark of happiness is like a punch, isn't it?" I pull my knees against the ache in my middle.

His head nods. "Being with her is all that matters."

"No judgment intended, but that perspective is utter crap. What if all the afterlife hype is a load of hooey and there's no big reunion waiting?"

"You don't believe in heaven?"

"I try, I do, but I think the odds that Natasha's spirit is here are ten to one over a mythical kingdom in the netherworld. And if there is another side, you won't get the welcome you're hoping for. Imagine, just for a second, showing up at the pearly gates and telling Nat you bailed on Alex and Joey. She'd slug you."

He snorts bitterness. "I know I cannot act on my despair, but . . ."

"Doesn't it have to be acted on? I mean otherwise you're just stuck in it."

"Tomorrow the sun will rise and I will have to face again she's gone."

I stand. "Sun rises in the east. My friends, Huey and the Missus, have fathoms of facing know how." He accepts a hand up. "You should go there. By the ocean, sound is swallowed by the waves. The boys can laugh. You can roar. Your missus can weep. All as much as you need."

A sour laugh escapes. "Strange you say this. Running is the only thing I can imagine right now. But the boys have missed much school. I've not worked since—"

"You making a fortune sitting here? The seahorse tells me that it's the best tact right now."

His steps become less stiff as we walk. "Why a seahorse?"

"Because it finds balance when it seems impossible."

"Natasha said you gave her the spirit of a dog."

118

"Not just any dog, a golden retriever. You have to know how much I love my dog to know how special that is."

We walk, block upon block, in silence. At a crosswalk he asks, "May I show you something?"

"Okay?" As we turn down his street, I steel myself for gut-ripping sadness: Nat's dream wedding planning book, her hope chest filled with porcelain teacups . . .

We enter the yard and go into his workshop. A bucket is half-full of buttons, ordinary buttons. Mr. Koshkin picks up lengths of buttons woven together with wire. "She was making something. I can't see what it was. Can you?"

"Maybe. I'll consult the clans while you're away."

TWENTY-SIX

Stretching out my long bones is a challenge in the boys' closet, but it's the safest spot for me to sleep and the vent on the floor gives my ear a line to the bowels of crapdom. I keep a pen handy to jot down names, dates, plots . . . Cigarettes coming from an RCMP dump are bringing in a tidy sum, but moving drugs across the lake is the real money-maker. My ears perk when talk turns to my eighteenth birthday next year. O'Toole says, "I got a doc in my pocket. He'll sign anything."

The Dick says, "That Cornish broad from the school called me in for a chat. She thinks the kid's a psycho dingbat."

*Think it's time we change my name from Jasper to Jesus, then talking to me will just make you a good Christian.*

*That may be our only hope.*

While the Dudley Do-Wrongs continue to plot my demise, the door whines on its hinges. Yellow light leaks in from the hall. There is no mistaking the stink cocktail that is Devil Girl: stale baby powder, cum, and weed. Her arm snakes behind the hung sheet, searches the air, then slithers under my bra. My scream is more a high-pitched squeak. Todd snaps on the light and says, "Ronnie, what the fuck? Get your ass outta here."

Ronnie plunks on the floor, bearing startling resemblance to a panda in her white T-shirt and Tork's black sweatshirt. "Ah, fuck off. I'm just asking Hari for a loan." On Fridays, I smooth my escape from crapdom with groceries and a couple of bucks for the Zanzibar and she knows my bra is padded to cover expenses. "You gotta help me."

*Bet she's knocked up.*

*Shhh.*

"Led Zep's playing Montreal on Monday. Tork scored wheels. You gotta help us."

"I'm not giving you my hard-earned money."

"Come on, you little Jew. Sell ya my ring." The ring. My nana's emerald diamond heirloom. The only Appleton remnant left. Given to me by Nana on her dying bed. Snatched by Mum and gifted to Ronnie on her sour sixteen. "Just five hundred."

"That piece of crap? It's just hunks of glass. I'll give you ten bucks."

Ronnie tugs it off her baby finger. "Three hundred."

"Fifty, tops."

"I can get a hundred at McTamney's."

If she ever was awake during business hours, she'd find she could get ten times that at the pawn shop. "I've got ninety-seven. Take it or leave it."

"Sold." She nabs the money, face sweetening as she scans

the oceanside mural we've painted on the wall. "Hey, that's real pretty. Remember when we went to that cottage, Toddie?"

"Yeah. You were the only one who caught a fish."

"Tasted good, eh?" She navigates to a stand, like a toddler trying to find her legs. "Bye, losers. Zep calls."

The silence in the room hums after she goes. My hand closes around the ring, a thing I'm not sure I want anymore.

*Nana was nice. She made fudge and sang Buffalo Gals.*

*She also made Daddy.*

Sleep hangs like an apple just out of reach.


Jennah arrives at seven thirty a.m. to drop off a travel activity bag for the Koshkin boys and an Adidas track suit for me and I wonder if any of the Appleton sisters ever really sleep. "I saw these at Eaton's yesterday." Out of all the stellar clothes Jennah has given me, this delights me most. "It'll look so much nicer than the ratty things you wear for volleyball."

Last year, the Jarvis volleyball champs made the papers and Jennah had nothing sporty in her closet to cover up my bruises. I haven't the heart to tell her that the season is cancelled. She ticks number four and five off her list of thirty things to accomplish today. *She is a marvel of precisely ordered discord.*

Aaron tuned up the Koshkins' station wagon. Sabina packed it with pillows and picnics. Now, Ellis gives Mr. Koshkin the key to their cottage near Trois-Rivières and we watch them down the road, astonished that the old Chevy is able to clear the asphalt under the weight of their grief.

"You know, Ari, Joseph couldn't've gotten behind the wheel and moved without this end. It's a mercy they don't have to endure a trial."

"Sabina gives me the same uplifting blather, but the sound of

ByBillyBob's head hitting the car is all I hear. I'm not who I was anymore."

"That's not necessarily a bad thing. Remember that poem you shared in grade nine? Be the unthinkable one. That's who this can make you: more expansive, stronger than you ever were. You're a lioneagle conquering evil."

"For frig sake, sir, ease up on the syrup."

"Yeah, made myself a little nauseated just now. Hey, I've got the grade nines starting on the diary assignment. How about you do it?"

"I still keep one, but giving you an unedited slice of my life would begin with Devil Girl's hand in my bra."

"Hmm. A tragedy? A comedy?"

"Horror. Sheer horror. Anyway, the printed word is eluding me."

"Makes sense, in a way."

"How's that?"

"If you're afraid that things really could be used against you in a court of law, I understand your psyche just spooling up thread that you can weave together later. But any way you spin it, your life's a writer's dream."


I leave my gift from Jennah in my locker and nab my ratty sweats. It's the beginning of track, and running feels like the only rational move left. I lap the class because I so badly want to escape. *The Koshkins are likely east of Montreal by now.*

*And we're running in circles.*

Another five or ten times around the track beckons but Coach Palmer sidelines me with a flick of her clipboard. She chitters while I cool down. "Monday, I want to see you out for track."

It's odd that a no-legged seahorse spins at the idea. "Maybe," I say.

A little energy fills my pores as I shower, shorting out when I discover my gym and street clothes are gone, gone, gone. Former volleyball teammates nonchalantly preen and adjust their skirts. *Can't believe I fell victim to such unoriginal torture.*

Jasper tails up. *You're not a cornered dog. Lioneagle up, Ari Joy Zajac.*

The underwear they nabbed is clean and snazzy. Purple with white daisies, matching bra, not pathetically small or sumptuously big, but a respectable non-padded 34B. My jeans are scribbled with quotes, the kind that would do a thief some good. *Let them hang them on a flagpole.* I cinch my towel, release my curtain of hair, and go confidently in the direction of my locker. In the hall, as classes change, I step into my new track pants, zipping the jacket over my towel before skimming it out. I'm in a black Adidas skin from ankle to chin. I grab Jillianne's advice, turn up the music in my head, slam into my boots, then jump, jump, jump, turning dervish circles down the hall. Gawkers part as I wah-wah-watusi myself to chemistry, then home.

Todd delivers the weekend forecast while exiting the asylum. "I'm in Rockton 'til Tuesday. We're out of bread, milk, and pretty much everything. And steer clear of the Dick."

"He get demoted?"

"For fuck sure that's coming but for now he's got the clap. So, chances are your mum, O'Toole, Ronnie, and company have it, too."

Mikey asks, "Do I have clap?"

"No. Only Dicks, pricks, and scuzzy chicks get it."

Todd hoists his pack over his shoulder. "Oh, and Laura's bailing. Sorry, Mike."

Mikey shrugs his way up the stairs. "Don't like that Delio, anyway."

"Delio?"

"Her milkman."

"Let's just make for Sabina's right now."

One minute less and we could've made a clean get away. The Dick pulls up in the blue sedan, rolls down the window, and hands me a white carton. "Get two into your mother. I'll be back in an hour. Tell her to be ready."

There's a tower of cartons in the hall: Brexton Picnic sets, Sail pipe tobacco, Ocean Fresh sardines . . .

*What kind of a day netted this crap?*

Mum wobbles from the kitchen in bellbottoms a mariachi dancer would envy, a fur-trimmed pink sweater, and what could be a feather duster in her hair. There was a time when every man sucked in his gut when Mum entered a room. In spite of her loathing of me, there was a certain pride that Theresa Appleton was my mum. "Oh, Jory, have you seen my box?"

I assess the box in my hand containing one hundred and forty-four penicillin tablets. "This one?"

"No, my, my—" She motions with her hand. "My box."

"Your purse?" She nods, wide-eyed, like it's what she'd said all along. Her eyes are still forget-me-not blue. "I'll find it. First come take these." She downs two pills. I give her a third because it makes her smile.

O'Toole animates off the couch. "You got the cure there, sweet thing?"

"Is putting pants on just too friggin' hard for you?"

"I'll show you what's hard."

*Walked right into that one.*

"Ari," Mikey calls from the front door. "Wendy's here."

The disgrace of the craphouse assaults all the senses: clutter and carelessness everywhere. Foul mouths overriding the constant hiss of the TV. Banisters, live with bacteria from unwashed hands. Mum's sickly sweet Shalimar masking stale smoke and vermin decomposing in the wall.

I step onto the derelict porch. "What new slings and arrows?"

"Just a sorry," Wendy says. "Heard what happened after gym today."

"Everyone hates me."

"Cassie buys the whole frame-up thing. Your stepdad being a cop and all. She and Byron were . . . you know . . . doing it."

"I suspected."

"I'm so stupid."

I absently peel a scab of paint from the rail. "He played everyone."

"Not like me. I'm such an idiot. We . . . He . . ." Her head drops to her knees. "I can't even say it."

"Nothing will shock me, guaranteed, and shit is better out than in. That way you can flush it."

"You promise you won't ever tell?"

"Word."

"We never even lip-kissed. All he wanted was for me to kiss his . . . his . . . thing. You can't even imagine how awful it was."

"Yeah, I can."

"Has it happened to you?"

"Yep."

"I cried. How pathetic is that?"

"Me, too." I don't tell her that I was seven.

"Worst is I loved him." She searches the abandoned nest in the porch light. "I loved, really loved someone who could do what he did."

"You loved the story he made up."

"You know, it drove him crazy that you never paid him any mind."

"I bought his shiny story, too." I study my over-long toes. "I steered clear because in my experience golden guys like him were only ever interested in Appleton tarts for a romp on the slutty side of the sheets."

"He was the rotten one, to the core. Detective Halpern thinks he did it because Nat said no. She dies because she was being good and I—"

"You're here and you're the only one at school being decent with me, so give yourself a break."

"This changes everything forever, doesn't it?"

I see, for Wendy, Nat's death is a tsunami. For me, it's just another breaker crashing on my shore and I don't know what that makes me. "My aunts say there's creative energy in everything that happens."

"Nat's dad gave me her bike. I could never ride it, but the stillness of it gives me the creeps. It would hurt him if I gave it back, wouldn't it?"

"Probably."

"Wish he'd just given me one of her buttons to hold onto."

"Ari. Ari!" Mikey's hollering levitates me into the house. Mum is standing on the rug, forearm to nose, blood gushing.

I back her into the chair and nab a towel from the sofa. "Mikey, get TP. Mum, tilt your head back."

Wendy says, "No. Head forward. Pinch her nose, here." She snatches the TP from Mikey, twists a plug, and shoves it up Mum's nostril. "Are you on blood thinners, Mrs. Appleton?"

"No. She likely just had a snort of coke to get herself up for a big night."

"Wha—? Geez."

"You mastered your first aid badge at Girl Guides, didn't you?"

"Pathetic, eh."

"No, appreciated." I keep the pressure on Mum's nose and offer my own first aid. "You should go before the Dick gets back."

"Okay." Her turn at the doorway is like a spent flower holding against a big rain. "I don't know how to get through this."

"Can you scope out where we might get some buttons?"

"What kind?"

"Um . . . every kind and colour."

"How many?"

"Lots. And bring Nat's bike to the art room on Monday."

"Okay?"

"And drop by Sabina's tomorrow. I have a button for you."

"One of Nat's?"

"I found it for her birthday. She'd want you to have it."

TWENTY SEVEN

Mikey tags along on my Sunday meet-up. Aaron absorbs the kid's slump and drag. "Hey, buddy. Thought you were at your mom's."

"Mikey made his own way from Laura's to the Riverboat last night."

"What? That's like two miles. You should've called me."

"Didn't have money." Mikey bites back his lip quiver. "Kira helped me find Ari."

Aaron asks, "You guys free for a while?"

"Free as wing-clipped birds."

"Okay, Mikey, pick an adventure: mountain climbing, trail-blazing—"

"The ocean."

"Get your imagination in gear and we'll go."

Aaron arms Mikey into the nook behind the seats. He's as pale as porcelain and blue just under his surface and I wonder if broken kids really can be pieced together and veined with gold.

As we drive east, Aaron asks, "Have you heard how Nat's family are doing?"

"Apparently her dad's stuck to Huey like a new foster kid. Her mom spends her days with the Missus, and the boys have made fast friends and situated themselves into school."

"Where're they staying?"

"Cap Harmer gave them use of a rental cottage. The men laid in wood. Ladies Aid stocked the pantry. I know the rough seas can't be changed, but maybe they'll find some way to navigate."

Just past Oshawa, Aaron follows a spring rough road down to the lake. Mikey launches toward it, rocketing the shore while we saunter along. Aaron asks, "So, what happened?"

"Laura's creep of a boyfriend locked him out and she was too wasted to notice. Mikey knocked and knocked, cried and pleaded. One thirty, he comes shivering into the Riverboat, barefooted, in PJs. He'd pissed himself."

"Does the Dick know?"

"Mikey begged me not to tell. He'd kill Laura. Friggin' pathetic parentals. I've got to figure a way to get him to the Butters."

He pockets his hands. "I know it's where you both belong, but I hate the thought of Toronto without you two."

"Don't get your sails in a knot." I link my arm with his. "Jasper says the winds will settle between this sou'wester and nor'easter before geography separates us."

"We are impossibly different, aren't we."

"Impossible or not, the fact of it is we are, we just are."

"Are what?"

"Connected."

"Jake doesn't mind this . . . um . . . connection?"

"Mind? He expects it. It's a little exhausting how much he thinks he doesn't deserve me." I keep hold of his arm because I need to. "I mean, how twisted is this? I'm a murderer and he's a saint. He tells me I'm clay and thinks himself dirt."

"You're not a murderer."

"A manslaughterer, then. I did whiplash BS to his death."

"No deal. You don't get to play this both ways. If Jasper and his friends are real, as you claim they are, the walrus clan did the deed." The smile between us is sweet as a kiss.

"Aaron West, are you ready to let that animal of yours out?"

"Is it an octopus?"

"Why would you think that?"

"You always say my hands are overfull."

"Connect with the ethereal, the metaphysical you, not the logical, man." I sing a clue, "You'd like to be under the sea, but an octopus is definitely not thee."

Mikey circles back with a little less burden. "Can we make a fire?"

"Can do."

"You have a dry log in that jeep, don't you."

Aaron winks. "And a pot, water, and dehydrated mac and cheese."

"Okay, practically speaking you might be an octoeagle, like I'm a lioneagle, but that's quite different than what your mind-bending animal is."

"You are delightfully odd, Ari Lioneagle."

"Thank you."

At the drop back into hell, I take in his good face. "Thanks for helping us navigate this day." It's rare, I think, for eyes to connect and remain held by the other. I know a dolphin and seahorse don't belong together but there's no denying the love that tangles us and the deepening of it.

Aaron breaks the spell. "Um, you think you might want to play some volleyball?"

"Every night I dream of smashing O'Toole's head. Why?"

"Someone in my class plays with a community league. They're short a full roster."

"Where?"

"Wednesdays at the Benson Building."

"Don't think I could swing it with Mikey."

"She has two kids who tag along with her. I'll send the details with Mikey on Tuesday."


Escape from crapdom on poker night to play volleyball is better than Christmas. Mikey and I scheme up a plan to make the Dick think it's his idea. We slap together baloney sandwiches while Todd goes to buy a case of beer. Mum sits on the wobbly chair waiting for me to fluff up her split ends, eating mayonnaise. She spoons up another dollop. "For Christ's sake, Mum, eat a sandwich."

"I like pudding."

As much as the Dick is inflating with his new "acting detective" status, Mum is deflating. I wait in hopeful anticipation for simultaneous explosion and implosion. When the Dick molders in, refreshments are piled and Mum is propped up with hairspray and amphetamines. He yanks up Mikey's chin. "What happened to your eye?"

"Got hit by a ball."

The Dick would be proud if he'd been in a scrap. He snaps Mikey's head away. "Pathetic."

Mikey backs away as planned and I say, "His teacher says he needs practice with hand-eye coordination."

"Baseball, that's what he needs. Or bowling."

"She recommended a program for kids over at the university. He'd have to try out though."

"When?"

"Tonight."

"Take him."

"Can't. I have homework."

It's been a solid year since the Dick has risked bruising me, but he yanks on my hair without thought or mercy. "You can do it there. Get."

Mikey has a Hardy Boys book. I have jitters and my new track suit as we hurry to the Women's Athletic Building at U of T. "I'm going to make a fool of myself."

Mikey swipes the black makeup off his eye. "You're the best player at Jarvis."

I wipe off the remaining smudge. "This is the big leagues."

I wander in and a woman, tall as a mast, smiles. "Ari?" I nod. "I'm Giselle. This must be Mikey. My Erika will be chuffed at having a friend to help with the ankle-biters." She points across the gym. "There're two bucks in it if you can keep that lot happy and off our court." Mikey rises to the challenge and Giselle sizes me up. "You play?"

"Just my school team."

"What we need most right now is a body or we'll have to forfeit."

For two whole hours, my history is absent. I just play, with abandon. After a thin win, at my serve, we drink banana-raspberry smoothies and talk. I hold my own with books read, listen in rapt wonderment to stories about careers and travel, and they ask me about making pots.

Mikey and I accept a ride to Wellesley and Jarvis, then meander home. "That was the most fun ever. Here fun, I mean."

"Yeah. It was."

"Erika asked if I wanted to come over and play sometime. Her dad's a geologist and has fossil rocks."

"Cool."

"I told her if she came to Pleasant Cove, we'd find fern fossils in the rock slide."

"Giselle said the kids have never been so good."

"I'm going to be a foster dad like Huey when I grow up."

"Don't let the Dick hear you say that."

"Kira's almost as good as Jasper at making up stories."

"Does she have one for why you need to come with me this summer?"

"Yep, I need to train as a sea cadet so I can be a marine cop."

"Excellent tact. I heard O'Toole say the new police chief is training a whole unit because of drugs going across the lake."

"Is the new chief going to protect us?"

"I tell you, Mikey, I can't sort the protectors from the predators."

The craphouse is so thick with smoke I can see it through the front window, like dense maritime fog. By now, O'Toole will be plastered enough to think I want to play poke-her. The Dick will be either in-the-hole pissed or winning-big bragging, and Mum will be puking in the sink. Mikey appraises the unidentified hulks planted on the veranda. "Who are those new guys?"

"Associates. Let's sneak in."

We head around back, nimble foot onto the porch roof and dive through Devil Girl's window. Mikey checks the hall, signals "all clear," and I dart into the boys' room.

"Go brush your teeth." I leave on my stinky volleyball gear and pretzel into the closet.

Through the paper-thin wall, I hear Mikey meet up with O'Toole. "Hey, ass wipe, Hariet in there?"

"No, she brought me home, then went to the library."

"Fuckin' liar. Library's closed."

"At the university it's open 'til midnight."

"She with that Aaron creep?"

"Her friend Giselle. She has a card she lets Ari use."

*He's a good story-weaver, eh, Ari.*

*Epic.*

I snug down with *I Know Why the Caged Bird Sings*, feeling still disassembled but hopeful that something resembling life can be pieced together.

## TWENTY-EIGHT

Monday, June 1st at three fifty-five, I approach the Shell Tower. Mr. Koshkin is sitting on the bench out front. He motions for me to sit. "This meeting must seem a strange request."

"What isn't off-kilter this year?"

"It's nine months since we were to meet Natasha here."

"I can't imagine the terror you've felt from that moment on."

"And now I must learn to meet life without her. For the boys, and for Katia. For my Natasha, also."

"She said you were brave."

"Tell me other things you remember of her."

"Um . . . She could say the alphabet backwards faster than anyone. We'd race. She'd be at A before I was halfway through."

His fisted hand steadies his lip quiver.

"She gave a Valentine to every single person in the school so no one would feel left out."

"I remember. She had me bring home two cartons of toffees."

"She welcomed me with a toffee. I was so unhappy being pulled from my old school, she saw that. She was the first person to talk to me, invite me to lunch, help me find my way to classes."

He's bent forward, studying his empty hands as I tell him all the sweet things I remember. His sigh is ragged. "We are moving from here, Ari."

"Sabina told me you're going to Guelph."

"Yes. A new job. Agricultural research will be a change, a necessary change."

"Candy to dirt. There's a poem in that."

"I need for you to hear me say this. There is mercy for me in his death. I don't care what difficulties he faced. I could not have tolerated excuses made in his defence at a trial. If he had a life, any life, no matter it be in a cage, I'd be consumed by bitterness.

133

And if Katia were to offer him sympathy or worse, forgiveness, and knowing her she would, it would break us." His veined hand pats my arm. "Live your life knowing my load, the weight on our family is less burdened."

"I'll let the walrus clan know they helped."

"All your clans helped."

"The Cove's a good place, eh."

"A hallowed place."

"True, eh? All I want from life is to get Mikey there and live out my days with Jake."

"It's a fine hope, but take it from me, your dreams cannot be dependent on another's presence in that life. Each morning now, I open my eyes, and an old dog, right in here"—he taps his chest—"says, 'Joseph, get up and retrieve what you can for Katia and the boys.'"

"There's been a spirited dog poking at me, too." I check the tower clock. "Can you come to the school?"

"Who's there at this time?"

"Just Mina, Wendy, and Ellis, but all Nat's friends helped make something from her buttons."

Near as I can describe Mr. Koshkin's face when he sees it is a golden retriever waiting for a ball to be thrown. Not a smile but anticipation, longing mixed with a little hope. "You did this with that bucket of buttons?"

"When something needs to be done and you ask Wendy to do it, it's like the loaves and fishes miracle. Half a bucket became trash-cans full." Natasha's bike is encrusted with buttons, spokes, frames, wheels, seat, basket to pedals. The form riding it is as real as it is abstract. There's no mistaking, from the flip of hair to flower-power sneakers, it's Nat. "We wired them together following the ones Nat started. Then used a resin to fill in the spaces."

Mina says, "When the sun catches it, it fills with light. We're going to coat it a few more times so it can handle the weather."

Mr. Koshkin asks, "Where will it go?"

Wendy says, "We're doing a fundraiser for a gazebo and benches."

He looks to Ellis. "Will you go and bring Katia and the boys? Please."

I duck out with Ellis. "What a lovely tribute, Ari."

"Mina's the mastermind and renderer. I swear Nat looked like a chicken before she fashioned it."

"That pup in the carrier is yours to the last button. His laughing mouth makes me smile."

TWENTY-NINE

Third Sunday in June, I watch Aaron stride toward me. Odd how I'm getting older and he isn't. We are tethered, a soul from too much order and a soul from utter chaos, finding equilibrium in the other. "So, Aaron West, you look in need of a long ocean soak."

"Lima is right on the ocean."

"Are you going to climb Machu Picchu?"

"Uncle Pete's coming in August and we might. That earthquake in Chimbote was devastating. We'll meet up with the Red Cross and see what help we can be before doing anything else."

"And July?"

"Course work. If you can believe it, I'll be getting paid to gather data on literacy." He peruses the wry smile on my face. "What?"

"It's nice to see you swimming in the right direction."

He digs one of Sabina's pastries out of the bag. "Did you know Linda's getting married?"

"I heard. You won't always be alone, you know. Jasper's never wrong."

"I'm not so much lonely for Linda as I am for myself and I'm not at the place where I can go and meet me, if that makes any sense."

"Everyone is held by something. Where my history is dung and I get mired in the shit, you're caught in a cage of spun gold. Yours is a harder escape, I think." My boot nudges his sneaker. "We're kind of at the same place. Theoretically we could just fly away, anywhere we please."

"So, what keeps us stuck?"

"The gravity of the question my old friend Chase posed last summer: What's the one regret you wish you could change when you're ninety? That's an okay stickiness to be in, don't you think?"

"Feels like ninety years have passed since then."

"The physics of trouble time."

"Speaking of trouble, how's your mum?"

"Yellow as a duck."

"What's going to happen to Mikey if—"

"Mum dies?"

"Sorry, I just . . . What will happen?"

"Reality is, if the Dick doesn't blow up his life, Mikey stays with him. Dick married Mum because he thinks it makes me—ergo, Len's money—his property. He's gathering evidence to have me committed on my eighteenth birthday."

"Could he?"

"Definitely possible. If anyone asks, you've only ever heard me talking to Jesus." I shrug. "I can help the kid while Mum's breathing and Len's money is in play, but after, I won't have a road in."

Aaron asks, "Is the Dick still being decent?"

"Halfway. O'Toole's got him jammed up with a lot of sketchy hombres, but he has a fresh murder to make him happy."

"What happened?"

"A ninety-year-old was strangled and stuffed in a closet. Earthquakes and all this other shit never end, do they?"

"Knowing that makes this peaceful moment pretty spectacular, eh?" He unearths a paper bag from his satchel. "Happy belated seventeenth."

Inside is a silky book of Japanese pottery. "Oh, this is so perfect. Where'd you find it?"

"Giselle tracked it down. Have to be honest, it was her idea."

"Ready for some serendipity?" I rummage through my pack to a carefully padded gift. "This is my first one. I wanted you to have it." A pot mended with spidery gold sits on his open palm. "Didn't know how else to tell you how connecting me to Giselle has been the only time I've felt close to normal this year." We shouldn't lock eyes, not when I love Jake, but sometimes eyes disobey hearts. "Are you coming to the final game?" I ask.

"Wouldn't miss it."


Stands have been rolled onto the side of the gym where the kids usually play. My supporters cheer as we own the last game of a round robin. I'm not the best player, but I'm the angriest and that alone racks up the points.

Post-game, Giselle gives out directions to her house. "Go on ahead. Door's open."

Aaron says, "Come on, Todd. Ride with us."

Todd straightens. "Me? Really? I'm invited?"

"Couldn't celebrate without you, bro," I say before heading to the changeroom.

I'm dabbing my scraped knees with Mecca, thinking about warmed brie and cold watermelon, when a card is flicked in my face. "Have you thought about where you're going?"

"Um, Giselle's party?"

"I mean, which university." A woman I don't know but have seen watching us play now and then says, "You could have a full ride to any school."

Jennah's minidress slips over my head. "I'm just going into grade twelve."

"Grade thirteen's an easy workaround. Other provinces and schools in the U.S. don't require it." She stands too close; there's a tiny blister on her lip. "I'd like to see you in training this summer."

I look at her card. "Sorry, Miss Strazda? I have a job in Nova Scotia. I leave on Friday for the summer and when I do go to university, it'll be there."

"No. McGill, maybe."

I so seldom feel clarity in my life. Right now, what I want, and what I'll do, is make my hair look pretty for tonight and go to Nova Scotia on Friday.

On the way to the car, Giselle says, "Keep that card, Ari. Strazda's pulling together a Canadian team to compete on an international level."

"Why me? Everyone on the team's better than me."

"In sports years, we're geriatric. You're young, you go all in and play your guts out. It's a great way to pay for school."

I stuff the card in my bag, knowing I'm not getting into any university based on my marks.

Giselle's home is big and moneyed, but not decorator-perfect like Jennah's. There's a weird pool, inside a solarium. Long and skinny. Mikey and Erika have their feet a-dangle and Giselle says they can go in if they can find a lifeguard in the crowd. Neither

138

Aaron or I are lifeguards but we're content to sit, soak our feet, and watch them start at opposite ends and race toward us in the middle. Aaron leans into my ear. "You moved like water and smashed like a wave on that court." For a dolphin spirit, that's close to saying I love you.

Getting his toes in the water is risky, perilous even. "I liked hearing you cheer." Our naked forearms touch as we splash in the other's eyes. His hair brushes my cheek as I look away. Mina's swapping travel stories with Sonja. Ellis is pummelling our best player at ping-pong. Todd is holding court with several people around a rattan table. I ask, "Do you know who Todd's talking to?"

"Apparently, there're plans in the works to bring a zoo to Toronto. They're picking Todd's brain."

"He looks so happy." My baby finger touches Aaron's. "After this awful year, I can't really settle into this calm."

"Just let go. For one night."

We both teeter between holding on and letting go. As the kids launch into another race, my inhale mingles with Aaron's exhale. He claims a little more of my hand. "Tell me we have next year. Even if it's just this."

"Yin and yang, you and me." My panties are purring, and my cheeks are as hot as my neon-pink bra. A whisper of space separates our mouths, tongue wets, lips connec—

Erika and Mikey collide with our legs, jumping up with a splash. "Who won?"

Aaron exhales. "It was a tie."

*I would've kissed him, Jasper.*

*Me too. These waves have knocked us right off our tail.*

*Get me home to Jake.*


Mikey is asleep before his feet are inside his tent. I pretend my closet is a dinghy and imagine I'm afloat, at rest against Jake's chest.

Todd chitters, "Those guys were from the zoological society. They couldn't believe that I'd bottle-fed lion cubs." Only outsider freaks can understand what it's like to be talked to like a person of more worth than trouble. "They're going to come to the safari for a tour next week." He talks and talks, sighs, then says, "Night, Ari."

"Night."

In darkness, it's difficult to sort sleeping breaths from sighs. "Ari?"

"Mmm?"

"What animal do you see in me?"

"A sea lion."

"'Cause of my blubber?"

"Inner animals size up with goodness. Sea lions live without complaint on rocky shores and in smashing waves. They've a thick skin and a soft heart."

"Are they smart?"

"Jake says they can predict earthquakes."

"Ari?"

"Mmm?"

"It was the best night I ever had."

In the morning I feel a little seasick when I climb out of bed. Todd is belly down, splayed on his too-small bed, looking more like a flying squirrel than a sea lion. Mikey's nine-year-long legs look thin as cords sticking out of his tent. I wiggle them. "Let's make an early break for it."

He stirs, mumbling, "Is it Friday?"

"Almost."

Some guy, undershirt cinched over his pecker, exits the bathroom as I step over debris in the hall. He grunts, "Hiya," and goes back into Devil Girl's cave. The door to the master dumpster is open. Under gray sheets is a mound of Dick. Mum sits on the side of the bed, looking at the clutter on the dresser or perhaps the stranger in the mirror. She looks out at me. "There you arm."

And here she is not. "Go back to sleep, Mum."

O'Toole is snore-drooling on the sofa. Tork is in the kitchen, jeans slung like a plumber with a heavy load. He pours milk straight into the Dick's box of Frosted Flakes. Mikey's jittery voice behind me says, "Let's just go."

The toilet flushes upstairs and no way are we getting caught in the middle of this cereal drama. We are almost out the door when the Dick grumbles from mid-stairs, "Where the fuck are you two off to?"

Mikey tucks behind me while I scrabble for a reason to be leaving the house at seven a.m. "Um, it's field day. Mikey wants to get in some practice laps." He chins us away and we're half-way down the block before I clue in that Mikey is in shorts three sizes too small, a green-striped T-shirt stained with condiments, runners held sole to canvas by duct tape, and slept-on swimmer's hair.

"I hate field day. Can I just go to Sabina's?"

"She has a doctor's appointment for her back today."

"Maybe my mom's?"

"She got that job at Dominion." He kicks at the gravel and Jasper kicks me, or tails me, hard. "How'd you like a day off from everything?"

His head snaps up. "Miss field day? Could I? Please."

"Possibly, but first you have to swear on your dragonfly that you'll never tell anyone where I take you, even if you're being murdered."

"I promise."

"I mean it, Mikey. No one can know. Not the police, your teachers, Todd, not even Aaron."

"Or Aunt Sabina?"

"She knows because Jacquie told her for safety, but she's trained in war resistance tactics. But it has to be a secret."

"I swear, on Kira's wings."

"Come on."

"What about school?"

"Marks are in. I'll get Jennah to call for us."

I stick to back streets, hoping Mikey will lose any sense of direction. "Where're we going?"

"A lioneagle's nest."

"Wow."

Wow. Wonder. Wander. There are filaments of a poem mixed with early light as Mikey circles the nest whispering, "Wow," and "Holy wow."

I dial Jennah. "Oh, you just caught me heading out the door."

"Mikey and I are playing hooky. Can you call our schools?"

"A pesky summer cold?" I hear her Rolodex whirl as she flips for the numbers. "I'm just finishing up the shopping for our trip. Anything you need?"

"You coming downtown?"

"I am."

"Mikey needs shorts and tops, sneakers, too."

"What size?"

Mikey's head is tilted up, taking in the totems suspended in the window. "Um, about the height of your Dean, but skinnier?"

"Measure him up."

"Hang on." Mikey's hand extends to an origami bird as I size him with a string and ruler.

He blows on the crane. "I, I dreamed here."

I arrange a meet-up with Jennah and find make-do clothes for Mikey. "Go have a shower and I'll make us some eggs."

We graze, draw, read, paper-fold . . . Our eight hours in the nest feels like a holiday week. "Do you know how to fold a dragonfly?"

"No, but I bet you could figure the physics of it out." I check the time. "Go get dressed."

Jennah did what Jennah does. I rendezvoused with her in front of the Riverboat at one sharp. She passed five bags from the window of her shiny car, waving off my attempt to give her money. "Can't stay, sis. Have a million things to do. Have a good, good summer."

The bags held three pairs of shorts, Beach Boy swim trunks, five T-shirts, underwear, flip-flops, and black canvas runners with white rubber toes.

Mikey comes out in black shorts and a green top. "Does Jennah know about my dragonfly?"

"She knows more than she lets on."

We wash the dishes, straighten the cushions, gather hand-made end-of-school gifts, and close things up for the summer.


When he settles into his tent for the night he says, "You made a room-poem and I got to fly in it for a whole day. That's bigger than a book-poem."

I tuck into my nook. Mum can be heard through the wall, singing, "This little light of men, 'til we go again, let it dee, let it dee, dee, dee me."

*She still has a sweet voice.*

*And a pickled brain.*

I snug back and look up. Suspended from the empty closet rod is a necklace, a honking gold heart. Written on the underside of the shelf, in black marker, are the words, "What a nice place to cum."

I rip the sheets off my mattress and ball my blankets on the floor. "That bloody O'Toole."

Todd gets up, takes in O'Toole's scrawl, and slides the bolt across the door. "Is a wanking fool."

Mikey says, "But we're cool."
*Ah, another room-poem.*
*I hate you.*

THIRTY

Last year at early dismissal, I waited here with Natasha. This year, only Mikey comes running out waving his report card.

"We're going home!"

I lift the red ribbon on his shirt. "What's this?"

"Won it for sportsmanship."

"That's the best award to get." He runs to keep up with my joy-long steps taking us to crapdom. "Go in and pack while I go see what Halpern wants."

He runs ahead. "Hurry fast, okay." He zips back and hands me the ribbon with a wink.

"Good thinking, bro."

Things are festive at police headquarters. Halpern spots me and brings me a Coke. "Thanks for coming."

"Why'd you want to see me?"

"At our last debrief, Cornish worried that you're a complete clam with her."

*What kind of a pathetic analyst takes me for a mollusc?*

*Shut up.* "I've a tribe that gets me to open up. And a two seventeen train that'll take me right to them."

"Okay, then. Just take this one word with you: intent."

"Intent?"

Halpern points to stacked cartons. "Intent. Big difference from making a mistake. Heck, I wouldn't even call what happened a mistake, more an accident you witnessed. Kid, bad shit goes down every day. Some of it's planned, but most of the time it's bad luck and unintentional fuck-ups."

"Is all this about Byron?"

"Nah. We're looking at every unsolved case. Given what we got so far, Montreal could've had him on several counts of statutory rape. He liked them young and worshipping."

"So, what was his intent?"

"Most telling was stuff he wrote after hitching the sneakers to the wreath. He thought Nat had a charmed life. Talk about resentment. 'She gets everything while I got shit,' yada, yada, yada. Bastard. He had more chances and more going for him than a lot I've seen. Heard you've been through the system. How'd that happen?"

"My dad worked away a lot. My mum would get herself into messes. My aunts usually took us, but when there're six, a kid can run out of relatives."

"How was it for you?"

"I managed. Most were benign, some deplorable, a few nice. It was never for long. We always got collected up and pieced back together. My sisters and aunts were always there for me. Still are."

"Good. That's good. You hear stories." He half sits on the table. "You know, back in fifty-three I worked a case. A teenager, Marion McDowell, disappeared. God, we worked it, night and day for a year, two. We even had a dick from Scotland Yard come, a psychic, tips by the thousands."

"You ever find her?"

"Not a hair. The mother went off her head. Dad moved out. The not knowing just destroyed them. Coulda been the same limbo for the Koshkins. This Smith kid was smart enough to erase his tracks and move cross-country. With one kill, there was nothing stopping him from offing the next girl to say no." He walks me toward the clutter of cops who are lifting a glass to the Dick. "You do okay at school?"

"I got through."

"You survived. Don't forget that. And next year has to be better than this."

"That's an assumption I never make."

"You need anything at all, just let me know."

The Dick has a new suit, charcoal gray, hoisted too high on his waist but he looks as nice as a greasy wart hog can possibly look in a suit. "Congratulations, Detective Irwin."

"With a commendation." He pulls at fake suspenders and smiles like a big plum-proud porker. "Doughnuts for the boys was a nice touch."

"Todd and Mikey chipped in."

"Appreciated."

"Um, Ronnie, too."

"Lying to a detective? Watch your step." He squares up the name plate on his desk. "Your mum see the doc?"

"Yes."

"And?"

Advanced cirrhosis, alcohol-related dementia, heart arrhythmia, chronic bronchitis . . . "She just needs vitamins and rest."

"Mikey see Laura?"

"Yeah. She's working at Dominion."

"I give that ten minutes. Better he's at that marine camp this summer than with that loser." I would've given the Dick maybe two minutes at being decent but Mikey and I have navigated this entire school year without a punch or kick. "You off then?"

"Afternoon train."

"Been a hell of a year, eh."

"Hell. Yeah. Mikey asked me to give you this." I hand him the ribbon.

"First? In what?"

"Um, hurdles."

He takes a ten from a wallet overfat with cash. "Give this to him for his holiday."

Money has passed from my hand to the Dick's more than a hundred times. With this giving, I've no sense if the planet has been righted on its axis or if the universe is haplessly off course.

As I head for the door, I notice O'Toole in an alcove, having a head-to-head with Dr. Cornish.

I exit, scanning the parking lot for Dr. Cornish's red Valiant. Last time I saw it was this morning at Jarvis. The top was down and she was loading banker boxes into the backseat. Every student has a file. Nat's was fat with commendations and perfect attendance; mine, with twisted troubles. I think of the evidence stacked in the piss-coloured room, then stride, with intent, over to her car, flip the lid, finger past Abrams, Adams, Anderson, and nab the Appleton file. *Shame we have to burn it. It's such a good story.*

*No way we can risk O'Toole sweet-talking her into handing it over.*

I turn and see Aaron standing by his jeep, hands in the pockets of his neat khakis. "Hey, cowboy. You here to help me make a quick getaway?"

"You need one?"

"Yeah, I just stole incriminating evidence."

"Get in."

I hop in. "Don't you have a plane to catch?"

"On my way. Just had to see you first."

"Why?"

"I know you said you'll be back in September, but after this year, well, no one is guaranteed anything. Every goodbye should be the last words you want that person to hear." He nabs a spot at the corner of crapstreet and I'm afraid he'll say words that can't be unsaid. We're eye to eye, the back of his fingers brush my cheek. "Ari, this world is a better place because you're in it." Not another syllable is spoken. The door opens without a squeak and we both move toward the first summer of a new decade.

*That intent was spectacular.*

*Yeah.* I walk to the craphouse trying to piece together "intent." *The road to hell is paved with good intentions. What does that say about heaven and bad intentions?*

*Let's just go and have a whole summer for "all in tents and porpoises." We'll sleep in tents and see dolphins. Get it? Oh, come on, it's a little funny.*

Mikey is packed and perched on the front steps. "Todd had to go. He said he'll come check on the garbage on his days off."

"Let me grab my pack and we're outta here."

Mum is standing in the upstairs hall. "Ready to go?" Her lucidity startles me.

"Yep."

"Do I need a sweater?"

"For what?"

"Shopping."

"We're not going shopping."

"I want a dress for my birthday."

"Your birthday's in October. It's June."

"Junie's coming?"

"Sure. Bye."

"You promised. I'm telling."

"Go, right ahead." I retrieve my backpack, force in the stolen file, scutter down the stairs, and make for the door. The sound of Mum going ass over tits down the stairs hits like bullets. Her head smacking the banister at the bottom is eerily close to the thunk of BS colliding with the bumper. In the ten-second pause at the door, "intent" opens like a time-lapsed flower. The story of a ruinous lipstick smear on Aunt Dolores's wedding dress. A suspected appendicitis attack that had Grandpa taking Mum to hospital and missing Mary's graduation. The phone call that misdirected Aunt Elsie to the wrong address for her final conservatory exam. A legion of stories of Mum intent on squashing joy. I open the door and step out without looking back. "Come on. Let's go."

Mikey run-walks to keep up.

*Intent.*

*Shut up.*

*On purpose.*

*I said, shut it.*

*A deliberate act.*

"Shut up. Shut up. Shut the frig up!"

Mikey stares, gap-mouthed. "Pardon?"

"When will she stop ruining my life?"

"Ari? You okay?"

"No, I'm not bloody okay. She toppled down the stairs."

Mikey sighs and turns us around.

I smolder the three blocks back to the craphouse. She is conscious and sitting against a carton when I go in. "Oh, Jen, I went here, here. I can't find my tree, my up . . . the feet thing."

"Oh, for pity sake. Mike, go see if Ronnie's upstairs. We'll pay her to call an ambulance and wait with Mum."

Mikey bolts up and hurries down. "She's not."

"Your legs broken? Can you stand?"

The bump on her head is the size of a lemon. "This forth, right? Bird, like this." She lifts her left arm and it's bent at a wrong angle.

"Should I call Pops?"

"No. He'll make us her nurse-slaves. If she can walk, we'll load her in a cab."

"I fell on stars. Down chairs."

"Oh, shut the frig up!" I secure her right arm and hoist her up. She emits a noise like a bagpipe inflating, but her feet seem to hold her. "Go call a cab."

Mikey zips off and returns. "They'll be here in ten minutes."

"Put a kitchen chair on the front lawn and we'll wait there."

"Shoes on? My shows?"

"Yeah, *My Un-Favourite Martian*."

"I happy it, like, like them." Her legs and hips are in working order and she's compliant.

Mikey asks, "What're we going to do?"

I check my watch. "We're going to miss the two seventeen, that's what. There's a five ten to Montreal. We're getting that."

Mum's brain is so scrambled, she can't match sounds with feelings. She sits, emitting a laugh-cry caterwaul, worsening when I stuff her in the cab. I give the cabbie a five-dollar tip for the three drops of blood that fell on his seat before I wadded a sock against Mum's nosebleed. Once inside emerg, I let it gush, because it moves her to the head of the line and off to a cubicle. The nurse writes down Mum's info and details about the tumble. "Has the patient been at this hospital before?"

"Yes, ma'am." Her disgraceful file will be next to mine, the one detailing the time she split my head with the dustpan. The nurse asks my name. "Um, Ar . . . ah, Ronnie Irwin."

"Relationship?"

"Stepdaughter."

"Emergency contact?"

"Detective Richard Irwin, Metro Toronto Police, Oxford8-2996."

"Have a seat in the waiting area."

"Come on, Mikey. I need to call Jennah."

She picks up on the first ring. "Ari? Why aren't you on the train?"

"Mum had a fall."

"Bad?"

"Walloped her head. Likely busted her arm."

"It's like she knows we're all going on holidays and has to wreck it."

"When're you leaving?"

"Soon as Wilf gets home. He'll have a coronary if we're a minute late for the tournament. Where're you?"

"East General."

"Well, that's fine then. Split before they tell you to take her home."

"Just ditch her?"

"Oh, like she never ditched us. Jory loves ministering to pathetic souls. I'll get her there."

"What if you can't reach her?"

"I'll hire a nurse. Leave my number with the desk and get yourself gone."

"You're the best, Jen."

"Go. Now."

"Can you let Jillianne know we're coming."

"Will do and I'll let Mary know you're delayed but on your way."

Mikey slips his skinny hand into mine. "You're nice."

*For all intents and purposes, she is.*

*Shut it. I'm in no friggin' mood.*


The Montreal delay is a gift. For years, I watched Jillianne Appleton wreck herself with drugs and boys. Now, I see my beautiful sister reborn as Anne Trembley, at her job. Witnessing her create gives me hope, as big as the sea-serpent costume we're wiring together. Destruction. Construction. She's content. Zen. Evolving. And there's a child. A little girl named Celine.

"Where's her mom?" I ask.

"Think she's dead, or good as. Her Uncle Isa, one of the dancers, was looking after her. He got a gig in Europe and couldn't manage. Auntie D and me were over the moon to get a kid without the bother of a man."

Next morning, at Central Station, Mum's oldest sister, Auntie Dolores, gives me a folio. "Heard you were looking for pictures of your dad."

"I—"

"Take a look. I insist."

The folio contains a wad of handwritten pages and several ancient snaps of a toddler and several of a small boy. The face, the mane of curls, the inward turn of the foot are identical to photos Mary has of me as a child. "No question I'm an Appleton, eh."

"I do question that. These snaps are your grandpa, Frederick Trembley. His friends called him Fish."

"Fish?"

"Fred and his big fish stories. He was so sick by the time you came along, I don't think you ever heard one. Thought you'd especially like this one. All the animals are talking."

I almost knock the alpaca in Auntie D off its skinny legs. "Thank you."

"It's nothing but some scraps of paper."

"Thank you for giving my sister this life."

"It's my treat having her and Celine underfoot. Go, get yourself home, Ari Joy Trembley Zajac."

"I'm trying, Auntie. Trying hard."

## THIRTY-ONE

There should be a poem in a journey home but my thoughts are as disjointed as the billboards streaking by: *You'll wonder where the yellow went when—Brylcream, a little dab will—on your way with Chevro—*

William stops, opens his palm. "I'll be taking that penny, little miss."

*Two pennies closer to home.*

*Bet Jake could turn that into a song.*

He pockets the one I hand over. "We clear on what this one's for?"

"The boy that I—"

"Not your doing. Remember? It's for the courage it took to search for who you are."

"How?"

He winks. "Just rest and grab hold of the joy ahead."

Nia picks us up in Sydney. "Hey, Mikey. Wait 'til you see the shirts Sadie's made for you kids."

"Can we earn badges?"

"You bet. Did you bring your compass?"

"Of course."

"Then direct us home and get started on your navigation badge."

"Thought Jake was coming?" I say.

"He's a little off his feet."

"Sick?"

"Heartsick, I suspect."

I nab the middle seat, one, so I can snug up to my white bear, and, two, so I can see Mikey's constant smile reflected in the side mirror. He asks, "Jake fishing?"

"He's over at Mabou. Salt Wind's playing a benefit for Chedabucto tonight."

"Can we go? Can we?"

"Tomorrow, there's a big ceilidh in Ingonish, with fireworks and all. Today's for getting your ocean legs back." Her hand encourages my knee. "Let all the heaviness go. Let it all go."

Welcomed silence takes me home. As we turn into the gravel driveway, a carving suspended in Skyfish's window shakes up the broken pieces in me. "Ohhh. Let me out." Nia is stopped before my words are out. I scrabble over Mikey and run. It's a fish, a leaping fish, three, maybe four feet long. The head half is etched clay, glazed the rainbow colours seen in a pearly shell. The tail half is a fluid curve of weathered wood. Most spectacular is the copper threading through its length, so finely embedded it looks not pieced but spectacularly whole.

"Mary and I've been having some kintsugi fun. Want to play?"

I back away, my hair pulled not by the Dick, O'Toole, or BS, but by the ocean. I outrun the dogs to the shore; boots, clothes falling away. I hit the icy water, emerging with a roar.

My head turns right. Sitting on the rock-fall rubble is the Missus, knitting while watching the flock of fosters skimming the shore. Kylie, the cranky babe from last summer, toddles over with an offering of slimy seaweed. "Fuzzy bunny." I accept the gift and she heads off for more.

The Missus offers a gritty blanket for my goose-bumped flesh. "Here's our girl, home to mends."

"Aye." I plunk beside her. "Last summer you said my world was going to break apart and I'd know how to piece it together. But I haven't a clue."

"Oh, those happenings weren't your breaking." She doesn't miss a stitch or take her eye off the kids. "It was the Koshkins' and that misassembled boy. You just got caught up in the landslide, all good for muscling up and moving the rocks ahead." In sky-blue Keds, puddled red socks, flowered housedress, brassy hair springing from an orange scarf, the Missus feels like the most assembled person on the planet. I'm guessing she sees the blackness of the year ahead.

"The doctor said Mum's got a year, tops."

"Nothin' will be okay, but everything will turn right." She whistles the kids and stands. "Can I asks a weighty favour?"

"Anything."

"Lets our Jake know you loves him, cracks and all. One day you'll thank me. A perfect man is no one yous can make a life with." She waddles off, seven ducklings follow.

*Is he drinking, Jasper? I can't spend my life with another Mum. I won't.*

*He has Jewel. She won't let him drown.*

A flat-edged red rock perfect for the fireplace catches my eye. A dozen, veined with mica, are strewn about. I scan the vertical distance from the shore to Moondance. We need to start on a new path up.

THIRTY-TWO

New things are being explored at Skyfish. Mary's pottery and Nia's carvings have merged in several pieces: a heron, a mermaid, a turtle . . . Tiny polished stones, sliced agates, metals intertwine organically in the clay and wood. Mary says, "You need to unravel before weaving something new." She places a lump of clay on my palm. I turn to the wheel, spinning through hours without a worry of who will take care of Mikey. I fill two trays with squat pots and marine shapes for Ari-Fairy chimes. While the kiln fires up, I sit across from Nia and paint sandpipers on weathered wood. She's hammering a twist of wire on a mandrel and I see the dolphin emerging. "When'd you start making jewellery?"

"Used to make trinkets all the time back in the day. When I picked up the wire for sculpting, it felt like I'd bumped into an old friend. Sadie takes bits and baubles to the fairs and the Butters get a little extra cash for their brood."

"I wonder how things would've turned out if ByBillyBob had landed with the Butters."

"Well, the name would be a treat." She seems to read the questions scrawling through my head. "Don't know if history is written or we write it. I suspect we're all just rocks being shaped by the waves."

"You can't argue, though, that some are sparkly quartz and some are gray lumps that catch unsuspecting toes."

"Look at the rocks you're gathering for your hearth. You're drawn to what's at your heart."

"My favourites are the fern fossils."

"They're testament to what happened in the past." She buffs and polishes a dolphin curve of copper-brass-silver that will circle any size finger.

"Does the past imprint people, too?"

"Inevitably, but expose those fossils, let the movement of the waves at them, and the defined edges change."

"Are the waves redefining something in Jake?"

"It's the way of things. Past two weeks he's been sadder than a hang-dogged hound." She looks right at me. "You do know, don't you, that boy has to break and deal with his shit."

"I don't know what I know, anymore."

156

"He's scared if he's not perfect, he's going to be left."

"That's a lot like Mikey. He never gives me a pebble of trouble."

"Mikey has a healthy dose of self-preservation in him. Like any respectable dragonfly, he'll eat up the pesky mosquitoes." Her pliers punctuate her thoughts. "Jake's so weighted with doubt. No one can keep up a dance like that boy does."

"So, what happened?"

She snips lengths of copper and silver. "Likely something as inevitable as a misguided roll in the hay."

"You mean?"

"That'd be my guess." She files a barb of silver and blows away the dust.

"Jake's always been my certainty."

"Only certainty is changing winds. Only control is deciding what you're going to do with the energy of it."

"No treasure blathering just now, please, Auntie." I'm tired. I'm pissed. And I am bloody well going to have my long-waited-for summer.

I make up the bed in the summer house with line-dried sheets, put on the nightie that swirls like mist, and drape the quilt over my shoulders. The rock Jake gave me for my sixteenth birthday sits on the acres between Skyfish and the Butters, saturated in moonlight. Climbing atop is tricky, but on it I'll be seen whether Jake turns right or left off the drive. Ribbons of mist slip over the grass and the ocean hush-hush-hushes through the dark. To my left are my queer aunties, to my right, acres of throwaways, and throughout the Cove are spirited people akin to me. I am home, and the hour spent waiting is like soaking in the Milky Way. Jewels gather in my hair and I wonder what the light does to them, when the old truck turns down the drive. Jake stops at the fork. The wait before he opens the door is an intolerable half minute. The engine stops. Lights disappear. Door opens. His shape moves across the dewy grass. Jake is more than six foot. His shoulders are hard-work wide. I see him. Not the breadth and width of him, but the vulnerability at his core. Aaron's right, nothing is guaranteed. Even rocks break.

His hair is a mess of unruly waves. In the light of a veiled moon, his face looking up at me is the storybook mariner rescuing the mermaid from the rocks. Before any hellos, I say, "Just tell me."

"Tell you what?"

"Do you love me?"

"More than life."

"Do you want me?"

"More than air."

"Well then, spit out what's stuck in your throat so we can breathe."

"What makes you think—"

"You didn't come running across the field, peeling down to your skin to meet me."

He looks at my bare toes poking out of the quilt, pockets his hands, and shrugs.

"There's nothing you can say that will end us. Nothing."

"You'll hate me."

"Left all my hate in Toronto. Is it someone from the Cove?"

"A—a gig in Halifax. Too much beer. A girl ducking into the room where we stashed our gear. Without even a 'how d'ya do,' she went down. I went up. My head left. I came." He looks into my eyes. "I hate myself for it."

My legs fold against my chest and I tug them against the hurt, the fear. *Too much beer?*

"I don't deserve you."

"Oh, for pity sake, Jake. Deserving has nothing to do with us. You told me that seahorses mate for life, and I'm sure as sure that's true for us, but we were fifteen and eighteen when you said I was the only girl you could ever be waiting for. Sixteen and nineteen when we promised last dance. There are years 'til we get there. I'm away more than here. You play love songs to an ocean full of seahorse predators. What warm-blooded hippocampus wouldn't have its head turned by a flashy angelfish?"

"I'm sorrier than I can say."

"Missteps are inevitable. Believe me, I know. We better settle on that right now."

He opens his arms and I tumble into terror-tight arms. "Just say you forgive me."

"I accept you. I forgive this. Trouble is, you're going to kick yourself 'round the trail and back, and the summer's too bloody short for it." I pull back. "Go shower. The sheets on our bed are clean."

Minutes later, the spring stretches on the door to the summer house. Jake's hand quiets its smack against the frame. The hairs on my skin startle up as his naked length slips next to mine. I savour the fragrance of soap mixing with ocean breeze, the featherweight of his arm slipping around me, his heart music felt at my back. At my turning he says, "Ari, I promise—"

I clap his mouth quiet, "Just promise that no matter how much we both mess up we'll fight for us, we'll work it out."

His hair is shower-damp and laced with moonlight. Before the long, slow kiss, his lips soft, minty, open, say, "I promise." His fiddle-fingers play down my body, along each rib. I shift under, wrap him with my legs, and he fills the hollows in me.


The old iron bed is positioned smack in the middle of the summer house. Fog, like smoke, slips through the screens. I spoon into Jake, away from the damp and the nightmare. He whispers into my fright of hair, "You 'right, love?"

"No, I need to throw some clay at a monster."

He lifts the covers for me to escape. I nab his sweater, step into rubber boots, and head to Skyfish.

I'm half-aware of coffee, muffins, lunch, Mikey going off to build a dragonfly nest.

It's the neck kiss from Jake that has me lifting my head to his question. "A monkfish?"

I survey the toothy creature encasing the pot. "It ripped off my ear in a dream. I'm harnessing it."

He says, "I'm heading over to the lodge."

"Already?"

"It's gone past six. You're coming, right?"

"Well, someone has to protect you."

"There's just a gig in Halifax July end. Rest of the bookings will all land me home after." His fingers dance through my hair without a bit of hurt in them. "I have something to show you. Later."


The moon smiles through a smoke of stars. Jake's grade twelve transcript is in my hand. "You're really smart, Jake."

His skin blankets my back. "Right. I'm past twenty and just finished grade twelve."

"Stop doing that. I'm proud of you."

"Truthfully, I kept at it in hopes of hearing that."

"How'd you manage it with your dozen other jobs?"

"Wasn't so hard, except this assignment where I had to write my earliest memory. I wrote about fishing with Huey, not about what I really remembered."

"Was it too sad?"

"No, too precious to give to a teacher pickled in Aqua Velva."

"Tell me?"

"I remembered sitting in the shanty, looking out the broken-paned window. Morning light made the face looking in empty, a space to be coloured how I wanted. I always made it my mum coming back to get me. In a way it was. It was Mary. She coaxed me out, washed a thousand bites." He inhales deep. "She warmed my toes in woolly socks, tugged a sweater over my head. While I shovelled in chicken and buttered bread, apple squares and milk, she fussed with my hair. She was picking nits, I now know. I still feel that salve soaking in behind my ears and along my neck." He turns, tucks his hands under his head, and stares at the roof bones. "The days my dad left me behind, I could count on her or Nia showing up minutes after."

"God, Jake, you have to write that."

"I'll leave writing to you. Science doesn't rip open your guts. I'm going to take some college courses after the freeze."

"For pity sake, start now. Stop worrying about making money."

"I'm building you a grand house with a big ocean-view room for you to write and paint."

"What do you want for you?"

"Just to make you happy, proud."

"Stop being so bloody pleasing." I sit up. "It's exhausting for everyone. M&N say you drive yourself 'round the clock. What is it that makes you think I need big stuff?"

"It's the life you deserve."

"Or is it a life that makes you feel deserving?" His scared face, the child looking out the broken window, looks full at me. "Why can't you hear why I love you?"

"Why do you, Ari?"

"For the small things."

He peeks under the blanket. "Ouch."

I whap him with a pillow. "Like when you hurry a stranded

161

herring back to water or sing a foster through fears." I settle back against his chest. "You're my last dance, Jake."

"What if—"

"There's no what if that doesn't land us together. Jewel must tell you that."

"She's not near as mouthy as your Jasper."

"She's just dizzy trying to keep up with you." My hand turns slow circles down his chest. "I need a rest in the seagrass, unhurried hours with you."

"You want me to step aside with Salt Wind?"

"No, not a single note. And I love talking dreams. Just be here when you're here, not thinking about more and more doing. Just lay with me knowing you're enough."

"Do you feel that you're enough with me?"

"With you is the only place I feel home in my skin, safe with the mess in me." My long leg twines 'round his. "Last summer, the fretting about me staying or going coloured every night we had. I know this September will take me back. Help me fill up these cracks before I do."

A dog barks, once. We're both asleep before the night answers.

THIRTY-THREE

Last summer I discovered imps and winged enchanters hiding in the clay. Now, the red mounds have a sinister sneer. Mary watches me just staring, hands inert. Softly she says, "Let them out."

"There're screams inside."

Nia's great white bear licks his lips. "Get moving. I want to see a scream on every shelf."

"It'll scare customers away."

"Only the faint-hearted."

Jasper lifts his snouty head, exhaling like a dragon with a fire wanting out. And so they come, pots swallowed by monster fish, toothy creatures evoking shivery smiles from one buyer to the next.

Mornings, I walk the shore with Nia, adding metal bits to our driftwood hunt. A rusty ten-inch spike clunks into my bucket. "That's a backbone for Lolita."

"That girl needs one. All girls do."

"I find it odd that people are snapping these up."

"I'm not. They're amusing and creepy, beautiful and piercing. They're sculpted poems."

The day, and everything in it, comes to me. Jake brings coffee and a kiss before heading out. This morning, to fish. The afternoon, a whale-watching excursion. Evening, a gig somewhere close. The nights are ours. Sex, often. A tired holding, always.

Through the window I see Mikey and his buddy Callum, barefoot and sun-brown, wobbling along, with a load shared between them. I stretch off my stool, working out neck-knots as I go meet them. "Ari, wait'll you see what we got." The crate sends up a puff as they plunk it down.

I tuck on my knees for a closer look at a motherlode of watch and clock parts and letter keys from ancient typewriters. "Boy, oh, boys. Where'd you find these?"

"Tim MacDonald's cleaning out his dad's shed. Sold 'em to us for a buck."

"They're just what I need."

"He's got a whole heap of stuff. Huey's gone over to haul a load of scrap. Said he'll bring you all the fish parts your net'll hold."

Usually I pay them fifty cents for a bucket of bits. Giving them two bucks each feels like a bargain at half the price. "Better shake a leg if you're crewing for Jake." They sprint away, sending grasshoppers jumping for their lives.

Even before Huey delivers the goods, striker keys are transmuting into fish spines, clock gears into fins, and springs into eyes.

Mary's squeal tells me the firing has birthed something evolutionary. "Nia, come see these."

Nia's laugh is husky and musical. I ask, "Is Lolita in one piece?"

"Nothing a little kintsugi won't mend. Love her underbite."

My current sculpture won't let me even sneak a look at another fish. It hasn't given up her name yet, but we're connected on a molecular level. I can look right through her, like in the bible storybook where an illustration gave a peek of Jonah inside the whale. I've cut away so much that it has no purpose as a pot. At most it could be a cage for a small candle. The tail is a fluted display, like seen on the fanciest fish. Copper veins hold where it snapped in the firing. The hollow inside has me itching. It's not long before the three of us are solving the dilemma. Nia's jewellery tools are skinny and long-nosed. Mary uses a pipette to place drops of glue. We fill it with polished stones, bits of sea glass, a fishhook, a tiny starfish, a rusty ginger beer cap, clock hands . . .

*You should fill up their bellies before you kintsugi it.*

*You might've suggested that yesterday.*

Mary steps back, tilting her head. "She really is extraordinary."

The dogs bark at a car turning in. "Keep at it. I'll see to the shop."

I set a tiny brass watch gear into a snaggletooth, like an amalgam in a cavity. Snip striker keys at varying lengths and fix them into the holes poked before the firing. Inside the protruding mouth, I glue four old typewriter keys: P, L, A, and Y.

It's long past closing but the night is too peaceful not to piece together a broken pot.

A flash of light and tires on the gravel suggests time has folded from nine p.m. to two a.m. and Jake is home. The bell in the shop rings and a man says, "Hello? Are you open?"

I poke my head out of the workroom. "Can I help you?"

"I saw the lights on and—" His gray head moves with the air of a diplomat. "Sorry, I was here earlier today. Bought some mugs for my daughters."

"Did you want to return them?"

"Oh, no. No. No."

Auntie Nia comes in through the back. "Thought I heard a car. Everything 'right?"

"This is rather silly. Got all the way around the trail and had to come back for that." He points to a shelf.

"You needed a teapot?" I ask.

"No, there was a, a thing there earlier, a speckled fish of sorts."

"Oh, Louis."

Nia says, "Sorry. It sold. Fast as they're done they swim away."

"Oh." He turns to leave. "Sorry to bother."

"Wait," I say. "What would make you drive back around the bend for a monster fish?"

"I suppose, my wife told me to."

"She's in the van?"

"No, she died months ago. I could hear her laugh as soon as I saw that, that whatchamacallit. She would've bought it in a flash."

"Where does someone put a monster fish?"

"Patty would've used it as a centrepiece for an important dinner or on a pedestal in our vestibule."

My head tilts and he follows me into the workroom. "And where would you put one?"

"Smack on my desk, maybe with a cigar in its mouth."

"Louis was more of a pipe smoker."

He smiles, accepting the offer of a stool. Nia plugs in the kettle and opens the cookie tin. "This is too kind of you." I pick up my palette knife to use up my mix of glue before it hardens and resume reassembling the broken pot. "Accident?"

"No. Meditation. Therapy."

"Beautiful." He near chokes on a macaroon when he sees Lolita and her friends on the rack behind me. "Oh, there's more? May I?"

"They're not fully evolved yet."

He helps himself to a long gander and picks up the one with a mouthful of PLAY. He looks at Nia. "When will this one be done?"

"Ask the creator."

His eyes narrow as he takes me in more fully. "This is your work?"

"They all swim out of my dreams. That one's just waiting for her name."

He lifts it like one might examine a new kitten. "It's Joy."

THIRTY-FOUR

I lie with Mary and Nia on the Skyfish floor feeling veined with East Coast gold. "I've run out of monster fish."

Nia says, "They were a limited edition."

"I'll miss this content and the long deep sleeps."

"I'll miss having you here to slow our Jake down."

"Hours this summer felt like when we were kids roaming the shore." I turn my head to Mary. "How's it possible Jake's mum never came back to even check how he was?"

"We tried to contact her but a cousin said she'd moved away. Started over."

"No matter how messed up Laura is, Mikey still knows she thinks he's a treasure. And as much as I wanted Mum to disappear, she always kept track of me."

Mary squeezes my hand. "There's beautiful wabi-sabi in the world because of your and Jake's mums."

"Jake isn't wabi-sabi."

"He just never stops long enough for his off-kilteriness to be seen more than a blink. Sooner or later he'll have to stop and face up to imperfection."

"Why does everyone keep saying that?"

"Weather forecasts are helpful. But new music will follow, of that I'm certain sure."

"You're such a treasure hunter, Auntie."

"Lots more to be discovered."

"Yeah, back to the bowels of the Earth to wait for Mum's skin to follow her lost mind into the great beyond."

Nia asks, "What did Dick say when you asked about you both staying?"

"That Mum's liver is shot and if I think he's cleaning up her shit I've got another think coming."

Mary surveys the roof. "Elsie and Dolores said they'd help."

"Mum's not my worry. It's Mikey. If I could arrange for the Dick to get Len's money, he'd give me Mikey."

"Len left that for your schooling."

"I could get a volleyball scholarship."

"Is that what you want?" Nia asks.

"I just might. Smashing balls for four years could be very cathartic."

"Agreed," Mary says. "But think this through. After he used up the money? Then what? You know he'd snatch Mike back 'til he'd rung everything out of you both." Mary rises easy, like a curtain going up, and I wonder what Mum could've become if she hadn't pickled herself. "Come on, Nia. I'm guessing there's a boy waiting outside the door."

Under the porch light, Jake leans, cap in hand. "It's a calm night. Thought I'd take Ari for a last turn around the bay."

Mary laughs. "Is that what they call it these days?"

We walk, holding hands through to the landing. "Jake, what if you didn't have to prove a single thing to anyone? What would you do?"

He breathes in the cooling air. "Go to school. Teachers told me time and again I could be a scientist. It always stirred something in me."

"We'll have more than enough money for our future. Do what's right for you now. That's all I want."

He steadies me onto the boat. "Okay, I'll go."

"Where?"

"Dalhousie. They accepted me."

Under us is water but the universe feels steady and in order. "Promise you'll go?"

"My word. But I'm not aiming for the top."

"Why the frig not?"

"Cause that's where I like you."

"Oh, Mr. Tupper, wind's comin' up."

## THIRTY-FIVE

Last September the return to Toronto hit like an earthquake. A catastrophic event that left a crack in the foundation of life and a knowing that aftershocks go on forever. As the train slows on Labour Day, 1970, Mikey, tanned, confident, solid, squares his shoulders. "Don't worry. I earned my exterminator badge."

"Be prepared" has a whole other scope when you're Dick Irwin's kid. I hoist my bag over my shoulder. "If the rats are back, we're going to Sabina's."

"Huey says we need to get a cat for mousing and a terrier for ratting. Did you know a group of rats is called a mischief?"

"Fitting."

We stop at the corner and assess the mischief out front of crapdom. The Dick shakes the hand of a guy in a fedora. He's in the same suit as the day we left, with more belly sloshing over the waistband. Three guys get into a black caddy and drive away. The Dick and O'Toole climb into the blue sedan and follow. "Well, that's a lucky start."

The kitchen chair is right where we left it eight weeks ago, but plywood replaces the cardboard on the broken windows and a spike has been added to the grassless lawn, securing a heavy chain with a spikey dog collar at the end. "Oh, Ari. We got a dog?"

"Stay back. Let me make sure it's friendly." I open the door a crack. "Hello? Here, boy."

Todd calls, "Hey. Welcome back." He bends so he can see me from the top of the stairs. "Chain's a ruse. Pop just wants people to think we have a guard dog."

"Is it bad?"

"There's weird shit going on."

Mum is sitting on the chenille chair. Wearing my blue gym romper? Her hair is teased up, but so thin I can see her scalp. She's looking at the TV, but it's not on. "Mum?"

Her head turns and she squints. "Hello? Say, you're that girl. That movie girl."

Todd ambles down. "She keeps calling me Mr. Fairchild."

"Any rats?"

"Just the Jimmy Cagney kind. Don't know what's up, but you can be sure it ain't on the up and up."

Mikey comes inside, taking our gear upstairs while I shimmy though boxes stacked like a warehouse. "What is all this shit?"

"I've been home two days and there's been like thirty guys coming and going."

We enter the kitchen and it looks pretty much like when we left. "Haven't they been eating?"

"Takeout. Paper plates. Only thing in the fridge is beer."

"The porch?"

"Go look." The back porch is a stash of boxed goods. Smirnoff Vodka, Buxton watches, Barbie dolls, London Fog raincoats . . . I smell smoke and follow it to the backyard. There's a new wood fence, high with a gate. Sheets of plywood have murdered the grass; a garden swing and two patio sets, complete with umbrellas, fill the space. Empty beer bottles and overfull ashtrays clutter the tabletops. Wisps of smoke escape from metal drums lining the driveway. "Figure they keep the fires going with trash so evidence can be burned quick."

"What happened to him being a detective?"

"No idea what went down, but O'Toole's running Pops like a whipped dog."

"What if we just turned them in?"

Todd snaps me around like a sling. "What cop are we a hundred percent sure of? Say nothin' about this to no one. Not Aaron, or Sabina, or your teacher friends."

"Halpern—"

"He couldn't see a psycho's hand down his own pants. You heard Snake say they're friends. Just keep low 'til we can sort out who's what. We're safe. Heard one of them say there's no better cover than a sick wife and kids. Pops ain't gonna do nothin' to cause any attention."

"You're sure?"

"We're in for smooth sailing. Come on, I'll treat you to pizza and we'll get a keyed lock for our door."

"Ronnie back?"

"Yeah, but no Tork. She's hooked up with Pinto."

"What? He's like forty."

"Welcome home."

Mum's remaining brain cells number less than a head of lettuce, yet she is oddly content in this vegetative state. She sits at the TV table, dipping puffed wheat into applesauce. I leave her watching Tom and Jerry while I hustle Mikey out the door. "Bye, Mark. Arriva diva, Ava."

Mikey says, "Least she got our names close."

"She thinks I'm Ava Gardner." I give Mikey an envelope. "Breakfast club money, Y sign-up, emergency form, and swim registration."

"Is there volleyball tonight?"

"Starts next week."

He slips his hand in mine and I feel the pull to our life away from here. "Could Todd ever live in Pleasant Cove with us?"

"After sacrificing his closet, he can have the pick of any room in Moondance." I tug him across the street, toward the here and now. "Do you want to join Scouts with Sabina's boys on Saturdays?"

"Oh, boy, can I?" Since the lockout, weekends with Laura

are something Mikey both fears won't happen and worries will. "What about my mom?"

"Sunday, we'll take her some groceries and see how she is."

Mikey dashes off to meet friends. My feet are stuck at the fork in the path. *Is this the calm before the storm, the eye of the storm, or are we really in for smooth sailing?*

It's disquieting feeling Jasper tip backwards off his tail, rolling with laughter. *Smooth sailing. Oh, Ari, you are too funny. We've eight pennies to go.*

THIRTY-SIX

Perhaps the grade twelve book list—*Things Fall Apart*, *The Crucible*, *1984*—should make me a little antsy, but Mikey and I are pretty much invisible. One week back and the Dick's only expectations are for me to take care of Mikey and put clothes on Mum. The latter being by far the greater challenge.

On Friday, we connect with Todd on the corner. Mikey asks, "What's the plan again?"

"You go with Todd to his work while I get you a weekend pass."

"He'll never buy it."

Todd arms Mikey away. "He might. Pretending you're taking up hockey will score big."

I push myself crapward. From the hall I see Mum standing in the kitchen wearing the blue sweater I gave her this morning and what looks like off-white seersucker pants. As my eyes adjust, her cottage cheesy legs and baggy bum skin come into focus. "Oh, for pity sake, Mum." She turns and her face is smeared with jam. "Get upstairs, right now."

She complies without a word. On the steps I find her underpants and polyester slacks. I assume she's had a romp until I see they're wet with pee. I load her into the tub and she says plain as Palmolive, "Some bubbles."

The Dick nearly drowned Mikey and me in this very tub and I wonder for a minute what Mum's face would look like under the water, eyes bulging, little bubbles escaping. I pour in a dollop of shampoo and agitate until there's enough foam to hide her skeletal frame. The yellow of her skin pops against the white froth.

I hear a bluster of cops and robbers clambering in and go down. The Dick's poker buddies, holding buckets of KFC, chorus, "Hey, Hari. Welcome back."

Poker on a Friday night is something new. The Dick says, "Tell Mikey chow's up."

"Um, I tried to call you at work for permission, but I guess you were out on a case. Jennah's taking Dean to try out for hockey. I thought maybe if Mikey went, it might get him interested."

Todd was so right on. The Dick puffs up like he might ejaculate a hockey stick. "He shoots. He scores!"

"If he plays, it'll eat up his weekends."

"Better hockey than stayin' with that cocksucker mother of his."

O'Toole says, "What the little ass wipe needs to man him up."

They all grunt and adjust their pants as they shinny up to the table.

I find a dress that will cover Mum's boney butt if her pants go missing again. I push her toward the bed. "Stay up here so you're closer to the toilet. You want some chicken?"

She articulates perfectly: "Cupcakes."

For *frig* sake, die already.

I retrieve Mikey and we catch the streetcar to Sabina's. "Ari, what if Pops wants to see me play?"

"We'll scheme something up. Jennah's got a team jersey for you and Aaron can teach you to skate a bit." Worry is felt in his tense arm against mine. "Right now, he's too all up in mafia mayhem to be bothered."

Mikey hesitates as I open the door to Sabina's Boutique. "What if I . . . if I . . . Can I stay with you?"

"I work way late." I crouch to meet his pale eyes. "Listen. Those new guys hanging around crapdom scare the piss out of me, too." His head hangs with the shame of peeing his cot this week. "Hey, let's nip down to the basement and find my old sleeping bag. You can roll it out on the floor and tell Sabina you want to pretend you're camping."

"Wish we could just run away."

"If it comes to it, we will." My knees complain as I straighten up. "Come on. You'll have two glorious days of peace here."

"Promise you won't go back there."

"I'll be safe at the nest."

There is never a molecule of resentment over the imposition Mikey and I foist on Sabina. Her welcome back is generous and genuine. I give her a dozen necklaces I made, hammered metal statement pieces, more suited for an upscale boutique than my usual flower-power love-beads. "Oh, corka, how beautiful. Customers have been asking what new is in store from my resident designer."

"As soon as I get some tools, I'll whip up more."

"Aaron left this." She hands me a note.

"You saw him?"

"He brought the boys each an arrowhead from Peru. He is such a nice young man."

"He just knows where his paczkis come from." I peek at his note.

*Ari, If you're reading this, know I'm smiling because you're back. I'll be at our bench Sunday. Hope you're free.*

*We're free. We're free.*

*Please don't start stirring all this up again.*

Being back at the Riverboat anchors me. Time in the nest works out the ache of empty hands and arms. *I need clay. I want Jake.*

Sunday morning comes too soon. I scan my clothes. Babcia's hand-embroidered peasant blouse slips over my damp hair. I appraise the fit of my jeans in the full-length mirror, pack chruscikis, and lock up.

Aaron is on our bench, head bent to a book. He checks over his shoulder, spots me, and hurries into an extra-long hug. "Geez, I missed you."

"Maybe so, but it's quite evident you spent the summer in your proper element."

We sit, side by each, his face shiny with adventure. "It's hard to describe where I've been." He lifts his head to a pair of geese lifting off the lake. "So many times I found myself thinking, 'So this is what Ari feels when she wakes up in Pleasant Cove.'" He places a perfect cowrie shell on my palm. "I picked this up one morning wondering what discoveries you were finding on a shore on the other side of the world."

"Once I figured out how to transmute nightmares into art, I finally got some sleep."

"And Mikey?"

"Tripped over joy all summer."

"And now?"

"I'm not sure what's churning in that head of his. His teacher does bloody 'current events' every morning. You know Mikey, he's likely the only fourth grader who thinks about what he's reading. He's scared Ricky's going to be sent to Vietnam. He frets about nuclear tests, hurricanes, downed planes . . . Maybe

175

it's just the weirdness in crapdom more than planetary turmoil, but he's a jitter of worries."

"The Dick isn't hurting you or Mike again, is he?"

"No. There's a new kind of mayhem. Not sure what's up, but I'm certain it's a house of illegal cards and the Dick is going to get royally flushed."

He tosses crumbs for a flutter of sparrows. "And your mum?"

"Her mind-melt is a horror. I prefer her mean and scrappy." I examine the shell's markings. Finger its smooth curves. "When she's gone and Len's money is out of the equation, what can I do? This is the last year I have to get Mikey out of that house."

"We'll run away to South America if we have to."

I want to ask if the "we" includes me, but I'm as afraid of a no as I am of a yes. "I do have a weekend escape plan. It's a long shot, or is it a slap shot in hockey? You up to whipping Mikey into a Bobby Howe?"

"That would be Orr or Gordie."

"I need both."

He stands, inviting me for a ramble. "I'll give it my best shot."

The sun warms my neck as we stroll the shore. Aaron gathers stones, giving five to me to throw, one each for grandma, Len, Iggy, Jet, and Natasha. "You've seen me through so many deaths."

"I was thinking about that this summer. I worked with people who'd lost their entire families in the earthquake and here I am, turning twenty-seven and have never had anyone close to me die."

"Not a grandparent?"

"Nope. They're all alive."

"Often I feel I attract destruction."

"Think it's more accurate to say you attract energy."

"Either way, nor'easters can kick up such a fuss, you lose all sense of which way is open water and which is solid ground."

He tucks his hands and his feelings in his pockets as we head toward the parking lot. "So, how's Jake?"

"He got accepted to Dalhousie."

"That's fantastic."

"Should be, would be, could be, but I called Huey yesterday hoping he'd heard how his first week went and he told me that school was on hold until after the freeze."

"Why?"

"A neighbour busted his leg and begged Huey to keep his boat running in return for half the haul. Huey couldn't let Cap down and Jake wouldn't let Huey go it alone or leave the Missus with the extra load." I pitch the last stone. "There're two dozen men that would've jumped at the work."

"It's easier to do what you know."

"What I know is Jake loathes fishing. He doesn't mind catching a meal to feed the kids but hauling creatures out of the ocean, the flopping and struggle for air, just wrecks him. He isn't following what he knows deep down."

We reach his jeep and he asks, "Can I take you to lunch?"

"Promised Sabina an autumn in Paris backdrop for her window. Come help and you'll get some cabbage rolls."

Day's end, Aaron drops us at the corner of misery and mayhem. "Um, I have a class at OISE on Wednesday. You guys want a lift home after volleyball?"

Mikey says yes before I can shake no.

Our walk to crapdom is like a pair heading to the gallows. Mikey asks, "Is it Mennonites that have lots of wives?"

"No. That's Mormons."

"More moms? Is there a fewer moms?"

"I'd join that church."

"Scouts was at a church."

"Did you like it?"

"A lot. A whole lot." Mikey ploughs open the door, walks past Todd watching *Hogan's Heroes*, Mum comatose on the chair, to the Dick.

"Hey, kid. Still got all your teeth?"

Mikey extends a hockey puck. "Scored a goal."

The Dick nabs it, roughs Mikey's hair. "That's my kid."

Ascending the stairs, I ask, "Where'd you get the puck?"

Mikey boldly runs interference with O'Toole's hand reaching for a tit squeeze as he descends. He fakes left, then skits right into the boys' room. "Bought it yesterday. I'm a boy scout now."

I watch him cross-legged on the floor finishing his diorama for school. He painted the inside of a boot box like an arena, crafted players holding balsa wood hockey sticks. Made a Stanley Cup from cigarette pack liners. A magnet underneath moves Number 14, Davie Keon, down the ice. What it demonstrates is not his love of hockey but his emerging brilliance at Dickhandling.

Todd picks it up for a closer gander. "This is genius. Let's show Pops."

I watch from the stairs as the Dick peers with rapt wonderment. "Holy Christ. Leave this here so I can show the boys."


Noise is a given on poker nights but not like this. Downstairs, clutter flies, glass breaks, voices bellow. I corkscrew into Mikey's tent and he curves into me like an armadillo into its shell. My heartbeat, ragged and off-beat, thuds in my ears. *I want Jake. Want Jake. Want Jake. Want, want.*

Come morning, I tip-toe down. The place looks like a cyclone hit. The Dick spots me and mutters "Christ. Look." I follow his gutted eyes to where Mikey's diorama is squashed on Mum's chair. "Pinto moved it off the table so we could play. That bloody O'Toole sat on it." He picks up his jacket, checking out before a faceoff with Mikey.

Mikey hovers at the top of the stairs in blue underpants, unravelling at the waistband, and a threadbare cowboy PJ top. "Is it safe?"

"I'm afraid your diorama took a body check." His shrug is absent of caring. "Get dressed and don't come down in bare feet."

He comes down carrying a popsicle stick schooner he constructed last year, drags his diorama like a dead possum to the curb, and heads to school in resigned silence.

## THIRTY-SEVEN

I fall asleep to the boys from Creedence Clearwater Revival jamming on the Riverboat's back porch. I wake to "Bad Moon Rising" looping through my thoughts. Across the China Sea, war rages. To the east, Jake is lost in a fog. West of the *Oh shit* point, Montreal is exploding with the FLQ crisis, and Toronto is a mafia minefield.

I head to the lake for some time with Len before Aaron arrives, rereading Jake's letter as I walk.

> *The other day I got swallowed by a fog. It rolled in so thick I couldn't get my bearings. I'd get myself tuned to the foghorn, then hear it behind. About midnight, I heard a shotgun, waiting for a count, then firing again. I knew*

*it was Huey signalling. Two things came to me so clear in
that mist: one, I'm best leaving the fishing to those with
a heart for it and two, I should've gone to school like I
promised you. I'm sorry. What if I told you the new term
will find me right where I should be?*


I'd say, I'll believe it when I live it.

"You're here early." I catch a whiff of lime-scented shaving
cream as Aaron sits.

"Jasper needed the sound of the waves."

*And our sou'wester to talk us through our sea of disquiet.*

Hours in, hunger replaces the roil in my gut. Aaron laughs at
my belly growls. "Let's get some lunch."

There is colour in the air, like amber glass and yards of
autumn-coloured leaves underfoot. Cattails and slender grass
plume from a gully. Red-winged blackbirds take flight as we pass.
I stop. Listen. Aaron says, "What?"

"There should be a poem in this. All I need is a friggin' haiku."

"For school?"

"Yeah. If you can believe it, English is my toughest subject
right now. I can't seem to write a bloody thing."

"You know why ninety-nine percent of what lands on my
desk is awful?"

"Why?"

"Because grade eights try so hard to be poetic. They think it
to death. Any string of words that reaches another person comes
from the gut, the heart, flesh and bone. Stop thinking about it."

"Oh, you're one to talk, Mister Lister."

"Number forty-two on the list happens to be: stop overthink-
ing everything."

An old man in a flannel robe shuffles toward the boardwalk.

A woman emerges from one of the lakefront houses and hurries to catch him. "Daddy!" When they meet, the curve of his shoulders matches the exquisite swell of her pregnant belly. "Come on, Dad. Tea's ready."

My hands lift, the right curving like the half moon of the man's shoulders, the left like the full moon of her belly. Aaron follows my line of sight. "What're you thinking?"

"I'm not, I'm seeing something."

"A poem?"

"I need gems and wire."

"First line of a haiku right there."

THIRTY-EIGHT

Sleeping in the closet, I gather intel through the vent in the floor when thugs are loading and unloading inventory in the cellar and through the paper-thin wall while persons wait for the toilet across the hall.

Last night I heard O'Toole growling, "Don't fucking mess this up, Irwin."

And the Dick snapping back, "I'm getting out of the hole, then I'm out. Capisce?"

"You ain't got a snowball's chance in hell of getting out of that pit."

Now, this morning in the hall, I hear Pinto say, "Wait 'til Tino gets a load of Irwin's girl."

And Snake says, "I wanna be around for that." There are

other possibilities, I know—Ronnie, Mum, maybe the Dick has a chippie on the side—but I have a niggly feeling they're referring to me.

I hear Mum exit the bathroom. "Mornin', you bug legs, beg lugs, big hugs."

Pinto says, "Mornin' Theresa."

Snake must turn his head to the wall, because "What a piece of shit" lands like bird crap on my chest.

The sadness is so gummy, I can't move. That my mum was a rare beauty was, perhaps, my only treasure of her.

"Ari?" Mikey peeks behind the sheet. "We're gonna be late."

"Just give me five minutes. Go pack your lunch."

I didn't undress last night so I'm ready in two minutes. I open the door and O'Toole is in the bathroom, pissing, door open.

I say, "You might want to have that checked. Looks like a bad case of smallcox." He elbows the door closed.

Todd walks with Mikey and me to the corner. I ask, "Have you figured out this expanded operation?"

"Snake's moving goods and O'Toole and Pop are just making sure the cops are looking the other way."

"What about this guy Tino?"

"Alls I know is everyone's scared shitless of him."

"Do you know how much money the Dick owes?"

"Gotta be a bundle. Long as I've been around, he's been betting on sure things."

"He's going to blow it, isn't he? The whole detective thing."

"Odds are fucksure. You have volleyball tonight?"

"Yeah."

"I'm working late. Meet me at the clinic so we can walk home together."

Mikey flaps his arms around Todd in a sincere hug. In my four years in crapdom, I can't remember seeing Todd embraced by anyone. I hug his upper half. "Thanks, Todd. You're a spectacular big brother."

Mikey hoists his droopy pack as we reach his schoolyard. "Make sure you eat your carrots, Ari."

"You put carrots in my lunch, bro?"

"And Frosted Flakes."

"That's grrreat!"

On the way to Jarvis, I count the syllables in fragmented thoughts, trying to find inspiration for a haiku due by two. *That's six syllables.*

*How about "Behind sleepless sheet*
*Wall listens, girl hears thug talk*
*Run before you're screwed"?*
*Terrible. Awful.*

"Hello, Ari."

I look up. *Oh bloody* . . . "Hello."

*That's five syllables.*

Detective Halpern leans against a shiny black car. "Got a minute?"

"No. I'll be late for school."

"I'll give you a lift."

"Not cool, sir."

He smiles. "How you doing?"

"Fine."

"School okay?"

I shrug. "A veritable equation of pluses and minuses."

"Life, eh." He drops his cigarette and crushes it out. "How's your dad doing?"

"Likely still giving all the fish in the St. Lawrence indigestion."

"Your stepdad. He still enjoying his new position?"

"You'd know better than me." I step backwards toward school.

"Hardly ever see him. Mikey and I are so busy—with sports and stuff."

"How're things at home?"

"Well, my mum's sick, so you know, up and down."

"Maybe I should drop 'round and see her."

I've no clue what web is being spun, but I'm not getting tangled in it. "Um, her hair's falling out. Visitors upset her." I back away. "Really, I have to go."

His voice catches up to me as I run. "Ari, be careful."

I bolt across the field, running into a few lines while I do.

*Melon collie girl.*

*Only dogs can be trusted.*

*Someone retrieve her.*

*Deplorable.*


By grade twelve and thirteen, so few girls are left taking phys. ed. that even with a combined class we only add up to fourteen. Kendra Blunt doesn't care that I manslaughtered BS; she's just happy that she has someone who can pace her around the track. In return for letting her run me into the ground, she gives me a marvellous comb, an Afro comb. "Your mama never teach you how to tame that mess?"

"Kendra, my mama didn't teach me shit."

She laughs and checks out my sweatshirt. "You goin' to UCLA?"

"No, my friend goes there."

"I'm getting a full ride to McGill. And you watch, I'm makin' it to the Pan Ams this summer." She nabs her gear. "Later, 'gater."

I sit on the hill, a milky sun drying my hair as this spectacular comb skates through, leaving a party of serpentines in its wake. An exquisite haiku is like a moth promising to land if I'm perfectly still.

"You should run cross-country." Riley Hollingsworth, in sweaty football regalia, plunks himself right where a speck of creative genius was preparing to light. "I'm having a party Friday. Wanna come?"

"I work."

"Come after."

I stand. "Thanks, but I'm never finished before two a.m."

He knocks on my boot, red cowboy boots that I found in Mary's closet. "I dig these." When he stands, we are the same height. "I dig you."

This guy is king of grade thirteen and I'm certain there's a plot cooking that will see me tied naked to the flagpole, or worse. "Ah, I'm late for class." I make like an atom and split.

*Could this day get any weirder?*

*Oh, Ari, you're so funny.*

I head to English and drop my crap of a haiku on Ellis's desk. He asks, "Your family in Montreal okay?"

"The army's put a lid on the pandemonium but they're still keeping low." Ellis is like me: Franco mother, Anglo dad. "How's your tribe?"

"Trois-Rivières is away from the heart of the storm." He picks up his book. "How about a little *Hamlet* to lighten things up."

"Ah, 'to take arms against a sea of troubles.'"


After school, the craphouse is echo quiet. O'Toole says, "Your mummy needs help upstairs, sugar tits." He nabs Mikey by the collar. "Girl stuff, ass wipe."

When you take in the bulk of the Dick, it's hard to imagine that he could get the jump on anyone, but I'm yanked, muzzled, and cornered in the bathroom so fast the floor spins. His hand seals around my nose and mouth. "Do I need to take out my gun?" My head jitters no. I meet him eye to eye, standing

185

dead still as his hand moves to my neck. "Why'd you meet with Halpern?"

"I, I didn't." His hand presses then releases, a little. "Just bumped into him on my way to school."

"Tell me every word that was said and do not"—his jaw grates—"do not fucking lie to me."

"He asked how I was. And about school."

"Was he waiting there for you?"

I'm certain he was doing exactly that. "No. He . . . was coming out of a house, glanced up, and saw me."

"What house?"

"Ah . . . maybe third from the corner?"

"And?"

"We talked about school."

"And?"

"That's all."

"Did he say anything about me?"

"No. Um, yes. He asked if you liked your new job."

"And?"

"Said you loved it."

"What else?"

"Just chitter, like Mikey playing hockey and stuff."

"Did he want you down at the station?"

"No. Said he might stop by for a visit." His hand tightens. Fingers squeeze. I lengthen my neck. "I told him Mum was sick and a visit would upset her."

"That it?"

"Offered to drop me at school and I said no. That's all."

When he takes his hand away, strands of my hair are tangled on his cufflink. "You see him again, you tell me, you hear?"

"Yes, sir."

"Listen. This is work stuff. I'm deep undercover. Big stuff's going down. Keep your mouth shut."

"Maybe we, um, Mikey shouldn't be here."

"Long as you keep your mouth shut, everything's copacetic. Capisce?"

I'd be impressed at his new big word if he hadn't pronounced it "cop" instead of "cope." "Yes, sir." I've been expecting the Dick to turn mean. Compared to his fists, this is Christmas. Admittedly, Christmas has always been a complete shit, but survivable.

His pressure lowers and he talks like we've just shared a nice cup of tea. "So, how's Mikey's hockey coming?"

"His hockey? Ohhh, great, just great." I glance in the mirror for a bald spot. My perfect spirals have exploded into a stress.

Mikey's voice follows a soft knock. "Excuse me. May I use the bathroom?"

The Dick opens the door, walking past Mikey like he's dust. Mikey scans me. "You okay?"

I see he's come not to pee but rescue me. "Sure. Good."

"Why'd O'Toole lie? Your mum's downstairs."

"She dressed?"

"In a red shiny thing with dragons on it."

*Fitting, she sure is a drag on us. Get it? Get—*

*Just shut up.*


Aaron is waiting to give us a ride home after volleyball. "Geez, Aaron, Mikey said you had a cold, but you look terrible. Why aren't you home in bed?"

"Said I'd give you a ride."

"We were going to drop this off." I hand him a care package: cough drops, tissues, and Sabina's voodoo tea concoction that packs a Polish punch to every virus known to humankind. "Put honey in the tea or you'll never get it down."

"Thanks." His voice is husky, eyes ringed. I want to spirit him to the nest and take care of him. I want his skin against my back like it is with Jake and—I don't want him around at all.

"Where to?" he asks.

*Pleasant Cove.* "Todd's work."

Past the windshield, I watch trees shake off the last of their leaves as Mikey jabbers, "Two ladies came to watch Ari play. They were all 'Wow' and 'Holy cow.'"

"Who were they?"

Mikey says, "Girl Scouts of Canada."

When we reach the clinic, Mikey runs ahead hoping for some dog therapy before returning to crapdom. I climb out on a sigh. "Thanks. Appreciated."

Aaron asks, "Did Mikey mean a scout for a university was there tonight?"

"Remember that woman who was at the closer last year? I told her I'd only go east for school and couldn't be convinced otherwise." The steel of his door provides an anchor for my hands. "She convinced someone from Dalhousie to come watch."

"And?"

"Think they're offering me a scholarship. And I don't need grade thirteen."

"Oh . . . that's amazing. Isn't it?"

"I love playing, it's closer to home, and . . ."

"Jake will be there."

"There's that, but I was going to say that the way I feel at Jarvis I wouldn't mind ditching thirteen, plus I've got to get out of crapdom. Mikey and me."

"Any escape plans?"

"Yep. I'm going to rat out the Dick and O'Toole."

"For what?"

"I know where they have 'acquired' property stashed."

"He should've been arrested two years ago for assaulting you and Mike."

"I was afraid then. Didn't know what cops to trust. Halpern's a good cop. I'm sure of it. He already knows something stinks."

"When?"

"Needs a bit of planning. I bumped into Halpern this morning and the Dick knew about it. So, am I being tailed or is Halpern?"

"Why on earth would either be the case?"

"The Dick's mixed up with some thugs and the new chief is on a dethugging rampage."

"Just make the call, then get on the eastbound train."

"To take Mikey east, I have to get legal papers."

"Go west if you have to. Stay with my parents. They've offered time and again."

"I have a place to lay low until I get a handle on the fallout."

"How can I help?"

"If you feel up to it, meet me at Sabina's on Friday and we can fine-tune when and how?" I test his forehead for fever, then my finger drifts along a wave of his hair. "I'm sorry to bale on us. Sorrier than I can say."

"Jasper's never wrong, remember? We'll find equilibrium." His hand connects with mine still in his hair, holding it like it's fine china, then he lets go.


The air has the October bite that Len and I loved and I'm buoyed knowing I'm still connected in spite of the eternity of distance that separates us. *I'll never lose all the years Aaron and I've shared.*

*The craphouse is going to explode. We have to go.*

"Earth to Ari. Are you stoned or something?" Todd waves a hand near my face.

189

"Just thinking."

"Good game tonight?"

"Really good. You in Rockton this weekend?"

"Yep, 'til Monday."

*Saturday night, Jasper. We'll send the troops storming.*

There are cars in the driveway and on both sides of the street. As we come into the house, Snake walks down the hall and says, "Look at them rosy cheeks. What you been up to, cupcake?"

"Played some volleyball while Mikey honed his skills."

"Right." He leans on the banister, blocking the stairs. "So, cupcake, know why they call me Snake?"

Mikey says, "Because of the tattoo on your arm?"

"Good guess, but last name's Flake. Cop just can't get no respect with a name like that. Right? Am I right?"

"You're right."

*Cop? Had him pegged as a robber. Hey, he's a cobber.*

"Mikey, it's late, go brush your teeth and get ready for bed."

"Night, Snake."

"Back atcha, Einstein. So, Ari, tell me again about this morning. Just need to make sure Irwin didn't miss any pertinent details." There's a little Jimmy Cagney "you dirty rat" in his voice. "What was he driving?"

"A black sedan?"

"Anyone else in it?"

"Don't think so. I didn't really look inside."

"Why'd he want to talk to you?"

"He'd talk to any of Natasha's friends if he saw them. Last year was shitty for all of us."

"You really don't think he was looking for intel?"

"No. Not at all."

"Listen. This operation is delicate and top secret, very hush-hush from the chief, so we never had this conversation, capisce?"

"What conversation?"

He winks, moves aside, and I start up the stairs. "Hey, you let me know if O'Toole gives you any grief."

"His grief I can handle, but I'd appreciate it if you'd tell him to keep his hands in his pockets and his pecker in his pants."

"Got yourself a deal."

The reek of piss hits me as soon as I top the stairs. Mum is curled on the bed, cocooned in grayed sheets. Skinny hands under her chin resemble a spindly insect. "Oh, Hariet. Is it snowing?" *Tonight, she knows your name but not that she's pissed herself?*

*We are so done here.*

I breathe through my mouth, unknot the sheets, and find her in Mikey's striped T-shirt and nothing else. "Oh, for frig sake, Mum."

"I'm icing."

She's hot to touch, clammy, and wobbly as gelatin as I wrestle off Mikey's top. Her skin doesn't fit her anymore and her belly looks pregnant, her ankles chubby. Through her glacial shivers, I force on leopard-skin stretch pants, a Christmas sweater, the Dick's work socks, his old uniform shirt, and a red toque.

I stuff the rancid sheets, fouled blankets, and plastic table-cloth in a garbage bag, spread a hefty bag on the mattress, cover it with the last semi-clean sheet. *With all the shit he steals, why the frig can't he pinch a washer/dryer?*

She totters to a sit. "You hungry?" I ask. She shakes no. "Water?" She nods yes. I give her a swig from the filthy cup and she pukes. Mercifully she hits the mounded laundry.

"I'm freezly, Jilly."

I tip her into bed, cover her with a car blanket and a moth-riddled floral curtain, brave Devil Girl's cave and snatch Babcia's cum-stained featherbed. I want out right now. *Please just let me go to Dal.*

*Oh, we might have a haiku.*

All night I turn and toss on rumbly voices and muted

movement under me. Before dawn, before the fishing boats head out, I call Jake. "Ari? What's wrong?"

"Something's right, I think, but I have to ask how you feel about it before moving on things. What if I was able to start at Dalhousie in September?"

"This September?"

"Yeah. Are you jumping or kicking?"

"Jumping. Joy jumping. How?"

"Long story. But you're sure I wouldn't be crashing something you'd rather have just for you?"

"No. I'd be over the moon."

"Okay. I have to go see if Mum still has a pulse. I'll tell you everything later."

Mum opens her eyes when I touch her forehead. The whites are yellow and unfocused. "Come pee before you piss your only pants."

She pisses less than a thimble and pukes up water. I decide my plan is less complicated if she's out of the house. Her feet have deflated a little and my flats fit. I sacrifice a black tank and tan blazer, which lend a little class to the leopard pants, not much, but it's better than the Frosty sweater and the Dick's shirt. A black cloche with a knit flower covers her disgrace of hair. She's a jittery mound of jelly to get down the stairs. The Dick's at the door. I ask, "Can you drive Mum and me to the hospital? She's not doing so good."

He tugs on his jacket. "No can do. Gotta be at HQ by eight. Call a cab." He yells like Mum's hearing is the problem. "You look real nice, Theresa."

Snake says, "At your service, cupcake." Mikey sits up front and I settle Mum in the back of his posh car. After dropping Mikey at school, Snake says, "Tell me the exact route you took yesterday." I know he knows it, so I don't lie. He drives down the empty street before taking us to emerg. I shake Mum awake. Snake Flake says, "Take care, cupcake."

*And there's our haiku.*

"Thank you. I really appreciate this."

"No problemo."

I wish Mum would have a nosebleed because I have to wait and wait and wait. I leave her snoozing and go call Jennah. All I say is, "I'm at East General. It's bad."

"I'm on my way in ten."

Jennah arrives before I have to face the shame of what Mum has done to herself. Mercifully, her chart gives the doctor the gist. I say, "She hardly eats. Water comes back up. Says she's cold but feels hot. Her belly and ankles balloon by night."

He asks, "Confusion?"

"Really bad."

"Trouble breathing?"

"Winded walking from bed to bathroom."

"We'll admit her. Run some tests." He is kind. Not blindsided-by-Jennah nice. Just kind.

Mum is either unconscious or asleep when an orderly comes to take her to X-ray. The nurse says, "It'll be a couple of hours before she's in her room."

"Thank you," Jennah says. "The staff here are always just wonderful." Jennah is only twelve years older than me. Yet she has five kids. Ten if you count the sisters she's raised. She mothers me out to her car. "You haven't eaten a thing today, have you? And you look the wreck of the helperus."

"Hesperus."

"I meant exactly what I said."

"I should get to school."

"Brunch and then I'll drop you." There's a striped shopping bag with a big red star on the front seat. "Merry Christmas."

"It's not even November."

"Well, I knew I'd find you dressed in a dog's breakfast. Besides, you'll be away over the holidays."

I hug the bag on my lap, knowing Jennah has chosen something spectacular for me. "You have your Christmas shopping all done, don't you?"

"Half at most. Picked that up on the club's annual shopping spree in New York. You can give yourself a splash and a swipe at the diner and try it on."

"I can't go to school in Fifth Avenue shit."

"You'll feel like a hip co-ed. Trust me."

My new underpants and bra are navy with tiny white stars. The jeans are black and tight. A steel-gray, buttery leather jacket tops a T-shirt printed with Georgia O'Keeffe's *Red Canna*. I don't need a mirror to see Ari Joy Zajac walking across campus. I tug on my red boots, braid my hair over my shoulder, and exit the ladies' room. I didn't cry at Mum curled on a stretcher but my lip trembles now. "Thank you, Jen. I love every last thread."

I cling to her until she says, "Tea's getting cold."

"I have some stuff to tell you." Food arrives and Jennah's choices suit me like these clothes. I tell her about Dalhousie. I tell her I want to head east and I tell her the hardest thing of all. "When I moved to crapdom, the Dick said he'd kill the J's, one by one, if I crossed him. His plan for you is to beat you to death. Set Wilf up to take the fall. Then he'll move into your house and wreck all your kids."

"As if that pig could pull anything over on this fox." She tops up our tea from a little stainless pot. "This tidbit is going straight to Wilf. My man may be a big gorilla but he's brilliant at business."

"This is brawn not business. What could Wilf do?"

She pushes cantaloupe in my direction. "Well, for starters, he'll take this threat to one of his judge friends, have it recorded and notarized, and let Irwin know it. What'd be the point of offing me if all pointed back to him? And I'll say that I don't feel safe and insist Wilf hide us for a time in one of those oceanfront places on Long Island. I'd move there in half a heartbeat."

"That takes care of you. What about Jory?"

"Didn't anyone tell you?"

"Tell me what?"

"She's gone and moved herself to a commune. Hooked up with some back-to-nature preacher."

"Where? When?"

"August. Um, Killalee? Killaloe? It's completely off the grid. Jillianne is living incognito as Anne Trembley. June's MIA. Jacquie's in Poland, so go, go, go, sis." She jams toast, cuts it, handing me the big half. "Does this deal come with residence?"

"Yes, but Jake—"

"Don't you 'but Jake' me. He can be your boyfriend but sneak him into your dorm and hang a sock on your door like regular kids do. Don't set up house yet. Please, Ari. You've had enough of it. I was eighteen when I married that jerk Roland. Wish I'd gone to school. I was smart."

"What would you've studied?"

"I'd have made a damn good lawyer."

"Then do it. You're only thirty. You'd be ahead of every woman in the class because you've already got the messy baby stuff done." I finish off the fruit, then the cheese, realizing I could eat more. "And by the time your delightful D's start messing up, you'll be in a position to get them off."

"Not going to happen." She punctuates with her fork. "Ever."

When you're charting your own course, taking steps feels different. I sign in at school, forgoing the overused sick mum excuse to cite cramps as the reason for my half-day absence. I schedule a makeup test in math and beg for an extension in biology. I map out each subject's assignments and tests. I want a transcript where people that matter won't think I'm dirt stupid.

*You're clay, not dirt.*

*Not according to my report cards.*

In grade eight, I was top mark at Oakridge. Since moving to

crapdom, my grades have roller-coastered from nineties to thirties, up and down, down and up.

In English, Ellis returns my haiku. I shake my head. "Never would've thought you one to give a mercy A."

"You had me at 'Melon collie girl.'"

"You, sir, are testing my faith in the honesty of painted turtles. But I'll take it. I really want to get my marks up."

"And yet, Mina said you were absent from art this morning."

"Had to take Mum to hospital. The doctor said her kidneys are shutting down."

"Oh, I'm sorry."

"She's such a disgrace. I feel like pond scum hauling her into emerg."

"It's her shame, not yours."

"Come on, sir. When a bird shits on your head, it flies off without a thought and you're left with a hot pile sliding down your hair."

"One bonus mark for that analogy."

"Appreciated."

"Anything we can do to help?"

"Are you free to meet me at Sabina's tomorrow night?"

"Could be. What's up?"

I check that no listeners are near. "I've a solid way to get Mikey and me out of crapdom."

"When?"

"Saturday. Execution and aftermath needs fine-tuning."

"Are you safe going home today?"

"We're fine." I stand tall in my new clothes, over-ready to go confidently in the direction of my dreams. "Um, will you tell Dr. Ventner that my mum really is sick and I do care about her class?"

"Trouble getting an extension?"

"She gave one but it had a squandering-my-potential smack

to it. Biology is the only science class where I haven't felt out of my element."

At the library, Mikey does his homework at a cubby while Ralph, Jarvis's math genius, gets me caught up on worksheets. He gives me a fresh stack. "Now, do the same ones again. It'll consolidate the theory."

I give him five bucks for the two hours. "You free tomorrow?"

"Not free. Same time, same price?"

"Deal."

I pass the table where Nat and I did projects. *I'm ready for a new library, Jasper.*

Mikey packs up and zips his sweater. "Is Todd home yet?"

"He's working until seven."

"Can I take you for grilled cheese at Woolworths?"

"You've got yourself a date."

We sit at the counter, swivelling on chrome stools. Mikey chitters, telling me that seahorses suck in food like a vacuum and dragonflies snatch their dinner and eat on the fly. "Erika's dad saw a dragonfly fossil with a two-foot wingspan. It lived millions of years ago. Do you think there were giant mosquitos, too?"

I nod while sucking up the dregs of my chocolate milk, sweetly imagining Mikey's evolution when the Dick becomes extinct. "Let's go, bro."

Snake steps out the same minute we arrive at crapdom. He's dressed in a sharp black suit, black shirt, and a pin-striped tie. He takes in my new gear. "Hey, cupcake. Don't we make a pair? How's your mother?" "Mother" comes out as "mudder" and it suits her.

"They're running tests."

"Good. Good. I'm around if you need anything." He leans into my ear. "And O'Toole's workin' another case."

"Pardon?"

He tips his fedora and winks.

*No. No. No. I need him here for the bust.*

The smell of Lysol hits like a slap. As I turn, it soaks in that there are zero boxes in the hall. The stack between the dining room and living room are gone. The pile beside the TV, gone; where the laundry is usually mounded is a floral slipcover. *Oh, no, no, no.*

A woman shaped like an egg walks down the hall on the shortest legs and tiniest feet I've ever seen. "Come on, Shirley. That's it for today."

Another woman descends the stairs, slightly younger and taller but without question related. Behind her, the Dick is carrying two hefty bags. "Oh, Hariet, meet Gladys and Shirley. They was just making things nice for when your mum gets home. Come on, ladies. I'll give ya a lift."

They giggle, all the three of them giggle, as they leave. I hurry to the kitchen. As much as shit can sparkle, it does. The porch is empty, except for one of the patio sets from the backyard, arranged like regular humans live here. Mikey sneaks up behind, whispering, "Ari, what's happening?"

I nip to the garage and peek through the window. The goods are gone. In the basement, Mikey's fort is empty. Emerging from the cellar, I see Cunt's cage draped with a sheer piece of aqua cloth; it's the skirt of a party dress Len bought for Mum. *What do we do now, Jasper?*

Traffic noise from the street pours in with the opening of the door. Todd says, "Holy Hannibal. We've got a couch?"

Mikey says, "We've been cleaned out, Todd." His scared hand tugs at me. "It's good they're gone, right?"

I pull away. Kick the chair across the linoleum, roar as I knock

198

a vase of plastic tulips off the hall table, stomp up the stairs, and brood in my corner.

Todd comes up. "Ari? What's wrong?"

"All that shit was going to trap the Dick. Why'd they take everything?"

"Must've thought their cover was blown. Before I went to work, Snake was all in Ronnie's face. He'd seen her talking to some cop. Next thing I know, Snake's on the phone. Broads in aprons show up and start cleaning while stuff goes out the back." Todd checks the hall. "Under all the sardines and Barbie Dolls was some serious shit."

"Where'd they take everything?"

"Cross border I'd guess."

Mikey quiet-steps in, puff-eyed and red-nosed, with a mug for me.

"I don't want any fucking tea!"

He whispers, "I'll make him cyanide coffee for you. I could. I really would—"

"Cheer up. They're gone and they ain't coming back." Todd crouches, something that's not easy for him to do. "Listen, stay outta Pop's reach. Seems housing them goods was part of a payback on what he owes. And that's gone."

"What was with the cleaning fairies?"

"Wiping out fingerprints, my guess."

"How'd you know all this?"

"*Perry Mason*, but not so much the show. I watch TV while they're playing poker. The more they knock back the booze, the more they see an empty chair."

"Fingerprints I get, but slipcovers?"

"Must've found it in the closet. My mom used to love that thing."

"That man goes through a lot of mothers, doesn't he?"

Todd says, "Motherfucker, numero uno."

"If Snake's gone, does that mean this guy Tino is, too?"

"Near as I can tell they're two different operations. Snake is in 'merchandising' and Tino's a money man."

"Like a loan shark?"

"Big fish."

"Oh."

Ten p.m., Mikey is deep asleep, having unwound into the emptied house. Downstairs, Todd is watching *It Takes a Thief*. I sling my pack over a shoulder. "I'm going to the hospital to see Mum. I'll be back in time to take Mikey to school."

"Right."

A black sedan is parked five doors down. I resist kicking the tires and telling the guys inside that they're too slow, too late, and are bloody pathetic detectives. My walk turns to a jog, to a run, ending with a sprint through the Riverboat to the nest. I triple-lock the door. *I can't take any more, Jasper. Tell me I can get on the train and go. Please.*

*Put the kettle on and let's just try to get caught up.*

I hang up my new coat, the scent of it reminding me of Aaron's leather jacket. I put on Len's PJ bottoms and flannel shirt. Cohen's *Songs from a Room* spins while I organize work into piles. Jacquie, the smartest Appleton, left a box for me, an academic survival kit. I dig through it for an essay. A note on the outline reads: "Remember different dates, same shit: revenge, power, money, love, greed, honour, valour, betrayal." *Pretty much sums up my life.* I follow her precisely ordered template and my essay outline on the Tudors is completed before midnight.

I lift the needle on the record player, setting it down again on "Bird on a Wire." *"She tried every friggin' way to be free" is going to be written on our tombstone.*

*No tombstone for us. We want to be thrown back into the ocean in eighty-three years.*

*Keep me alive 'til I'm one hundred, Jasper, and I promise I'll do that for you.*

I put extra care into my biology write-up, drawing the frog's anatomy with the precision of an Audubon print. *I'd take this at university if I could be assured of never having to pith another frog.*

*My kin, pinned right between the eyes.*

It's two a.m. and I survey the remaining piles. I pick up my math text, move to my comfy chair, opening it to this gem on the first page: "Algebra, from Arabic 'al-jabr' meaning 'reunion of broken parts.'" I hear Uncle Iggy say, "Sleep, corka." His strong hand reaches beyond absence, encouraging my head to his shoulder. "'Tis okay. All will be okay."

I descend to somewhere without dreams and surface to sky a shade lighter than black. It's five a.m. I shower; detangle my hair into spirals; pick ladybug underwear, black T-shirt, my new jeans; and gather my completed assignments. My new jacket squeaks as I tug it on, the lock clicks, and a V of travelling geese honk in a silver sky.

The Italian bakery is open and I nip in. Dom smiles like a gap-toothed marmot. "Bella, where have you been?"

"You know, busy. I'd like six sausage rolls; um, make that eight. Can you wrap them by twos in four bags?"

"Some pagnottini, no? It is"—he kisses his fingers— "magnifico."

"Sure, one in each bag."

In one bag he drops two. "You need two, bella."

"And two coffees. To go."

I juggle my load, while Jasper lists: *Math work sheets, then study for test on Tuesday.* Hamlet *essay on revenge and justice. Lab write-up on water drop analysis. Book report on* Le Petit Prince. *Then, yippee, our art assignment.* For art I have to draw ten distinct eyes on postcard-sized rectangles. They'll be installed side by side in the hallway with my classmates'.

*Can you imagine what it'll be like to study art at university?*
*You're asking me if I can imagine something?*
*Well, then, imagine up another way out.*

The blue sedan is alone in the driveway and the house feels like an eviscerated animal. The Dick's butt can be seen sticking out of the fridge door. He stands, scowling at me coming in at seven twenty a.m. "Where the fuck you been?"

"Hospital."

He humphs and snatches the coffee from my hand like it was meant for him. "Pea-brained Newfie, ya forgot sugar."

"Mikey has extra practice. I'm taking him right from school."

"More practice the better. Am I right?"

"You're right." I head upstairs thinking about how easy it would be to poison him.

I set the other coffee on Todd's nightstand and wiggle Mikey's foot. "Go have a quick bath while the tub's clean."

Mikey looks like he has parents who give a shit, with clean nails, groomed hair, milk in his thermos, and hand-me-downs from Jennah. On the walk to school he asks, "Is your mum gonna come out of hospital?"

"Don't know."

"Will you live at the nest if she doesn't?"

"Maybe."

"Can I live there with you? I'll sleep on the floor."

"When needed, I'll stash you there, but we need a legit solution."

"Just sneak me to Huey and the Missus."

"They're government-approved fosterers. We can't risk messing things up for them."

"Aunties M&N?"

"They're not allowed to have kids."

"Why?"

"Law says they're not suitable."

"And my mom and pop are?"

"Yeah, go figure." I pat down his cowlick. "Go have a worryless day."

I hand in assignments, ace a French quiz, and inform Mina that my window of opportunity for escape has been thwarted and she doesn't need to come tonight.

"Just because you don't need help doesn't mean I don't need a dose of Sabina's cooking. See you at six thirty."

I change for phys. ed., lockering up all my new clothes. Coach Palmer drags in a bag of volleyballs. You'd think I'd be piss happy, but ninety percent of this class remains cemented in their Ari-hate. Coach says, "Cassie, Kendra, on the court. Heads or tails." Kendra calls tails and loses first pick.

Cassie says, "Nora." Kendra picks me. Cassie choses Barb. Kendra picks Wendy. Cassie says, "Tanya."

Kendra calls, "Stephanie."

Stephanie says, "Coach Palmer, I hurt my knee." Gerry and Debbie have similar excuses as to why they don't want to be on my side.

Coach Palmer is about to blow her red-headed stack when Kendra says, "Cassie, you can have everyone else and we'll still wipe the floor with you."

Palmer smiles and blows her whistle. Wendy is the kind of player who shares and is more than happy to set. Kendra is a rocket. I am pissed. And it turns out, eleven people on the other court is not very efficient. They're left wondering what hit them. After class, Coach enters the change room, stands like Wonder Woman, words spitting like bullets: "Do not ever bring your petty grievances into my gym again. If you can't conduct yourselves in a manner befitting the sports program at Jarvis, then do not set foot in my gym." She snaps around. "Appleton. In my office. Now."

I follow her across the gym and into her miniscule office knowing I'm a two-thousand-word paper on the Mechanics of

Movement in arrears. "I'll have my essay on your desk Monday morning, I swear."

"Close the door." I do and she dances like footballers do when they score a touchdown. "What in holy hell have you been doing?"

"Pardon?"

"Your game. What I saw out there just now."

"Been playing with a community league."

"Where?"

"U of T."

"Wow. I mean it. Wow."

"Um, I kinda got offered a scholarship."

"To where?"

"Dalhousie."

"Oh, boy, oh, boy. They've a hot team. Wouldn't surprise me if they go all the way this year."

"I told them you were my coach. They said they'd want to talk to you." She smiles with her whole face and I ask, "When you talk to them, can you tell them that I'm not dirt-dumb, but that there's just been a lot of crap with Nat and stuff."

"You bet. Would you go next year?"

"I'd like to, more than anything."

"You should. You have to." She nods. "I'm proud of you, Ari."

I'm still smiling as I claim the unoccupied end of the uncool table in the cafeteria. I pour tea from my thermos, unwrap the sausage rolls, and begin the climb out of the academic hole I'm in. I've labelled my muscled runner and am a good seven hundred words into my movement paper and halfway through my pagnottini when Riley sits down across from me. "Hi, Ari." I keep plodding and he picks up my drawing. "How can you do this?"

"How do you sticky-finger a football on the run?"

He nudges my hand with a pencil crayon. "So, you free this weekend?"

"Not even a minute to piss."

"Don't you ever just have fun?"

"Oh, my life's a laugh-a-minute amusement park."

"Go out with me."

I take in his ruddy, team-captain face. "I have a boyfriend."

"A thousand miles away. Where's the fun in that? So, how about tonight?"

"Work."

"Saturday?"

"Homework, homework, and work."

"You don't work Sunday."

"I do. I make jewellery for a boutique."

"I'm going to keep asking 'til you say yes." He tilts his head and I just know there's a bet on the line and a plot being hatched.

After dinner, as Sabina's Otto helps the boys make birdhouses for their woodworking badge, I lay out the highs and lows of my week.

Ellis says, "Snake? A guy named Snake's living at the house?"

"Snake and his snakelets are many rungs higher on the evolutionary ladder than the *copper*heads."

"The whole lot are venomous. We've got to get Mikey to the Butters and you to Dalhousie."

"What the Dick really wants is to be a detective, but he owes so much money he can't get out from under. The answer lies in Len's money."

Mina asks, "How much money is at stake here?"

I shrug. "No idea. He and O'Toole talk about a hundred thousand dollar windfall, but there's no way. Len left me ninety-eight. Mr. Lukeman has sent two hundred fifty dollars monthly for almost four years. Then how much are lawyer fees?"

Ellis asks, "How can that bastard think the money's his?"

"Because he married Mum and she told him he could have it."

"It's not hers to give."

"When has rationality ever defined Mum?" I stretch my long bones and take dessert plates to the sink. "I should get to work."

"I'll give you a lift." Aaron is quiet all the way to the Riverboat. "How're you feeling?"

"Sabina's brew knocked the cold out." He zips into a parking spot.

"Want to come in and listen to some folksy jazz?"

"I've an essay and I'm still kind of wiped."

Knowing Aaron, his essay is typed, sourced, and has five appendices. "I really make your life chaotic, don't I?"

"Yes." He smiles, a sad smile. "I want chaos, Ari." In a blink, like a curtain closing, his want disappears. "And I want you safely settled where you belong."

I hop out before I churn up more turmoil. "Thank you. You're a friend in a million."

"Can we connect Sunday?"

"If you're up for a study date at Sabina's."

"That works. I'll bring Mikey the book he needs on the Great Lakes."

I watch the jeep slip down Yorkville. *How does one girl meet two perfect guys?*

*'Cause you're a cracked pot and there are pieces of you in two places.*

THIRTY-NINE

I can't remember the last time I slept until ten. I remain in bed savouring the quiet of my nest until the ringing phone shatters my Zen. *What new peril, Jasper?*

"Hello?"

"Nothing's wrong. Everything's right."

"Jake?"

"I have a 'what if' that can't wait for a letter."

"What?"

"Duncan's parents rent a flat. Small, but close to campus. Cheap. I wouldn't ask this now but it's coming open and I have to let them know by Monday. Do we want it?"

"What do you want?"

"For you to be free to choose."

"Jennah thinks I should be a regular kid in residence."

"It's okay if you want to. Just being in the same town will be something for us."

"If I did, where would you live? Residence?"

"Oh, that'd be like a submarine full of teenage fosters. No thanks. Duncan's aunt has single rooms for rent. Call me tomorrow."

"I will."

I hear his smile when he says, "We're so close to everything, I can taste it."

"It's sweet, eh."

As I redeem all the minutes of the day, it's like Jake is here with me, barefoot, blue-jeaned, sweet and salty, toes touching as we read on either side of the bed. He hums. I draw. I know what Jennah thinks, but I don't want to live with a bunch of volleyball girls. Don't want to share a room with any messy devil girls or find a strange boy in my bed.

I know it's dinner-time confusion when I call the Butters. "Hi, Huey. Jake there?"

"Hang on, he's half out the door."

"Ari?"

"What if I said I don't need until tomorrow to know I want to be with you every minute I can?"

"Really? You sure?"

"What if I said I am?"

"Then I'd say hot damn."

FORTY

Two weeks of dry-cleaning, draining, and nourishing gives Mum more life to waste. She shuffles in like an anorexic penguin and looks at the sofa. "Oh, look, a new cough. He gets me pretty things." The only man who ever gave Mum pretty things was Len: dresses, furniture, flowers . . .

The hospital sent Mum home with eight hours of nursing, which Jennah organized into two hours, four days a week. Wilf's faults are many but generosity isn't one of them. He's paying for six more hours of nursing and arranged the loan of a Morris Minor car, old as me but shiny as mint. It's the colour of sky and taking pissed sheets to the laundry is no longer an Everest of a chore. I park it around the block so the Dick doesn't see it as his property.

There's a sense that a sinkhole is about to swallow the craphouse whole. Mikey, Todd, and I are poised to bail. It's seven a.m., Mum is in her bed crying, or more snivelling. *A lament over a lost red shoe?*

The Dick is somewhere downstairs, quiet, too quiet. He came in at three twenty a.m. and his rage in the cellar with O'Toole could be felt through the vent, the only clear words being "fuck" and "fucking fuck."

I wake Mikey. Tell him to keep low and silent while I head downstairs to scout for crapmines. O'Toole is passed out on the sofa. The Dick's suit is a heap in the hall. He's standing at the sink in plaid boxers and a filthy muscle shirt. An angry outbreak of pimples circle his neck. He scrubs his bristling head under running water and mops it with the tea towel. "Morning," I say, small and unobtrusive.

"Oh, you. Make coffee, would ya." Disappointment leaks out of his every pore.

"I'm doing laundry after school. Just throw what you want washed in the hall."

He says, "Thanks." *Dick Irwin said thanks?* "Take my suit to the cleaners? Tough case last night. Got blood on it."

"Sure."

I make him Nescafé and take tea up to Mum. She amounts to nothing more than a smear of mustard in a nightie. Mikey stands behind me, making sense of things as he does. "You know about forces? Pull and push?"

"Sorta," I say.

"Last year was gravity. Everyone pulled together. Least that made the awful feel a little okay. This year's like same poles of magnets pushing everything apart."

"Yeah. It does feel more unsteady."

I rummage through the closet in the alcove and find Todd's navy blazer and gray suit pants that fit him when he was thirty pounds heavier.

The Dick has moved to the cluttered table. I hang the suit on the pantry door. "This might do until your suit's ready."

"Yeah. Good. Can you spot me a ten?"

I sacrifice ten bucks. Before I can skedaddle out the door, O'Toole is polluting the hall with a wonky boner under his tighties. "Mornin' pussy pat."

"Go fuck yourself."

"Be more fun with you."

*Seven weeks until Christmas break.*

*Things are going to blow. I can feel it.*

The doctor told Mum she'd die if she didn't lay off all shit, especially booze. I'd make her one-hundred-proof tea if I didn't know I'd be the one cleaning up bloody vomit. She's weepy and whiny without her chemical props, and her despair isn't about a wasted life, it's over the Dick's abandonment.

The nurse got her bathed, diapered, dressed, and planted downstairs, where she sits crying into a pair of substantial white panties. "Ava, I found these by the bed. They aren't mine."

Lucid moments are so rare and this is what she clues into? "Probably just Ronnie's. Most the time she's so wasted she doesn't know where her bed is."

"Ronnie lost her arm."

"What?"

She yellow-eyed stares. "Gone." Patches stain her face and her hair has turned witch-straw.

"Mikey needs his hair cut. Come with and Francine will do yours, too."

"That'd be nice, Jen."

Upstairs, I tell Mikey to go call a taxi. He says, "But we have a car."

"One, I'm not having Mum piss in it and two, we don't want anyone here knowing."

I poke my head into Devil Girl's cave to see if she's in possession of her limbs. She looks up from her sulk on the bed. "Whadda you want, bitchface?"

"Taking Mum to get her hair done. You want to come? My treat."

"Why not."

"You okay?"

"Pinto dumped me. He's a total fuckin' perv." She struggles her odd body into a lime sweater dress. Ronnie is bum, belly, and boobs connected by skinny legs, arms, and neck. She wipes smudges from under her eyes and adds makeup to an already caked face, then shoves bare feet into scuffed go-go boots.

Considering what could go wrong, the outing is stellar. Mikey and I go to the deli and buy turkey clubs, broth for Mum, and sweet rolls for Charmaine and Francine. Mum doesn't barf, she pees—mercifully in the toilet—and hums to the music playing. Charmaine gives Ronnie a makeup lesson in hopes that she'll purchase some product. For sixty-seven dollars, including tip and taxi, bellies are full, spirits lifted, and I get a thank you from Ronnie who happily clutches a zippered pouch with new blush and lip gloss. *Two Irwin thank yous in one day? Watch out, Ari.*

The taxi returns us better than we left. Mum has a teased-up 'do that hides her baldness. Ronnie has a shiny bob. Mikey looks handsome and somehow taller, and my mane is trimmed up six inches and hairdresser silky.

By the curb is a black Lincoln. On the porch stands the Dick and two fine-suited men. The shorter of the two looks us over, then over again. The Dick says, "Tino, these are my daughters, my wife, and my son. This is Mr. Constantine."

Mikey, with his I'm-never-getting-hit-again savvy, extends his hand. "Pleased to meet you, sir."

Ronnie opens like a flower on a hot day. "Hi, I'm Ronnie. Veronica, actually."

Mum says, "It's fin, feen, fine."

It's the last of the fresh cool before winter's cold. "Yes, it's a fine day. Very fine." Mr. Constantine motions a tip of his fedora and lays claim to my face. "And you are?"

"Hariet." I want to say Ari Zajac, but I'm not giving this creep my cherished name. "Excuse me. My mum needs to get off her feet." Being a head taller than Ronnie makes disappearing impossible and I wish I'd dressed Amish instead of in tight jeans.

*I need a shower, Jasper.*

*He's the one the Dick owes big.*

A hearty goodbye can be heard at the door. Before I can say, "There's a sandwich," the Dick yanks me by the hair into the pantry and pincers my ear. "Don't you ever disrespect Mr. Constantine like that again, you hear."

"How did I—"

"Walking away like he was nothin'."

"Didn't think you'd want Mum pissing on his shoes."

His clamp eases. "Listen, I just need you to be nice."

Todd answers a ringing phone and yells, "Pop, it's for you."

"Not home."

"It's Providence Villa."

"Tell 'em to call Edwin."

Twenty seconds later Todd stands at the opening. "Grandpops croaked."

The Dick's hand drops. For a millisecond, his face is an eight-year-old's discovering his dead puppy. His voice projects inward. "Did you tell 'em to call Ed?"

"Yep."

I say what people always say. "I'm sorry."

"No skin off my nose. He's nothing to me."

"That's when it wrecks you most."

"Shut the fuck up!" He points a finger at me, then Todd. "I'm not here. Clear?"

I've had only three face-to-face encounters with the Irwin patriarch during my incarceration in crapdom. Deplorable sums him up in a word. "Who's Edwin?" I ask.

"Pop's brother."

"Didn't know he had a brother."

"He's got two and a sister and there's, like, a ton of cousins."


Third Sunday in November, Aaron brings the coffee and pictures of Zodiac sleeping by the fire. He asks, "How was the funeral?"

"Weird. Pathetic. Beside the Dick, Todd, and me, there were only six people there. No flowers. No eulogy from his kids. Not a tear shed. The reception was whiskey, packaged cookies, and lies. The Dick said Todd was a vet. Ricky, a race car driver in California. Mum was in Europe visiting her daughter. He let people think I was Ronnie and said I was a volleyball champ."

"And Mikey?"

"The whole reason he let me leave him at Sabina's was so he could say Mikey was playing hockey and he had to make a quick exit to get to his game. The only emotion I saw from the Dick was terror that he might get stuck with any part of the bill."

"That's the most depressing send-off I've ever heard of."

"Not me. My dad was unceremoniously disposed of without ritual. Jennah was adamant that he be cremated and buried in a lead box, numbered rather than named."

Aaron's head tilts with the weight of caring. "Understandable given how he treated all of you."

"But how do you ever resolve anything if you burn it, bury it, and refuse to name it?"

"I took psych for four years and that astute question never would've occurred to me."

"That wisdom comes from studying boat restoration with Huey Butters."

"Did Ricky come home for the funeral?"

"Todd called him, but he said he's waiting for a bigger crowd to make an entrance."

"I'm still not clear why the Dick finding out that Ricky's in the army is such a big deal."

"Well, apparently, it was the Dick's dream to be a soldier but he was triple-rejected. Ricky's coming back in full uniform, when everyone will see he's better than the Dick."

"What a family."

"That's the thing. Todd has evolved into a tub of kindness. Ricky is GI-go-go Joe. Mikey is, well, Mikey." I snug up closer to absorb his warmth.

He does something easy and without hesitation: puts his arm around my shoulder. "Let's go somewhere with heat."

I happily move toward the warmth of Sabina's. "Think I might take psychology next year. I need to sort the nature versus nurture confusion."

"No one can because it's not either/or and the weights are always in flux. Like, you're a volleyball ace because you're tall and athletic, also because a coach saw potential and you practise hard."

"And because so many people piss me off and you set me up with Giselle." I keep hold of his arm. "Maybe I should return the kindness and set you up with Mikey's teacher."

"She a match for my animal?"

"She's a manta ray. So, no, not an exact match. But she's gentle and graceful."

"Check with me in the new year when my course load's a little lighter."

In two months, I sense there will be a new excuse why this odd tango is where we both need to be.

## FORTY-ONE

The absence of mayhem is like being on an ice floe: it seems solid but you know there is open water underneath. A chunk can break away without warning, setting you helplessly adrift. For three weeks, there has been bliss in crapdom. Instead of a funeral bill, the Dick received a cheque for three hundred and eighty-nine dollars as his share of what was left in his father's account. His wallet is fat with twice that and hope runs big that he's well on his way to a day of reckoning with his employer.

One of the cleaning fairies, Shirley, continues to come one, two, sometimes three times a week. I don't care that she and the Dick are adulterating right under Mum's nose because Shirley leaves the sink and toilet sparkling. O'Toole is nicely constricted by Snake and back with his wife, now pregnant with another hapless child.

Every morning the nurse comes to clean up Mum, and wonder of wonders, Devil Girl is a Florence Frightengale. For two bucks a day, Ronnie insists Mum onto the toilet until she pees, doles out her two o'clock pills, and snaps open a vanilla shake for her. It's the only constructive thing I've ever seen Ronnie do and it makes her kind of smiley.

I'm caught up at school and actually getting that P = Q. In fact, Ari Joy Zajac is on the honour roll.

I tuck in my nook with letters and books while Mikey places his pillow outside his tent. "Will I ever be able to come stay with you and Jake in Halifax?"

"Lots. Jake says there's a Murphy bed."

"The kind that folds into the wall?"

"Yep."

"Could it ever snap me inside?"

"No."

"I wouldn't be scared to be trapped with you guys." He mashes the pillow under his sunshine head. "Do I have to go to my mom's for Christmas?"

"You know that under all your mom's messed-up shit, she really does think you're special."

"I guess. But what if I get locked out and it's snowing? Could I go to the nest?"

"Bet if I asked, your mom would be happy for you to have a holiday with me."

"For real? Would you?"

"Sure."

"Can I bring her my present before we go?"

"After school, Friday. We'll catch the Saturday train."

He sighs deep. "We're the luckiest in the world, aren't we?"


I ace a pop quiz in math. Collect poetry threads in biology: light, energy, transformation, fuel . . . Dr. Ventner winks a smile returning my lab, one hundred percent, and my test, ninety-three percent. *Definitely taking biology at Dalhousie.*

During my spare and lunch, I head out like Jennah with a list: pick up Ice Capades tickets for the Zajac clan; a brass compass at Taylor's Antiques for Aaron; paintings from the framers—for Ellis and Mina, a Dali-esque turtle stack holding a wonky wonder-full world on their backs, and for Jake, a seahorse pair in a tangle of seagrass titled *U of Us*. I pick up my mail and rush to Checkers for the lunch special.

I settle into a booth, opening letters while waiting. I read Jacquie's first.

*Hey Sis: Miss you. Oh, this baby can't come soon enough.*

216

*I pee every two minutes. It's another girl. I'm certain. What do you think of Leona for her name?*

*I haven't written much about the unrest here, but the turmoil and disquiet has rattled me down to the marrow; Franc, too. I asked Babcia if there was peace anywhere on this planet and she tapped her heart. That's something, eh. The horror that she's lived and her heart is a peaceful place. At Babcia's request, I've rummaged through boxes, gathered pictures, and filled a steno with notes. She says they're for you. A story ready for writing. I'll bring them in the spring . . .*

My letter from Jake is plump.

*Ari: I open my eyes these mornings and as sleep dissolves, I see I'm waking to dreams. I hardly dare to believe this is happening. Just school, without the worry of kids. Don't get me wrong, I love the nippers, but imagining time to discover how things work feels like new music. There are tons of gigs to be had in Halifax. I'll make more than enough weekends to see us through. And no fishing for a spell. I really hate it. I know you know that but it's some-thing for me to say.*

*To think that you'll be coming in the fall. The place is small, but close to campus and not far from the shore. Duncan's parents have bikes that are ours for the loan. If we give the flat a lick of paint, they won't charge rent for the summer months. The kitchen needs a couple of shelves. Maybe over Christmas we could steal away for a day and you can tell me where you'd like them. The Missus and Mary have packed up boxes of wares . . .*

*He's as excited as a new bride.*

*The universe is in a perfect spin.*

I finish my pie. I'd lick the plate if Riley Hollingsworth wasn't at the lunch bar swivelling to catch a look every five seconds. I leave a two-dollar holiday tip.

Riley spins on his counter stool as I pass. "Hey, Ari. You heading back?"

"Yep."

"Can I catch a ride?"

"You promise it won't land me with glue in my hair?"

"Pardon?"

"Is there a plot to torture me?"

"I just dig your wheels and it's snowing."

"Okay. But no laughing if I stall on a hill."

"I'll show you a way back that avoids all hills."

"There's no such route, Riley."

Mina, the principal, and the secretary are huddled like the Bermuda triangle when we pull into the parking lot. Mina's colourlessness when she looks at me makes my pink cheeks blanch. "Ari, lock up. You need to come with me."

"Is my mum dead?"

She encourages me toward her car. "No."

"Auntie Mary? Not Nia? Zodiac? Jacquie? Not Arielle?"

She sits me in the front seat. It's warm from the waiting.

"Did something happen to Mikey?"

"Mikey's fine. Aaron'll pick him up and take him to Sabina's. Jake's had an accident."

"What?"

"He's in hospital in Halifax."

"Oh . . . no—no, no. Take me to the train."

"Ellis is going to drive you."

"How?"

"School's out tomorrow. Classes can take care of themselves."

218

My shivering won't stop. "Is he going to die?"

"It's not life-threatening, but it is serious. A cable snapped, injuring his hand and eye."


Ellis pulls into a stop for coffee, returning with tea for me.

"He's hurt bad, isn't he?"

"Mary wanted to tell you, but I think the miles to process this is needed. He'll likely lose vision in his left eye and . . . his right hand was severed."

"Severed? Can they sew it back on?"

"It was lost, in the ocean."

"But we have a little apartment and bicycles and . . ." I pull my knees to my head. "I give up."

"Didn't you tell me your Uncle Iggy lost both his legs and still danced his whole life?" My shivering starts again and Ellis unearths his sweater. "Tell me more about your uncle."

"He was a hero of three wars . . ."

"Three? Korea?"

"World War One, Two, and Applegeddon."


Jake's bandaged arm looks like a giant Q-tip across the hospital gown. Gauze half swallows his face; blue leaks out. I look to Huey. "Can I touch him?"

"Come over to here and hold his hand."

I take it, careful not to mess up his IV. He says my name, muttering he's sorry. I whisper in his ear, "I'm sorry you're hurt but I'm not sorry I love you."


Jake moans and I scurry off the middle-of-the-night chair-bed. "Jake? It's Ari."

"Hand's killing me." He searches my face with underwater eyes. "Is it okay?"

With the bandage so big, any doped-up person could believe his right hand hadn't left. "You're here. I'm here. So, everything's okay." I push the nurse-button and tell her Jake has a lot of pain.

Maybe because doctors have big brains, their hearts get short-ended in blood supply. Dr. MacAfee stands at the end of the bed delivering Jake's odds of left-eye blindness like it's a small pepperoni pizza, then proceeds to slice Jake with the sharp truth. "And with rehab and prosthetics, you should have no difficulty carrying out activities of daily living." He has no clue this news snip, snip, snips away more than a flesh and bone hand. Jake holds with that hand, builds, provides, makes music . . .

Jake glares at me, then at Dr. MacAfee. "A what? With what?"

"It's remarkable what's being done with biomechanics and artificial limbs."

Jake curls into a heavy ball, muscles pulling away as I stroke his back. His first words in two hours are "Leave me alone." I stay because I know he doesn't mean it, sitting quiet with him through the closing of the year.

I've never known Jake to be a speck impatient or a mote unkind. When he says, "Leave me the fuck alone," I don't. When I tell him I'm never leaving, he leaves me, into silence, long silences.

I cry myself to sleep in the room Mary rented near the hospital, then go back for more.

He says, "Go. Just go."

"You don't really want me to."

He clears the side table with a sweep of his arm and descends into his pillow.

220

Auntie Mary says I need to go back to school. Auntie Nia says I should give him some space. Huey pleads, "Give him some time, but please, Ari, don't give up on him."

"I never could, Huey."

Second week of January, they send him to rehab. Sabina calls and I know I have to go back.

Jake stares out a big window at naked branches and frost-killed gardens. A red poker chip flips along his left fingers and I wonder if they're remembering the music.

"Jake, the Dick broke Mikey's arm and—"

"What?" He folds the chip into his palm.

"He's losing it again. I'll come back soon as I can." I take a kiss from his cheek and settle on his ear. "You lost pieces of yourself that we can find a way to live without. If you shut me out, how will I survive without my heart?"


Aaron meets me at the train. "Geezus, Ari. I'm so sorry. How's Jake?"

"Sad. Mad more than anything. What the heck happened to Mikey? Thought he was at Sabina's."

"Todd said the Dick dragged him out of school. Figures he did it to make sure you came back. Arm's broken above the elbow. Mikey says he fell tobogganing but the hospital sent a social worker in, so I don't think they believe his story."

"Have you seen him?"

"He hasn't been at school. Todd says the Dick's unravelling."

Like a seagull's scream, "Fucking, fucking hell!" rises from my gut.

## FORTY-TWO

When I first landed in crapdom, Mikey didn't talk, not a peep. He's back to his silence, clinging to me like a bloody traumatized squid. He goes to school, does his work, and waits for me inside the front doors, heading straight up to his tent when we walk through the door.

Mum wheezes from her chair, "Nice cream."

"Get it your bloody self." I straighten my shoulders, stretch to my full height, striding to where the Dick skulks in the kitchen. "Just letting you know, I'm done here."

His head, heavy as rock, turns on his neck. "Don't fuck with me."

"My friend's sick. I'm going home."

"You're not leaving me with a sick wife and kid."

"Jennah's arranging a home for Mum. Mikey can come with me."

"Not happening."

"You have no say over what I do." He takes a step toward me, fists tensing. I stop him with one finger. "And if I die, every penny of Len's money goes to Arielle."

"I'll kill every last one of your fucking sisters."

"You know how many judges Wilf plays golf with? He has a lock on you if anything happens to anyone I care about."

"Fuck you. Mikey ain't going nowhere."

"Your call. Good luck." I turn slowly, knowing a "wait" is coming.

"Hang on. He can't even zip his fly with that contraption on his arm."

"Whose fault is that?"

"He's clumsy."

"Bull-fucking-shit."

"Watch your mouth."

"You watch your step. One mark on me and I'm going straight to Halpern with detailed evidence I've gathered since you forced me to live in this hell."

"No way. I've been over every inch of this house. Shirley's very thorough."

"You think I'm stupid enough to keep it here? You may've gotten rid of the goods, but not before I took pictures of every box in this house, garage, cellar . . . Got a dozen of you with Snake and Pinto hauling smokes through the back gate. And think about all those whispered meets in the cellar. Astonishing what my recorder picked up through the vent in Todd's room. All in triplicate, to be sent on my say so, or my demise."

*Why didn't we think to really do that?*

*I know, right?*

"You think for a minute that you could get anything past my guys at the station?"

"Good point. Thanks. I'll turn it over to Snake, say I found you keeping the goods on him."

"Okay, fuck it." He plays his only card left. "Stay 'til school's out and I'll sign any custody deal you want."

I know full well in May, on my eighteenth birthday, his gift to me is a committal to Queen Street, but for now I'll take this until I can figure it all out. "When you're on nights, I'll sleep here until Mum's placed. But if O'Toole shows, I'm gone and you can change her bloody diaper."

"No funny business or I swear I'll kill you."

"At this point I really don't care." My leg lifts, foot connecting with the table rim. It rockets across the floor, toppling Cunt's cage, launching shit in all directions. "I am so done with this fucking house and everything in it!"

The one time Mikey decides to come out of his room lands

him in the hall. I know by his face that he's heard the whole exchange.

"Get your boots."

He stands like a scarecrow stuck on a cross.

"Move it, Mikey. Coat on." I push him out the door, coat half on, tears freezing on his cheeks, a whimper catching in his throat. "Get in the car. Now." Gears grind as we make for the nest. Once inside, I force Mikey's head up to look at me. "I'm on my last nerve so just give me a friggin' break." His shoulder-to-wrist cast guts me as he flings one scrawny arm around my waist. "Christ, you stink."

I hefty-bag his cast and insist him into the shower. In a box from Jennah are thoughtful clothes: track pants without zippers, T-shirts and sweatshirts with domes along the arm and side. In silence we eat toast with Sabina's soup. Mikey curls on the bed, his cast propped on pillows. I turn out the light, letting a joint take me from smouldering to mellow.

With a solid sleep, breakfast, and a peaceful weekend ahead, I say, "Tell me what happened."

He shakes no.

"Talk. Now. I'm barely hanging on here."

His voice is small and shaky. "Can I stay here?"

"Until I get things sorted, yes. Now tell me."

"I didn't do anything. I didn't."

"What set him off?"

"He was on the phone, yelling. Then he smashed the receiver, yanked me off the sofa, and said, 'Get that little b-b—'"

"Bitch?"

He nods. "Said if you didn't come back, I was dead."

"Why didn't you tell the social worker?"

"He was right there when the lady came, and he said he had Jake hurt and he'd do the same to you if I told."

"He had nothing to do with Jake's accident. A worn cable snapped. It was just terrible timing, that's all."

"Is Jake going to be okay?"

"Don't know. He's wrecked inside and out."

## FORTY-THREE

Jake doesn't answer my letters or take my calls.

Mum's liver, kidneys, and heart are failing. My grades are close behind.

The Dick is drowning in a mafia mess and I have the sinking feeling that Mr. Constantine would take servicing in lieu of cash.

*I wonder what an ulcer feels like.*

Mum decomposes on the couch while we eat. The Dick moves noodles around his plate. "Ronnie, listen, I need that ring Theresa gave you. Just for a time. I'll give it back."

"Hariet stole it, Daddy."

The Dick fists up my hair and I fist my fork. "You really think I have the balls to mess with Ronnie?"

He smashes his plate against the wall as the phone starts ringing. "Answer the fucking phone."

In the absurdity I've come to expect, it's Mr. Constantine asking me if I'd accompany him to a Tom Jones concert.

"Sorry, sir, I'm not allowed out on school nights and I work weekend nights."

"If you asked your father, I think he might lighten up on the rules."

For once in her pathetic life, Mum helps me. "Go pee pee."

"Excuse me, sir. Have to go help my mum."

I hand the receiver to the Dick and push Mum upstairs, land her on the toilet, then dump her in bed. The Dick is lurking in the doorway when I turn around. "Ari, it would mean a lot to me if you went out with Tino. Just once." As soon as "Ari" came out of his mouth, I knew I'd been offered as payment.

Friday night, Mr. Constantine saunters into the Riverboat with a glamour gal whose face-gunk hides her twenty young years. I pace in the kitchen. Crystal says, "Girl, you're killing me. Get out there."

"That man at the corner table thinks I'm payment for a debt."

"Worst thing you can do is show him you're scared. Players like him take whatever they can, but they respect ballsy women."

*Do seahorses have balls?*

*None to boast about. Best go with the lion in you.*

I adjust the growing situation in my pants and head out with a tray. Before he can eye-undress me I grab a chair. "Why the hell are you here?"

He closed-mouth smiles. "I like jazz."

"Bullshit. If you think you're buying a young virgin with that Dick's IOU, you can just keep your wallet and everything else in your fancy suit."

He laughs, a head-back laugh, and sends his bimbette to the little girl's room. "Your father just thought we might—"

"That Dick is not my father. My dad blew his brains out and my mum killed my papa, and I swear if you come anywhere near me, I'll cut off *your* dick and shove it down your throat."

A slow draw makes his cigarette fire. "One dinner and a single dance."

"I'm seventeen. What the hell's wrong with you?"

226

"You have a certain"—his head shimmies—"je ne sais quoi."
His French has a distinctive Bugs Bunny ring to it.

"Merde." I push away from the table. "Vous êtes un cochon
dégoûtant."

*You're right, he is a disgusting pig, but . . . Ari, he might be just
the ticket for saving our bacon.*

He stays until closing, leaving a hundred-dollar tip. Crystal
follows him out, waving the bill before stuffing it in her shirt.
"Thanks, appreciate it."

Two fingers graze his eyebrow in salute before he gets in the
back of a shiny black car.

FORTY-FOUR

With his cast, Mikey can't swim or play hockey, so Aaron and
I take him to a movie. After, at the diner, Aaron says, "Sorry,
guys. Who knew that a Disney film with animated cats would
have mayhem over an inheritance?"

Mikey's take on *The AristoCats* is a relief. "But the cats got
home and the bad guy got his comeuppance."

"True." Aaron nudges my plate closer. "Would you rather
try soup?"

I force down a bite of grilled cheese. "No, I'm good."

At the drop-off, I say, "Thanks. We both really appreciate
this."

"You free Saturday?"

"Free? No."

"Available?" I nod, my cheek tilting to meet his hand reaching through the window. His fingers slip through my hair. "You need an escape, even if it's just for a day."

Saturday morning, Aaron drives north through snow-sugared trees, giving the gift of unquestioning miles. We come to a gallery nestled in nature's art, and for unmeasured time I'm lost in lines, colour, motion, shadow, light . . . The paintings speak with clarity and mystery. I'm inside *First Snow*, *Pic Island*, *Algoma Waterfall* . . . I resist as Aaron nudges me to the exit. "If you eat, I'll bring you back until closing."

The restaurant is cozy, the air bready. The soup and crusty rolls would've sated me, but the cheese-stuffed pasta and winter squash is ambrosia. Aaron talks about a meal in an ocean village called Positano. "It's on a cliff; below, the sea was more green than blue and my uncle said, 'Let's go rent one of those boats and sail off the world.'"

"You spent a summer in Europe? You're an odd Amish, Aaron West."

"Mennonite. My Uncle Pete said he needed to go back as a pilgrimage after serving there during the war."

"Again, weird."

"Dad and him were medics. No bearing arms. Anyway, he sold my going and seeing the world as educational to my parents. I think they knew I'd explode if they didn't give me some openings."

"You're having the longest rumspringa in history, aren't you."

"That's more an Amish thing, but my family does expect me to come back and settle down."

"The earliest I see you doing that is when you're eighty-two, even that's an outside shot." I mop up sauce with bread. "Does your uncle have a family?"

"His wife died before I was born."

"No kids?"

"Me and my sisters are his kids. He's had a girlfriend or ten, but everyone pretends they don't know a thing about them."

"I like him."

"He likes you, too."

"You talk about me?"

"He's the one who told me that this friendship was the most valuable thing in my life and not to lose it."

"He did not. Did he?"

"He said you get me, more than I get myself." He checks his watch and looks for the waiter. "Shall we go back?"

"I want some gelato first."

On the drive home, trees are underlit by the setting sun. "How do I thank you for this?"

"It was nice having someone to enjoy it with."

"Can we go again?"

"For sure." He reaches over the seat and nabs a white paper bag. "Here, just in case you need an escape before we do."

Inside is a book, *The Group of Seven* by Peter Mellen. I flip it over, scanning the artists. "Aaron, this one looks"—I tilt it to the last of the light—"like the man on the cedar bench, the one I sat beside."

"A.Y. Jackson is often there. Did you talk?"

"I said, 'This is nirvana, isn't it.' He just smiled into my bliss."

As we enter the city, Aaron asks, "Where do you need to go?"

*The ocean, the potter's wheel* . . . "Work. Just drop me around back of the Riverboat."

He opens my door like his mother taught him to do. Aaron is a paradox, his face is soft and strong, boyish with the five o'clock shadowing of a man, he's bound and boundless, set in stone and fluid. As I step from the jeep, I slip into a hug, long and longing. "I really, really needed this today."

He holds me for sixteen beats of his heart, then his lips brush my forehead. "Me, too. See you tomorrow."

FORTY-FIVE

Mum is home after a week in hospital. Cleaned out, she's pitifully more tuned in. She's curled on the couch, crying, "Richard doesn't love me anymore."

I tuck the shawl under her chin and answer the knock on the door. An explosion of roses appear to have hands and legs. "Delivery for Miss Irwin." I take the heavy vase, hand the guy a buck, and read the card. *Miss Irwin: You are fireworks in a night sky. Tino.*

*Irwin? Oh, as if we don't have enough trouble keeping food down.*

"Who's there, Elsie?"

"Look, Mum. The Dick sent you flowers."

"No. Did he? What say the card do?"

"Theresa: You are fireworks in a night sky, love Richard."

Big tears spill as she sniffs a pink rose. "I have to pee."

In three months, I'll be eighteen and I need a solid plan. On the way to the bathroom, step one comes into focus: get Mum out of the equation. "I'm going east next week. I'll take you to your sister's for a holiday and pick you up on the way back."

She shakes at her reflection in the mirror. "I'm nothing but a rag hag." It's the closest thing to poetry I've ever heard come out of her mouth. "What'd I ever do to deserve this?"

"Really? You had big brains, Mum. Where'd you think this road would land you?"

She turns, slaps me with the force of a baloney slice. It hurts more than anything the Dick ever dished out. I leave her on the toilet and call Jennah to ask permission to drive the car to Montreal.

"When?"

"Saturday. I can't wait for a nursing home spot to open. I'm taking Aunt Elsie up on her offer to help."

"What about school?"

"Nothing adds up without Jake. I need to see him."

"You're not losing that scholarship. Let me call the school. I'll tell them Mum's at death's door and get a list of what work needs doing. It's the only way I'll agree."

"Okay."

I lie and tell the Dick that March break is early and take Mikey to Sabina's.

Eight a.m., Saturday March 6, I realize the value of planning and lists. *She's going to piss in our car.*

I nab the red-checked oilcloth from the kitchen table and spread it over the tiny back seat. *We'll have to crack her legs to corkscrew her in here.* I'm in a bit of a sweat when I crawl out and there, pulling up to the curb, is Jennah in her shiny silver car. Sitting beside her is Jory.

"You can't drive that wobbly bucket on the highway." Jennah directs Jory to move gear from the Morris to the precisely ordered trunk of the Cougar.

"Jen?"

"Road trip. Jory and I'll drive. You'll study."

Mum has the whole back seat if she needs it and we have more music, laughs, and crap food than anybody deserves. The last hundred miles, Mum reclines, head on my lap, taking in the blue sky. "I meant to be something else."

"Pardon?"

"Something Mary could never be."

"What?"

"One summer I was a Double Bubble Girl at the CBB."

"The CNE?"

"Mm-hmm. Pink short-shorts and candy-striped top." Her lucidity makes me think this is a final neuron rally before lights out. "I was fourteen, earning a dollar a week until this man said I was prettier than Jean Harlow. He put me in a flexy red dress by a Ford Super Deluxe for five whole dollars a day. A trade show's where I met my Vincent. Said he'd buy the car if I came with it. Oh, he was a looker, like Cary Grant."

My hand hushes her arm. "I never knew that."

"For two yams I neared fame, in magazines and everything. Then babies came . . . and the war." She drifts to Elvis singing "Love Me Tender." "He was raised from the dead?"

"Elvis?"

"No, Vincent. When he was small as Marky. He was out for three days, then woke full of life, like Jesus."

Jory turns around. "I heard that one."

"From who?" I ask.

"Nana Appleton. Grandpa crowned him with a full bottle of Crown Royal."

"Is Nana expecting us?"

"No, Mum, Elsie."

"Won't Grandma be surprised?"

"Yeah."

Auntie Elsie swallows her horror as she helps Mum out of the back seat and into the house. Jillianne scans the near corpse on the couch. "She's done, isn't she."

"Yep," I say.

"Are we supposed to care?"

"I say focus on the living."

I snap around to the long-missed voice. "Jacquie? Oh, Jacquie."
"Surprise!"

I cling to the solid and soft of her. "How?"

"Franc wanted to do some work on the Toronto boutique before we move there. He's gone ahead with Babcia to Sabina's. We're staying here for a bit."

"Where's my new nephew?"

She hushes with her finger and we tip-toe over to the pram in the sunroom. "Ari, meet Leonek Ignatius Zajac. We call him Leo."

I scoop up the tiny sleeping bundle. "Hello, little lion. I'm your auntie." He's the sweetest-cheeked baby I've ever seen, and by the shine on Jacquie's face, I know he's a bit of gold filling the crack in her heart. "Where's Arielle?"

"Over at Auntie D's playing with Celine. Mum is no one and nothing she needs to see."

I have much to learn from my sisters about erasing Theresa and Vincent Appleton from mind, body, and soul.

Auntie Elsie keeps Mum and shoos us to Dolores's house. "Go have a bit of fun."

We are five sisters tucked on comfy seats in Auntie D's rec room. She comes down, opens the fridge, and loads the coffee table with sundae fixings. "Lambs are asleep. I'll bring Leo down when he's ready for a feed."

Jacquie says, "We'll hear him. Believe me. Stay. We're missing our sixth."

I'm usually the one pining for the missing sister. When Dolores sits, Jennah lifts a spoon of butterscotch ripple in a toast. "To June, and to Auntie D, standing in for the walls of the sister-house."

"Say what?"

Jory says, "I'm the roof. Jen's the windows. Jill—uh, pardon me, *Anne* is the floor. Jacquie's the door and June the walls. Ari built it."

Dolores fills a bowl with Neapolitan. "Given how your home was always falling apart, I can understand why you would. And what part of the house were you, Ari?"

Four sisters chime, "The electricity."

Dolores smiles. "Mary, Elsie, and me are so proud of you girls."

Jacquie splits a banana and loads her bowl. "The best three out of the four Trembley sisters ain't bad."

"That mother of yours has always had her heart turned in on herself. She's not a reflection of you, and not a one of you are a reflection of her."

Anne says, "It's astonishing, really. I mean, what are the odds that five of us would be sitting here living relatively unfucked lives?"

Jennah says, "Let's give credit where credit is due: I raised your sorry asses and did a damn fine job." We raise our bowls to Jennah. For as long as I can remember, there has been a chasm between sister number one and three. Anne speculates it's because Daddy replaced Jennah with Jacquie as the apple of his eye-rection. Jennah stands. "But I wasn't the only one. A toast to Jacquie. Ballsy at business. Mother of three beautiful children. Wife to Franc, a man as gentle as our Len, and, and, and—the one brave enough to open the door and tell the world our truth. I don't believe in all that God stuff that was crammed down our throats. Sorry, Jory. But the truth set us free."

Jory says, "Amen."

"Daddy fucked us. Mum fucked us over." Jacquie smiles at Jennah. "Yet look at us, we're fucking awesome."

"Oh, I fucking love you girls." It's the first time I've ever heard Dolores swear. "Don't know if this is the time or place,

234

but when your grandma died, your mum made her own wishes known."

Jacquie says, "Don't tell me. A gold casket with eight buff, naked men carrying her."

"She was definite that she was not to be burned or buried. A mausoleum suited her. In Montreal, not Toronto near Grandma. Oh, and she said she wouldn't be caught dead wearing black."

Jory, who hasn't a spiteful bone in her skinny body, says, "So, I propose cremation, a black urn, and burial in the same plot as Grandma. All in favour, raise a spoon." Six spoons lift. "Motion carried."

Six a.m., Jennah gives me her keys. She feels both fragile and invincible as she hugs me off. "I'm pulling for you. Go get him."

Pleasant Cove appears like a storybook village. As I have aged, I've come to see the imperfections: poverty, bitter wives, wayward children, and many salty dogs. Still, it's the best place on Earth, filled with music, art, and neighbourliness. *Can't quite fathom that Jake is one of the ones wandering on the dark side of the moon.*

Jake sits, staring at the waves, looking thin and weathered. Many times we've leaned against this log and dreamed. Today the sand chills my bum. He folds his arms against the March bite. "Jake, wherever your journey takes you, I'm at the other end waiting."

Quiet hangs for as long as it takes the sun to fall. "I don't want you there."

"Knock it off. You don't mean that."

"Don't tell me what I mean."

"What the frig, Jake. You're throwing all our dreams away because you lost a hand and eye?"

"Maybe I see inside now, what I really am."

"Bloody fool. You can't see anything at all." The sunless wind chills me to my marrow. I stand. "I'm sure the Missus has the kettle on." He sits, unmoved. "Get your sorry self up. Now. I'm cold."

I wade through days of too many pills and ocean big silences.

He lies beached on the bed. I snug up beside him. "I have to take the car back tomorrow."

"Ari, let me go."

"No."

"We're done."

I sit up. "Never. Now, you get yourself back to rehab. We're going to school in September."

"I'm not going."

"Why? You didn't lose your brain or your heart. Stop this. Please."

"I don't care about any of it anymore."

"I've thought hard about losing one of my hands. How big the loss would be if I couldn't turn pots. But Uncle Iggy would spirit-kick me 'round the planets if I didn't use what I had left. You'll figure out how, but you have to do something first."

"There's nothing to be done."

"You've been waiting for a reason to say, 'See, told you I'm not good enough.' When you stand nose to nose with your father and tell him he's a big fat liar and you're deserving of a thousand Ari Zajacs, then everything you set your hand to will make music."

"If I'd gone to school like I promised. If I had—"

"You'd still have that fear in your belly. Keep your promises now. You promised to fight for us no matter what."

He drowns his face in the pillow, escaping into jerky dreams. Pain wakes him in the emptiest hours of the night. He

236

hunches over the side of the bed, moaning and rocking. Huey lumbers out of his room with Jake's pills.

"Wait. When Uncle Iggy had bad pains, Len joined him up with his legs."

Huey says, "Did what?"

Jake doesn't pull away from my hold on his arm. I whisper, "Jake, this is your right arm, feel it unknot all the way down to the tips of your fingers, stretched out whole and free, flowing like water." I feather his arm in a light scratch. "Lay back and we'll swim long lovely strokes with two whole hands." Through a quiet hour, I talk him back to sleep.

In the morning Huey and I reanimate over coffee. "What you did really seemed to help, dolly."

"Want to know what worked best? If Len sat on the end of the bed with Iggy on his lap." I pause. "Sounds squirrelly, I know, but it worked like magic. Iggy would look in the mirror and see Len's legs as his own and all the terrible cramps would ease. Len said the brain couldn't miss something it saw right in front of it."

Huey's big hand covers mine. "And how's the dolly right in front of old Huey?"

"Joy less and full."

"Well, ain't those just the very things to keep a boat from tipping." He kisses my forehead. "We'll keep things afloat 'til the storm calms."

Jake stirs. I take his left hand, willing hope into his right. "Jake, I'm taking the car back to Montreal. I'll come back by train tomorrow."

His head shakes for a time before he forces out, "No."

"I'm coming."

Tears won't stay down when he spits words heavy as stones. "For Christ's sake, I don't want you here."

"Be as big a mule-headed jerk as you want. Soon as I get things sorted, I'm coming back."

237

Two seconds into Skyfish and I blow like a beluga. Nia hushes my stress of hair. "We're going to take good care of him. This is his dark place, his treasure hunt." She puts me in the passenger seat and Mary slides in behind the wheel.

"What're you doing?"

"I need to see my sister."

I'm more bone-weary than I've ever felt in my seventeen-and-three-quarters years on this earth, driving from a heart-break mess to a pathetic mess to a mortal-threat mess. Pictures from the March highway blur grime to gray. I cocoon into a knitted shawl and hear Uncle Iggy in his marbly voice say clear as spring, "What is behind and what is ahead is small compared to the Jewel within . . ." Sleep hits like a blind fall over the edge. I wake outside a coffee shop in Truro. Mary asks, "How're you doing?"

"Good, I'm good. I'll drive for a while."

"You want music?"

I don't know what I want or how to start unraveling all the wool in my stomach. "I want Jake. This isn't him at all."

"No, it's not him, but these roots have been growing his whole life. Now, the rock's broke. There's a lot of chipping away that needs doing." Mary plunks her foot on the dash like she's twenty. "I remember him, maybe six, on the dock lifting this heavy crate. He got halfway before spilling its load. His father yanked him up by his ear, calling him a useless good-for-nothing shite pile. That was his constant before he went to live with the Butters. The minute he got into that house, he searched for ways to please. He's been a godsend to Nia and me over the years, but I'm seeing we fed into his belief that he needed to do something to be loved. He's never felt loved just for being."

"He has. Of course he has. He remembers you coming every day after his mum left."

"I've never once seen him cry. Can't remember hearing him

238

laugh out loud either. You, on the other hand, opened like a book inviting us inside."

"I don't know where I'd be if not for all the caring you heaped on me."

"Ari, there's so much on your plate right now."

"It's always overfull. Ellis says it's a writer's dream."

"Is a writer what you are? Or a potter?"

"Honestly Auntie, I don't know what I am. Lately, writing has been nothing but coercing words out."

"I'm certain at this time in your journey, you're a potter. And you know the clay has to be right before you can turn it. Open your hands and let go of Jake for a time. He has some work to do on his own."

I look as far ahead on the road as I can. "He needs me."

"What he needs is to shatter and let light into that wounded place. He just can't bear to have his father's ugly hatred of him out in the open, but he's feeling it every minute. Thinks he's rotten at his core and believes it's a mercy making you go."

"I can't let him go. He's my last dance."

"I believe he is, but let him sit out the middle ones 'til he finds new legs."

"What about school?"

"Maybe he'll be ready. It's six months off. Figure out what you want for you. The only life you can be responsible for is your own."

"That's not true. Mum's only lived for herself and that's made for a pretty shitty life."

"You're mixing up selfishness with responsibility." Auntie Mary opens a bag of Fritos. "Though your mum is both selfish and irresponsible."

"Tell me something I don't know."

"When she ran off with your dad, we all said that was it, no more catering to her, she needed to grow up. That lasted until we heard she was pregnant. Grandma took her groceries. Cooked meals. Grandpa fixed up their apartment. Elsie and Dolores were over there every day cleaning up her mess, and there was Elsie pregnant herself, and Dolores wanting a baby so bad. I got off easy because she wouldn't let me in."

"She hated you back then?"

"Can't remember when she didn't. But your dad coming into the picture took it to a whole new level."

"Is it true that Daddy loved you?"

"Love? No, no, no. He'd just never come across a female who didn't melt in his presence." She offers the corn chips, holding the bag at the steering wheel until I take one. "I despise your dad for what he did to you girls. Would've killed him if I'd known, but strangely we got along really well."

"How so?"

"He was so smart. Brilliant, really. No matter the topic, I could have an intelligent conversation with him. I loved that. And musical. Never heard anything so infectious as him singing and playing the piano. He'd tell you girls stories, bundle you up, and take you to the park."

"I remember his niceness, too. It makes it harder to sort out other things."

"What things?"

"Raping my sisters."

"I've never pushed you to talk about what he did to you, but you can tell me anything."

"I've told you he just always wanted to be touched."

"I've worried after all that fuss getting you to the dentist when you were small that he pushed you further than you ever said."

"I know you figured out he stuck his dick in my mouth. Really, Auntie, what's the good in giving voice to that shit?" I wash the sawdusty chips down with tea. "Please, can we talk about something else? Tell me about Grandpa Trembley."

240

"He was a master mason."

"How'd he land in Toronto?"

"He got offered a good job and he grabbed it. War fractured him; laying bricks, row after level row, calmed him."

"I get that. Dolores says I'm like him."

"You are. So am I."

"Is it awful for you that the youngest Trembley sister is going to die first?"

"I'm just sad that I've never had anything with her like you have with the J's."

In a pretty blue room, with clean sheets, Mum's three sisters surround her. She's dressed in a white nightie with little pink rosebuds. Mary sits on the bed, reminiscing. "Remember that time Mummy was planting rhododendrons and Daddy said, 'Just put Theresa out there, she puts all the flowers to shame.'" Mary's hand gentles Mum's bruised arm. "Theresa, please, can you forgive me for everything I've done to hurt you? I'm so very sorry."

Mum pulls away, turns her face to the wall.

Jennah wants to slap her, I can see it; instead she kisses her cheek. "Okay, Mum. We'll come back middle of next month."

I sit on the bed. "Bye. I'll take care of things while you're away."

She pulls me close with a grip on my sweater, a closeness I've longed for since my evolution began. I lean in for something sweet. "Promise me you'll not go to Mary Catherine's when I'm gone. Promise me."

"No, I'll never promise that." She coils into terminal disappointment and I let go.

## FORTY-SIX

When I imagine the last chapter in the craphouse, it involves a messy trial where the Dick's dicking makes front-page news. I go to Mr. Lukeman with my file of documented shit. "Ari? Thought you were going away."

"Went last week instead."

"How're things?"

"Titanic. Wilf's car is gone."

"I heard."

"I never should've left it out front of crapdom."

"You had a lot on your mind. Was it insured?"

"Yeah. Wilf's good that way. I just loved the thing." I hand over the folder. "Can you look at this and see if there's anything here that could help me get a custody deal for Mikey?"

He shuffles through my Nancy Drew sleuthing. "No question he's a bad cop, but there's nothing concrete. It's all circumstantial. I've discovered he's deep, deep in the hole. He's going to lose the house. Is Mikey at Sabina's?"

"The Dick's nabbed him back to keep me close. What if he told the truth about the busted arm?"

"The report's in. That social worker would have to say she missed it and that wouldn't look good on her, so I doubt she'd go to bat for a kid who changes his story."

"Have you discovered anything that could get O'Toole out of our hair?"

"My connections say his name is all over several investigations into missing drugs but I'm not privy to what's been uncovered."

"Um, have you ever heard of a Tino Constantine?"

"He's in the business of, let's say, high-interest loans. Irwin owes him big. Why?"

"Seems he has a crush on me."

"He has children your age."

"It's just in us Appletons to attract worms. Listen, can you advance the Dick my next expense cheque so he can throw some money at this thug until I can get us out?"

"Let me look into it. Where can I reach you?"

"I'm giving Bernie some extra shifts over the break."


Before the Riverboat opens, Bernie calls me into his office. "Sit down, Ari."

Mr. Constantine stands, hat in hand, by the bookcase.

"Why?" I back toward the door.

"Relax, Tino and I go way back. Sam Lukeman called, filled me in a little. Tino wanted to set things straight." Bernie looks at the fine-tailored thug. "Ain't that right, Tino."

"It was never my intention to frighten you, Ari. Irwin can't pay his debt with something that doesn't belong to him. You've got nothing to fear from me." Mr. Constantine shrugs under his cashmere coat. "Though, I would enjoy just a conversation over dinner."

"You old goat. Stop torturing my employees." Bernie arms him to the door. "Get yourself home and give my regards to Gloria and the kids."

I watch him out the door. "What just happened? Why're you talking to my lawyer?"

"I've known Sammy Lukeman since he was knee-high to a cricket. He knew I had Constantine's ear and thought maybe I could smooth things out. Tino's a filthy bastard, but he's got principles. Family's sacred. The fact that you stayed on to take care of Mikey scored big. Not to mention your sacred papa dead and your sainted mother dying. He's a sucker for a hard-luck bootstrap story."

"You think I could get him to murder the Dick?"

"How'd he get his money if he did that?" Bernie brushes my nose. "Just about broke his heart when it sunk in he wasn't adding you to his string of working girls."

"What kind of work?"

"Oh, nursery school teachers, librarians, things like that."

"Thanks, Bernie."

"We got your back."

The Riverboat is changing. The hippie spirit pretty much disappeared with the sixties. It's still a full house for a Tuesday and I could dance. Relief does that to a body. Instead, in between dropping off orders, I have my nose in study cards for a chemistry test.


A thin pink light wakes me just hours after I crash-land in the nest; it's the colour hope might refract. I seize the hope of getting caught up at school.

Three thirty, I jump to a knock on my door. Through the batik covering the window, I see Mina on the stoop. I hug her in. "Why aren't you skiing?"

"Came back early."

"Oh." My prickly neck hairs tell me that I don't want to know why. I pour her tea in my favourite mug and put Sabina's chruscikis on a plate.

She studies the assignment on my easel: an ancient tree, its naked branches bent to the lake, flourishing under the water with leaf-faerie life. "Ari, this is magical." She stops at Len's pot and fingers it. "Mary asked me to come. Maybe you should sit."

I wipe the counter. Line up papers. Shine the faucet.

"Your mother's gone."

Gone doesn't mean much when a person has always been absent. Gone means too much when all you've ever hoped for was a moment of her presence.

Mina opens her arms. I step back into the coat rack holding Len's fedora, a little feather we picked up on one of our walks still tucked under the band. Her hand is ice through my sweater. A little pull moves me. A slight push folds my knees and my chair catches me. She gathers things into a bag. "You're coming to stay with us until Mary gets here."

"I have to type my essay and study for chem before work."

"Here, put on your coat; there's a chill in the air, but I did see a robin this morning."


Arrangements are made and mourners arrive. Really, there isn't a person in Sabina's apartment who doesn't feel the relief of this passing. Rambunctious kids are not hushed. Sisters and aunties eat and laugh. I'm stuck in the injustice: Uncle Iggy dying from a bashed-in head; Len, an exploding heart; Natasha, a crushed neck; and Mum quietly slipping away while watching Jacques Cousteau.

Ellis calls me, "Ari. Ari, there's a call for you. Quick." He hands me the phone.

"Hello?"

"Ari, it's—"

"Jake? Oh, Jake."

"I'm so sorry. I never want you to hurt."

"You'll never know what this call means to me."

"I . . . I'm—maybe—I—"

"Just tell me there's a hope for September. Please, Jake."

"I'm trying. I'll try. Just take care, okay."

Mary pries the humming phone from my hand. "Time to go."


For the final farewell, Mum is in a black urn shaped like a pickle jar and I'm surprised there was enough of her to fill it even half up.

Cops are a brotherhood, showing in full force, all spit and polished. Halpern bolsters my arm with a kind hand. "Tough break, kid. I'm really sorry."

I feel a great deal for the Dick: contempt, hatred, repulsion . . . maybe a grain of pity when he gets pummelled. First jab, Halpern bypasses him without uttering a single word. Second, Tino strides in, a goon on each side. And knockout, Ricky, the soldier boy, ribboned and in full dress makes his entrance.

The chapel fills, a gathering more to support the living than to honour the dead. How awful, how bloody mortifying to fill half a jar at the end of your days and have blaring silence when the hired officiate asks, "Does anyone have anything they'd like to say in remembrance of Theresa—wife, mother, sister, friend?"

There must be a witty story from Dolores. A touching anecdote from Elsie. A memorable roll in the hay from one of the Dick's buddies. The silence threatens to rupture my ear drums. Frig, frig, frig. I stand, telling my feet to bloody well move.

*Mum was a pathetic bitch is all I've got.*

*Whiny's not a good colour on you.*

From the podium, I survey the empathetic faces, startled to see the Jarvis volleyball team stretched along a row and warmed by my community league behind them.

"Um, Mum . . . my mum was colourful, no one can argue that. She could be Grace Kelly in the morning and Cher by nightfall. Maybe that's where my love for colour began.

"Often, I've felt her length was all she gave me, but on the drive to Montreal, she gave me a treasure, one for all of us, a caution really, to live the life you've imagined, so that 'I meant to be something else' aren't the words spoken on your final journey." I scan faces, some blank, others confused or thinking about refreshments, but most are open and exquisitely present. "This week, there have been rescuers at my side and I have to say I'm truly thankful for the treasures Mum brought into my life: five

246

sisters, rare jewels whose courage and tenacity fill me with hope. My aunties, Mary, Nia, Dolores, and Elsie, my spirit mothers. I simply wouldn't have survived without your care.

"Mum sent me many places, one of which was the east. No one can understand the gift that is until it has seeped in through your toes. She brought Len Zajac into my life, my spirit father who redefined me as beloved daughter and with Len came an extended family that makes me believe the world would be a better place if everyone were Polish. At least there'd be no hunger if Aunt Sabina were in charge.

"With five sisters, I sometimes thought brothers would be easier. Because of Mum, I have Ricky, Todd, and Mikey, three soldiers who have protected and enriched my life. She gave me more schools than would appear good for any kid. But at them I received lifelines: Belle, Aaron, Mina, Ellis.

"Life with Theresa Appleton wasn't easy but to borrow on words given to me, Mum, you were clay, not dirt." I smile at my tribe of supporters. "You are her spectacular creation and I'm blessed by all of you."

At the cemetery, Mary has my back. The sun warms mercifully. The breeze carries away the freesia stench. Aaron stands on the other side, but his eyes stay with me and I'm missing Jake so much if I don't get to him to fill up the holes, *I* will die.

Now, too many comforters comfort and I can't breathe. Human kindness sucks the oxygen out of every corner. I open the door to the little room that once slept me, folding into the corner where the walls meet, absorbing the dark for a peaceful long while. Mary opens the door, speaking across the dim light. "Can I get you anything?"

"Yeah, get me out of here without huggy goodbyes."

"Just lay down here. No one will disturb you."

"What I need is a lay beside Jake." The wanting-out tears swell in my chest, displacing oxygen.

"He's not the one to help you through this."

"He called me."

"He did and I'm proud of him for doing that, but he's too embroiled in his own war to help you through this. I'll get Mina to take you to her place."

"I need my paints and memory clutter."

"Right, I'll get your coat."

Aaron returns with it. "Your aunt wants me to drop you somewhere." I climb off the bed and we slip out the back door and into his jeep. "Where to?"

"The Village." My calloused hand reaches for his. "You're the constant in my life."

"You're the colour in mine." He keeps hold of my hand as he shifts gears. Outside the window, dropped-out humanity congeals in alcoves. He says, "I envy these kids, living wild with no boundaries."

"Most of them are fried from all the shit they've taken and don't have anywhere else to go. Anyways, you're the wildest guy I know. Dropping out is easy, nothing so hard as climbing a mountain. Turn down here."

We crawl along the alley. "Where am I taking you?"

"A friend's place. Let me out here. It's just up top this flight."

He's around to help me out before I manage it on my own. Me, standing on the bottom step puts us at exact height. The angle of his face makes me want my pastels. "Did you have a horse back home?"

"Not my own, but I rode."

"I can imagine you on one. Like a cowboy in the movies." He looks lost on the vast prairie as he studies my eyes. I shrug. "Don't know what I'm supposed to feel right now."

"Understandable. It'd be terrible to lose my mom, but it would be a grief with something real to get hold of. You have an absence in an absence. What is that?"

"Disorienting. Exhausting."

248

"Is your friend expecting you?"

"I've a key." I touch the light shining from a window onto his cheek. He leans into my hand. "Do you ever wish there could be more between us?"

He searches my face and exhales.

"Wait, don't answer. Don't want to hear no—or yes on a funeral day." I back up the steps.

"Um . . . I-I . . . wait, Sabina sent leftovers." I descend, meet him halfway, knowing if he reached the top, today I wouldn't let him go.


The aroma of coffee arrives ahead of the knock. Nia says, "Ari, we've come for breakfast. Sabina sent all the good food with you." I open the door. "Gracious, girl, were you still in bed?"

I straighten the quilt and throw cushions on the bed. "Stayed up late painting."

Auntie Mary spreads food like a picnic. I have a comfy reading chair and two mismatched wooden chairs, one robin's egg blue, the other chili pepper red, but we all sit on my bed talking, laughing, crying, joking . . . opening, opening, opening. My head lands on Nia's lap. "Does death scare you?"

"When death comes, I'll meet it with the same awe and gratefulness with which I hold this moment."

"Honestly?"

"Fearing what's to come costs me the joy I feel in this present with you and that's too much to pay."

"I've eight cents of fear for things to come."

Jasper flicks my forehead. *Huh, didn't know Hariet was on this bed.*

*Give me a break.*

*Okay.* Jasper sings in my ear: *niaminamaryari, niaminamaryari. Your names make music.*

249

I pick at a puff pastry. "Auntie, how come you shipped me off with Aaron last night?"

"I didn't want you to be so lonely."

"He was my teacher. Anything more than what we have would wreck his life, wouldn't it?"

"The two of you are nothing of teacher and student anymore. You're friends. There's nothing improper about what the two of you share."

"He's so much older than me."

"With the life you've lived, you're by far the older one."

Nia says, "People don't grow so well in constant light. Why'd you think he creates his own darkness? Think about the places he travels."

"But Jake—"

Mary asks, "Why'd you want to come here last night when there were so many around to comfort?"

"Just needed to ponder perplexities on my own."

She touches my nose.

"But I still knew you were there. Jake needs to know I'll never leave him, no matter what. I could get through anything because I knew you'd never let me go."

Nia's head wobbles. "What the blazes are you on about? We released you time and time again. With every toss over the precipice, you opened your wings and soared."

"What if he crashes because he feels he's lost everything?"

"That's exactly what the boy needs. Aaron's overdue for a sound cracking, too."

"Aaron's perfectly assembled."

"Maybe so, but"—Nia braids my hair—"this nor'easter has him so stirred, that that westwind will drift forever, never able to settle, always wondering what if." I shake no. Nia bobs yes. "This old bear thinks right now the two of you would do each other a universe of good."

"No way could I bear the weight of shattering his moral rightness. Besides, I've decided to offer the Dick ten thousand for Mikey and just get the hell out of here. Forget waiting 'til June."

Nia says, "Let Sam work out a legal arrangement. Stay out of it and away from that house."

"The Dick's way too jittery. Until I've got a signed deal, he has to believe I'm within his grasp. Mikey's his insurance."

Mary snorts. "What a waste of flesh he is. Who was that with him at the funeral?"

"Shirley, the new duchess of crapdom."

FORTY-SEVEN

At school on Monday everyone is full of condolences. Throughout the day, teachers are generous with compassion marks. I do my utmost to channel an Anne of Green Gables tragical-face, but all the sympathy pushes me precariously close to smashing my fist into the brick.

The soldier boy is waiting by the front door of my school. He's still James Dean cute, a go-getter, too, racking up certifications at rocket speed.

"Come to say goodbye?" I ask.

"No, Todd's in hospital, hurt, bad."

"Our Todd?"

"Yeah."

"No. What happened?" I follow him out to the blue sedan.

"He's got a busted leg. Shoulder's ripped out of its hinge."

"How?"

"Two thugs on his way to work."

Todd is a pulpy mess when we arrive at the hospital. "Oh, geezus, Todd. What the hell?"

He blubbers. "If I say anything, they'll kill me. If Pops doesn't pay up, they'll kill me."

"Who?"

"The guys he owes. I'm gonna lose my job. Talk to Dr. McKay. Tell him it's not my fault." Todd winces as he tries to sit. "I got eight hundred bucks stashed in the lockbox at the clinic. Get it. Tell 'em not to murder me. You gotta tell 'em, please."

"Um, okay?"

"We'll sort it, man. You rest." Ricky walks soldierly beside me. "Did you see them burns up his arm? Fucking bastards. Any idea who did it?"

"Yeah." I stop at a phone in the lobby and dial the Riverboat. "Bernie? It's Ari. Where can I find Constantine?"

"He has a construction company on Main near Danforth."

"Construction? Oh, for god sake, do thugs have no friggin' imagination?"

"What's up?"

"I'm going to go murder him." I hang up and scan the yellow pages for the address, then snag Ricky's arm. "Come on. Look muscled up."

As I storm into Constantine Construction, the back of the door hits the wall. "Where's Tino?"

A Lucille Ball double looks over her magazine. "In a meeting." I fling doors. "Stop. You can't go barging in." I open a storeroom, moving on to the next as Lucy sizes up Ricky. "You a cop?"

Jasper sniggers. *Lucy and Ricky, pretty funny eh, Ari?*

*Shut up.*

The next door bounces. I smack its rebound, marching in with hellfire. "You—you goon! You enormous horse's fart." Lurch and the Hulk step forward, stopping with a hand signal from Tino. "You lying bastard. You gave your word you wouldn't touch me."

A twitch, trying not to be a smile, holds the corner of his mouth. "I didn't—"

"Any man of honour, any monkey with half a brain would know if you touch my brothers, you touch me. And if you had a molecule of insight, you'd know the Dick doesn't give a flying fuck about his kids and you just did him a favour by cutting down on groceries. Shit, you really want to make his day? Murder this one here." Ricky follows my yank on his arm. "He double hates Ricky for being better than him."

"He owes—"

"Would you expect your kids to pay for your mistakes or would you man up and take care of the mess yourself? I swear, you touch my family again, I'll send you on a date with my mother."

"I'm a businessman and —"

"Are you starving? Out on the street? You going to die if you don't get your money today? Listen here, mister, you're not getting it from me and you sure as hell aren't going to hurt the people I care about for something that useless Dick did. What kind of a monster are you? Todd takes care of puppies, for god's sake. How could you hurt someone like that?"

"If you'd let me finish a sentence, I'd tell you that Dick Irwin owes a lot of people and I'd never hurt a kid." He moves a gold toothpick to the corner of his mouth. "And I was going to say I'm a businessman prepared to buy up Irwin's markers so all his business would be with me."

"Why?"

"For the pleasure of owning a cop, and so you'll have dinner with me."

"What the hell is with you?"

He half shrugs. "I like what I like."

"More, you want what you can't have. Friggin' toddler. Define dinner."

"Good food. A little wine. Nice conversation."

"Why?"

"Can't say why I'm stuck on this deal, just am."

"I'm never sleeping with you."

"Just dinner."

"You swear you didn't hurt Todd?"

"Swear on my mother."

"You'll call off all the goons?"

"Done."

"No one touches his kids or my relatives, which, by the way, includes every Polish person in the country. Hands off everyone on the East Coast, my teachers, my aunts, and they better not even look at my sisters . . . Oh, and my dog."

"Anything else?"

"Make it somewhere nice and if you touch a single cell on me, you'll be eating your balls for dessert." Lurch folds his arms as I stretch my full length. "And don't you be messing with me, you stupid friggin' ape. I've murdered before and I'll do it again." I look back to Tino. "I have your word?"

"My word. Thursday?"

"Moronic testosterone-loaded boys. Nia and Mary are the only ones with any sense." I pull Ricky by his epaulets. "Come on, we'll take Todd a milkshake."

"Army sure could use a girl like you."


Morning after Todd's pummelling, I take a beating of my own. Shirley, six inches shorter and forty pounds heavier than Mum, dressed in Mum's leopard capris, hands me a red beaded pouch containing Theresa Appleton's treasures, unearthed from an underwear drawer.

From her forty-seven years on this Earth she held on to a clipping from a 1940 *Telegram*, her in a slinky gown draping the hood of a sleek car. A page from an Eaton's catalogue, Mum modeling a polka-dot dress. Three satin ribbons holding fake gold medals, "Ontario Musical Association, First—Girl's Duet." Four letters from my dad sent during the war. An adult tooth and some photos: one of Vincent Appleton, movie handsome in his uniform. I think the second is Jennah until I check the back: "Theresa, 1939." I calculate her age in my head, fifteen. On a satiny bed she reclines, naked, head propped on one hand, top leg draped over the bottom. The last picture is Mum, Dad, and my sisters on Aunt Elsie's sofa. The J's have colourful silk scarves. Jory and Jillianne wave theirs like pennants. June's is balled around her fist. Jennah's and Jacquie's hang limp. *Where were you?*

I estimate ages, figuring I would've been six or seven. *No idea, Jasper.*

I swallow acid rising from my gut and unfold the letters. The first from Sherbrooke, November 1941, starts poetic—*My dearest T: How I long for just one taste from your sweet neck*—quickly turning into a long complaint about army food and the injustice of basic training. From England to Italy then France, I search for the poignant, the profound, the deep pool of wisdom that comes from war, finding less than a mud puddle. The last letter closes: *I keep thinking about that night in Detroit. It gets me through the cold nights. Hearts to love, V.*

I tuck it all back inside. *Detroit, Jasper? A night in Detroit gets him through? What is all this stupid shit?*

I catapult up the stairs to ransack every corner and crevice looking for what she really held onto, the cards and letters from us, a repentant suicide note from my father, the macaroni necklace I made her for Mother's Day, the journals where she really lived. The Dick fills the doorway. "She was a good woman, kid. Best I ever knew."

I walk Mikey to school, surfacing when *he* hands *me* a lunch. He says, "At least eat your apple." From his porcupine hair to mismatched socks, he looks as unmothered as I feel.

"You bet, cadet."

I ditch school and go to Jennah's. She peruses the contents of the pouch. "It's all a lifetime ago, dead, dead, dead and gone. Stop dwelling. Just enjoy the present."

"Do you enjoy your present?"

"Yeah, sis. For the most part I do." She struggles with the lid on a jar of pickles. "Except for this damned arthritis." I pop the lid, wondering what she did to set Wilf into doling out a dose of "arthritis." "We bought a camper. We're all going to the Carolinas. You should come with."

"You really think Wilf would survive travel with a nor'easter?"

"Not well, but the kids would love it."

"Would Wilf let them come to Skyfish for a visit this summer?"

"Not likely."

"You could tell him you're sending them to a camp that teaches discipline and refinement."

"They're all lit up and chattery after being with you. Wilf would know." She checks the time on her jewelled watch and I take the hint.

"You named your girls Darcy and Diamond. They should be lit up." I twist up my confusion of hair. "Could you fix me up for a fancy dinner on Thursday?"

"Now you're asking for something I know."

I go to the boutique to catch Jory before she heads back to

nature. The Garden of Eden tattoo on her right arm and the dove on her left looks like she's wearing an ink sweater. I ask for insight. "Don't you hate Daddy for messing with you and Mummy for not doing a bloody thing to stop it?"

She outsights, "Jesus has washed everything away, turned all the black to snow. Come stay at Morning Glory with me and be washed in the blood."

"No. I prefer baths in mud."

Jacquie pokes through the jetsam. I ask, "Do you know where I was when this picture was taken?"

Jory scans the family portrait, minus one Apple. "Daddy brought us those scarves from New Orleans. He was working there for like six months."

"Did he bring me one?"

The way Jacquie says "Oh, I'm sure he did" tells me he didn't, and my absence from the photo suggests they hadn't gotten around to picking me up from whatever foster farm they'd dumped me at. "I can't be bothered with this crap. I'm long done with the both of them. You gotta do that, too, sis. Just grab hold of life and love wherever you find it." Her words I can't discount because Jacquie has done exactly that. "Now, shouldn't you be at school?"

"I try. I do, but the shit just keeps coming."

I head toward school but get off the streetcar at the bookstore and buy Jillianne a book of Charles Worth designs. *Anne, you are a creation more beautiful than all the dresses in these pages.* In the same package I wrap the beaded pouch for Auntie Dolores. *Auntie D: I haven't cried for Mum. Maybe because I don't know who I'm crying for. These are the treasures she kept. Of all Mum's sisters I think you're the one who will tell me some truth, any truth as she sees it.*

I send June another postcard, a toothy beaver on the front. *You are the bravest Appleton of all to have bitten the snake that fed you. With love and missing, Ari.*

257

I skip tutoring and take Todd a milkshake. I tell him his job is waiting and all the hounds have been called off.

"You positive?" he asks.

"Only rabid hog we have to worry about is the Dick."

"Doc says I can go home next week."

"I've a few ideas that are going to end our time in crapdom for good. Just rest."

I head to the pool to watch Mikey back at his swimming lessons. Aaron smiles, then blanches. "Ari, have you slept at all since the funeral?"

I fill him in on the whole mess. "No sooner do I get Mikey out of his friggin' cast then Todd's in one."

"Does Mikey know?"

"Does that kid need anything else to worry about?"

"No, he doesn't. And you cannot go out with that guy."

"Tino's actually my best shot at ending this. I think he'd kill the Dick if I asked."

"Then ask."

"I'm just not up to more blood on my hands, even if it is the Dick's. With Len's money only nine weeks away, Mikey and I are safe as houses. The Dick really needs it and he needs me alive to get it."

"How can he?"

"Easy. Commit me and administer it on my behalf. If I go missing, start looking at Queen Street, then Whitby Psych."

"He can't do that."

"You never see the movie with Elwood and his imaginary rabbit, Harvey? There's documented proof that I have animated conversations with a seahorse."

"You got rid of that."

"It was just a partial file. Besides, they'd have no trouble forging something."

"Do you have to go back tonight?"

"All we have to endure is ten-minute check-ins after school."
I nudge his arm. "Sabina made perogies."

Ari Zajac should go to the workroom and do homework.
Instead, I shower, put on comfy clothes, and join a real family
around the TV. I'm adrift before *Green Acres* ends. I'm not sure
who gives me the blanket, but I know it's Aaron coaxing my head
to the pillow, and maybe, just maybe, I feel his lips on my forehead and "Goodnight, sleeping beauty" in my ear.

I look like the cat spit me out when I drag myself into school
on Wednesday. Kendra cheers, "She's here. Told you she would."

*Frig, Jasper, what's on today?*

*OFSAA round robin, maybe?*

Coach Palmer says, "Grab your gear, get on the bus, and play
today like persons who could change the course of your stars are
watching."

My gear has been in my locker, unwashed for almost three
weeks. It could be on account of my stink, or my rage, but the
Jarvis seniors are undefeated going into the last game. I scan
the stands and see my coach with Strazda and a tower of a man.
Rows below, I spot Ricky. I peel over before the game starts.
"What's wrong?"

"Nothin'. Just went to see Todd and he said you were playing. He was really hoping to come to this one."

"Thought you had to be back on base."

"Not 'til twenty-one hundred."

"Could you go meet Mikey and bring him here?"

"No prob. And pizza on me after?"

A uniformed soldier makes for a prickly hug, but an impres-
sive one nonetheless. When I take my place on court, Cassie asks,
"That Jake?"

"No, my big brother."

"Cool." She smiles at him like she's reclaimed the chunk of
her soul BS butchered. *It's the way of shit, eh, Jasper.*

*Yeah, it stinks less the further you get from it.*

Post-game, I'm summoned. Tower-man is from the Canadian Volleyball Federation. He states more than asks, "June first, there's a four-week clinic at McGill. I want you there."

Palmer says, "I'll arrange it with school."

Strazda asks, "Ari? You in?"

I, Ari Joy Zajac, am distancing myself from Irwin shit, ASAP. "Barring mayhem, I'll be there."

FORTY-EIGHT

On Thursday, Aaron is waiting outside Jarvis. I sigh. "What now?"

"Thought you might need a lift."

"You scared the shit out of me."

"Well, you're scaring the shit out of me."

I stop, sharp. "Aaron, you swore? Why're you scared?"

"You can't go out with that guy."

"Don't worry. Tino's the man of my schemes. I'm going to start dating him." Aaron looks like he might hurl as I tug him onward. "Strictly for protection. When the Dick sees we're an item, I'll become the crown princess of crapdom. Why aren't you in school?"

"Said I had a headache. I haven't taken any sick time in five years."

"So, I've got you lying and swearing?"

260

"I do feel sick about tonight." He pulls away from the curb. "Where am I taking you?"

I finger count. "Pick up Mikey. Crapdom check-in. Jennah's to get stuffed into fine-dining gear, then to some place called Winston's."

"Swanky place."

"You've been?"

"Not on my budget."

When we arrive at the craphouse, Mikey asks, "You want to see my tent, Aaron?"

"Oh, let's leave that for a day the Dick isn't home," I say. I know from my Zodiac pictures that Aaron grew up in a pretty house, simple, ordered, godly clean, likely smelling of lilacs in the spring and apple crisp in autumn, and I can't face the shame. "Stay here while I give the Dick his distemper shot."

Mum's stained chair is at the curb for trash day. *I don't miss her, do I, Jasper?*

*Dunno. Don't miss the piss stink for sure.*

The Dick opens the door. Face chalky, lips pale as lard. "You still on with Tino?"

"Yep."

"You got a minute?"

"Just."

I've never known an Orco to last more than five minutes in crapdom, but there're a dozen plated between us as we sit at the stained table. "Um, just want you to know I'm makin' a new start. Tino and me settled on terms. End of April we's movin', Shirley and me. When Theresa's money comes in, you do right by me and I'll let Mikey decide where he wants to be."

"What's right?"

"Fifty-fifty? 'Course most of that'll go in the bank for Mikey." He dips a cookie in cold tea. "I'm on track at work, hundred and

261

ten percent. Closed that case of those hookers who were roughed up. And that bloody O'Toole's finally off my back."

"How?"

"He knocked up the wife's sister. Carmie's so pissed she's gonna spill all she's got on him to Halpern. Hell, he's likely half-way to California by now." A cookie hunk blots out his front tooth. "Whaddaya say?"

"Sounds reasonable. I'm going to be late for my date."

When I return, Mikey asks, "What took so long?"

"It's a chess game. Just studying the board for our next move." From the side mirror I watch Mum's throne diminish as we pick up speed. *The queen is dead. She's really gone.*

Mikey hops out at Sabina's. "You coming here after?"

"No, I'll sleep at the nest. Jennah's giving you a lift to school tomorrow, so be ready by seven thirty." He accepts without a gripe being shuffled from place to person and waves bye.

Jennah is waiting on her steps, like a kid excited about her new life-sized, dress-up Barbie.

I say, "You've got to make me look like a hundred thousand bucks."

Aaron sits on the clean sofa, entertained by the twins while Jennah goes to work. I'm taller than Jennah, so her black velvet dress comes above my knees and my boobs plump out of it, just a little. Whatever she puts on my hair makes it a party of serpen-tines, half up and half down. "Hold still, Ari."

"Easy on the war paint."

"Just a little glow and sparkle. Now my diamond drop." She fastens the platinum chain and the stone looks like an arrow pointing to my cleavage. "Where's Nia's ring?"

"In my pack." Satiny legs and polished feet slip into patent pumps.

She fishes it out, slides it on my finger, then turns me to the full-length mirror. "I'd say a hundred million bucks."

Aaron glances over his shoulder, nearly dumping Dylan into the coffee table when he stands. "Holy." He swallows. "Holy." He inhales, exhales. "Hoooleee."

"Stop singing the doxology, man, and get her to the restaurant." Jennah hands me a shawl and a little purse. "Knock 'em dead, sis."

"I need that box I left here." She retrieves the black box and I'm ready to make a deal.

Aaron drives in silence to the restaurant, runs around, and opens my door. "Maybe I should wait out here."

"I've money for a cab."

"You going to your friend's place after?"

I nod.

"You scared?"

"Yeah, of walking in these shoes." I inhale seeing Bernie and his wife heading into the restaurant. "Is it seven forty yet?"

"Yes. Why?"

"Jennah said I should be at least ten minutes late."

*Okay, Jasper, let's net him.* A girl knows when she looks good. She knows when men are looking at their dates with one eye and her with the other. It's a fancy-schmancy place with a tuxedoed man ready to help. "I'm meeting Mr. Constantine."

"Right this way, miss."

Tino stands, drinking me in from toe to tit. Tuxedo man pulls out a chair for my box, then one for me. "Would you care for something from the bar?"

"Club soda, please."

Tino shifts in his seat. "You look va-va-voom."

"You're spiffed up pretty fine yourself."

"Are there sharp objects in that box?"

"Just a little gift. Best pot out of the east."

He loosens his collar. "I-I'm not into . . ."

"You should be scared. Look inside." Cautiously he uncovers one of my best pieces, terracotta and turquoise bleeding through

263

moon-white glaze. He reads the card: *Every being born from this earth is clay, unique, priceless, and easily broken. Handle with reverence.* "I made it."

"It's beautiful." He bites his cheek on the inside while fingering the sea spirit climbing over the side. "I seldom receive poetic gifts."

"Everything's a poem if you let it be. Neruda wrote an ode to his socks."

"What you said at your mother's funeral was poetic."

"Have to say, it was weird seeing you there."

"Just paying my respects."

"Liar. You were protecting your investments." Another Tuxedo comes with my drink, menus, assorted bread bits, and fills Tino's glass. Tino motions to my empty wine glass. My hair dances when I shake no. "Never touch the stuff, and if you don't want to piss me off, you'll go easy."

"You're very sure of yourself, aren't you."

"You kidding? What-the-hell-am-I-supposed-to-do-now is my middle name."

"But that doesn't stop you from moving forward."

I should never read and speak at the same time. "It does exactly that. I don't look behind to the dwindling fires or ahead to the looming inferno. I just go for a little internal dip, with a seahorse." His loud laugh makes Jasper jump. I fold the menu. "You order. I just don't like bloody meat or any organ that once thought, spoke, saw, or purified."

"What about smelled?"

"They serve noses here?" He hides his smile behind his elbows-on-the-table hands and settles into getting his money's worth in questions about my life. I answer all the usual small talk intrusions. "Okay, my turn. Are you happy?"

A swig of wine swishes back and forth in his mouth. "You don't start small, do you. Are you happy?"

"I keep at least one room inside open for happiness."

He taps my ring with his fork. "Is there a young man in that room?"

His neck blooms when I lift my eyes full in his face. "I have spectacular people in my life. This was a gift from a woman who took me in when I was a scared kid; she gave me the earth, sun, and stars and never asked for a thing in return."

"And who put those exquisite hands on a hot stove?"

I turn my palms up to the old scars. "I went into fire for something I wanted."

"What?"

"A treasure box of hope."

"Hope?"

"Letters from my aunts. So, answer my question."

"Why'd you want to know?"

"People are stories. I can't write without barging in past the front door. Could've asked if you're sad, pissed, scared, or constipated. Happy seemed a more palatable appetizer."

"You want to be a writer?" he asks.

"You have a pen?" He slides a sleek gold beauty out of his jacket and I write on a scrap of tissue. *You should be a righter.* "A teacher told me I should be a writer and this is what I thought she meant and I knew just what that was because every night my aunts whispered in my ear, 'Everything will be all right, Ari. Dream.' And I thought what a great thing it'd be to be righters like them."

We talk through his steak and my chicken stuffed with creamed heaven and potatoes so tiny they must've been grown on a leprechaun farm. Despite journalistic probing, he reveals nothing about what makes him work, but I sense doors opening under his fine suit.

"Eat your vegetables. The asparagus is spectacular." He declines and tuxedo man takes our plates. "Please tell the chef he could give my Polish aunt a run for her cooking crown."

The waiter smiles like he has a cozy house and kids happy to see him. "Would you care to see the dessert menu?"

"I'll have the chocolatiest thing in the kitchen, please."

He bows a little to Tino. "Mr. Constantine?"

"A brand—uh, make that two chocolate things and coffee."

"Tea for me, please."

"I imagine you're quite the dancer, Ari."

"And why's that?"

"The way you move is mesmerizing."

"You can ease up on the flattery 'cause there's not a chance of any sheet-shimmying between us."

He smiles. "If I thought there was, you wouldn't be nearly as intriguing as you are. Bed partners are a dime a dozen. Good dance partners are rare."

"I know, right?" Jennah told me to leave a little on my plate but the fluffed-up chocolate has me wanting to lick the unforkable bits and snatch Tino's, too. I steal a bite from his plate. "My fiddler's got the moves, but he's always making the music. I haven't had a spectacular turn around the floor since my papa was alive."

"So, you do dance."

"I have Poland in one foot and Nova Scotia in the other, so I more fly."

"I know the agreement was dinner, but would you come to my club? Just one dance? Night's still young."

I tip his almost ten o'clock watch. "Obviously you don't have to get up for school tomorrow." He nods and lifts his hand for the check. "Are there ladies peeling off their knickers at this place?"

"No."

"I'll make *you* a deal: give the waiter a good tip and a dance is yours."

A tidy stack slides out of his wallet and into the folder. We stand, and in Jennah's shoes I top him by inches. He motions to the door. "Shall we?"

Our Tuxedo lifts his voice over the silvery music. "Sir?"

Tino looks back. "Thank the lady."

Entering his sparkly club, Tino puffs up proud. To write him into a story, I'd have to shave off the clichéd edges: the coat over the shoulders, the stripe in his suit, the big gold ring. I'd give him a little more height and free up his hair, but the nightclub would be this: 1920s wood and chintz meets 1970s neon and chrome. Swing jazz explodes from the band and my feet fire remembering the times Len danced me like loose spaghetti to like music. I edge toward the floor. "Well, man, can you dance or what?"

"Not while there's a no touch rule in place."

I nab his hand. "Armistice 'til midnight."

I don't mind being with the big cheese bully because the sea of people part, giving us the floor, and if he thought he got his money's worth over dinner, he hits the jackpot with the dancing. By our second dance, my shoes are off, his jacket gone, and the man dances like a little of Fred Astaire lives in him.

By half eleven, he's panting and I say, "I have to go."

The band slows to some Ella Fitzgerald seductive blues and he extends his hand. "Not for any deals, just for the love of the music." His scent is subtler than expected, fresh citrus. We drift around the floor, and with his arm around my waist, I feel his want.

I remain in his embrace while the walls absorb the sultry afternotes. "You can dance, Mr. Constantine, so there's happiness in you somewhere."

His hand lingers on the small of my back. "A drink?"

"No, a cab."

"I'll drive you."

"No. This is where we say goodnight."

"Tony will take you." He floats Jennah's shawl over my shoulder. "Thank you for the finest evening I can remember"— lips brush my cheek and my name on his exhale trickles down my neck—"Ari."

267

In the back of a big black car, the hides of selfless cows cushion my bum. *He's hooked, Ari.*

*Having a shark in our corner suits me just fine.* "To the Riverboat, Antonio."

Tony squints into the rear-view. "Boss said take you to your door."

"Well, my good man, I'm in charge of where this lady goes."

I climb out and down the stairs to a coffee house half-full of people with no better place to go. I exit through the back, walking barefoot down my alley in the cool spring air. I'd swivel and bolt if I didn't recognize the shape sitting on my bottom step as Aaron. "Hey, cowboy. What're you doing here?"

"Just had to make sure you got to your friend's."

I boldly go where no Ari has gone before and tuck between his knees. His hands span my waist, forehead nuzzling my velvet-covered belly. Over my bottom, down my legs, his hands slide. Longing shoots up my thighs. He looks up. "Ari . . . I . . . I should go." He stands, stepping onto the ground and I help myself to a hug, wondering if velvet under a man's hand is like touching the veil between heaven and earth. "I, I'm sorry. I have to go."

"Why're you sorry?"

"I'm crossing a line."

"Because you were once my teacher?" He nods. I chase his eyes. "It's a chalk line, Aaron, not a permanent one. That isn't the line separating us now."

"Then what is? Jake?"

"You're a wind heading southwest and I'm a nor'easter."

"They can't mix?"

"Nor'easters really mess things up. You might think you want no boundaries, but the unsettling will shake you to your core." I release him, backing away. "Go sleep. You have work tomorrow."

"Um, your birthday falls on a Sunday. Can I take you somewhere special?"

"Depends. Am I an ex-pupil or a friend?"

"Friend. You, Ari, are my best friend."

"Then I'd like that."

"Will you wear that dress?"

I nod, smiling until I'm locked inside.

The kettle boils as I shower. A confusion of scents peel away: Mummy reeking of Chantilly. Daddy's Old Spice on his hands as he held my head right where he wanted it. Memories slip down the drain. *I miss Jake's quiet scent, Jasper.*

I climb into my clean bed, naked, mould into the pillows with my unfinished letter to Jake, and reread the pleadings.

> *There's no logic to your thinking. Do you believe I'm destined to become an addict? A child abuser? What about Mikey? Is he doomed to become the Dick? Did you ever once think that Danny deserved his father's unkindness? You tried so hard to cut away the tangle of lies that caught him up. Why can't you show yourself the same mercy?*

I crumple the page and begin again.

> *Spring woke me this morning. A single crocus under my step poked out the palest mauve face through a crinoline of sun-missed snow. I went to school with muddy knees because it needed a sniff, that lovely whiff of spring. Not fruit or sugar sweet, just a hint of green. In every class I opened windows for more. Ellis has a terrible cold. He said he was embracing the respite from wet wool and the stench of sneakers.*
>
> *I get that joy in absence, a rest from the assault. This evening saturated me in smells, all a bit dizzying. Somewhere, right now, music is playing, smoky jazz and heated blues. An emerald-dressed woman drenched*

*in Ma Griffe is circling the dance floor with an American
drowning in Jade East—olfactory offenders in a gangster's lair.*

*This day is long overdue its ending, but I need time
to desaturate. Jennah's dress is suspended like a stranger
by my open window, with it hangs the hope that a night
wind will snatch the confusing tangle of Chanel, Aramis—
chalk, too—and get it out of my nest.*

*The float of peppermint tea and the quiet knock of
the clock letting me know I have this moment is spectacular, rendering me gratefully senseless. Inhale and dream,
Jake. Your Ari.*

I pull the brass chain. The nest goes black, warming to pewter as I settle under the featherbed. Radio from downstairs leaks
in, "Come fly with me, let's fly, let's fly away . . ." Jake is with
me as my hand slips over my breast, circling my belly before exploring. Jennah's dress flutters and I close my eyes, letting Tino's
hands move to the places he'd wanted. We climb, muscles tensing, then it's Aaron's weight on me, his lips kissing my neck as
my head arches back, moans mingling with the distant music,
"Once I get you up there where the air is rarified, we'll just glide
starry-eyed . . ."

I turn, hug my pillow. *Stop messing with me, Jasper. I'll only
ever love Jake.*

The phone slaps me out of fitful sleep. "Hello?"

"Hey, dolly," Huey says, "just wanted to catch you before
school." I blink my clock into focus, seven fifty. "Had to tell you,
Jake's going back to rehab."

"When?"

"They's got a spot for him a week Monday."

"Can I talk to him?"

"He's out walking the shore. He tolds me not to tell you, but givin' good news is only fair after all the hard things."

"Oh, Huey, you've made my day."

I seize the clay of this Friday: go to school, make a list, then a sublist, using my spare and lunch to get things done. I hide in the back corner. Food is not allowed in the school library, so I get a little misty-eyed when Miss Gulliver quietly places a Tupperware bowl of homemade rice pudding on my worktable. "I always find this goes down easy. I make it with almond milk."

"Thank you." I refocus on my assignment. *Jasper, I must look like death.*

*Just a little chartreuse around the gills. Hey, I never knew almonds had teats.*

After school I wrap and post my belated Christmas gift to Jake, the painting, *U of Us*, with a note: *For our place. We'll find a new cozy space.*

*Oh, Ari. Is the poetry coming back?*

*It might just be.*


At work Bernie calls me into his office. "How was last night?"

"I have a lot of rescuers, but Tino might be my best ally yet. Thanks for chaperoning."

"What? Just wanted a good meal." He hands me a velvet box containing a thin string of sapphires.

"Whoa, Tino sure has good taste. Can you keep it in your safe until I can return it?"

"Sure thing, doll."

"Men sure are complicated creatures."

"Naw, we're just stupid."

"You're one of the smartest people I know."

"Back to work. I don't pay you to stand around gabbing."

"A lot of the time you do."

Saturday, I return the necklace. Tino smooths his grease-slick hair. "You don't like it?"

"It's exquisite, but I can't accept."

"No strings. I just want you to have it."

"But then you wouldn't know I had a nice time without you having to give me anything. Give it to your wife."

"Not got enough shebang for her."

"Well, it's got too much shebang for this down-home girl."

"What do down-home girl's like?"

"This one just wants to unload the friggin' eight pennies in her pocket and go home."

"Not sure how that's done, but Bernie says you're pinned down with Irwin's kid. Why ain't he with the mother?"

"When he was small, CAS seized him a half dozen times. Courts decided the Dick was the better parent. She tries but she's as dependable as a candle in a windstorm."

"How 'bout I just off Irwin?"

"Tempting, but corpses, even rotten ones, are heavy to schlep around. The Dick's scared of you. If you insisted, I wager he'd sign an iron-clad custody agreement."

"If I did, might I get another dance?"

"I'd give you another just because we had fun."

"You're an interesting human specimen, kitten."

"Likewise, Tino Constantine."

"First name's Theo."

"Suits you."

He walks me to the door, hesitating before opening it. "Irwin ever hit you?"

"You don't have to fight that battle for me."

One finger traces the old scar over my eyebrow without touching it.

"A whack with an andiron and it's pretty much the only connection my mum and I ever had."

## FORTY-NINE

Monday, I return to crapdom to find Shirley and the Dick hoisting Todd up the stairs, like Laurel and Hardy moving the piano.

"Heard you showed Tino a really good time." The Dick's fat nose shines redder than usual and the pores on his face are so big fruit flies could breed in them, and a few likely do. "So, when you goin' out again?"

"Meeting for drinks tonight."

"Good show."

I check on Todd. "You okay?"

"I'm good. Wish they coulda put on the walking cast, though."

"When will they?"

"Next week. Hey, you seen O'Toole around?"

"No. We've been at Sabina's. Heard he's on the lam."

"Halpern came to hospital with a shitload of questions. O'Toole's going down."

"And the Dick?"

"Hard to say."

"Um, I have to run a few errands. What can I get you?"

"Piss bottle?"

"Right. I'll be back in an hour or so."

I meet with Laura. In return for signing custody papers, she asks not for money but mercy. "Ari, I heard O'Toole's in hot water. Don't give police anything on Dick. Promise. For Mikey's sake. I know what it's like to have a daddy in jail."

I'll take freedom at any price. "Sure. Fine."

I place an order at Smitty's Appliances, buy comic books, snacks, and a bed table at Woolworths. On my return to crapdom, the Dick gives me a once over. "For Christ sake, fix yourself up before you go out."

"Roger that. Can I borrow your thermos?"

"Long as you don't spit in it."

I nab pillows from Ronnie's room, tuck them under Todd's leg, then fill the cooler with snacks. "I have to go on a pretend date." I place the Dick's thermos on the nightstand. "Piss in this."

"You coming back?"

"Late. Can you manage?"

"No prob. Pass me my pills?"

"Does it still hurt?"

"Not much. They just help me sleep."


Three a.m. I leave the nest. My hair is washed and tamed. I teeter between classy and sexy in a black camisole and leather jacket. I have eight tasks ticked off my list, best of which is my creative writing assignment: "Becoming Unthinkable." When entering crapdom, the Dick wakes in the chair and I wonder if this is what it feels like to have parents who give a shit. "Good time?"

"A real blast."


After school, Tuesday, Todd says, "Ari, I'm going crazy in here. Help me downstairs."

"If there was a bathroom, I would. I'll be back in a shake with something that'll help."

I take Mikey's wagon to Smitty's Appliances. "Afternoon, Ari. It's all set. All you have to do is plug her in."

"I brought the wagon."

"Nonsense, delivery truck's heading out." His son emerges from the back with a Zenith Chromacolour portable TV. "Set it up for her, too, Norm, there's a good lad."

A flame creeps up Norm's neck, igniting on his cheeks, when I say, "Thanks." A nod is the most conversation he can muster as we drive to crapdom. He hoists the TV out of the back and follows me up the stairs.

Todd's voice wobbles as Norm sets the TV on its stand. "Ari, what'd you do?"

"She's your very own. Happy birthday, merry Christmas, Easter tidings, and get well soon. Mikey, help Todd eat, then get your homework done." He gives a thumbs-up but is already lost in the blue light.

I ask Norm, "Can you drop me at Maitland Street?"

He nods, or maybe he's just shaking.

At the door the Dick nabs my braid. "Where're you going?"

"Out." Nosing up to him, I spit. "You ever touch my hair again and I'll have Tino's barber scalp you. We clear?" He releases.

Norm eases his grip on the steering wheel as we near Maitland and the terror of having a girl in his truck comes to an end. "Night. Thanks."

Todd's boss, Dr. McKay, keeps his clinic in an old house. He peeks out of a room when the bell clatters. "Ari, good, come lend a hand."

In the little treatment room, a dizzy man regroups on a chair while I stroke a stressed boxer. "It's okay, you lovely soul. The doc will have that leg fixed up right quick."

He stitches, bandages, then lifts the dog down. "There you go, laddie. Stay away from sharp fences now." He settles the bill and says, "Hope you've come to tell me Todd will soon be back."

"He gets a walking cast next week. Um, I know sometimes Todd sleeps here when critters need watching. If I could set up a room upstairs for him, you'd have a built-in night shift in return for lodgings."

"Would Todd agree to this?"

"There's no place he'd be happier."

Dr. McKay takes two steps at a time to a room loaded with

275

cartons and a small cot. "I save the boxes for take-home beds. Folded down they'd fit in the storeroom. There's a kitchen downstairs."

"That a yes?"

"Get him back here soon."

FIFTY

What does it say about Dick Irwin's pathetic life when I'm the best next of kin Halpern can find? I call Constantine after getting the news that the Dick took a beating. "Tino? What the hell? He would've signed the agreement."

"Got nothing to do with me, kitten. Swear on my sainted mother."

"Then who?"

"The guys lookin' for O'Toole. Listen, when Halpern hauls you in, you heard nothin', saw nothin', know nothin'. These guys don't mess around."

"Oh, please just get me away from this friggin' shit!"

"Did Laura sign?"

"Yes."

"Meet me at the hospital at noon."

Thugs really do break kneecaps. An overhead bar hammocks the Dick's right leg. When he sees me, growls escape his wired jaw. "I'n 'oing to keel you, you 'ucking cunt."

I turn to Tino. "Did he say he's going canoeing?"

"Goin' up the river, Irwin?"

276

"'ucking 'astard, 'e had a 'eal."

"I always honour my deals. You know who eats canaries? Snakes. That's who. Now, here's the new deal. You're going to sign these papers and I'm gonna put the word out that you'd never sing. O'Toole takes the heat on both sides." Tino shoves a pen in the Dick's hand and holds the custody agreement taut. "Sign here, here and here."

"'crew you."

Tino leans on the rail. "Irwin, you notice that the only thing on your miserable person not incapacitated is your right hand? Things are that way so, one, you can fuck yourself, and two, sign these papers. I strongly recommend it for your health."

It's done, easily done.

Mina finds me sitting on crapdom's stoop, reading the mail. "Anything good?"

"Did you know Jake's going back to rehab?"

"He talked to Ellis after your mum's funeral. It's a good step, but Ellis thinks he's doing it for you, not for himself."

"If it gets him moving, I'll happily be his motivation. He so needs to exorcise his dad's meanness."

"It's his mother leaving him behind that gets me." Mina rights the house number. The 7 falls back down, numbering crapdom "LO." "How does a kid process being deliberately left in hell?"

"He excuses her. Says his sisters were all her arms could carry. But he was forever waiting for her to come back for him. I want Jake to clean out the mess, but I'm scared he might get so lost he'll disappear, like June."

"The greater risk is him never finding his true life because people held him together."

"Have you found yours?"

277

"For the most part. Really it's a journey, with right turns, wrong paths, backtracking, rerouting, redeeming." She tips my envelope and checks the sender.

"Auntie Dolores has been sending me Appleton slices."

"Any revelations?"

"She says under my dad's shine was the most splintered person imaginable. Unbordered in his emotions. When I wasn't the longed-for son, he smashed his new car with a tire iron. Barely acknowledged Mum's existence after. No wonder she hated me so much."

"Both of them were selfish idiots for not loving the gift of a child."

"Dolores says Mummy had brains, beauty, talent, but whenever she made a right turn she'd back up, fast as lightening, to find the wrong one. At sixteen she packed a bag with Auntie Elsie's best clothes and ran off with my dad. He was twice her age." A bee, reanimating in a sun-warmed spot, butts against the peeling rail. "How'd you figure same seeds and growing conditions produced Dolores, Elsie, Mary, and Mum?"

"What's that saying? 'Same sun that melts wax hardens clay.' Those who are amazed at it all become. The blind pitch what they've got."

A lady pushing a stroller along the sidewalk bristles as her toddler tucks to examine ants. "Kurt, I swear, if you don't listen to Mummy, I'll . . . Move it, now. One. Two. Thr—"

"Seven, nine, twelve." He springs up, bopping forward like a kangaroo.

I half smile. "I'm sorry you never had kids."

She folds onto the step. "It used to feel more bitter than sweet but it's brought us to a good place, right for Ellis and me, a jitter of possibilities."

My arm weaves through Mina's. "Half of Jarvis call you Mum and Dad, you know."

"Yeah, we have some pretty spectacular kids."

"I never knew Auntie Dolores had four miscarriages or how hard it was for her that Mum reproduced easier than bacteria. Mum used to parade us in front of her, 'Aren't they the most beautiful jewels.' I'm no closer to understanding Mum, but I get my aunt better. I'm glad she has Jillianne."

"And I'm glad I have you. I came to invite you and Mikey to crash at our place."

"Mikey's at Sabina's. I'm Todd's gopher until I get his room set up. Should be able to move him out on Saturday."

"Where's O'Toole?"

"Gone underground."

"Appropriate for a rat. So, a custody deal's set?"

I nod.

"What can Ellis and I do to get you to Dalhousie?"

"I'm going to fail chemistry and I'll be lucky to scrape through math and I missed a big history test. If I don't pass with a sixty-five, I'll lose the scholarship."

Mina bolsters my sags. "I'll work something out with your teachers. I'm sure they'd be willing to provide some assignments for bonus marks."

"It's a good thing I can play ball because according to my paper records, I'm dumber than depleted dirt."


Friday, I do something I can ill afford: skip school. It's a universal disappointment to collapse the boxes and find peony wallpaper. I strip it off, unearthing Pepto-Bismol-coloured walls. I mix half gallons of white and blue paint and roll it on. *Mauve?*

*If you can't say it's gray, then just keep your snout shut.*


Before sunrise Saturday, I trek to Sabina's, scavenge furniture from the basement, load Otto's truck, snatch some Polish delicacies, and head to Aaron's.

He opens the door a crack at my quiet knock. "Ari? Everything okay?" He opens a little wider and I see his PJ bottoms.

"Sorry to come so early, but I really need help moving stuff into Todd's room." I offer pastries. "Brought breakfast."

"Um, sure. How about I meet you downstairs."

"Oh, geez." My peripheral vision blurs, narrowing to a blue dot. I bolt down the stairs.

"Ari." He catches me on the sidewalk. "Wait."

"Sorry. I should've called." Too little sleep, too much mayhem makes me all quivery.

"Come back. I'll make coffee."

"Do you have a naked girl in there?"

"No."

"A boy?"

"What? No."

He leads me back and I hesitate at the door. "Did you send her out the window?"

"There's no girl. I just didn't want you to see what was on my table."

"Pictures of naked girls?"

"Your birthday present from Zodiac." On the table in his apartment a helter-skelter of paw prints cover a canvas. "When I went home at Christmas, my cousins' kid was making handprints. Zodiac stepped in the pan and the idea was born." His hands light on my waist from behind. "There's the photo."

I lift a picture of Aaron holding Zodiac's blue paw up in a wave. "I was at rope's end and you just gave me miles to go on." My back rests against his chest as I scan his Amish-sparse apartment. "Where're your travel treasures?"

"Storage. My lease is up. I'm going to crash at a friend's 'til school's out."

"Then?"

"Peru. Then back to finish my master's. I won't be able to afford this place."

"Hey, that's the picture I made for you in grade eight."

"I wasn't ready to pack everything away. I've always thought it was spectacular."

"Please let me paint you another one. That heron looks like a whooping ostrich."

"Huh, I always thought it was an emu."

"Smartass, so you going to help me or what?" My face tilts back, kissable-close. Our inhales catch the other's breath. We swallow in sync.

"J-just let me get dressed."


Dr. McKay surveys the cozy haven. "Is Todd ready to manage?"

"His doctor said he needs to move more." I check Aaron's watch. "I've got to get the truck back, feed Todd, shower, and get to work."

Aaron tugs my braid as he follows me out. "Then what?"

"I really should study."

FIFTY-ONE

Midnight and the Riverboat is a jump of bodies. Aaron steps through the door looking like a minor niner on the first day of high school. I sidle up, tank top to T-shirt close. "Hey, cowboy, can I buy you a drink?" He bites on his smile as I usher him to the stool by the cash. "What brings you here?"

"Didn't want you going back to that house so late on your own."

I kiss "Thank you" to his ear, lingering a half moment on his neck. "Enjoy the music."

As I deliver orders, I watch him listening only with his ears. Not even his toe moves to "Light My Fire." I know where this set ends. I slide over, flirty-girl-like because music and this man moves me. "Listen to this one with me." The tilt of my head lifts him off the stool. I turn, fusing back to chest. Thirty seconds into "The First Time Ever I Saw Your Face," his body relaxes into mine, hips sway in sync. A minute in, and his arms are full circle, his hand opens on my belly and the music slips past our ears, down our necks, through our chests. I lift my face back to meet his, a spark arcing from his mouth to mine. He turns me, swallowing me in a hug, fists gathering my hair as his mouth heats my forehead. "I-I want—"

The fear in him, in both of us, makes me step away. Our eyes continue the holding. I've seen that same desire on Jake's face and I feel the biggest loneliness of my near eighteen years on this Earth. "Lemonade? I'll get you one."

He waits and drives me to the craphouse. "I don't want you staying here."

"Todd gets scared all alone."

"Where's Shirley?"

"No clue."

There's no sense arguing about him seeing me in. Todd welcomes the doggie bag in his hand. "You need help with anything before I go, Todd?"

He talks, stuffed-mouth full. "I'm good."

"See you tomorrow, then. Eight thirty." I follow Aaron down the stairs with my hands on his shoulders. He turns at the bottom step. "Maybe I should stay."

"You're a cruel man tempting me like this, but I'd never ask someone I love to stay in this house." His eyes widen like I just gave him a puppy and a kick in the gut at the same time. "Oh, as if you don't know. Go on."

I cut the seam of Todd's pants and wake him. "Get dressed."

"Where am I going?"

"To your very own nest complete with a stocked fridge and a dog or ten."

"Really? What about my TV?"

"Aaron will carry it down."

"Ari, I take back that you're a meddling idiot. You're the best thing that ever happened to the Irwins."

"And you turned out to be a spectacular treasure in this dark, Todd."

Sing-dancing down the stairs sets a body right off-kilter for an ambush, especially by a cop with sneak-tactic training. From the shadowy hall, he captures my left wrist with handcuffs, bull-dozing me backwards into the front room, securing me to the radiator under the window.

"O'Toole, you friggin' asshole, take this off."

"Just collecting a little down payment from Irwin."

"Fine. Unlock me and I'll write you a cheque."

His mouth contorts with the scratching of his bristled chin. "This payment I'm taking in services."

"Tino will kill you if you touch me."

"Think you're so dammed smart." His elbow presses into my chest. "You think the guys in my pocket don't know how to part a smartass girl from her money?" The smirk oozing across his face spills into my gut. "You see, when a cop kills a bad guy in the line of duty, they call him a hero."

"You don't have to hurt anyone. You can have the money."

"Damn straight, it's mine." He fingers the steel around my wrist, snakes up my arm, hooking the neck of my T-shirt before ripping it near in two. "With interest."

I go for his eyes with my free hand. He snaps my wrist with his right, backhanding me with his left. An armageddon of screaming, hitting, hair ripping, scratching shakes the walls. My knee connects with his balls, reeling him backwards. The only thing in my reach is a heavy-bottom pole lamp. I grasp it and I swear Jasper speaks, *He's ready for it to come right, swing left.* I swing away from him, smashing through the front window. Glass falls like spring melt off a roof. A neighbour screeches, "What in heavens?"

My arm remains attached to the radiator inside but the rest of me hurtles to the veranda, screaming. "Help! Fire, fire, fire!"

Then I hear Todd clambering down the stairs. "You filthy bastard. Keep your fucking hands off her." Fight ruckus and flying clatter spill from inside.

I scream, scream, scream. "Help! Please, help!"

Then an explosion silences everything. O'Toole's boots cross the veranda, slow, like a run through water. The space around me pops, shakes. Lightening sizzles through my hair, burning my shoulder, exploding my foot.

I descend into the ocean, tangle in the weeds. My bum feels wet and when too much of you spills out, you get very sleepy, drifting away on the back of a little seahorse and you feel boys you love rock you in the waves.

"Jesus, oh God, no. Ari. Ari! No. Don't leave me."

## FIFTY-TWO

Part of me gets why Mum loaded up on dope. I don't have to speak or hear or feel. I open the eye that can open and Aaron's face floats over me.

"Hey, you."

"Todd?"

"In surgery."

"Mikey?"

"With Sabina."

Men in suits appear around the curtain. "She awake?"

"In and out."

I recognize Halpern's voice, close my eye, and disappear.

"She say anything?"

"Just asked about Todd and Mikey."

"Ari? Ari! Who did this?"

"O'Toole."


A cast fixes my O'Toole-delivered wrist fracture. A bandage covers a bullet graze on my bicep. My left arm has fifty-eight stitches from ripping over glass when I heaved myself out the window. I would've thought a bullet through the foot would hurt more, but it doesn't come close to the wrench in my shoulder. Auntie Mary braids my hair and washes my purply face. One eye is swollen shut and my lip puffs fish-fat. My tongue keeps worrying the split in the corner. "How's Todd?"

"Not good."

"I have to see him."

The nurse tries to shoo us away when Nia wheels me to intensive care. "Please, it'd be good for both of them."

Todd took a bullet right in his stomach. Tubes squirrel in

all directions. His eyes stay closed, but they flutter when I talk. "Todd, get better. Please. Your new home is waiting."

A doctor comes in and the nurse drives my chair into the hall.

Nia says, "The doctor's willing to let you recuperate at home. We're going to take you to Mina's."

"No. Todd doesn't like being alone." I glance at the elevator opening and my lip hurts to smile. "Tino?" I struggle to stand.

"Christ almighty. O'Toole did this?" Tino wrestles down the cry in his throat as he eases me down. "I'm gonna rip that bastard's liver out and stuff it down his throat."

"Theo the thug, meet Nia, giver of earth, sun, and stars."

"Pleased to make your acquaintance, ma'am. How's the kid?"

Nia's head shake is heavy.

"Anything you need, kitten?"

I push down the Jell-O quaking up from my stomach. "Can you get me a book called *The Incredible Journey*? I'd like to read it to Todd."


This journey, my journey is incredulous. For Hariet Appleton, there's no physics, no mechanical laws that stop shit. No benevolent force triumphing evil. Prayer doesn't work. Cheaters do prosper. Bastards get away with murder. The wages of sin is not death. Bad guys get their pensions in the end. These are the realities with few exceptions.

Four weeks ago, soldiers from Ricky's platoon, all shiny and polished, carried Todd out of the church. Policemen stopping traffic at every light saluted him through. The news called him the brave man who loved animals and gave his life saving another.

Nia drives me to the cemetery gate every day, because I'm supposed to walk and it's the only way anyone can get me to move. I sit on the wet grass. "How can this be your ending, Todd?" Words are garbled through my tears, tears that I just can't get a lid on. "I make all this shit happen."

"Enough." Nia hoists me off the ground, moves me toward the gate. "You just landed in a life so shit-loaded, you couldn't help but get covered in it."

"There's no denying I'm at the core of this."

Nia snaps my shoulders.

"Ow, that hurts."

"Good, now listen to me. Your mother made terrible choices and you got dragged into it and your whole life you've been swinging right trying to fix everything and please everyone."

"You always swing right."

She rattles my shoulder a little more. "Sweet mother earth, if I hadn't smashed windows all my life I wouldn't have my Mary. Always righting is lopsided and exhausting for everyone. I love you all the more for swinging left and saving yourself. Now, are you going to pick up the treasures here or wallow in this shit?"

No matter what the aunties say, I know I am a catalyst, a chemical reactor causing death. We return to Mina's, me all red-nosed and puff-eyed. Aaron walks down and helps me up the steps. "Just came to see how you're doing."

"Fractured beyond knowing where to start repair."

Aaron sighs. "I'm so sorry you're going through this. My gut told me not to leave you there that night."

I sink on the plump sofa. "You tried. I sent you packing."

Nia says, "Hindsight. There were a thousand nights she was at risk. There isn't a gut in this room that didn't know that."

Mina asks, "Can you come Friday for early birthday cake, Aaron?"

"I'd like that. Um, Giselle wondered if she could come by."

"No. I'm too miserable that my volleyball days are over."

"You don't know that. Give yourself time to heal."

"The doctor said with this tear I'll be lucky to get my arm

over my head. I saw the report before he sent it to Dalhousie. My scholarship's gone. My marks are crap. And the unbearable worst, I got Todd murdered." I push hard against another dam-burst of blubbering.

"Maybe we should postpone this Sunday."

Nia says, "Absolutely not. Life has to be lived no matter how impossible that seems. Take her somewhere back into life. That's an order."

"That okay, Ari?"

"Nothing's okay."

"Can I bring Mikey to see you?"

"His brother's dead because of me."

"Todd's dead because of O'Toole. What Mikey sees is that Todd saved you."

"I came back to Toronto to help and I've just made a mess that can't ever be mended."

Auntie Mary hands me a white pill and an inch of milkshake. I swallow, then curl into Aaron's lap, pretending to sleep so he'll gentle my hair for a long while.

## FIFTY-THREE

Six weeks after the shootout, I turn eighteen. Pesky helpers push me out of my despair using a whopping dose of weed. I don't know where Nia got it, but I'm grateful, grateful, grateful. It smothers the pain in my shoulder and the ache in my chest better than hospital pills.

Jennah comes over to cover up evidence of my near-murdering. She says, "Sam Lukeman got a call from the Dick this morning."

"Why?"

"The thoughtful man remembered your birthday. He's suing for his share of his wife's estate."

"That bloody money started this horror. I'm setting a match to it."

"A narcissistic piranha started this." I quiet, sinking into the buzz. *Huh, Jasper, after all our looking, Jen just nailed Mum's animal.* "Sam told him you'd donated every dollar to the humane society in memory of Todd. What sticks in my craw is him getting his pension. Sam said they can't disprove his claim that he got injured in the line of duty. And he was in hospital when hell broke loose. Now, enough of him." Jennah assesses her handiwork and gentles my cheek. "You made it to eighteen. Our beautiful wreck of the helperus."

Jen zips up the softest boots any cow ever sacrificed its life for. A black skirt floats to mid-calf. A camisole and plum-coloured jacket make me look like a fashion model. Nia lifts my chin, looking past me, right to Jasper. "Let the darkness go, for a few hours. Today needs a little celebration."

Aaron arrives, pausing when he sees me. "You look . . ."

*Do not say beautiful.*

"Kintsugied."

On the drive he gives me a package. Wrapped in tissue is a small stone sea lion. The note says, *Happy birthday to my spirit-sister. I love you more than oceans. Mikey.*

I'm mercifully numb and wish I had a couple of joints in my purse instead of the white pills.

"Mikey said it's for your absent present window. What'd he mean?"

"I'll show you one day soon. Is he talking?"

"Yeah, we talk. He said to tell you that sea lions have winged feet. He's trying hard to keep his heart above water, but he believes you being hurt and Todd dying are all his fault."

"What?"

"Think about it, if not for him, you'd be out east and Todd would be in Rockton."

"What an awful, awful mess. Can you bring him over tomorrow?"

"That'd be a good start. Now, close your eyes for an escape. We've a bit of a drive."

I drift through miles on the last of the high.

We picnic at Niagara-on-the-Lake, a fancy basket lunch that I'm certain Sabina packed. "Can we see the Falls? I've never seen them."

He pulls two tickets for the Shaw Festival out of his pocket. "Later."

"We're going to a play?"

"*Getting Married*, then we're going to the Falls. Does that scare you?"

"Right now, anything resembling life scares me."

The play makes me laugh—almost. The Falls make us dreamy. Someone tapping on Aaron's shoulder makes him turn. "West? Wow, Aaron. Great to see you, man."

"Uh, Dave? What're you doing here?"

"Sales convention." He takes me in, forwards his hand, and shakes my cast. "Dave Harcord."

"Sorry, Dave, this is Ari." Aaron stuffs his hands in his pocket. "Dave and I are friends from high school."

"Nice to meet you."

"So, how about joining me for dinner?"

"Ah, another time would be better. I'll be home July. Okay if we catch up then?"

"Sure." He play-punches Aaron's shoulder. "You old dog, you."

The elevator glass mirrors us as we ride to the top of a high tower for dinner overlooking the Falls. Bottom floor, Aaron's head focuses on the floor, travelling upwards with the ascent of the car, his eyes meeting my reflected ones by mid-journey. "I am an old dog, aren't I."

"You are who you are and nowhere close to who you'll be. Besides, I love dogs."

"Who I will be is what scares me."

"Expand."

"I sometimes wondered about a September where you came back and told me that you weren't with Jake. It's sick, I know, but I wondered where we could go."

"If you really think we're sick, I'm walking home right now. By myself."

"I just mean that you and I are outside the lines."

"Well, that's your own bloody fault for staying inside the lines for twenty-seven years. Your psyche has to go for something big to break you out of the wading pool you're in." The hostess leads us to a table. "Besides, in lioneagle years, I'm forty-two."

He half smiles, his dimple like a period on the end of a happy sentence.

I near collapse into the chair. "Would I wreck things if I put my foot up beside you?"

"You want your boot off?"

"That'd be like milkweed coming out of the pod. I'd never get it back in." The pain in me is startling, stretching toe to tip. I leave the pills in my purse, needing the way pain masks the ache in my chest. "Are you thinking all this line stuff because your friend saw us?"

"Scared me a little."

"Because he'll tell your parents?"

"No. They know how important your friendship is to me."

"Do they disapprove?"

"What they know is you protected your dog, and Mikey. Besides my mom's years younger than my dad. They get it."

"So, then?"

"It was more I didn't know how to introduce you. Unlisted, undefined things make me feel shoved underwater."

"Jasper, does this man need a swim with a seahorse or what. We'll take you for a dip after dinner."

"In the Falls?"

"Don't be daft, man. I carry my ocean with me."

"Actually, I'd welcome Dave suggesting I'm dating. There's a girl believing I'm coming back to settle down."

"You've never mentioned anyone."

"Emily. We dated through high school. Probably would've married if I hadn't stumbled upon her and Dave in the hay-loft."

"Ouch."

"Luckiest break ever. Settling down scares the life out of me."

"Mayhem-free settling is all I want."

"With Jake?"

"If I could mend his life, I would, but, I can't navigate my own sorry self."

"Would you ever go back with him?"

"I'll end up a solo seahorse if he doesn't find his way back to our shore, but he has fathoms to travel, and I've been told, or more warned, to let him go so he can dive where he needs."

"Will he be there when you go this summer?"

"He's taken a job on a troller. Huey thinks it could be good for him, but I don't. He hates hauling live creatures from the ocean and mariners are a rough lot."

"Losing his hand, his music must be devastating."

"Music's in the soul, not the hand. It's not lost; he's just bloody set on proving to us that he's like his dad."

"What is it? Why? I mean why do you love him?"

"Imagine a little kid who only wants to find a home meeting someone who looks into all the rooms inside you and says, 'I know this place, it's the other half of *my* house.' Jake and I've always had this connection, like he's my front door and I'm his, and on opening we never feel any fuss about the mess, just open arms inviting the other in."

"I've never felt anything like that, not even Linda."

"You shouldn't. Your match will be the one jumping over the threshold into the great unknown." I check his face. "Made you shiver with anticipation, didn't I."

"Thought opposites attract."

"If you're an ion maybe, but in the animal world an inchworm does better snuggling up to another wiggler than an elephant, don't you think?"

His mashed potatoes flatten under the weight of his fork.

"You and Jake are eerily alike."

"Alike?"

"I used to think the fog rolling in was his kindness spilling out. The kindness from you these years has soaked to my dry roots. Without you, Mikey and I would've become dust." His hand feels fragile in mine. "You and Jake are the same good clay, but the elements have shaped you differently. Your solid life has given you wings at your core and Jake's life on stormy seas has given him an anchor at his. And there's the music situation."

"Music?"

"You're afraid to let yours out and he's terrified to keep his in." Candlelight pools in the water glass. "And you know why that is?"

"Fear?"

"You both know that when the music ends, you come to a silence where there's no option but to listen to your inner animal."

"You still believe I have one."

"It's getting harder and harder not to reach in and grab hold of it."

The napkin spirals in his hand. "Are you caught between an anchor and a wing?"

"More suspended. You're both the loveliest bits of my past. Jake, I hope, is my future." My eyes lift to meet his. "You, I think, are my present."

His smile is small, like a new leaf. "Is your foot up to a stroll?"

"Long as I have you to lean on."

We walk, arms linked, stopping at a little jut to soak in the coloured lights. The spray makes me shiver and my hair party. "This has been as perfect as this birthday could be." I tip-toe up and kiss him soft on his lips. "Thank you." He wanders my face, risks settling in my eyes. I taste the salt on his thumb as he touches the healing line on my mouth. The pull of his hand under my chin brings my lips to his. Jasper whispers, *Everyone needs a kiss on their birthday*. I receive the gift, open and long. He gives more and more and I respond with a tiny bit of tongue. *You're allowed eighteen kisses.*

"How . . . how can I be doing this?"

My fingers feel the racing in his chest. "According to a wise bear, you have to, like taking medicine." He takes a big dose and licks the spoon.

The years of longing in us, colliding with the feeling of my house being swept over the Falls, leave me trembling. My knee buckles.

"Come sit down. I'll get the car." He parks me on a bench, drapes his jacket over my shoulders, and runs.

On the drive home, as he talks me around the world, I'm thinking about his lips on mine and that I'm a few kisses short of the eighteen allowed. He helps me to Mina and Ellis's door. "Ari? You okay?"

The anticipation of more kisses is snuffed by a shoulder aching up into my ear and a foot throbbing like an abscessed tooth.

"I ask this in the most unromantic way imaginable, please throw me on a bed."

## FIFTY-FOUR

Dead men, lost men drown me in terminal sadness. Mina stuffs my backpack and nudges me out the door. "Go with Mikey and Aaron. Mikey needs to see you're breathing. The fresh air will do you good."

Aaron is wilderness man. Everything he does—tent raising, snatching fish out of thin water, gathering wood, making fire— both anesthetizes and puts me in heat. I tame my hair and crawl out of the tent. Aaron asks, "Mikey asleep?"

"Sound."

He invites me to a sit by the fire. I curl close, absorb his good- ness. His chest is solid beneath my cheek and his heart beats: want-want, want want. I take in the stars over his head. He ex- plores them in my eyes. "What're you thinking?" I ask.

"Nothing." Sizzling sap spits.

"Liar, liar, sweatpants-on-fire."

"You really want to know what thought flew through my head?"

I nod.

"You'll think I'm nuts."

"Then maybe I won't feel so lonely."

"I didn't write a list."

"What? There's no list?"

"No, I don't mean *the* list. I mean for this weekend. I just threw stuff into the jeep and picked you up."

"Are you saying there's no food?"

"There's food, but it's the kind of unlisted mess that has us eating hot dogs and chips for breakfast."

"That's a bad thing?"

"Not having a list scares me and the fact that it scares me feels an awful thing." He leans against the log, holding me, nuzzling my head-top, searching for a way to lay out the tangle in his head. "When I was ten, I was painting my uncle's shed. The sky was loaded with these mashed clouds and I said, 'I wonder what it'd be like to go right into them.'

"Uncle Pete put down his brush and said, 'Whenever there's wonder, you gotta go right into it.' We just got in his jeep and left. Approaching dusk we stopped. He lifted the seat, tossed out gear, and we were set up in a wink. Next morning, we sat through that hour when the air colours and I had my first coffee ever and we grabbed handfuls of nuts and seeds from this big bag liberally peppered with Smarties. I marvelled that a man could eat such a thing for breakfast." Aaron snugs me closer, pulling the sleeping bag over my wrecked shoulder. "We drove until the mist of cloud surrounded us. The falling sun caught the wet air and I felt like I'd entered a hidden dimension of time and space."

I savour the slow drift of his hand down my body and back up to my cheek, lifting off my skin with each pass over my breast. Jasper meddles, *Go into the wonder, Aaron. Go into the wonder.*

*Stop it. We won't ever betray Jake.*

Twenty minutes into a log-leaning, fire gaze, he sighs. "Never had that feeling since. I'm forever circling the wonder, watching like a spectator, never venturing into the heart of it." His finger traces the scallop of my bra, venturing a quarter inch under the lacy wave, like a balcony sitter moving down to the second row.

I tilt my head back. "Are you wondering right now?"

"More than I ever have."

My lips slide into the curve of his neck. One button slips away, two, three . . . four. I kiss his chest. He inhales with my hand's descent, his leg opening, extending as I stroke his thigh, each ascent bringing my hand closer to where he's swollen beneath his sweatpants. His face lifts to the bend and sway at the top of the trees. He makes not a single sound when I venture under, taking him in my hand, leaf on water light and slow. He lets me bring him to the mountaintop and push him over the edge, drawing in great wafts of air as he tumbles like a rock off a mountain.

I snatch the towel drying by the fire to mop him up, lean back against his naked chest, pulling his paralyzed arms around me, breaking a long silence with "You think your sleeping bag's zipper is compatible with mine? I really miss being held."

Middle of the night, sandwiched between him and Mikey, Aaron pulls me close, his hand venturing under my T-shirt, opening full on the lace covering my breast. "I can't—"

"You don't have to."

"No, I can't stop wanting you. I try, but I can't."

"Stop torturing yourself with the past and future. Just hold me now, please."

When light surfaces me, I wait under the warm sleeping bag, weighted under the feathers of a dream, Natasha on the swing, *Oh, Ari, look at the trees waltzing with the wind*. My wooden lids lift. Aaron and Mikey are gone. I braid my forest-wild hair, swipe my teeth with my T-shirt, and crawl out.

The trees are heavy with dew. "Where's Mikey?"

Aaron hands me coffee and points to a rock where the boy sits hopeful with his fishing pole. "I'm worried about him. He hardly talks."

"He lost his brother."

"And he almost lost you." Aaron looks at the lake, not me.

"Aaron, please don't pull away from me. I can't handle losing anybody else right now."

"I shouldn't have . . ."

"I did the doing."

"But I—"

"I warned you, Westwind, nor'easters mess everything up." My blue enamel cup fits in a knot on the log as if a fallen spruce comes with coasters in Aaron's camp spot. I head into the woods.

"Don't get lost, Ari."

"I already am."


Mina turns on the hall light and finds me huddled in the corner. "Another nightmare?"

My head wobbles. "Len left me in a church. He didn't want me anymore. There were hands waiting to grab my ankles if I got off the pew."

"In dreams we replace what we're most afraid of with the person we feel safest with. It helps us work things out in a safe place. How old were you in the dream?"

"Li-li-little." I blubber, stutter. "I want . . ."

"What, Ari?"

"To be held."

"By your papa?"

"I want Jake. I want Aaron to give back my dog."

Mina helps me off the floor. "I'd hoped O'Toole being arrested would make the nightmares stop."

"It's just made everything bigger." I despise the whiny snivel my voice has these days. "I keep seeing Todd's little room. He never even had a chance to be happy."

Mina settles behind me on the bed. "I had Todd in grade nine, the kid most destined to die confined to a La-Z-Boy. He wasn't the chubby guy that people liked. Kids tortured him. When I saw him at the volleyball party, I couldn't fathom it was the same person. Don't tell me he never had a chance to be happy."

"He was discovering his happiness, and when it comes to the root of why he'll never find it, you come to Hariet Appleton."

She turns to the ceiling. "Do you know how many times I've asked myself why I didn't think to include Todd the day I came to invite you and Mikey to join us? If I had . . ."

"He was an unlikely white knight, but he protected me and Mikey all the time. Whenever I thanked him, he joked that his size was useful for something."

"That the most unlikely among us can be the greatest hero of all is, I believe, the most precious gem ever unearthed. Tell his story with pen or paints. Make something about this redemptive, please."

"That's a big sadness, too. Words and colour have left me. Like they're disgusted with me."

"They're just giving you a little time and space." Gently, she massages my shoulder. "How was your camping trip?"

"Mikey had a little rest from all the horror."

"And you?"

"Aaron can't get past the *shalt nots*." I tuck my loneliness under the quilt. "I'm so heaved up inside, it's just best not to get mixed up with me. If I lose him as a friend, I couldn't bear it."

"Are you coming back to do grade thirteen?"

"Dalhousie doesn't want a broken volleyball player. Jake is breaking my heart back home. Aaron can't love me here. I just want to run away and find June."

"Only one anyone can find is their own self." She captures my hand reaching for the pills on the nightstand. "When has there ever been a time for you to just love school?"

"Not since landing with M&N when I was eight."

"There's no high school in Pleasant Cove. Come back here

299

and get your marks up. It'll give you options to forge your own destiny."

"Seems anything I forge dissolves to ash."

"Lioneagles arise from ashes."

FIFTY-FIVE

Aaron West is an unlisted wreck. He opens his mouth to speak and ends up chewing air. He moves in like a kiss might be coming, then dusts a used-up eyelash from my cheek. I bring lemonade to his table. "I asked for Coke."

"Good lord, West, as if you need more caffeine." I ignore the other customers and sit. "Let this worry go. We'll sort things out in September when you're one hundred percent student, not a teacher."

"You are coming back?"

"I've no clue where I belong."

"Me, too. I feel so stuck and at loose ends."

"Wait 'til after my shift. We'll talk then."

I should've kept more of an eye on a boy at loose ends. Guys like Lewis always have shit to sell the knotted and unravelled. I touch Aaron's shoulder. "Okay, I'm done, let's go." He's picking something off the table that isn't there. "Aaron?" His head lifts like a swan unfolding. Pupils eclipse his irises. "Aaron, what did you take?" I fight for the bamming in my chest to stay out of my voice. "Tell me what you took."

"Communion." His eyes ratchet from my face to my shoulder to his hand.

"On your tongue?" I snap to Lewis. "You gave him acid?" One step and his shirt provides a choke hold. "You bastard, did you?"

"Just a hit."

Crystal shows Lewis the door. "Can you manage, Ari?"

"Yeah." He's willing to be led. "Aaron, come with me."

I coax him along the dark alley. He stops where light from a window arrows the ground. "Where does it end?"

"The ocean."

He reaches down, touches the dirt. "I love you."

"I need you to come with me." Every friggin' thing distracts him. "Come on, you like mountains. Let's climb one." I push him up my steps. "Stop looking down and I'll show you an eagle's nest."

"Whoa, look there."

*Stupid friggin' idiotic* . . . "It's beautiful."

"What is that?"

"Trees. Climb higher." Years in the Village and drug-dropping sisters make me an expert on riding out this shit. I open the door. "Go in, it's safe." I sit him on the comfy chair, turn on the soft light, then move everything I don't want toppling in a "Oh, God look at all of them."

"I'm going to take off your shoes, okay?" He bends over, mesmerized by his socks, and I wonder what Neruda was on when he wrote "Ode to My Socks."

I watch him through a night of wondering, murmuring, sitting, wandering. He picks up a red tea towel. "God said this, didn't he? I should've . . ." He drops the towel, fascinated by the appendage underneath. "Whoa."

I capture his bewildered hand. "God says you should sit and let me hold you."

He teeters on a floor crack.

"If you fall in, you'll only float." I put on trip-tranquilizing music, sit at the head of the bed, and invite him to me.

301

"Whoa, the walls?"

"They're singing Pachelbel's Canon. Drink this." I lift orange juice to his lips and he drinks.

"Did God say that?"

"God says it's okay to let go and not be afraid."

He rubs a spot on my arm. "Oh, geezus."

"It's just paint. There's nothing wrong."

"I can do this better."

"There's no better to be done. Just follow the colour." I drift. He takes a long time to let go. Light is seeping through the windows before he rolls to the wall and sleeps. A muddy muddle stirs in my belly. My shoulder and wrist ache, hedging the pain in my chest. I look at Aaron in my bed, feeling like someone has left me again.

*It's the first time in his whole life he's ever messed up. Don't say goodbye.*

*But he messed up because of me.*


He rolls to a sit, capturing his head in his hands. "God, what've I done?"

"Acid."

His head droops as he contemplates his socks, which likely don't look so special today. "I can't believe I did this. I'm . . . I-I'm . . ."

"You're through the trip, but I'm guessing you're going to have a hell of a time collecting your luggage."

He reaches for his shoes. "I should go."

"No. You're staying here and working through whatever made you do such an idiotic, lame-brained, friggin' stupid thing. Go have a shower while I make some bloody tea. I put some clothes out for you."

He obeys like a guilty dog and comes out all little-boy tousled. "Whose clothes am I wearing?"

"My old friend Chase's. Come eat."

He sits on the red chair, lowers his mouth to the blue mug, then lets his head fall to the scarred yellow wood. Our hair connects as I search for his ear. "Aaron, if you screwed up and screwed up and screwed up again, this friend would still love you. In this room all gods that stand in judgment say not guilty."

He looks up at me. "I'll only believe that if you say it's true for you."

"Inside these walls, yeah."

When one's foundations shift, constructing new rooms, tearing down others, it gets crowded inside. "You need some space. There's an empty journal by the chair and food enough to last a week." He looks as if I'm leaving him smack in the middle of the Sahara with no water. "I'm going to do laundry and get groceries."

"What if the owner comes back?"

"I am coming back."

"This is your place?"

"Jacquie gave it to me."

He moves to the window. The sun bleaches his face leaving his back stained with shadow. "Have you ever taken . . . ?"

"Couple of times." He has the lonely sigh of a man that has no one to share an honest thought with. "It's okay if you liked it. You just have to look smack at why."

"No, I . . . I . . . Did you?"

"Mushrooms freed me some, but acid, I hated. Life on the outside for me was out of control. I didn't much care for that on my insides, too."

"Nothing was defined. Everything was moving."

"Don't throw it away."

"What?"

"Whatever's opening up in you. Listen to the voice in here."
I nudge the spirit living inside him. It remains as still as a gray
rock.

Jasper pipes up when I hoist up the laundry bag. *Know how to
wake a sleeping dolphin, Ari?*

*Yeah, I know.*

"Wait, take the jeep." His head cranks around. "My keys? My
wallet? My jacket?"

"On the rack. Lesson one: that shit makes you friggin' stupid."

I take the streetcar because shifting and clutching are impossible in my present state. There's a laundromat closer than
going to Sabina's, but Mikey needs to see I'm moving as much
as I need to hear him talking.

Mikey is pale as milk and clings to me like a persistent cold,
helping me do laundry, when he could be riding the bike Otto
fixed up for him. I ask, "You all caught up on your worksheets?"
He nods. "If you want to go to the Butters now instead of June
end, I'll take you."

"Would you stay?"

"Mina's helping me get all my school stuff done. I'm so far in
the hole it's going to take me a few weeks."

"I want to go when you go."

"How about I ask Aaron if he's up for an adventure tomorrow?"

His smile is small but there's a little life in it.


On return to the nest there are washed dishes in the rack, journal fanning from pen-plumped pages, and Aaron curled on my
bed, arms wrapped around my stuffed Zodiac. *I'm so lonely,
Jasper. I want to climb in and have him turn all sleepy and open
to me.*

I shower, and when I contemplate the underwear basket, Jasper pokes, *The lacy ones.*

I cook quiet, but the spiced air wakes him. "What time's it?"

"Six."

"P.m.?" He rubs his jumbled head. "What time do you work?"

"I'm only working one shift now, remember? Because of my shoulder."

He tries to order his stressed hair. "Every time I think about what happened to you and Todd, I can't breathe."

"Is that why you took it?"

"I guess. You mind if I have another shower?"

"Help yourself."

"Thanks for taking care of me last night." His finger lifts mine from its red pepper cutting and he gives me a small kiss on the forehead before disappearing into the bathroom.

*We love Aaron.*

*But I love Jake.*

I love the smell of my plain soap. I especially like it on Aaron. "You hungry?"

"Yeah. It smells good."

"It's amazing what I can do with a wok on a hot plate."

"Sounds painful."

"Set the table, wise ass."

It's telling that he matches up the plates when I mix them up on purpose. Every bite yields a question. "What was that?"

"Water chestnut."

"Is this a cashew?"

I nod.

"What are these?"

"Rice noodles. What do you eat, Aaron West?"

"I'm a farm boy. Meat and potatoes."

"What about all your travels?"

"I pack crackers and peanut butter."

"There's a lot of work to get you ready for living in the southern hemisphere. We'll start with paella."

He cowers behind his inside rock.

"Relax. I'll leave out the squid." I fill his mug with tea and plunk down a slab of fudgy cake.

"Sabina make this?"

"Yep."

"How's Mikey?"

"Processing. Apparently, the Dick called Jennah looking for Mikey."

"What'd he want?"

"Last thing I expected. Help picking out Todd's gravestone."

"Weird."

"Yeah. Jenn said the Dick genuinely seemed sad. Sabina thinks Mikey should see that."

"Don't trust him, Ari."

"I don't. Tino knows a guy. He'll drive them. I'm going to get Mikey's schoolwork for the rest of the year and keep him at Sabina's, so the Dick can't have him nabbed from school. I'll go and work on my stuff with him."

He takes a big bite. "I'll come after school in hopes of more cake."

"Stay here and you can have some for breakfast." Chocolate freezes on his lip and I can see his heart lub-dubbing against his T-shirt. "What? Your stuff's in storage. Your friend's couch hurts your back. Stay here 'til you go home. I'll crash at Sabina's if you're scared of me."

"This place is like being inside a whole other world."

Light splinters off his shoulder. "Oh, Aaron, look." I go and open the door. A sky saturated crimson backlights the greening trees.

He stands behind—close, inhaling my coconut-scented hair.

"I've witnessed a thousand sunsets, but this might be the prettiest I've ever seen."

*Push him from shore.*

*Stop meddling.* I pull the door closed, slide the bolt and turn. "Why'd you take it?"

"I had 'one reckless thing' on my list." He stacks the dishes. "And I guess the thought of you moving east is—I know life's going to take us in different directions, but I don't want to ever say goodbye to you." Silence hangs as I put away food and he scrapes and rinses. I hoist myself onto the little counter, drying the dishes he passes my way. He looks up from the soapy water, full in my face, like a diver preparing to do a double-back three-and-a-half full reverse. "I took it because I hoped it'd give me courage."

"To love me?"

"Every woman I meet, all I think is she's not you." I stretch forward by fractions. He leans in by micro-fractions. The air between us stirs like a hummingbird waiting, weightless, for a drink of nectar. When we kiss, the way we kiss, I know he's entered the water. His wet hand weaves through my hair and the fuse is lit. Small kisses trail his whispered words. "Ari, this is crazy."

"Be crazy." My head lifts, neck opening. "The wise teacher doesn't wall you in the house of wisdom. She leads you to the threshold of your own mind."

He tucks up to the counter, between my dangling legs. "Pardon?"

"Gibran. It might sound tempting but be warned, this nor'easter will leave your solid house of wisdom in shambles."

He inhales. Exhales. "Blow."

I pull my blouse over my head, then lift Aaron's T-shirt over his. Hands drift up the sensitive skin along my sides, thumbs making my nipples startle up under the silk, strap falling away

307

as he kisses my shoulder. He unhooks my bra and takes hold of the wonder.

His moans spill over my breasts as I unzip him, slipping my hand down his belly to where his penis is trapped like an inflated raft in a closet. My tongue brushes his lips, bringing his mouth back to mine. He dances out of his jeans, kicking away his boxers. I navigate my skirt over my head, barely disconnecting our lips.

I kiss. He kisses. We kiss. Borders cross, disappear. He quiets, like stepping into the storm's eye. Looking down, his hands explore my naked thighs, fingers tracing the rise of lace like a moon over my hip. He tugs my panties. I lift for their removal and—the meeting of the winds is on. My legs snap 'round him as he gathers my naked skin against his peeled self with more Oh Gods than is heard at the First Pentecostal on resurrection Sunday. He aims us for the bed, landing us on the chair. I kneel, painting from his neck to his chest to his belly with my tongue, then kiss where he's wanting, wanting, wanting. I meander my lips back up to his face. "Last chance to take shelter."

One sweep and he lands me on the bed, and we are the untamed spring storm that turns the world green and live. I guide him in, fly him away, tossing him barely conscious on a mountain peak, in an eagle's nest under my feathered wing.

One forty-six, I sense him staring, open-eyed at the ceiling beams. I turn, studying the shadows above us. "Please don't tell me you're sad."

"Just scared. I wasn't thinking straight."

"I was. You don't have to worry about any little squalls."

"How?"

"The pill." My hand searches for his. "You and me like this has to stay inside these walls, just for us to know. I can't wreck your life. Promise me."

"Promise."

When I wake again, he's looking at me and I wonder how

long he's been waiting like Zodiac the obedient in the presence of prime rib. He moves hair from my shoulder, kisses it, then unearths my neck.

"Hang on, sailor. This vessel has taken on water and has a dead mackerel in her mouth." I've never seen my bum walking away, but I suspect it might be a good one. Though maybe glimpsing any girl's ass under a waterfall of hair lures a guy out of bed. He nabs me when I come out of the bathroom. A scratch of new growth prickles as I kiss my way to his ear. "Go shower and get ready for church." Likely he's heard those words a thousand times in his life and I feel big disappointment.

Pachelbel's Canon fills the nest when he returns. I slip the button on his fly. "You're wearing the wrong suit for this church."

"When do we have to pick up Mikey?"

"Three hours. Let us pray."

"Amen." A slow loving begins, the kind that lingers on a soft thigh, listens to whispered prayers, takes communion from skin, shoulder, breast, hip. He hesitates to shadow me with his body, but the joining is faith—seeing without eyes, feeling without hands, hearing music resonating in bone. He pulls back, willing the divine not to leave him just yet, but the muscled longing in me draws him in, filling me and forcing the dolphin's cry from his depths into the light.

"Jesus, Ari, Jeeesus." His neck lengthens and a graceful leap breaks the surface, leaping again and again. He splashes down, floating on me, ocean soaked. "God. What'd you do to me?"

"That was your doing. There's a dolphin been wanting out." I kiss the salt from his forehead. "No wonder you've been so closed up. A boy from the prairie just wouldn't know what that was."

"You are miraculously strange—and astonishingly spectacular, Ari Nor'easter." He drifts on the afternotes of sacred music for long sweet moments before reaching for his jeans

309

crumpled on the floor. He retrieves his wallet and unfolds a hundred-times-folded piece of lined paper.

"Is that the list?"

"You get to cross one off." He releases it to me.

"Which one?"

"You'll know it when you see it."

I turn on the pillow and scan the rows. "Do something reckless?"

"No, I did that idiotic thing all by myself."

I forge on through seven wonders, writing a novel, sky diving, then arrive at it. I read and reread number seventeen thinking it must be something about getting lost in Virginia. "Holy schmoley, Aaron." I sit up. "I deflowered you?"

FIFTY-SIX

Monday morning, Aaron slides the knot up on his tie.

"Better hurry yourself out the door before I rip that shirt off you."

"Tell me this is okay."

"I'm partial to the leather tie."

"No, us."

"In the nest, nothing is bad. It just is."

He picks up his gear. "Grab your pack. I'll drop you at Sabina's."

"No thanks. It's too close to Oakridge. I'm not having Thornton messing up your last couple of weeks at school."

Tuesday, he nimble foots up the metal steps like a horny mountain goat.

Wednesday, I take Mikey to the museum, then back to the nest. "Help me pick the spot for Todd's sea lion." He hangs it close to the dragonfly. I ask, "Where'd you find it?"

"Aaron took me to, like, thirty places. We found it in an aquarium store." We tuck on the bed remembering Todd. "He told me it was you that said he should take care of dogs."

"I did. We'd go over to the Humane Society when the Dick was totally off the rails. One time there was an ad on the board for a vet assistant. I told him treating dogs would be better than sitting around being treated like one."

"He really liked that you came to live with us. He told me."

"Let's make a pact. I'll keep telling you that it's not your fault and you keep telling me that it's not my fault and we'll keep doing that until we both believe it."

"Can we plant a tree for him at Skyfish?"

"How about a dogwood?"

"Yeah." He fastens his twig arms around his stick legs. "I never, ever want to go back to that house."

"We never will. The bank owns it now."

"Where will Ronnie go?"

"Shirley's taking your dad up to Sudbury until his knee gets better. She invited Ronnie to go with."

"Will O'Toole go to jail forever?"

"I have a rule about the nest. Any and all shit stays outside. That way it's always clean and safe. We can talk about anything, but not here."

"That's going to be my rule in my dragonfly nest."

"You hungry?"

"For grilled cheese." We spin Neil Diamond because he

311

was Todd's favourite. I type an essay while Mikey completes his project on dinosaurs. Then we write letters, mine to Jake, Mikey's to Alex. "Can we plant a dogwood tree for Natasha, too?"

"Tell Alex that we'll plant it this summer and he can come see it one day."

"Can I make a party for my mom before we go?"

"Sure."

By the time Aaron arrives at the nest, we've perfected dinosaur pancakes. "Oh, hey, hi, Mikey." He tucks his testosterone and disappointment in his pockets.

"Mikey offered to bolster me through the sadness of missing volleyball tonight."

"It's nice you'll have company since I've a class."

Sitting at a table, eating, talking, listening is akin to medicine. I realize it's been six hours since I popped a pain pill.

Aaron's keys are on the counter. I slide a key onto his ring. "Just in case we're asleep."

"You sure?"

"As sure as I am about anything."

Mikey is asleep on the air mattress and I'm propped on the bed reading *A Place on Earth*, for pleasure, not academics, when Aaron returns. He quiet-steps over Mikey, gives me a kiss and a pastry box. "From Giselle."

"The kiss?"

He shakes his head and heads to the bathroom. The note atop is as sweet as the date squares.

*Ari, we all miss you. Come September we've decided on a Monday night swim. Sonja tore her rotator cuff two years ago and swimming helped her get good movement back.*

*Remember, we play for fun and that's the important thing. Anyway, I'm sure you could play better with one arm than most do with two. See you in September. Be there, or we'll come and get you.*

Aaron, in PJ pants and a black T-shirt, feels normal in this place. I snug up to the wall. He says, "Maybe I should stretch out beside Mikey."

I lift the covers. "I'll behave."

"Don't know if I can."

"Eat a date square. It's almost as filling."

He nestles in. "This, here with you, is the best adventure yet."

"I'm dropping Mikey off at Sabina's after we hand stuff in at school. Will you be home for dinner and maybe a sundae with an Ari on top?"

"Give me that friggin' box." Until this moment, I've never seen Aaron utter a word with his mouth full. "Get comfy and I'll read to you."

On Thursday, Aaron comes home later than usual, showers 'til the hot water runs out and doesn't ask for the sundae.

"What's wrong?"

He crumples on the chair. "Belle. She's really upset."

"Why?"

"She came to my room after school and asked straight out if I . . . if we . . ."

"You told her?"

"Jeff mentioned I wasn't staying at his place anymore. Guess my face told her the rest. She . . . slapped me."

"What?"

"Said she thought I was different from the rest of the pigs. She's right. I know what you've lived. I should've been the one man that didn't take from you."

"Don't. Don't you dare try to be a father to me." I move to the counter, slicing onions with the biggest knife I have. "And don't make her propriety or your guilt mine."

He sighs into his hands. "I've always known this was wrong."

"You're not dumping your shalt nots on me. This is the rightest I felt since Jake left. I love you as a boyfriend. I love the loving and," I wipe my nose on my sleeve. "I need the holding." He walks 'round the counter, takes the knife from my hand, and hushes my hair. "Don't leave me, Aaron. Not yet. Please."

"I couldn't, even if I believed I should."

Midnight, I slip out of the knot of arms and legs and stretch the phone to the stoop. I wake Auntie Mary and sigh. "Why does knowing me wreck things?"

"What's wrong?"

"Belle hates Aaron for loving me. Aaron feels like shit."

"He's becoming his own man, and it's about bloody time. Get some sleep, then make them talk things out."


Friday, I open the door, recognizing Mr. Lukeman's shape on the other side of the knock. "Hello, Ari Joy Zajac."

"A lawyer making a house call. This can't be good."

"Had business with Bernie and thought I'd stop up and see why you're avoiding me." He sets down his briefcase. "So, why haven't you returned my calls?"

"One, because you want to give me Len's money. And two, you're going to tell me that I have to relive all this horror in open court."

"What I most want to give you is this." He hands over an envelope. "Your new name, legal and official, from A to J to Z. You are Appleton-free. And more good news: O'Toole's pleading guilty on the murder charge in return for protective custody. So, no trial."

"Did he turn on the Dick? Snake?"

His head shakes in the negative. "Serves him best to keep every ally he's got. I did meet with Irwin. Extinguished every last hope he had for a payout. God, he's pathetic."

"Can you believe my mum screwed over Len for him?"

"No. Speaking of which." He sneakily slips in a portfolio. "I know Len's money has caused so much turmoil but that's behind you now and—"

"I don't want it. It's blood money."

"Best way to get the blood off it is do some good with it." The math in my head says ninety-eight thousand, minus three thousand a year for four years, minus lawyer fees, leaves maybe fifty thousand dollars. He shows me a page with the bottom line of ten thousand six hundred dollars. "Ari, would you like me to continue administering it for you?"

"Um, how much does university cost?"

"There's more than enough for a PhD if you want."

"I want enough for Mikey to become an astrophysicist."

"You let me continue to invest this and there'll be money for his schooling. This is your time to rest, free from worries. I'll be in touch."

I watch him down the stairs while Aaron gathers the papers. "This is amazing, Ari. A hundred thousand will go a long way to caring for a hundred Mikeys."

"What?" I tilt the papers and the one hundred and six thousand registers. "How?" I fly down the steps. "Mr. Lukeman, how's there more than we started with?"

"Good market. Great investment advice."

"Do I pay you enough?"

"Nia's a good friend and you're the most entertaining client I have."

"Wish all kids with twisted messes could have a lawyer like you."

Saturday, Aaron checks another knock, paling at Belle's outline through the curtain. "Why's she here?"

"I asked her to come."

I never realized how loud my clock tick-tocks until we all sit staring at the floorboards for two hundred and seventeen seconds. "Sooo, Belle, before we start dissecting how disappointed you are in Aaron, let me first say that he has never been a father figure to me. I've always had rescuers, lucky, lucky kid that I am, but I've only ever had one counterbalance. Aaron's always been the one solid person equalizing all my chaos with goodness. He's not taking advantage. There's no improperness."

Her head wobbles in the direction of no.

"For ten months, he was my teacher. For forty-eight months after that, he's been my friend. Please. For pity sake, math has to be on my side for once."

"It's not right."

"Aaron officially resigned as a teacher two weeks ago. If I thought this would wreck his career, I would've gone home with Mary. He doesn't belong in a brick building. He needs open water."

"It's not right for you."

"Tell me what about my life is right? There're so many corpses, I don't know how to navigate life. I can't reconcile that first love for Natasha ended in death. And sex? My father so scrambled the rightness of it that I don't know how to rewrite it. It's like reading Rumi without translation from the Persian. And presently my last dance is so mixed up there's no hope of him screwing anything straight."

They both bite back a smile.

"Tell me, Belle, who better to heal that part of me than Aaron? What better man on this earth is there?"

She looks at my face.

"Don't hate him for loving me. It's breaking his heart and mine."

She chews the inside of her cheek.

"Besides, think of him. If I don't teach him a thing or two, he's going to end up with some mouse named Sister Beulah who wears a girdle and an unremovable brassiere under her nightie."

Weights shift in the room.

"Will you stay for supper?"

"I suppose."

## FIFTY-SEVEN

As promised, Mikey's mom is waiting on the sidewalk. She struggles with the door to the jeep. "You have a car?"

"Belongs to a friend."

"Where're we going?"

"When's the last time you treated yourself to the hairdressers?"

"Gosh, before Mikey was born."

I work on a book report while Francine conjures a Doris Day 'do on Laura. Her gum snaps as she scans her makeup sample kit. "Now, for a little colour." She blushes up Laura's cheeks and swipes her eyelashes with mascara, then rummages for a tiny tube of lipstick. "Here it is, Angel Kiss. Perfect for your colouring."

"You look like a million bucks, Laura. Let's up it with new threads."

I drive her to the boutique and she hesitates at the door. "This is too swanky for me, Ari."

"My aunt wants to meet you."

Sabina hurries over, warmly welcoming Laura. "So happy to finally meet the mother of such a wonderful boy."

"You know my Mikey?"

"He's good friends with my sons."

"This your store?"

"Yes, and I have something that will look stunning on you." Sabina picks a brown suit, polyester for easy care but beautifully made, and a teal blouse.

"Oh, it's so fine. I couldn't."

Sabina says, "Please. I can't afford to pay Ari for all the stock she makes for me. This reduces my debt, a little."

If I worked night and day for twenty years, I could never re-pay this family for what it's done for me and Mikey. "How about you give us a taste of whatever smells so good and we'll be even."

We head up the stairs to the table set with the fanciest dish-es. Mikey jump-jump-jumps, more animated than I've seen him since Todd's death. "Happy birthday!"

"Mikey? Oh, my goodness. My goodness. What's this?" Laura's hug is shaky. "My birthday's in August."

"But I always miss it. Aaron and me made cake."

She lifts her head to the counter. "You're Aaron?" He nods. "Thank you. Really, thank you."

"All Mikey's idea."

When I drive her home, she fingers the new locket around her neck. "I know it's all them folk from your way that's made Mikey the boy he is."

"You have, too, Laura."

"If only I could shake this. For good like. Then I could care for him like should be done."

"You have the number for Springwood."

"I'll go this time. I will. These folks where he's going will take care of him, right?"

"You've not a single worry he'll be loved in the most nurturing place on Earth."

"I never had nothin' like that. Left home when I was fifteen to get away from my stepdaddy. Never had no princess life like that girl who died." She blink-blink-blinks, her eyelash catching a tear. "But my boy made me feel like a queen today. You hear him say he wants to be a rocket scientist? He's smart, eh?"

"He's one special kid."

"If he sticks with me, his lot will be baggin' groceries at best. And with that father of his, soon enough he'd turn mean. Dick wasn't always so off his temper, you know. He worked good. Never missed a shift. Don't know how that upstart, O'Toole, got him so wrapped around his little pinkie. The O'Tooles lived on my street growin' up, did you know that?"

"I didn't."

"His daddy was so nice, always buying us treats from the Good Humor truck. Never heard him yellin', not like my daddy. O'Toole was two years ahead of me in school. Oh, did the girls hang off him. Everyone did. Got so big of himself, he lost himself."

"That's a gem of an insight, Laura. Mikey gets more of his smarts from you than you give yourself credit for."

"Pish-posh. Ain't got a brain in my head. You'll bring him back on school breaks like you said?"

"Promise. And when you're ready, I'll take you east to see him."

"You mean it? I ain't never had a holiday."

"Mikey can't wait for all the Cove to meet you."

"Tell him I'm letting him go because I know it's best for him right now."

"Every day."

"Let me off here." She shimmies her shoulders after stepping out. "I want to show off the new me. Bye. Keep our boy safe."

I merge into traffic, reluctantly turning right until I'm on crapstreet. There is a metal bin on the craphouse lawn, plywood over the front window, and workmen pitching out the toxic waste of Dick Irwin's life. Poking out of the top of the bin is Cunt's cage, Mum's party skirt still atop.

I head to the cemetery, placing dog treats on Todd's grave, hoping some gentle creatures will come and visit. "I'm so sorry, Todd. I miss you more than I have words to say."

FIFTY-EIGHT

I love how sex surges over the absences in my life. I soak up the escape in it, letting the bed become my ocean. Aaron and I barely make it to shore for sustenance from mid-June to end.

The fan skims our post-rapture, stripped-bare skin as we pillow talk. He sighs. "Can I stay here next week and feed your fish?"

"One, the fish are made of clay and two, you need to find equilibrium with your parents before heading south."

"They won't accept this."

"You're nearing twenty-eight, man. What's happening between us doesn't have to be confessed. Just go and be their son and love them like you do."

"They'll see the sin written all over my face."

My body tucks to a sit. "You think we're sin?"

"I didn't say that. But having sex outside of marriage is my parents' definition of sin."

"So . . . this would be the thing that makes me bad in their eyes?"

"It's a big thing with them."

"Your mom sent a letter after I toppled ByBillyBob into the great beyond, full of blather about forgiveness and another after I put Todd in the path of a fatal bullet. I'm innocent in those things and wicked for loving you?" I pull the afghan around my naked self. "Please don't tell them. Having Belle disapproving just about beached Ori."

"Ori?"

"Your dolphin. The middle of 'glorious.' Kind of like us, don't you think?"

"I know that we, us, are the middle. If things work out this summer for you and Jake, don't hesitate, not for a minute, to do what you need to do for you."

"Dalhousie is lost for me, but I hold a filament of hope that Jake will find his way there." I finger his good face. "If Jake turns about, I will turn with him."

"I know. I do know that."

"Wherever I land, this place is still yours for the year."

"Go home knowing that I'm not hiding this from my parents. I'm not hiding us from anyone, and if one day I find there's a god and he judges me for having completely loved someone, then he's not anyone I'd want to hang with for eternity." He kisses the smile on my lips. "I'll call in August and you can let me know if I should bring Zodiac back with me."

"Holy dog. It's safe for him now, isn't it."

## FIFTY-NINE

Her name isn't Lucy, it's Muriel. I bring her a coffee, four sugars, two cream. "Hi, Muriel. Tino in?"

"Let me check, hon." Her nail spears the button on the phone, then red lips wax wide. "Mr. C. says go right in."

Tino stands. "Hey, kitten. How's the foot?"

"Not so bad. It's the situation of having worn my arm backwards that's giving me trouble." I unload a pastry box on his desk. "Thanks for not murdering the Dick."

"You have too big a heart."

"I just figure scaring the shit out of him for the rest of his days has it over a quick end. Besides, Mikey has plotted the Dick's death so much, I worry the actuality would be too much with his current guilt-load."

"I got eyes on him in Sudbury and we made a little deal. Knocked ten thou off his marker, he agreed to stay the hell away from you."

"Wow. You are a softie."

"What are the chances I'm going to see jack-shit of what he owes? This way we have control." He polishes off a second cream puff in two bites. "These are gold. I could make Sabina a rich woman."

"She already is."

"The kid with her?"

"Until school lets out."

"Let me know if you need anything. Anything at all."

"You already gave me something."

"What's that?"

"A string of words. So much better for this girl than sapphires."

"Words?"

"Did you know your first name means gift and your last means steadfast?" He seesaws his head in a yes/no. "I think you're poetic in your own way. Unlikely heroes make great characters for a book."

He makes more room for ego by loosening his tie. "You don't say."

I place "Constant Gift" on his blotter. "Save a spot for me on your September dance card."

*Weighty work waits*
*while they midnight dance.*
*Muscle in him knows*
*feet step best when heart is light*
*when right turn, balances left.*
*He dances*
*in hidden rooms. She knows.*

*Falling moon melts silver into dawn*
*spilling through a now-windowed space.*
*Light waking waits*
*for his day dance*
*and she knows*
*each sunrise is a constant gift.*

*Tino: This potter knows good clay. Ari.*

## SIXTY

The rhythm of the train pounds out, "And the beat goes on, and the heart grows strong . . ."

William Walrus slows as he walks the aisle. There's softness in the way he leans over the seat. He opens his palm. "So sorry about your mother and big brother, little miss."

From the pouch, I give him two cents. "Mikey tell you?"

"Old William sees things, you know that."

"Tell me what you see?"

His hand remains open for another penny. "I see you got broken, but not beyond repair."

"I feel an utter ruin, William."

"You know what happens to wrecks in the ocean? They become a reef, a refuge teeming with life. But only with time. Stay open. Rest in your ocean."

"How do I do that when Jake is at war with it?"

"Never met a war that didn't end in peace." He waits for another penny.

"So, William, last year, Nat and BS cost me only two pennies and this year's a four on the Richter scale?"

"By my counts, it's a five."

I flick fingers. "Jake, Todd, Mum, my scholarship, and . . . ?"

"Fighting for Mikey's freedom is, I suspect, the heaviest penny you'll ever spend."

I unload the seventh penny. "So, I'm just three pennies from home?"

"Old William sees good ahead. Now, let it all go and just take care of your own self." He winks. "Say you will."

"Could I start by getting some ice?"

"Shoulder makin' a fuss?"

"Did Mikey blather everything?"

"Dragonflies never tell secrets. I'll be back in a whisk with that ice."

*This is too weird. Jasper, I know you're my imagination. And William's not really possessed by a walrus.*

*Do you know for sure that parallel universes don't exist?*

*Quiet. Now my head's aching, too.*


*I can't face them.* Jasper pushes me toward the Butters' house. The Missus runs out for a hug before I make it through the gate. Inside is eerily quiet. Two fosters nap. Four are berry picking with Mikey. I rock a baby while the Missus stirs a foul-smelling concoction. "Spits out the trouble."

"I betrayed Jake."

"Someone warming the lonely spaces?"

I nod.

"Women likes us have needs." She spoons gloop into a gauzy bag.

"Us?"

"The stormy years landed me in some tangles, both sweet and thorny. Messes of my own doing and those blown in by the winds. Now, puts the baby in the cot and takes off your shirt." I comply and she secures a poultice with what looks like an old girdle reconfigured into a shoulder brace.

My shoulder throbs, warms, tingles, settles, the stink transmuting to cucumber-mint. "This year was worse than last. I'm more bewildered than ever on how to piece my life together."

"You was caught in the Irwin's quake and Jake's earth split. You can only work with your own rubble. That's all anyone can dos."

"You can't possibly mean there's a worse breaking coming to me."

She laughs like a happy bird. "Heavens no. It'll be a teeny splinter. You've been through so many doozies, I worry you'll miss it."

"There's not enough gold to fill the chasms I've got. I'll happily miss a tiny crack."

"It's nicer sittin' without a sliver in your bum." Her floury hands dust my face, thumb printing the tiny scar on my cheek. The memoried pain caused by that micro fleck of rock rushes back. "No worries, lamb. Everything will turn right with Jake."

"Huey forgave you when he found out about someone warming the lonely spaces?"

"Asks him."


Huey's shoulders bend like a sunflower in heavy bloom and I worry he'll break under the weight. "You hear from Jake?" I ask.

"Through the Captain. He says, even one-handed, Jake beats two men."

"Is he drinking?"

"Yep." Huey's laugh is sour. "Cap says he's never seen a man who hated it more."

"What can I do? He never answers my letters."

"He reads them. And Cap says his nose is forever in a book. There's big hope in that."

"Do you know much about building houses?"

"Why would you be wantin' that, dolly?"

"I'm feeling a strong need for a solid house of my own."

"You haven't given up on my boy?"

"He's my last dance, Huey. Will he forgive me for not sitting out a middle one?"

"Alls I know is fear of losing the finest woman on this earth woke me up, got me moving back to home. You have a hammer?"

"Doesn't every girl?"

"Let's get started, then." I tuck my hand in his as we walk the rocky cliff. He asks, "What is it you call this piece again?"

"Moondance."

"That has a big hope to it, doesn't it, dolly."


Hard mornings give way to solid summer days and soft nights. In my cedar-scented room, I age back hearing, "You're a good girl and nothing that happened was ever your fault."

*What is my fault, Jasper?*

The deer gather outside my window. I join them, letting the day rise in my bones. I feel the breath from a doe's velvety nose as she plucks an apple from my hand. "You know, girl, it's Todd I can't bear. He came down those stairs to fight for me."

"Yes, he did." I turn to Nia standing in the new light. "And there's the biggest treasure yet."

"There's no treasure in it, Auntie."

"It's the crown jewel." She perches on the picnic table. "Learning that you can't control or fix everything and, the biggest gem, compassion for yourself for being imperfect. Imperfections are the sweet spots, the openings where life gets in and love gets out."

"Todd had such a beautiful heart."

"There's nothing, nothing that can change what happened. So, what are you going to do with the force of that reality? Since coming home, you've turned perfect pot after perfect pot. That seems a bit of a lie."

"My wrist hurts and my shoulder never stops aching. My body won't let me into my crazy-making space."

"Does the brace help?"

"Some, but it throws off the spin. What really helps is weed."

"Caution, miss."

"Yeah. Seeing what Mum did to herself . . . it scares the shit out of me what I could become."

"Know how I define DNA? Do not assume. Don't assume you're destined to become your mum and dad. And never assume you're immune from becoming them."

"How, when everything is so utterly wrecked, do I sort myself?"

"By paying attention to the moment you're in." Nia's hand gentling my hair is a perfect present. "How about we work on something together? I can be your shoulder when needs be. What's Jasper got in mind?"

"A sea lion."

"What medium do you fancy?"

"Don't know. Something light, pieced together."

"Let's go see what the ocean's left for us." Dew shimmers as deer startle away through the treeline. "Will you be planting a tree for your mum?"

"Haven't decided."

"Consider it. Talking to a tree is good. Yelling at one's even better."

"Maybe I'll put a hawthorn over by daddy's linden." Along the shore, I gather bits of driftwood. "Will these split if I put holes in them?"

"Not if you use a fine drill."

"What glue holds best?"

"I've a polyvinyl that weathers any weather." I stand on a big cache of gnarled wood. Nia asks, "What're you seeing?"

"Bones, feathers, scales, necks, wings, arms, heads, bellies, hair . . ."

"You see sea lion bones?"

"Not yet. But I spot a seahorse snout."

"Pile up what you want and we'll send the boys down to collect them."

"Jake always did that for me. I miss him so much."

"Me, too."

"Have you talked?"

"Mary and I tracked him down after we came back from seeing you. He was shaken something terrible over what happened."

"I was sure he'd come."

"He's trapped in that same terrible thinking—that he's the root of everything that's wrong."

"Will he come home at all this summer?"

"He has his whole history to untangle and rewrite." We fill the bucket with what I imagine could be eagle feathers. "For now, just let your mind rest and your body heal."

"That's pretty much what the Walrus said. Should I go back to Toronto in September?"

"No need to decide any of that now, but it's a good option. There's no boy more solid for you right now than Aaron."

"This is going to hurt Jake so much."

"Don't fret away this day worrying about ever after." Nia tucks the seahorse snout under one arm and tugs me with the other. "I have to admit, though, I worry about your next year."

"Frig. You and the Missus? What's coming now?"

"You're overdue for a dirt year."

"A what?"

"Every seventh year, the field lies fallow and replenishes. No toiling, no loss, just a quiet rebuilding."

"Sounds spectacular."

"Peacetime is tough for those who have known war for so long. Most think that's where the story ends."

A curve of wood with a knotty hole catches my imagination. "Look, it's an eye. Jasper's eye."

"Why, that biggity bugger wants us to start with him."

"Does the bear in you really believe Jake will find his way home?"

"He's as certain as I am of Mary having breakfast ready." She whistles for the dogs and turns toward home.

It takes two weeks to gather sea lion makings. While waiting, I explore my new medium, puzzling together driftwood eagles, seahorses, a variety of fish and wind chimes, some with dragonflies, others with turtles. Bits of sea glass add sparkle and colour.

Nia rigged a pulley from the workroom rafters, so my creations raise and lower and I never have to lift my arm higher than mid-chest. The sea lion has grown as tall as me and fatter than a fridge.

Mikey and his crew scour the shore. Today they have a driftwood cache riddled with holes, maybe from nails or worms, several resembling misshapen tears. I lift one to the light. *It's a dragonfly wing.* Mikey winks a smile and runs toward more discovery.

It's not unusual for customers to watch. There's something hopeful about debris being pieced into something. A little girl asks, "Could you do a giraffe?"

"If the parts ever wash up on the shore, I'll put it together."

The mother asks Mary to add an Ari-Fairy clay chime to her order. "I love the look of the driftwood ones but the sound of these is prettier."

I wrap her purchases. "You've just given me an idea to blend the two."

"Oh, could you do that? We're heading out whale watching. I could come back."

"I'll give it a go." As the newspaper curls around the mug, the words in a headline pop. "Oh no, Jim Morrison died?"

"Weeks ago. Drug overdose, I believe. You mind if I pick these up when I come back for the chimes?"

"They'll be behind the counter."

I've no idea who I'm crying for as I fasten ceramic sea shapes to driftwood dragonflies. Mary says, "I'll finish this. Go take a break."

One, maybe two hours later, Nia finds me in the summer house. She folds like a yogi at the end of the bed, legs bending like she's half her fifty-some years. "Life really is just one damn thing after another, isn't it?"

"Morrison sent me a postcard from Paris, thanking me for the boots. Said he fell asleep with them on and woke to stars falling from my hair." I scratch Spinner's silky ear. "Why does his dying have more of a wallop than Mum's?"

"Maybe because he was a creative soul or because you'd already grieved your mum for eighteen years."

"I miss her. How crazy is that?"

"It's like an amputation of a gangrenous toe. You're healthier with it gone, but there's an empty space and your balance is thrown off." Nia's paleness is lit by sun. Her uniform is jeans, so faded they near milk, and a white shirt, clean and pressed. Her hair, colourless and ponytailed, has a defiant flip. Even with all this ethereal light, to me she's mother earth, rock solid.

"Do you think meeting me jinxed Morrison?"

"Get over yourself, Hariet Appleton. You're not that powerful, or that important." Spinner's tail thump, thump, thumps against the quilt as if applauding. "And if you persist in thinking you're a bad seed, those thoughts will root into belief, grow into conviction, then to condemnation. You'll look back and discover you've abandoned truth for a pile of horseshit."

"How do I get to where you are?"

"You start by rooting out that arrogance that you have the most fucked-up life. Just circle this cove, look through the windows, and know how bloody blessed you are."

"I just have to look right in front of me." I know Nia's mum and sister didn't survive childbirth, her aunt was a spare-the-rod-spoil-the-child tyrant, her uncle raped her night upon night, and hiding her love for Mary is the only way the world accepts her.

"Then damn well see that I'm not a victim of my past or my circumstances."

"Do you forgive your uncle for what he did to you?"

"I forgive myself for not being strong enough to stop him. But he's just a severed gangrenous toe."

"That's pretty much how the J's dispose of Daddy."

"And you?"

"Honestly, I don't know how to reconcile how utterly I despise him with how I adored him. Or sort the way he was with me, both the sweet and bitter of it." *Such precious little hands. Touch Daddy nice.* My hand leaves Spinner's soft fur and pulls at the ache in my shoulder. "I'm, I don't know, ungathered. Mum's dead. O'Toole's caged. The Dick's defeated. Mikey's safe. Aaron loves me. I'm here and can stay as long as I want and I feel farther from myself, from knowing anything, than I ever have."

"Imagine how it felt after the wars. The ecstasy of victory. The relief and absence of fear. Then looking around and seeing the destruction. Sons, husbands, daughters, family, and friends, gone. Art and architecture reduced to rubble. And what did they do?"

"Raged?"

"They picked up one stone and placed it on the next."

Spinner sits, ears peaked, hearing Mary pulling the rusty-wheeled wagon down the path. As the sun slips into the ocean, lanterns are lit and a supper picnic is spread on the bed. Mary says, "Huey and Mikey dropped off a load. You've enough driftwood to make a whale. What is it you see in this lot?"

"Won't know until I pick up one piece and place it on the next."

"He also said the roof trusses will be delivered tomorrow. You're moving ahead on the house?"

"I am, Auntie. I am for me."

## SIXTY-ONE

On the shore, great silences fold into the crashing of the waves and Mikey, running like a stallion in the surf, has joy tripping at his heels. Mary asks, "What'd he call his pup?"

"TV, for Todd Victor. A dog named after him would delight Todd." My head finds the sweet hollow of her shoulder. "I'm trying, Auntie, but I can't get his blood off my hands."

"What a waste that'd be. Let it colour what you do. You ever noticed how I reach for the crimson glazes?"

"What wrong could there possibly be on your hands?"

"The rescued seldom sees the flaws in the rescuer. I often wonder how different your life might've been if I'd been kinder to your mum growing up."

"You're the definition of kind."

"The magic of kintsugi, my girl." I lean into her gentle kneading of my shoulder. "Until Theresa came along, I was daddy's girl. We'd tinker on broken radios or go on hikes searching for fossils. Your mum was shockingly beautiful, gifted, too. I hated, hated, *hated* how Grandpa lit up when she entered a room. Did everything I could to keep her out." I study the small lines around Mary's eyes, iceberg scars running deep below the skin. "Theresa found a trilobite fossil once on holidays. A perfect specimen of something I can only describe as an ancient sea beetle. I snatched it, ran back to the campsite claiming I'd found it." Mary stands, offering me a hand up. "We were eight and ten that summer. Instead of telling on me, she smashed Grandpa's cherished ivory pipe, said she saw me do it. My act started a crack that, no matter what I did, spidered into more."

All my life I've known Mary as creator. Mary as savior. It's stabilizing, walking side by side with Mary, lump of clay. "You can't fix another person's fault lines."

"But I—"

"Come on. Mum was suspended from kindergarten for chronic meanness. She had a piranha in her. If you'd given her an opening, she'd have moved in and consumed everything, then she'd have shat you out."

"Still—"

"Listen here, ma'am, there was nothing as messed up as the sister competition with the Appletons. 'Pick me.' 'Screw me.' 'No, me, Daddy, me.'" I bolster Mary's shoulders for a change. "None of us blames the other. We just made what we could out of it."

"When'd you get this wise?"

"Oh, as if you don't know, great mother of the universe." An ancient Wabi and an arthritic Cork welcome us with tail thumps. I fall to my knees and give thanks to the guardians at the gate. *What a place for a dog and a boy to live, eh, Ari.*

*Shut the frig up.*

"Aaron called again." Nia looks up from her bench, searching my face. "Didn't you call him back?"

"No."

"Everything okay?"

"There're just some words I don't want to hear come out of my mouth."

"Ari, don't tell me you're ending this. You need each other next year."

"Not him, Auntie. Jake won't or can't be with me right now and I plain don't want to be alone. I'm going back for a dirt year."

"Are you going to show us what's had you locked in the workroom before you do?"

"It's almost done." I pick up the phone and dial Aaron.

"Hello?" His voice gives my heart purchase. "Ari?"

"Sorry I didn't call."

"I heard there was a hurricane. Did you have much damage?"

"Maritimers are used to big blows and I got a treasure trove of driftwood from it."

"Jake okay?"

"Huey got word he was battened down in a safe harbour." Him asking about Jake makes my two-timing feel more like a threesome. "You at your parents?"

"Yep. Landed Tuesday."

"Good adventures?"

"Amazing."

"What's Zodiac doing right now?"

"He's tired from his walk. He's in between my mom and dad on the glider."

"You absolutely have to bring me a picture of that. Tell him he's the best dog on Mother God's earth and I love him."

"What're you saying?"

"How can I lock him alone in an attic all day when he could be chasing butterflies?"

"You sure?"

My words waver between longing and knowing that letting go is sometimes the best way to love. "Resolved."

"Dad said Mom's been crying all week."

"Yeah, he's that kind of dog. I'm going to need a mountain of comforting to numb this pain."

"I'll be there for you."

"Your sails are rising right now, aren't they?"

"See you in two weeks."

"Barring mayhem."

All my Skyfish summers have ended with a down-home party at Skyfish. This year the fiddles sleep. Huey and three strapping lads help me install Mikey's surprise out by the newly planted dogwood trees. We cover it with a sheet and head inside. The gallery's great room is a high-raftered expanse. Huey asks, "Shall we put it smack in the middle?"

"No. The floor needs to be open for when the dances start up again. The windowed corner, I think."

The guys roll a giant slab of polished cedar into the corner. Seven pieces of precisely placed rebar stick up, waiting. The mummy-wrapped sculpture is positioned on designated spikes. The bars disappear and the piece stands rock solid. I give them each five bucks and Rusty complains, "Don't we get to see it?"

"Not before Mary and Nia."

They leave and Huey helps me unwind the wrap. "How'd that load of spit-up wood become this?"

"Piece by piece."

The assembled driftwood is clearly two women, shoulder to shoulder, joyfully lifted by an ocean breeze. Rooty curls of hair flow from one. The other's hair is a wind-blown ponytail. Every wood sinew is live with motion and, most beautiful, every crack is veined with bronze. One uplifted arm has a quarter-inch split studded with garnet chips and on the outstretched palm is a lump of clay.

From base to fingertip, it's maybe ten feet. Huey shakes his head. "I'd say they're dancing, but it's bigger than that."

"They're creating."

"Let's gather everyone before light's gone."

Mikey verges on tears as he takes in the funky sea lion, nose lifted to commune with a dragonfly. TV pads over, lifts his leg, and christens it. Mikey laughs and cries in the same breath. "Todd loves this. He does."

"Right he does." Huey picks Mikey up, easy as a dime, easing the hurt with a mauling hug. "Now, let's see what else we can see."

I knew Mary and Nia wouldn't burden me with tears. Their joy is electric and birthing with new ideas. "Do you have its name?"

"Earth mothers."

## SIXTY-TWO

Are dirt years counted in acres? Fields? Plots, perhaps. Plot, meaning a small piece of land. Plot meaning a storyline.

*With how shit follows us, I'd say plot, a nefarious scheme.*

*I have a year off, remember.*

I'm content in this small attic. Aaron studying while I sort through Babcia's box of Zajac history. I read her journals, a life spanning two world wars, her losses equalling millions, compared to my ten pennies' worth. On a card she writes:

> *Dear one: Jacquie told me you worry your pen cannot tell the Zajac journey with justice. As I near the end of my days, I can say, corka, there is little justice in this world, but there is great hope. Tell our story, that my brother, Ignatius, and my precious Leonek, your papa, will be known. I remember your delight at Iggy's quotes to you. Begin with this one from me, Aurelia Zajac: history defines what we live, but it does not decide how we live. The ending is up to you.*

I dig in, unearthing treasures, learning that after the war, Len shovelled through ruins to find the assets the Zajacs hid before the invasion. With them he procured sacks of flour, chickens, whatever else was needed to bake bread. From the rubble he cleaned bricks, built an oven, and opened a bakery, knowing bread was worth gold, jewels, art . . .

*Huh, would've imagined Len finding desperate souls and giving away food.*

*Why do I feel more balanced knowing he grabbed all the dragon plunder he could and got his family here, Jasper?*

*Because cracked pots are more beautiful than perfect ones.*

I sit at the old Underwood, tapping out the Zajac story until Aaron's restless dolphin needs open water. We swim. Meet friends at the pub. Hike. Days, weeks, months stretch like sweet taffy. Then the calendar turns to June.


The Dick's blue sedan sits outside Jarvis with Ronnie stuffed behind the wheel in a pink velour track suit. Everything about the Dick is smaller, except for his nose. He leans out the window. "Where's Mikey at?"

I remain an arm's grab distance from the car. "Why?"

"Laura and me's givin' it another go."

"Laura and—pardon?"

"Got a place over on Shuter. Mikey belongs with us."

"I'll send him to Australia before I let the two of you use him up."

"Your nose got no place in our business no more."

I bend. "Hi, Ronnie." Her complexion is gray as smoke and her hair is a matted nest. "Where're you staying?"

"Here and there. Was living with Carmie O'Toole for a time, watchin' her kids."

"How are they?"

"Went into care."

"Them poor kids is without a father because of you." The Dick's face prunes up, exactly like his father's. "You're poison. One way or another, Mikey's coming home." His hand smacks the car in a let's go command and Ronnie pulls away.

I head to Sam Lukeman. He reassures. "There's nothing to worry about. Everything goes through me. They don't know Mikey's address and the courts would never—"

"Sure they would. They're his biological mum and dad."

"They can't look after themselves. Why would they want a kid?"

"Likely want his liver."

"Did Laura see Mikey at Christmas?"

"No. She cashed in the ticket."

"Poor kid."

"Mary and Nia brought him to Quebec. Aaron and Ellis organized a ski holiday. He had a blast." I stretch out of the chair. "I'm just giving you a heads-up, so they don't slip anything by you before I get things sorted."

I head to Tino, a more hands-on, helpful kind of friend. "You want I should kill him?"

"Tempting, but . . ." I give him a photograph. "This is my Uncle Iggy. He was murdered in a robbery on the Danforth in 1968. I know the Dick set it up. Figure you can find things out better than cops ever could."

"If the goods are out there, I'll get 'em."

"Thanks, Tino. You up for dancing this weekend?"

"You bringing that cowboy again?"

"Be nice."

"He's okay, but can't dance worth shit." He pinches my cheek. "Bring along Ellis and his lady, though."


Aaron drives me to the basement apartment on Shuter. We sit, waiting for the Dick to go and get tanked. On cue, he struggles along the walk with two silver canes, then slides straight-legged into the car.

"Geezus, how does he drive?"

"On ethanol."

We venture into a different place, same shit, especially the familiar craphouse stink. Laura welcomes the sugared coffee and iced doughnuts we bring. Her first words are "I'm clean. I swear."

"That's good, Laura. Mikey will be proud of you."

"I need him with me, Ari."

"He's happy. Settled in school. I asked him. He loves you but he doesn't want to live here."

"We need him. I can hardly see straight with these headaches and Dick can barely get around."

"Is this really what you want for him? Running to get you smokes and the Dick a bottle? For god's sake, Laura, mother up, for once in your life."

Her head bobbles. "I'll talk to Dick. Can you spare a ten 'til the cheques come?"

I take eighty-five from my pocket, hoping it's enough to kill her and the Dick.

SIXTY-THREE

Aaron lifts his head from the pillow to me packing lunches. "What time's it?"

"Five thirty. Get up."

He leaps like Zodiac at the possibility of a ramble. "Where're we going? What're we doing?"

"You're bloody exhausting. You know that, don't you?" I top the thermos with coffee. "Just hope Mina and I don't kill you and Ellis today."

As we drive north, Ellis asks, "What're you two up to?"

Mina says, "Ari and I discovered that you and Aaron have the same wish and Aaron's graduation warrants a big celebration."

I check to make sure I haven't made a disastrous miscalculation. "Are all the things on the list stuff you really want to do or were you just pulling ideas out of thin water?"

"Everything came out of dolphin jumps, though at the time I didn't know what they were."

As Mina pulls down a drive, little planes and a silver half moon building come into view. "Here're your lunches. We'll be back at three to catch it on film."

"Skydiving?" We hardly get a kiss before they fly away.

Later, watching them tumble toward earth, I see first what I always see, Jake falling, his brilliance pickling with the herring, his sweetness turning to salt in the gray ocean. Aaron's shoot opens and I imagine what he feels floating down into a world saturated with spring and I get why someone might want to jump—*ah, no, I don't.*

*Me either.*

I expect Aaron's four a.m. restlessness to have him nuzzling in, hoping for more graduation sex; instead I hear him slip out of the nest. Five a.m., I join him on the stoop. His face is lifted to the black sky, remaining there as he settles back against me. "You know that Lennon song, 'Imagine'?"

"Yeah."

"I lived that yesterday. Up there, I imagined one world, no religion, peace."

My arms circle him. His heart beats under my hand and I know this nest won't hold him, nor should it. "Oh, Aaron West, you are a dreamer."

"Am I the only one?"

"About skydiving you are."

"How do I let go of this?" His fingers tangle with mine. "Of you?"

341

"I'll stay with you through summer if you want."

"You mean it?"

"Pick something on that list of yours and we'll cross it off together."



June end, we drive my very own little truck to Pleasant Cove. The setting sun spills dragon treasure along the coast. So many times, Aaron was here in my dreams, now his knee beneath my hand feels less permanent than the ribbons of fog retreating to the ocean.

Late day, Nia drops us at the ferry in North Sydney. My eyes adjust to a man on the bench, reading *Walden*. I walk over. "William? What're you doing here?"

"Meetin' an old friend." He stands up, smiles wide. "There's something us shore creatures love about dolphins, eh, little miss." He tips his hat to Aaron. "Quite the feat, diving into the Atlantic to surface in the Pacific."

Aaron flubbers. "How . . . but . . . I . . ."

I push him past his bewilderment. "Don't try to figure it. Walruses know secrets." We board a ferry that's more a floating hotel. "This is number twenty-one on the list?"

"A step toward it."

Waiting for us in Newfoundland with Aaron's jeep is Libby, my favourite person from his study group. "Please don't tell me it's a threesome. I really like Libby and I think lesbians are the best thing ever created, but I'm not up to it."

"This is Libby's hometown. Her driving the jeep home was a win-win."

"Knew I liked that girl. There's more east in her than in me." Libby's natural beauty, inside and out, makes khaki shorts and steel-toed hikers look better than a red carpet occasion, and Aaron, so true and straight, doesn't see a speck how much she loves him.

342

Her dad pours over maps with Aaron while Libby shows me her shore. Jasper says, *She's a dolphin.*

*Shut the frig up. This storm hasn't blown itself out.* "So, Libby, what're you doing with your shiny new degree?"

"Got offered VP here but the thought of staying makes me crazy. My dad says it comes from giving me the name Liberty."

"Your name's Liberty?"

"Yep. I'm thinking of taking a post in Labrador."

*Ask her, ask her, ask her.*

*Shut your snout.*

Aaron collects me and hugs her. "Thanks for everything. I'm sure going to miss you."

Jasper weedles until I say, "Tell Libby she should check out teaching in Peru before deciding on the Great North."

"Oh, it'd be great having a friend there. Would you come and check it out?"

She looks at me, eyes as wide as a kid face to face with a wish-granting Ari. I nod. "You should."


Fitting that our journey starts in Conception Bay, the eastern-most point of Canada. Tomorrow we'll head west until we reach the other side, Atlantic to Pacific.

I fail spectacularly as navigator because I'm so busy gawking at every little bit of story happening around me. "There. There. There. Down that road."

Aaron turns right or left accordingly. Usually the road ends in a dump or a "No Trespassing" sign, but sometimes there's some-thing spectacular: a ridge, or a waterfall, or a silent lake where we pitch our tent, light a fire, catch dinner, skinny dip, kiss, and spark, then count meteors skating across the black sky.

On the road, he absorbs my sun-pink face whenever the moose threat is low. Today, he doesn't ask me to read the map; he just veers south, looking sleeve-rolled-up relaxed. We stop at the end of a long driveway.

I read the name on the mailbox. "Aaron?"

"Zodiac wants to see you."

"You'd let your parents meet me?"

"What? Why wouldn't I?"

"I'm not the kind of girl you take home to a nice family."

"Ori's going to take you skydiving if you don't smarten up. You're the best person I know."

"You mean that?"

"How can you even ask? One thing, and don't you dare take this as meaning I'm ashamed of anything between us, but we can't sleep together. It'd upset my parents." I catch a flash of gold and jump out. "Ari?"

"Brother Aaron, I'll be the epitome of Amish. Excuse me. I've another love to hug." One whistle and Zodiac stops his play, lifts his head, searching the air. Then the moment becomes the Hollywood run between lost lovers, ending in a dive into his fur, ecstatic wiggles tumbling us onto the grass.

A man who can be none other than Aaron's father smiles down. "You must be Ari."

The mature woman in me dusts off my jeans and extends a hand like a lady. Mr. West bypasses it for a meaty hug. "Can't say how happy we are to finally meet you."

Aaron's mom comes hurtling across the lawn to get her hands on her boy, then seizes me with goodness in one arm and kindness in the other.

By evening, we've washed off the road and grandparents, sisters, uncles, aunts, cousins, first, second, third, and fourth fill the yard for a barbeque. Luke, six, looks me over.

"Are you the Luke who helped Aaron with the Zodiac painting?" I ask. He nods. "It was the best present ever."

He saddles up close, patting Zodiac's head at rest on my lap. "Is it true you got caught up in a gunfight?"

"I did."

"Did it hurt?"

"A lot. But kind people helped me feel better."

His pudgy hand pats my foot. "I'm glad."

"Do you think we could paint something together before I leave?"

"Could you do a dragon?"

"They're my specialty."

He scrambles away. "Mummy, Ari paints special tea dragons. Can she come play tomorrow?"

Uncle Peter nabs the empty spot beside me and Jasper spins in the salt of him. *Aaron's the spiriting image of him. See, Ari, we're more set in water than stone.*

"How is it this prairie birthed two dolphins?" I ask.

His dimpled smile is exactly like Aaron's. "Many times, I've despaired that Aaron wouldn't find his way out of this land-locked sameness. I'm so grateful to you."

"Grateful enough to do me a favour?"

"Anything."

"Go visit Aaron when he's in Peru? Stay awhile if the loneliness is too big?"

"My bag's always packed."


Sunday morning, Aaron knocks and opens the guest room door. "Breakfast in thirty."

Zodiac jumps down to see if there might be a pre-breakfast bacon bite. Aaron hesitantly hangs our garment bag on a hook. "Um, it'd mean a lot to my parents if we went to church."

I sit up. "Is it head-covering Amish?"

"Just a gathering of non-judgmental saints. Except Emily. She'll be judging without mercy." He opens his hand. "Would you consider wearing my school ring?"

I rise and rummage through my pack for Nia's ring. "How about I sport this?"

He nabs it, slips it on my left hand, moves in for a kiss. "Oh, baby. Thank you."

"Go on. I've got work to do."

Unclasped and unzipped, I turn helpless circles as my shoulder refuses to go over my head. I need Aaron or at least arms that bend back. His mom pokes her head in. "Breakfast's up." My face nears Madame Tussauds' wax works in a hot sun. "Here, let me help." She hinges my bra, zips my dress, tamps my face, and makes my hair look party perfect.

Aaron, white shirt and tie handsome, looks ready to sing "Holy, Holy, Holy" again when I enter the kitchen. His sister Katie says, "That's the prettiest dress I've ever seen."

"My sister has a great closet to raid." A white sundress with scattered sprays of navy flowers fits me spectacularly.


I like the plainness and the light wood, the simple hymns, the way Aaron sits close, whispering memories in my ear. I like, too, that Emily is one row behind.

After church, a lunch extravaganza unfolds. Ladies cluster around a great island, organizing food on platters. Margie, the church lady who needs to know everything, observes. "That's a lovely ring. Did Aaron give it to you?"

"He slipped it on my finger, for certain sure."

Emily looks ready to murder a loaf of multigrain when Margie asks, "So you'll be marrying then?"

"Aaron's taking on a big project in Peru and I'm going back

346

east to school, so the future's one that will be full of the twists and turns Aaron loves."

Margie snits at Aaron's mom, "Don't know where you went wrong with that boy. A man who can't settle is one with a troubled heart."

"Oh, ma'am, have you got things muddled. Believe me, I know about parents going wrong. The Wests are as close to perfect as I've ever come across. It's because Aaron's been so nurtured that he takes risks, jumps at challenges. Everywhere he goes, he makes the world better. Do you know how many master's theses mildew on shelves? Not Aaron's. He's applying his and thousands of children who've never held a shiny yellow pencil will."

"All fine and good, but a man needs a family to be complete."

"Not all men. Not men who think more about what the world needs than what they want for their own self." I schlep a heaped bowl of potato salad to the table. Aaron's mom follows with cold cuts.

She plunks it down. "I really hate ham."

"What? Me, too." She half smiles into my face and I see a mom who loves her boy. "I know it's hard to let him go but he'll always come back. True home has a way of doing that."

She shakes no.

"Shake your head all you want. I've seen the list. You and I both know Aaron will accomplish everything he sets his heart to." We head back for more bounty. "Did you know last month he jumped out of a plane?"

"Dear Lord Jesus, give me strength."

"Ask the god of our mothers. I find her more hands-on helpful."

Zodiac and I lie listening to worms whispering under the grass. Aaron obliterates the sun when he stands over us. "What'd you do?"

"Well, certainly not you. How do Manitoba Mennonite maidens maintain morals with all this fine-bodied horse flesh around?"

"Stop being so Ari-sistible. What'd you say to Margie Klassen yesterday?"

"Did I say something wrong?"

"She's always needling Mom about something. I'm told you put her gently in her place. My parents also just said they support my decision to go to Peru and they're proud of everything I've done." He helps himself to the other side of Zodiac. "Feeling like I'm disappointing them is the one thing that beaches me."

"If your parents weren't walking across the lawn right now, I'd kiss you."

His dad calls, "We're just going to town for groceries. You kids want to come?"

"Thanks, but Ari needs more Zodiac time before we meet everyone at the Ranch House." Aaron waves at the truck pulling away, then whips around quick. "Fifteen minutes to town, twenty to shop, at least ten to gab, then fifteen back. There's something not on the list, but I've dreamt of happening on that single bed of mine since I was fourteen."

I leap up. "Zodiac, guard the perimeter."

"Will you wear my basketball jersey?"

I handle his ass. "Let's play ball."


His mom discovers me in the yard with Zodiac. "Ari? It's four a.m."

"My shoulder kicked me out of bed."

She pulls up a chair and massages the ache. "I don't know how you've survived all you've been through."

"I've had more people pulling for me than anyone deserves. You've helped me more than you'll ever know."

"Me?"

"You raised Aaron to be who he is. Whenever I landed smack in the worst of the bad, he'd sit with me on our bench just letting me absorb his good."

"I don't understand why you're letting each other go."

"We'll never let the other go. What we share won't be troubled by mountains and oceans."

"I just see how much you love each other."

"Exactly. That's why I could never ask him to stop at the ocean's edge, and he wouldn't ask me to ride any more tsunamis." Her hand rests on my hair and I relax into it.

"Ari, if you need to take Zodiac, I'll understand."

"I know how being uprooted feels. This is his home."


As distance separates us from the prairies, I understand more why a child raised on the vast constant of good yearns for rugged mountains. With each mile, Aaron becomes more fully Aaron. More than the guy I nested with in Toronto. Greater than the son held under his family's wing.

In the after-quiet of a heavy rain, he weighs on me, full and satisfied. Fat drops tap out improvised rhythms on the canvas above us and the river kicks up a fuss. His breath heats my cooling skin as he asks, "Are you scared to have things change between us?"

His hair, rich with the dirt of our day, feels mouldable beneath my hand. "I'll not let how much I'm going to miss your physical presence touch me right now. It'd cost me this moment." He elbows up to take in my face. Clouds have moved on and moonlight mixed with shadow splits him in two. Nia is right about things missed in the light. "Aaron, if I didn't know for certain your North Star pointed south, I'd grasp onto you with every muscle of Jasper's tail."

"I've been thinking deep on this. What if I just got things

349

set up, then came east while you go to school? I could teach in Antigonish. A dolphin would thrive so close to the ocean."

"No need. I've decided not to go to school. I'm going to Peru with you. Exquisite pottery comes out of the south. I'll find someone to study with there."

His mouth readies for protest.

"How'd hearing that make you feel? In your gut."

"It's what I've been hoping for and—it feels like dirt, not clay."

"Yeah, what you said made the salmon in my belly start swimming upstream." I pull him close. "The only option for a dolphin and a seahorse is to discover a whole new dimension to being."

SIXTY-FOUR

I know that no homecoming waits at the end of this drive. People in Coombs told us that a woman matching June's description left long ago but an Ian Mercer might know her whereabouts. I knock on the door. A flame-haired woman with a baby in a hip sling says, "Can I help you?"

"I-I'm looking for my sister."

"Just Ian, me, and little Raine here."

"The lady at the general store said Ian might know something."

"He's in the shop." Her chin lifts to a log cabin. "Hope you see something to buy while you're fishing."

Ian looks up from his work bench, swallowing as he takes in

my face. "Oh, I-I'm—hello." He has animal sprits bulging from his coveralls, squirreling out his hair. "Shop's open. Come on in."

"I . . . um . . . Do you know where I might find June Appleton?"

"Who?"

"Blonde hair, child named Spring."

"Who's looking?"

"I'm Ari, her sister."

"Amber said she had no family."

*Oh Ari. One by one, the J's are becoming A's.*

I touch a wolf so perfectly carved I near feel its breath on my cheek. "It's just easier to scrap us than to explain us."

"Amber followed a band outta here three years ago."

"What band?"

"Crow. Took our Spring and headed to the States. Minnesota, maybe. Haven't heard a word from her since." Dust shimmers as he sands the arc of a crane's graceful neck. "Thought we had a good thing."

"June wouldn't know what to do with a good thing for very long. Pain was more her barometer of what's real."

"Makes no sense."

"Prickles make no sense to a sunflower, but thistles get them."

"Pardon?"

"Being stung was June's measure of being here on this planet. Is that totem behind you for sale?"

"Why that one?"

"I can't tell where the east ends and the west begins in the carving."

The flame-haired beauty brings us lemonade in mismatched glasses. She says, "It's four hundred."

"Well, that gives you maybe a nickel for each hour's work." I write down Skyfish's address along with a cheque. "Can you ship it here?"

351

The woman nods. "Freight will likely be another fifty."

"Just let me know and I'll send a cheque and a picture of where it lands."

Ian says, "I'd like that."

"If you ever do hear from June or Spring, please tell them they can find me at that address." I turn at the door. "You should know, it wasn't you she ran from."

Aaron stops the jeep at Ian's holler. He puffs over and drops a patchwork book on my lap. "Eileen thinks I burned this, but I couldn't. Her family should have it."

"Thank you. You really captured her likeness on the totem."

We take a slow trek across Vancouver Island, stopping for the night at Englishman River Falls. Smoke rises like a Japanese brushstroke as Aaron blows on the kindling. The fire catches and he settles beside me. "Where's June's book?"

"In my bag. I've spent so many years creating a safe world for her. For now, I need her there and . . ."

Numbness spreads from my shoulder into my hand and I can't feel Aaron's thumb drawing circles on it. "And what?"

"I'm afraid I'll see me mirrored on the page. I never thought I looked like my sisters, but I saw myself in the faces Ian carved on that totem."

"Ian saw June's face in yours the minute he lifted his head. And it's inevitable you'll see flashes of your life in whatever your sister wrote. Even if it's not there, you'll write it in to make meaning of what she left behind for you."

"Do you think I'm running away?"

"Wish I could say yes, but honestly coming with me would be the running."


In Tofino, my country farthest west falls into the ocean. From our cabin bed, we witness the heavens change. Light has long been swallowed by the ocean, and now, like ideas, stars turn on one by one. I don't ask how long we have or what happens when he points the jeep south. I just hold him, knowing not many on this planet get to ride with a dolphin for so long. He asks, "How is this, this connection between us, explained?"

"Can't define it, but I'll be grateful all my days that I took hold of it."

His head settles on my belly. "This has been like skydiving every day."

"Wait 'til your dolphin shows up and takes you ocean diving."

"I think there will only ever be you."

"Don't you dare burden a little seahorse with that."



I collect shore bits, pictures, and poetic thoughts. Aaron walks toward me looking *Sea Hunt* fine in a wetsuit get-up and what could be a gigantic kazoo on his head. "Suit up. We're going kayaking."

"We're going on the ocean in that vessel?"

"Come on, it'll be fun."

*Libby would in a minute.*

*Shut up.* I struggle into something more like a hot water bottle than apparel. *Stupid friggin' men that have no sense.*

Sea kayaking is a little bit fun, but to be honest, I don't love it. Jasper also wishes he'd kept his snout shut. Aaron, on the other hand, disembarks whooping happy.

A man from the lodge sets up a breakfast. We picnic on our little piece of the shore, the winds still stirring between us; suspect they always will. Aaron releases his chest from the suit. I tug slow—very slow—on my zipper. Aaron rushes in, peeling me like a banana. "I added 'naked on a beach' to the list."

"Get a blanket; there's no romance in a butt full of sand." I fold on a rock while he launches into the cabin.

Jasper hides in the hair flowing over my shoulders. *What if somebody comes along?*

*Just be thankful he didn't want to do it in that skinny boat.*

Aaron stands, staring, and I lift my face. "You, Ari, are the most magical creature to have ever inhabited this earth."

"No, West, I'm just a cracked pot."

He spreads the blanket against a rock, inviting me to his lap, parting the sea of hair covering my breasts. "If anyone spots us, they'll think I've landed a mermaid."

After the climb, the shuddered cry, the long after-holding, we eat and chatter, then come to a silence. "Bet you'd like some coffee."

"Coffee would be good. I hear the best cup I'll ever get is from Peru. Go." He pulls on the T-shirt I made him years ago, slides into his jeans, tossing me his UW sweatshirt. His perfect self disappears through the cabin door.

Offshore, birds dart and dive. *How are we going to survive this present to absence, Jasper?*

It feels an eternal sit, grief flowing and ebbing with the waves.

I study the couple walking down my beach, recognize the familiar shapes. Hear their voices. "You wanted a coffee?"

Their legs feel real, but I can't bring them into focus through the big tears. "Ellis? Mina?"

"Aaron thought you might need company."

"How?"

"He knew we were on Queen's Island."

"He's gone?"

"Just." My legs are jelly as Ellis helps me stand. "Never seen Aaron anything but rock solid, but right now he's broken wide open."

"A dolphin needs that, right?" I sponge up my snot with the too-long sleeve of Aaron's jersey.

"Right."

"Don't know what I'm supposed to do now."

"Aaron took care of everything." He tucks an envelope in my hand. "He said start by reading this."

> *Ari: You knocked down the walls and set me free, so I can do nothing less than listen to Ori whispering inside. That night at Lake Louise, I heard her voice, more of a song singing, that I was to let go but never ever say goodbye. Before you, I was bound. The unravelling has loosed a spirit thread, the end of which Jasper holds. When a dolphin and a seahorse fall in love, the only possible outcome is ever-changing magic in an unfathomable ocean that fits in a pocket of wonder.*
>
> *No matter my location on this planet, Sunday will always be yours, in my thoughts, my pen, my voice— however I can reach you, I will. Aaron*

*That's a clean break, Ari. It will scar beautifully.*

Like a sturdy bra, Mina and Ellis give comfort and support from Vancouver to Halifax. Somewhere over the prairies, my lungs feel like a depressurized cabin. *Tell me I did the right thing, Jasper. I could grow to love Peru.*

*Peru is his hop to his next step to his next jump to his next hop, step, jump . . . leap, glide, flip . . . You see how he loved us. He'd swim in the bathtub for the rest of his life if we asked.*

There's an infusion of oxygen as I sense Aaron discovering the list I tucked in his backpack: Gray Rock, Sunday, Listing, Dirt Year Clay, Freedom Love, Dolphin Shower . . . I sense his one-dimple smile as he reads the poetry he stirred in me.

355

*Freefall*

*Hesitation, at the open door*
*in the long uncertainty passion growing*
*until gravity*
*pushed.*
*Some freefall through air*
*he, through ari*
*like wind through aspen, sun through water.*
*Who flies without first the climb,*
*the leap?*
*And who absorbs the passing magic*
*without looking up to his descending grace,*
*that warm sou'wester, stirring, settling,*
*forever freefalling in my soul.*

Ellis moves the arm rest and holds me through the descent.

SIXTY-FIVE

William Walrus punches my ticket. "Imagine, our little miss off to university. No better place for a seahorse than Saint FX."

"Oh, come on. How the frig do you know I decided not to go to Dalhousie?"

He smiles, returns my ticket, and opens his hand like he's owed a penny.

"No, William. It was a dirt year. No disasters."

"You, little miss, took hold, riding a wave that you knew would break your heart. It cost you."

"Aaron?" He nods and I hand over a penny. "You're downright spooky."

"Eight down, just two cents to go."

"I can handle that, eh?"

"On my whiskers, little miss. You're well past the *Oh shit* line now."

"Who? How?"

William winks and moves along.

I'm not surprised to find Aunties M&N and a lanky boy who prefers being called Mike Butters now setting up my new nest in Antigonish. The corner with the best light provides a little studio. On a pudgy red sofa is a gift from Aaron, a little mottled pup, maybe a beagle, spaniel, poodle combination. Too small to make the leap off the sofa, she soft-tumbles, then waggles sad-eyed over to me.

Mary skritches the pup's dangly ear. "You have her name?"

"Sunday."

Lying in the dark, snug in my featherbed, I understand pain as catalyst, pushing me from sleep to the blank page, then light cutting through the window, moving me to my sketchbook. Always, the lines, the shadows and light falling on the page, make his face. Sunday paws at my leg. "Hey, girl." She's grown too big for my lap but it's her preferred perch. "This is Jake. He knows the language of a thousand creatures." Her paw chases the pencil. "Just two classes, then we can head to Skyfish for a long weekend. Maybe by some luck he'll come home for Thanksgiving."

357

I collect my professor's scribblings—fresh, innovative, quirky, insightful—tucking them inside my gem room. Usually, I bump into one of them while reading my way across campus. My nose sniffs through *Waiting for Godot* while my belly thinks about second helpings of turkey. "Hi, Ari."

"Libby? What brings you here?"

"Aaron sent me info on Peru. I-I . . ." Never in a million years would I imagine Libby to be the kind of girl to blubber. "Climb Every Mountain" seems more her anthem.

"Come on, my nest's just over this way." I link arms with her. "Face it, girl, he's your match."

She snuffles her nose on her sleeve. "What?"

"Any woman with a single adventure cell couldn't help but love Aaron."

"I-I shouldn't've come."

"No sense delaying the inevitable." She follows me up the stairs. Sunday stretches from her sleep off the couch and Libby goes right for a snuggle and I know—really know—I don't want Aaron to be alone. "Had all your shots? Passport up to date?"

"He loves you."

"He does and I love him, always will. You up to sharing him with me? Because there's a thread connecting us that can't ever be broken." She must have been holding in the tears for a year. "Come to Skyfish for the weekend and we'll settle these winds."

I load her in the truck and Sunday has a lap for the journey. She finally talks to the side window. "If I could have a finger of Aaron or a single minute, I'd take it."

"Libby, you're looking at a lifetime of hoisting yourself up mountains and plunging over waterfalls in rubber rafts. And a finger isn't going to cut it; the boy will have you doing it on a zipline over the Urubamba Gorge."

"How can you let him go?"

"I'm not. I'm letting him grow."

"Without you?"

"No, separate from me."

"I don't understand."

"Not sure we fully do either. It's like . . . Last Christmas, we were in the Laurentians. At the end of a packed day, all our senses teetered on overload. As we watched the sun fall, we inhaled and at the exact same instant said, 'Tomorrow we go home.' My exhale was coloured with contentment, his with disappointment." I wait for a face-connecting stretch of road. "What kind of love lets a person live their wrong life?"

"I'd listen to him talk about you last year. You'd become mythical in my mind."

"Everyone's mythic, but most never see it. I think you see your mythic existence. You should go. Dolphins do better in pods, than alone."

"A-a-after school? You'll get back together?"

"Not like we were. We're exploring new spatially expansive, inner outer, planetary, microscopic cell terrain."

"Oh. How . . . what do . . . wh—?"

"I see you understand about as much as Aaron and I do."

Mary comes out in response to the canine chorus. "Ari, you brought a friend."

"It's a dolphin for Aaron."

"You shipping her to Peru?"

"Yeah, the meddling seahorse is sticking his snout in again."

Libby bites her lovely lips. "Aaron will never look at me the way he does you."

"You're right. When he looks at you, he'll see open water. I'll never see that look in his eyes."

"He's blind to me."

"No. His eyes were just stuck on shore watching out for me. Aaron's not drawn by normal girl bait. You have to lure him with

359

things like . . . you long to teach devastated humanity the physics of hope while living in a treehouse." I ready for explanation; instead she nods. "Good Lordess, I just quoted one of your diary entries, didn't I." I locate pen and paper and write.

> *Westwind: The trouble with a nor'easter is she keeps stirring things up. This one is to settle hearts where they belong. Remember our conversation over dinner in Niagara Falls? Well, look who's jumping over the threshold into the great unknown.*
>
> *Now, knock off all the 'I shouldn't, I can't' and leap. The only way to betray a seahorse is by not embracing love when it lands at your front puerta. Ari*

SIXTY-SIX

A letter from Libby tells me she's left for Peru.

Post from Sadie, Jake's foster sister, spills that Jake is shacked up with a jaded old fox.

And, strike three, Jillianne has a stroke.

Auntie Dolores uses gentle words like "mild" and "transient." "She was seeing spots, her speech got slurry, then she said her world tilted, but it's passed."

"How, Auntie? She's just twenty-two."

"They found a tiny hole in her heart. Let me see, I wrote it down, a 'foramen ovale.'"

"Can they fix it?"

"She'll have an operation on Friday."

"I'm on my way."


The surgery was invasive, but by Sunday Anne is sitting, smiling, eating pudding. The intern stays, answering questions, I think because he's never seen so many pretty girls in one hospital room. Jennah points to me and says, "Tell that one right there that her sister's going to be fine."

Dr. Adorable says, "She shouldn't have another concern related to this."

I ask, "What caused it?"

"It's congenital. All babies have it, but the hole usually closes with the first breath."

Jacquie hands me my jacket. "Jennah, Jory, and I are staying until there's nothing that needs doing, so go back to school without a worry."

Anne says, "Hey, Ari. I have a kintsugied heart. How about that."

"Think maybe all of us sisters do."

Sunday is wearing a bonnet and dress when I go to pick her up. "Far out."

Celine says, "She can keep 'em."

"Thanks."

Arielle says, "Wait, I'll get the panties."

"Awesome." I stuff them in my pack. "Give Leo a big hug from me when he wakes up."

Dolores provides a care package, not just driving snacks but home cooking to last me a week. It's something all my aunties do, and Mum never did.


November sludges in, damp, gray, and ugly, and with it comes a weightiness I've never known. Ever. Not even when Len died.

*What new hell is this?*

Jasper is quiet, see-sawing between panic and despair. *Jake's with Dulcie? The name sounds like the sad tunes he used to play.*

The floor of the sister-house has recovered, yet I can't shake the feeling that it is riddled with holes. Nothing feels safe or solid.

And nightmares arrive, ones I never had back when Nat was found, stranglings and being stuffed in a vent. I wake, choking, reaching for air. *What the hell, Jasper?* I turn on the lights and wait for morning; too many mornings I sit, and sit, and sit waiting for night.

My paintings are twisted and screamy, my writing black, and sometimes Sunday pees on the floor because I forget to take her out.

Whenever the fragrance of a summer fire wafts through the window, I climb onto the small balcony and my neighbour, Greg, passes his joint through the bars. He sits easy against the cold brick. "Professor Anderson posted the psych results. You got top mark."

"No great feat when your family wrote the book."

"Really?"

The weed fires red. "Yep." I've read my psych text cover to cover. Went searching for more. Until now, "troubled" labelled my family. In this place of higher learning, Appletons are called what they are—deviants, narcissists, incestuous, addicts—and hearing voices is a whole other kettle of crazy. The diagnoses decompose like beached whales in my head.

"What'd you do your English essay on?" He passes me the rest of the joint and lights another.

"*Call It Sleep.*"

"I just reworked an essay from high school." His head twitches with his laugh. "Bad idea. My mom's going to pitch me in the gulag at my grade."

"They don't send report cards home at university. Lie." I

pick blisters of rusty paint from the railing and memories of the craphouse fester like an abscess.

"She'll find out. She teaches Russian lit here. Wanna come over?"

My head folds to my knees. "I just want to sleep."

I see the rabbit in him: the silence of his hop over the rail, the softness of his hair, the twitch of his smile, his longing to copulate. Rabbits are no match for a lioneagle, still I let him push me inside, pull off my sweater and jeans, and kiss my neck. We drop to the bed like the last leaves clinging to the November maple.

After he's done, the line of his back looks broken as he sits and pulls his shirt over his head. "Gotta go." A string of light snakes across the floor. "See ya." He steps across it, disappearing through the window.

I leave my window open for a boy without dreams. He hops in and out of my bed, disrupting my nightmares and filling empty space. Term end, he helps himself to two hundred dollars stashed in Len's pot. "Makes us even for all my dope."

The pot tilts, graceful and slow, hesitating at the shelf's edge. I dive, desperately trying to cushion its impact. A dozen pieces scatter like a spent blue rose. I lock the window, then gather every shard and sliver.

Mid-December stings white, crisp, and blue-skied. A package arrives from Aaron full of pictures and shore treasures. He looks tanned and joy full. *Ari: You won't believe this. Tino arranged for supplies to build a school.* I eat an entire tin of Mary's fudge that I brought as a gift for my favourite professor. *I feel sick.*

*Least you feel something.*

I pick up the ringing phone. "Merry Christmas, kitten. Found what you're looking for. Irwin did set up that store caper."

I swallow fudge-flavoured acid. "Oh. Hang on to it for me."

I sponge up tears spilling down my cheek. "I got a letter from Aaron. That was really nice of you."

"A perk for being in the construction business. Have a good little holiday."

"You, too."

Mina calls, inviting me to visit. "Can't, Mina. I have a ton to do."

In truth, I'm ahead. Working at the easel fuels the pain in my shoulder, so I do it, hour after hour after hour. Biology, like a scab, is a thing I can't stop picking at. Library shelves groan with devastating accounts of humanness and inhumaneness. My classes—English, sociology, psychology—reward exploring especially dark themes.

Mina says, "You sound kind of blue, Ari."

"What luck for an artist, eh?"


Classes end on a Friday and an expanse of three weeks at home is mine for the nabbing. I'm marooned on the bed. Only Sunday's whining gets me up. I have weed. I have Dilaudid. I prefer the pain. Raising my arm is as good as cutting used to be, but without the mess.

Monday morning has the painful stab of brightness that new snow brings. I open an eye to Sunday's sad-eyed stare and Jasper poking. *Get up, get up, get up, get up, get up . . .*

*Shut up.*

*Know what we know?*

*You're going to bloody well tell me, aren't you.*

*There're a lot of ways to die, and there's not much control in it.*

*What's your friggin' point?*

*Dying is pretty random. How we live, not so much.*

*That's it, library ban for you.*

*We know this, not from books; we know from Appleton to Irwin, Koshkin to Trembley, West to Zajac; there're a lot of ways to live.*

*So?*

*So, get up, get up, get up, get up, get up . . .*

It's like a mosquito I can't crush.

*Get up! You are Ari Lioneagle and Sunday and me are your side-kicks.*

I haul myself to a sit. *Please, please, just shut the frig up.*


Mary tries to enter my silence over Christmas. "What is it, Ari?"

I shrug. "I just feel so weighted. I've lost Aaron. Jake."

Nia sits on the coffee table. "Losing love isn't what's pulling you under. It's time for you to exercise your limbs on your own. University is your time to open windows, sort through rooms, study treasure maps, look behind doors, explore new corridors."

"I was loving school until I got those letters from Libby and Sadie."

"And you got that call about Jillianne." Nia says.

"She had a little hole and they fixed it."

"The tiniest of holes can cause a great deal of damage," Mary preaches, "And before you can mend a pot you have to know where the crack is."

"I do know. Jake has fractured me beyond repair."

Nia says, "The Ari we know can rise above a lost love."

"So, what's this shit I'm sinking in? Mikey's off my back. Mum's ash."

"My guess is there's a fracture in your own core that you couldn't tend to because you were so caught up holding everyone together."

"But I don't stuff anything. I rage against the dying light all the time."

"Good." Nia hands me my coat. "Wood pile's low. Get out there and split some logs."

Sunday stays curled by the hearth when I whistle her to the truck. I think maybe Jasper prefers Skyfish too. *Right, I do. But you're stuck with me.*

My English professor hands back my essay on *Revolutionary Road*. "Maybe the most depressing thing I read over the holidays."

"Glad I could counterbalance all the merriment, sir."

"You really believe nobody ever lives their dream?"

"Maybe the ones who sleepwalk through their lives."

He buttons his coat while following me out. "What made you choose Yates?"

"The subject matter suited my state of mind."

"Where would you rather be?"

"Maybe Peru, instead of drowning in nightmares."

"And what would have a talented young woman drowning in nightmares?"

"Oh, nothing, my life is a rose garden."

"My question wasn't me being incredulous that you are such stuff as nightmares are made. Your writing would indicate you've encountered a great many thorns in that garden."

"None worth talking about."

"I've never met a conversation not worth having."

"Are you a cat or a dog person?"

"Dog, unless it's in the wild, then I like cats."

"My brother worked with wild cats. Lions."

"Worked? What does he do now?"

"He died."

"Oh, sorry. How?"

"Saving me."

"We've something in common, then."

"I very much doubt that."

"My big brother worked so I could go to school. He got drafted and I got a PhD."

366

"He died in the war?"

"He did. Losing a sibling throws the universe off-kilter, doesn't it?"

"Especially when he'd be alive if I'd done things differently."

"I'm a good listener if you need someone to talk to."

I like his name, Professor Eagleston. I like his peppered hair and black turtleneck worn with faded jeans. "You have the ocean in your pocket by any chance?"

"No, it's at my front door."

His house overlooks the bay. He reheats beef stroganoff while Vivaldi skirts around a silky fire. Subplot and subtext are obvious as we play author alphabet. I say, "Austen."

He says, "Brontë."

I eat a slice of orange. "Camus."

He licks his lip. "Dickens."

"Eliot."

He moves a rogue spiral of hair from my cheek. "Faulkner."

"Goethe."

"Homer."

"Lawrence."

He lifts a clichéd strawberry dipped in warmed chocolate to my mouth, finger lingering with an imperceptible tug on my lip. "Margaret or D.H.?"

I follow him to his bed.

Straddling his pale body, my hands skate across the silver hair on his chest. He cups my breasts. I kiss his neck, inhaling the scent of fresh lime. He enters me, adding fingers to the mix until I hum and he praises the gods—then it's over. Emptiness remains, but I don't ache as much marooned in his arms.


We talk about books and dead siblings, cooking and art. I return night after night, through to February. He kisses the moon-spill on my shoulder. "Let's go somewhere hot for reading week. Bahamas, Jamaica."

"No. The cold suits me better just now." I sit up. "I really should go and study."

He tugs my arm, gently. "Come back and keep Daddy warm." The way I catapult up scares him. Terrifies me. "Ari?" My sweater snaps over my head. My jeans find my legs as I hop to the door. "What is it? What's wrong?" I scramble out of the house, to my truck. He nabs the door. "Wait. Why are you crying?"

I wrench my arm from his grasp. "Get your fucking hands off me!"


How I navigate the truck to Skyfish I don't know.

The axe from the woodpile is in my hands, thud-thud-thudding against Daddy's linden tree. As the fragrance of fresh-cut wood hits, thunder roars from my gut. Mary and Nia appear, standing witness to a primal scream, spreading like fire over dry grass. Then I'm empty, body folding like a spent sparkler. "Let it out." Mary touches my back. "Let it all out."

Nia asks, "Did a memory climb up from the depths?"

I blubber, hard and messy. "I-I-I . . . I just saw, I saw me back then, saw the crack in my small self."

Mary hushes my hair. "Ari, did your Daddy rape you, too? Is that what you saw?"

"That's the thing, Auntie. He didn't."

"Ohhh." Nia's breath curls in the cold, dissipating like maritime fog, and there she sees me, the misnamed, unclaimed child. "Come in now, out of the cold."

The fire sparks. I'm suspended somewhere between numb and thawed. "How's it possible I feel, I don't know, betrayed? Left out?"

"You *were* left out. Your mum, and your dad, set you apart from the J's all your life. What set you on this road tonight?"

"Remembering a night the week Daddy died. Jillianne was snugged with me in our couch cave, on the edge of sleep. Then she was being lifted. Daddy was home after what seemed like weeks. He whispered, 'Hey, Jillibean, come keep Daddy warm.' I was sad, sad because he didn't want me. Then Jillianne was screaming. And, and, Jacquie . . . got backhanded."

Mary says, "He hit her?"

"No. Mummy did. The rest you know. Next day, Jacquie told Aunt Elsie that she was pregnant. That all the J's were broken. Then Daddy checked out. Mum cracked up. And the sister-house collapsed." I poke at the flames. "How fucked is it that being the *least fucked* Appleton makes me so sad?"

"Because it is sad." Mary makes tea in Grandma's Brown Betty pot.

"But *I* shouldn't be, I got sent here and—"

"For god sake, Ari, I swear if you were handed a cookie chocked with shit chips, you'd be, 'Oh, well, least I got some spectacular crumbs.' It's nauseating, and exhausting, really. Be sad, bloody sad. Hell, be furious. It doesn't negate what you're grateful for."

SIXTY-SEVEN

Five a.m. The fire shimmers low. Sunday tucks her soft self on my feet and Jasper pokes me. *Open it, open it.*

The fragrance of June arrives on turning to the first page: weed, cedar, strawberry, and that smell air has before it rains. I lift the book to my face, placing her hand-touched page on my cheek.

> *This book is for treasures, something a lioneagle set me hunting for. I'll start with my garden. I thought, on principle, everything I touched would croak but up come bushy leaves: beans, tomatoes, pumpkins even. Everything is growing, my garden, my belly, my hair. Will you think I'm crazy for wondering if my sugar snaps hurt when I bite them? I chew soft, thankful for what they give to this seed growing in me . . .*

I fan through pages, plump with seed packets, Shakespeare in the Park tickets, a photo of Yellow June smiling down at her baby, bits of hand-dipped cloth . . .

> *Ian hates the markets but I dream of winter's end and weekend noise.*
> *Tree, silent bark.*
> *Lake, mute liquid.*
> *Sky, deafening blue.*
> *Radio, dead.*
> *I'd kill for a battery.*

"Nice to see that smile, eh, Mary." I look up to M&N watching from their bedroom door.

"Just reading June's awful poetry. Yellow June is in here, side by side with Black June."

"Dark and light." Nia revives the fire and Mary makes cinnamon French toast. "C'est la vie."

"Would you guys mind if I went to Toronto for the rest of reading week? I want to share June with the sisters."

"Depends. How're your grades?"

"Aces. Despair has served me well." I force down bites of toast to ease Mary's worry. "I actually love my classes."

"What's your favourite course?"

"Geology."

"Really?"

"You'd think a rock is a rock. But igneous rock can change into sedimentary rock or metamorphic. Did you know, depending on what chemicals are thrown in and how quickly magma cools, during the transformation of igneous rock, sapphires are made?"

"I do know there's a hell of a lot of heat and pressure to birth a gem."

"If a rock can change, then people surely aren't set in stone. Gives me hope that Jake will find Jewel."

Mary says, "Fill your boots with hope for him, but for goddess sake, learn to dance on your own steady feet."

"And you get yourself grounded, miss." Nia waggles her fork. "Don't think we haven't seen you've been higher and more off-key than the soprano section of the Presbyterian choir."

"Murdering that linden felt like removing that rock splinter from my cheek. Now, I think I'll butcher Mum's hawthorn."

Mary says, "Then we'll line the shitbox with the pair of them."

"You know what I know, M&N?"

"What's that?"

"I'm not the name I was saddled with. I know whose daughter I am."


I stop in Montreal. Sister five comes with me to the river, to the place where Daddy blew his head off. I expect waves to surface. In unison we just inhale and exhale, then meander across the park

where, as kids, we walked the dog, somersaulted, sang for pennies. Anne says, "Do you feel like we've outgrown a childhood
illness? Holes closing like should've happened at first breath."

"Filling with gold. Can you drop me at the train?"

"Not driving?"

"No, I owe a walrus a penny."


"Ari?" Ellis near trips over his painted turtle. "Mina. She's here."

"Who's here?" Mina pokes her head from the kitchen, phone
in hand. "Ari? I just dialled your number."

"Did M&N call? I swear I'm on steady feet."

Ellis scoops me toward the sofa. "No, no, just some things I
wanted to talk over."

"About what?"

"First things first. What're you doing here?"

"Revisiting the sister-house."

"And?"

"The architects are dead and it stands; astonishingly, we all
stand. Why were you calling?"

"About Jake." Ellis sits on the old trunk. "You know that
from our first trip east, he and I connected. We've written these
past years."

"He answers your letters?"

Ellis nods. I fold away. He turns my face. "I was keeping a
promise to him not to tell."

"Does he know I betrayed him?"

"So, you dated Aaron," Mina says. "Get over it. Jake broke
things off. How's that betrayal?"

"In his last letter," Ellis says, "he wrote that all he wants is to
go home but he's stuck in one of those rip currents, so close to
coming out but completely exhausted. I'm going to go see him.
Can I tell him there's still hope with you?"

"I tell him in every friggin' letter."

"He's turned a corner, I think." Mina passes me a letter, back-folded to a starting place. *How is it that the faintest remembrance of her keeps me from stepping off the world?*

I search their faces. "Why can't he say this to me?"

"He's put it in writing." Ellis seals my hand around the promise.


Through the February window, I take in the blank canvas stretching the miles back to Montreal. William smiles down. "Well, little miss, how was your visit?"

"A pilgrimage, paying homage to the sister-house." I look to his face, leathered like an old bible. "Can I tell you something terrible?"

He stretches his hand for a penny. "Why'd you think I happened on this run?"

"I broke my papa's pot. The one he left me when he died."

"Something in it must be wanting out."

"What?"

"I suspect it's your own self."

"Pardon?"

"There's nothing, no thing, no person, as grand as meeting your own self, and welcoming that self inside. Your Jasper has set up some fine rooms."

"Really, William, how do you know all this shit?"

"Magic."

"Surely it's time I transitioned into reality."

"No, no, no, you're nearing the big magic, when the whole world tilts right." He points to the pouch. "Have a peek at what remains."

Out of the pouch slides the last penny, shiny as mint, 1961. At our very first meeting, William wrote 1961 on my palm and said,

"See, little miss, the whole world can turn upside down and still land right."

"How? This isn't what was here."

He winks, turns.

"Wait. Please, William tell me how to navigate this last penny."

"Set in place your own walls, doors, and windows, truth by truth."

## SIXTY-EIGHT

Professor Eagleston knows it's me knocking, but the door remains closed. I shiver on a rock near the water's edge, waiting. He gives in around midnight and comes out, remaining a safe distance. "What're you doing here?"

"I needed to see you before classes start, let you know I'm dropping your class."

"And say what? I attacked you?"

"What? No. There's no trouble to be made from this."

"You're crazy, you know."

"I am, but not because I freaked." He braves looking at my face. "My dad he . . . he did things that he shouldn't have done. This hole in Jillianne had me on the edge, you calling yourself 'Daddy' sent me squirrelling over."

He tugs his hair through his fingers. "Don't drop my class."

"It'd be best."

"And what do I say when the dean asks why my brightest student left my class? Reconsider. Please."

"If I hand in a spectacular essay, how will you mark it?"

"With the same appreciation I've had for all your assignments."

"What if I give you a shitty one?"

"D for disappointment."

"Okay, I'll stick it out."

"You're shaking. Come inside and warm up."

"My dog has me on probation. I need to go let her out." I back away. "You asked me before if I believed that no one ever gets to live their dream. That shouldn't even be the question."

"What should it be?"

"Does anybody really live their awake? Most are asleep and call it a life."


A salting of snow floats past a spring moon. Through another power outage, I warm under Babcia's feather wonder. The shelf seen from my bed holds gold-veined pots, stories written in cracked lines: absences, wounds, mistakes and misfortune. Kintsugi wasn't right for Len's pot. The fractures were too beautiful to fill. A candle burns inside, scar lines dark where the glue held, light escaping through cracks and tiny holes. My favourite bruise is a bit of turquoise glaze that remains where a chunk of clay has fallen away. Beside it is an unfinished work, about a quarter done, like me. It looks like a cupped hand.

Noise—knuckles rapping on my door, a party in the apartment above, the crunch of chips between my teeth—weaves into my book. *Hey, Ari, here's an Iggem: the world breaks everyone and afterward many are strong at the broken places.*

I close *Farewell to Arms* and snug down with Sunday. Moon shadows puddle on my art assignment— *Crapdom*, oil on canvas. For art class I had to capture a house I once lived in from memory. Three weeks ago, the craphouse seemed a subject of interest, a contemporary tragedy. Now, it sits on the easel like a smug lie. *No one ever lived there, Jasper.*

The schlepping in of tidy masterpieces by classmates has me calculating how long it would take me to go back and grab *Crapdom* from my easel. My professor asks, "Where's your assignment, Ari?"

"In the truck or at my apartment. Haven't decided."

"Which one will be here before class ends?"

"With a little help, the one in the back of my truck."

Tyler helps me haul in *The Sister-House*, acrylic on closet door. We lean it against the windowed wall.

"What the . . . ?"

"Sorry, it sacrificed itself when the story wanted out."

Tyler says, "You must've been on some weird shit."

My professor studies it slow, starting at the bottom where bodies, layered like sedimentary rock, pepper the grass with what they've seeded. Hell-edged grace is as near as can be described. He moves up to Jillianne, jigsawing through the cracked floor—to yellow mortar interrupting black June—then windowed Jennah, skeletal beneath sunlit gossamer—up to Jory, snaking rainbows from the roof—settling on Jacquie, my solid yellow door. Around the edge is a Rumi quote: "I have lived on the lip of insanity, wanting to know reasons, knocking on a door. It opens. I've been knocking from the inside."

"You once lived . . . here?"

"Resided." My sigh settles the chatter but not the current in the room. My professor bends forward to the door's keyhole and meets the child's gray eye looking out.

## SIXTY-NINE

I never tire of ocean pictures as I drive, or weary of Sadie's jabbering as I give her a lift most Sundays as far as Port Hawkesbury. "Saw Jake at the Dublin House last week, cryin' in his full mug, but it wasn't 'cause Dulcie's gone. It's that he doesn't know how to set things right. He up and left without downing the ale or chaser. That says a whole bunch, more than a dictionary, wouldn't you say, Ari?"

"I would."

"It's Huey that sets me worrying most. His fiddle never comes out the box no more. I told Jake if he didn't start the mending, this birthday would be Huey's last."

"What'd he say?"

"That he wasn't so important as to cause such a thing. So, I said that it had nothing to do with importance and only everything to do with love. He swallowed that into his gut. Could see it plain as when the Missus spooned in the castor and held Jake's nose 'til he swallowed."

I write my last exam, then drive to Halifax to see Jake's old therapist at the rehab centre. Ryan works on my shoulder, moving it in ways that hurt so bad Jasper near bites him, but then he rubs it for a long while in a way that feels almost good. "Are you swimming?"

"I was marooned for a bit but I'm back at it."

"I want you in the pool, four times a week minimum. We can get more range of motion back but you've got to put in the time." He plunks a heated bag on my neck and Jasper ponders "range of motion." *You can't ever have everything back, but you can have more than you have and it's up to you to get it.*

*You're more annoying than an ear-buzzing mosquito.*

"So, did Jake really say he didn't know how to set things right?"

"He told our friend all he wanted was to go home."

"He could fiddle again, play keyboard. I've worked with several amputees who picked up their instruments again."

"Really?"

"Jake could play with his toes if he put his heart to it."

I half search on the drive back to Skyfish, stopping at random bars, but Jasper says Jake is making his way to Pleasant Cove for Huey's birthday.


Mary and Nia survey my gathering of rocks in the truck. "Be careful of your shoulder unloading those."

"Ryan said it would be good for me to push it more."

"Lifting rocks?"

"Why waste money on weights when the shore gifts me with them?"

M&N arrive at Moondance an hour later. "The electric get hooked up?"

"Yep."

"Mary and I were going to run the power lines in for your birthday gift."

"I've always lived in houses that other people constructed for me. Bringing the energy here feels important to do on my own." Along the wall where I'll build the fireplace is my broken pot and my scarred lioneagle treasure box.

Mary unloads tea fixings and a plug-in kettle while Mike struggles in a fat weathered length of barn-board.

"Oh, Mikey, I love that."

"It's a piece of Skyfish for your mantle."

The new town doc follows with a rock the size of a lemon. "Where should I put this?"

378

"Outside with the others, there's a good lad." Mary winks at me and mouths, "Think he has a crush."

Mike turns on his way out, the aura of a mystic dragonfly surrounding the skinny twelve-year-old. "I'll come back later to help."

"Go play. Nothing needs doing."

The doc tips an invisible cap. "Save me a dance Friday?"

"Um, okay?"


Jasper dizzies himself on the wheel while I experiment with wabi-sabi pots. Mary loads the kiln. "You don't have to come tonight, Ari."

"Yes, I do." I unstraddle the bench. "Lioneagles are made for battles such as these."

"Be prepared. The two years since you've seen Jake have carved away at him. There's nothing left of the former boy."

"Isn't that what all the letting go has been for?"

I manage two lead-footed dances with Dr. David Macpherson. The ruckus at the door pulls my arm from David to dock-muscled, life-whipped Jake Tupper.

He manages a sloppy roughing of Mike's hair. "Hey, Mikester." I decide a daylight reunion the better and turn from the crowd. "Too good for a hello, Ari Appleton?"

Saltwater courses through me as I near him. "A hundred unanswered letters, more unreturned calls gets a girl thinking a boy isn't much interested in a hello." His chest stiffens at my touch. "And I, sir, am Ari Joy Zajac and I've missed you, Jake Butters."

He backs away, grabs some random girl, and kisses her.

Mike launches, fists flailing at Jake's back. "You . . . you ba-boon. Friggin' baboon. Why you being a jerk to Ari?"

Huey gentles the rage. "Whoa, son, let Jake sleep it off and we'll see to this in the morning." Huey's voice quivers. "Doc, be a good man and see Ari home."

Jake pitches a half-empty bottle into the night and David takes my arm. I take it back. "I'm going to catch up to Sadie. Would you mind letting my aunts know?"

David scuffs his hair. "Sure."

I wander to my rock, sitting until spring damp threatens my bones. *That was a pitiful show at being a pathetic drunk, wasn't it, Jasper.*

*He can't fool us. Let's go get him.*

Jake's boarding house rivals the craphouse. From Sadie, I know I'll find Jake second floor, second door on the right. Sad souls line the steps. One tugs my leg. "Spare a dollar?" I pay for passage up and find Jake passed out, fully dressed on a filthy mattress.

On the dresser are twine-wrapped stacks of well-read letters. When night-gnawing starts in the walls, I tuck on a wooden chair and wait for the half-waking moment when first light shines into cracks made by the swell of regret.

In the gray dawn, he blind-shuffles to the bathroom, returning his storm-weathered self to the edge of the bed. He whips a boot at rustling in the corner.

I shiver-whisper, "Please tell me that's just a very large mouse."

"Jesus H. Christ, what the hell?" Weariness weighs him like a dinghy loaded with boulders. "Get outta here."

"You forget I'm a stubborn, independent woman? I'll go when I'm good and ready."

"This is no place for you."

"I've been in worse."

He coils small on the bed. "Please, please just go."

"Can't."

"You'd be surprised how fucking easy it is."

380

"Easy? What you're doing is killing Huey. I get you needed time for a big tantrum but it's time to stop this wallow."

His body pops a little. "This can't be changed."

"There's nothing that can't be changed, especially considering what I know lives in you. Three small words will stop this spin and start turning things right." He rolls onto his back, covering his eyes with his arm. A stink, like sour milk and mildewed rags, hit. "Huey's dad was a messy drinker like yours."

"I know."

"Did you know Huey was, too?"

"You don't know shit. Huey's a saint."

"He's a crap-dumped, flawed person same as you and me. You know their middle boy, the one lost at sea? Huey's the one who lost him."

"Bullshit."

"No, human shit. He'd taken him out on the boat. He was so pickled he didn't even remember him going over. Wasn't sure he'd gone out with him or if he'd dreamt it."

"Not possible."

"Any one of us is capable of royally screwing up. Huey went into a death spin after and it was you that started the healing."

He turns to the wall.

"You were not yet four. Huey was on the dock, saw your dad deliver a backhand that knocked you off your feet, then set off without you."

"Tell me something I don't remember."

"Do you remember Huey going to you? Something happened that day."

"What?"

"He ran into some small magic. You found—"

"What words? What three words stop this?"

"Just saying, 'I am sorry.' It'll take a million tons off your shoulders and start the move out of this."

"I can't face him."

"Huey said that he could scarce face his own sorry self, but the sight of you alone on that dock got him up off his ass. He's never forgot the feel of your scared hand in his. He thought if he could just take care of one small boy, then maybe he could let his heart beat and his lungs fill again." I climb off the chair. "One sorry, then you can go jump back in the ocean if you need more wallowing, but you're coming with me. You owe him this." I gather up filthy bits of laundry. "Where can you shower around here and do you have any clothes that don't stink like dead cod?"

"Tomorrow."

"Today's Huey's birthday and you, boy, are his present. Get yourself out of that bed or I swear I'll give every man on the steps ten bucks to load and tie you in the truck."

Outside, I scan the weathered houses, heading for the one that looks not so pin-perfect I won't get past the front door and nice enough that they might have a washer/dryer. I knock and a plump, friendly type answers. "Morning, ma'am, I have a man situation. I'll give you five bucks for a load of laundry, another five for a shower, and five more for putting some breakfast into his pathetic belly."

She smiles, woman to woman, while tucking the cash between her mountainous boobs. "Bedder makes it two loads and adds the bleach." I hand over an extra five. "No, didn't mean for more."

"I'll likely need your help to haul his ass down the stairs." I head to the door. "Stupid friggin' thick-headed male. Was there ever a dumber creature."

"Not that I'm awares, dearie."


As easy as moving a paper boat, I push him along and load him into the truck. "One small step, Jake." He closes his eyes and we drive up the coast in silence.

Nearing the Butters, he says, "I can't do this."

"You'll be astonished how friggin' easy it is."

"I've no right."

"Maybe not, but Huey has a right to hear it."

He remains stuck in the truck, but Huey's arms are long enough to reach in and pull him out and the "I'm sorry, I'm sorry, I'm so sorry" damn bursts.

Jasper spins around my hair. *Ah, some saltwater for my Jewel.*


We meet not a hair of resistance ringing out a man over-ready to be wrung. For three weeks, he's soothed through shakes and jitters as the Missus spoons in special concoctions to clean out and build up.

The newest foster, a saggy-diapered fellow, climbs onto Jake's lap for a rest. It's innate for Jake to comfort small broken creatures with a finger dance. Mike calls this tyke Puffin because of his wheezy chest. I snug under Puff's legs and say, "Huey, tell Jake what you saw the day the two of you met."

Less weighted, Huey's shoulders circle back as if pulling oars through the memory. "We was cuttin' through seagrass toward shore. Jake's wee head was fixed over the edge of the skiff. He said, 'Look, my baby dragons.'"

Mike asks, "What was it?"

"Two seahorses. I'd never seen any in these parts, only ever heard Granny Clease tell of spotting one. I said, 'Where'd you suppose they came from?' and Jake said, 'They jumped outta my pocket.' Then of all things we heard a baby crying, and didn't we find one beached on the sand. And wasn't it the little bundle of joy sitting there beside him now."

If we'd thought it flooded before, this time the damn explodes. All the gods and goddesses move in. Mike takes Puffin. Mary plumps a pillow on my lap. Nia lifts Jake's legs onto the couch. The Missus covers him in a quilt and Huey fiddles him to sleep.

The new day is maybe four hours old. Jake whispers, "Don't know what I'm supposed to do now."

"Sleep. Rest. All the excavating's done. It's time to chip away and polish the treasures you've unearthed."

"How?"

"I'm driving you to Halifax. Ryan can't wait to get his hands on you."

"It can't ever be the same for us, Ari."

"Hallelujah." My hand drifts along his hair and down his arm. "All these years you've danced like a scared monkey, for the Butters, for M&N, for me. I want you to dance *with* me. Wait 'til you see how seahorses dance: they grasp a blade of grass with their tails, spinning, changing colours."

He sighs into the pillow. "I know and I've ruined it, ruined everything."

"You've just burned off the crap through this scorching. It'll take time to regrow." I trace the scar across his eyebrow, following its curve around his eye. "Can you see any from this eye?"

"Blurs, light and shadows."

"Can you see how much you're loved?"

"I'm so ashamed. All Huey and the Missus have been through and they never . . ."

"Your time with them has been more in their light. You just never witnessed where the darkness took them."

"All the awful things that've happened to you and you've never once let it swallow you."

"Lord, Jake, I'm swallowed all the time, but every time I get spit out with a big mucky slug in my hand, M&N are there saying, 'What a magnificent treasure you have, let's see what we can make of it.' I've blathered and painted and written my way through the dark. You've kept everything locked deep. Never hearing how you fill treasure rooms in me."

"I heard you and I threw it away."

"No, bastard voices rewrote my words into 'Maybe one day you'll be good enough.'"

"After what I've done, I really am not good enough."

"Right here, right now, I love you. Not for who you were or who you'll be." My finger silences the protest trying to get past his lips. "I don't care what or who you've done these years past. You haven't wrecked us. For the first time in my life, I'm looking ahead on the road and seeing our home and the family where I belong, we belong." I need him full in my arms. "Can I stretch out behind you? My bum's gone needles and pins."

He stands. "You sleep. I need to walk a bit."

"Take Sunday. She's good company."

Huey appears, hurrying on his boots and coat. They return an hour later, Huey's cheeks coloured with a little hope. Mike shovels mush into Puffin's mouth while outlining his project on whales.

"Pick Jake's brain on this one," I say. "All I know is they have lovely tails. He knows how they think." I kiss all around and hug Jake. "I'll be honking at six a.m. tomorrow."

His arms don't return my hug but his body feels a little less like holding a rock. "It's a long drive to Halifax. I'll find my way there."

"Nonsense, I'm saving M&N a delivery run."

When I arrive home, Mary is on the phone with Ryan, like a Rottweiler with a bone of education. "And get him started with some courses. Tell him it's part of his rehab program. We'll cover his expenses."

Nia asks, "You steady?"

"Jasper won't friggin' shut up about Jewel, and I can't get any peace about Aaron and Libby doing it on a jungle vine."

"Go get your hands on something solid."

I turn to the wheel and my mouldable partner, clay.

If I'd known the doc was coming, I wouldn't be skirt-hoisted, silky-legged straddling the bench. The tips of my hair are clay dipped as I pray over the wheel. He silent-watches the birth until my head lifts.

"Is everything sorted out with your friend?" he asks.

"A seahorse took a small step."

"Pardon?"

My bare feet kiss the wood as creator and created move to the workbench. "Want to watch me do surgery?" He nods. "Pull up a stool." I study David Macpherson's solid face. I write "oak" on a scrap of paper. "What's your favourite tree?"

He thinks for a long while, like facing a test he's afraid to get wrong. "An oak." I show him the paper. "How'd you know that?"

"I'm a sorceress. Bet you've never seen an oak sprite." I coax away bits of clay. "It's the spirit under the bark, in the heart of the tree." He moves around to witness the imp escaping from the clay. "I'd say this one's more three hundred years old."

"I know you don't really believe all this folksy claptrap."

"Gotta get this boy in touch with his own horse sense, Jasper."

"Do what?"

"Just consulting with the seahorse. He says you need to do some horsing around."

"You're pulling my leg, right?"

"Not a chance of me doing that, doc."

As the hour passes, I feel his breath behind me and sense him inhaling my hair. I mould a few oak leaves with my fingers, working them into the pot so the spirit peers through them.

"It's magnificent."

"Wait 'til you see it glazed and fired. Then it's yours, if you want it." I slip off the stool. "Come see what came out of the kiln." He's more interested in my face than the beautiful pots.

386

"Doc, I'm telling you right up front, there's no sense getting tangled with me. Another man has my heart."

"You can't mean Tupper. He's a drunk."

"There's a big difference between a bona fide drunk and a man who's just trying to convince himself he's a drunk." I study his square face. "No question there's fine horse flesh in you, but I'm sorry, it's not a match for the sea kind."

SEVENTY

There are hugs as the Butters send another son to war. Sunday settles on his lap while Jake takes in the breaking light along the shore. I catch the gray on his face and the rocking, like when Iggy had cramps. "Jake, I'm not being unkind when I say this: close your eyes and scratch Sunday's ears with both of your hands."

"I'm gonna be sick." I slide over on the shoulder. He hurls out the window, then plunges into his pocket for pills.

I take the water. "Try this first. Just try. Look at my face." He fumbles with the bottle. "Jake, touch my hair with your left hand." Sweat bubbles on his forehead. "Touch my hair." His hand trembles over the curls. "Now, close your eyes and feel my hair with your right hand."

"I don't fucking have a right hand!"

"Yes, you do. It's in the ocean, changed to a different energy, reconnect with it, feel all the fosters you've guided holding it." He forces breaths in and out as he lifts his right arm. "There's

387

the silk of it under your fingers, all the dips and waves of a calm shore."

Breathing slows as he drifts for a long while with both hands. His eyes open, lost somewhere between wonder and disbelief. "How?"

"No idea. Len's discovery. He'd get Uncle Iggy stretching out his imaginary legs in sun-warmed sand or dipping toes into a tropical surf. Iggy said it turned all the pain into electricity. Bet a scientist could figure out why."

He holds onto Sunday and a thread of hope through the long miles. I pull up at an old low-rise where M&N arranged a flat, give him the keys, and hop out. "Ryan will meet you tomorrow at the centre."

His eyes escape to the ocean seen a short way off.

"What're you going to do when things get tough here?"

"Maybe I'll get a dog to pat with both hands."

*Hello, Jewel.*


Dr. McPherson finds reasons every day to drop by. Huey sees him courting and makes excuses to check in. "Ari, lass, I've found what I think might be a moon. Come see." Huey tips his hat to David. "Afternoon, doc. Everyone in health?"

"Just bringing Ari some liniment for her shoulder."

Huey steps lightly, so I'm not afraid to ask, "How's Jake?"

"Ryan says he's mining deeper and climbing higher every day. He's started classes. Imagine my boy at university."

Huey unloads. I return to the gallery, Sunday on one heel, David on the other. "Can I take you somewhere special for dinner tonight?"

"Sorry, doc. Promised the Missus a hand. Two new fosters arrived."

From his pocket, he unearths a diamond the size of a tuna. "Ari, I want you for my wife."

I squint at the boulder. "Are you daft, man? You've known me less than two months."

"I've been looking for you all my life."

"Then you need spectacles. I'm not your match."

He tries to convince me with a kiss that has the delicacy of a Clydesdale smooching a shrimp. "Give us a chance. I can make you happy."

"Stupid friggin' horse. Gotta get Sadie back here, Jasper. She's the best filly there is."

"I'm David."

"What makes you think I'm talking to you?"

I hightail it back into the shop and eyes turn, like a pink giraffe wearing a kimono just stumbled in. Which I'd prefer seeing that one of the men present has seen me buck naked. "Professor Eagleston?"

"Ari? Oh, ah, hello. You work here?"

"Live."

"Ah, sorry, Ingrid, this is Ari, a former student. Ari, this is Dr. Long. She teaches Russian lit."

"Ari Zajac? You're the one who painted that door hanging in the Bloomfield Centre. You know my son, Greg."

I back behind the counter.

Some random customer says, "You're Ari? We're looking for you." He spears the space between us with his hand. "Holt Andrews. This is my wife, Sarah. We saw your work at an associate's house in New York. A toothy fish thing. Sarah had to have a piece."

Auntie Mary says, "You're getting quite the reputation, Ari."

I bolt to my cedar-scented room.

Auntie Nia's steady hand wakes me. "Supper's up."

"David?"

"Steered him away. Told him there's a disturbing cluster of mental defects in your lineage."

"Thanks, appreciate it."

"And we appreciate you. The Cheshire catfish and the piranhas left with the Holts. Your professor bought a driftwood eagle and a cracked pot. Mary could barely shut the cash drawer when we closed."

Mary appears in the doorway. "Sam Lukeman just called. Seems Dick and Laura are going after 'what's theirs.' Surely the courts would never give the pair of them custody."

The earth feels off-centre as I sit. "Oh, no, Auntie. They'd never do anything as stupid as putting an impressionable child with them."

Mary depressurizes with a limp laugh.

"If he pushes, he's going directly to jail. My worry is Mike going back on his own. Laura's guilting him closer with every letter," I say.

Nia stands. "We need a walk before supper."

We traipse over to the Butters. Mike is slumped on the corner of the veranda with TV by his side. By human count Nia is fifty-five, but by her new-every-moment measure she's just born. "Mike, I'm thinking that Lake Ontario would be a whole lot better if it became saltwater like our ocean here. I have two sacks of salt in the shed to make licks for our deer but I'm thinking it'd be better used if I dumped it in the lake to make it salty."

"That's just stupid."

"Is, isn't it. Would make as much difference as you going back to Toronto to take care of your mom."

"But she's my mom."

"Exactly. You're not hers. If I believed you should go back, I'd tell you so. Even if it was the hardest thing on earth for me to do."

His knees swallow his face. "Ari went back and took care of her mom."

"Ari went back because she was forced by law. Not to take care of her mother."

He shakes his head. "She went back when she didn't have to."

"I went back for you, not my mum, bro." Shore birds a long way off fight for scraps. "Is your treasure in helping Huey catch dinner for this lot or is it in a basement on Shuter Street running to the store to get the Dick a bottle and your mom cigarettes?"

"It's here. But what if they make me? What if they come and steal me?"

"We'll stash you in Peru before ever letting that happen."

The sun is nothing but a scrape on the hill when we reach home. Mary rushes into the ringing phone. "Ari, it's for you. Aaron."

My belly does a backwards two and a half flip. "But it's Friday." My hand shakes. "Aaron? What's wrong?"

"Just happened by a phone. We're in Lima today." He stumbles around chapter-ending words. "Libby had an appointment. Um . . . we're . . ."

It's inevitable that thirtieth birthdays would have them throwing caution to time-sensitive items on the list. "Did you know a baby dolphin is called a pup?" I say. "Could there be anything better to add to this planet?"

Who'd have guessed how many tears hid inside over this? Nia pushes me to the great curved gnarl Huey delivered earlier. We hoist it onto the workhorses. "Do you know what's in this one?"

"Yes."

"Let it help. Let it heal."

The crescent moon emerges with little coaxing. The knotted dancers rooted on top will pose the challenge.

Midnight, Mary and Nia lead me to a feast ready by a steamy bath. They say they built the hot tub for their aging joints, but

I know it's for my shoulder. Naked, three earth women slip beneath the froth. Sacred music harmonizes with night songs. My heavy heart floats. Grief dissolving like the clay set deep in the lines of my hands.

Next morning, Mike rises, his feet on Pleasant Cove rock, head in possibilities. For years, my perception of Mikey was that he was a mirror image of Jake, but he's not. He's a self-preservationist as much as he is giving. He does more than his share of chores and helping with the little fosters. But he plays, laughs, learns, and retreats for the sheer joy of it. The know-how absorbed working on Moondance, he's translating into his dragonfly nest, a ten-by-ten stone footing, tight floors, snug insulated walls, sleeping loft. Huey salvaged a big window and already Mike's totems number two dozen. He spins a skeleton key hung by fishing line, similar to my totem for Sabina. This one has a filigreed clover on top. "This one is you, Ari. My lucky key."

"I'm honoured, bro."

He is the child of a brute and an addict. He's known chaos and corruption, bereavement and beatings. Yet, here he is. Here we are.

SEVENTY-ONE

The same minibus Franc long ago fitted for our Expo 67 trip rattles to a stop in front of Skyfish. The door opens and my Toronto females stream out: six-year-old Arielle, Jacquie, Sabina, Belle, nine-year-old Darcy, and eight-year-old Diamond, followed by their sun-glassed mom, Jennah, then a tattooed toothpick, Jory, with her adopted delinquents—fourteen-year-old Lila and twelve-year-old Kansas—and finally the driver, Mina. "Road trip before school starts."

Following is a VW van with Dolores, Elsie, Anne, and Celine.

It's the best of weeks.

Holiday end, five sisters walk the shore. Jory says, "You ever thought of opening a camp?"

"Yep, Camp Wabi-sabi for cracked pots."

Jennah says, "What a time these kids have had. Only wish June and Spring were here."

Anne says, "Me, too. I miss her."

Jacquie watches Arielle atop a tangle of driftwood, hands raised in an empress pose. "That girl is so much like you, Ari, it makes me dizzy. I ask her who she's talking to and she says Othello."

"Ah, yes, her otter. All these kids are so lucky. Having you for sisters was the most spectacular break of my life." I help myself to Jacquie's arm. "How'd you guys know I needed this?"

"ESP: extraordinary sister perception. Which now senses Jake and you are still unanchored?"

"He came home four days ago. Hasn't given me so much as a call since starting rehab."

"So call him. You can't get your footing if you don't know where you stand."

"I'm afraid to hear that the future I've fought so hard for isn't going to happen."

Jennah says, "What you've fought so hard for is finding your own self and that's dependant on no man—or woman."

As they pull away, I wander to the edge of Skyfish. On the shore below, I spot Jake studying the ocean's size, bare-footed, jeans rolled up, white T-shirt bright as only the Missus can get laundry. He's changed, like the Pinocchio puppet swept out to sea and the real man returned.

I walk the ridge, passing through the six newly planted sister birch trees marking the property line, then journey through the bare bones of rooms wanting to be fatted, skinned over, and clothed pretty.

Jake crests the ridge same instant as I step onto the porch. He releases an orange rock onto the growing pile, then tilts his head. "Seems I have a trespasser."

I sit on the steps. "I own this piece. You gave it to me."

"As I remember it, that rock over there is what belongs to you."

"Guess you should've checked how deep and wide it ran."

Jake laughing out loud knocks Jasper right off his tail. It's a sound neither of us have ever heard before. "Mind if I sit on your steps?"

"It's your wood. Seems we have us a situation."

"Seems so." My skin shiver-bumps as he eases down beside me. "Thought for sure you would've painted that door yellow."

"Yellow belongs on the sister-house. White reminds me of the moon."

"I know I've no right to ask but I, I heard the doc asked for your hand."

"Aye, he asked." I wiggle the naked fingers of my left hand. "I didn't give."

"You waiting for Aaron?"

"Someone been filling your head, Jake Tupper?"

"Sadie talks the hind leg off."

"She does at that. Good thing I've found her a Clydesdale to work her magic on." I nudge his arm. "You've read my letters. You know my heart is yours. Always has been. Always will be."

He talks to his knees with the conviction of a legless shoe salesman. "Ari, you shouldn't wait around for a wreck. You deserve the best man there is."

"Ari waits for no man. I can dance on my own if your journey carries you away." My head nests in the dip of his shoulder. "But last dance with you is the only end I want."

"Can I ask why it's not Aaron?"

"When I was with him, he'd wonder at my cracks and say, 'Oh, how beautiful.' It always left me longing for what I had with you."

"What?"

"Someone who really saw me and understood what the fractures meant. Everyone wants to be seen, to be loved for the real of them, not the myth. He's a lovely, lovely man but he can't ever know what you and I know."

"I don't know much."

"You know the riptide that drags you under and the grace that pushes you to the surface." The wind lifts my hair, whipping it 'round. "I'm grabbing hold here. No wave is ever going to push me where I don't belong. If I'm not with you, then I'll swim alone."

He wanders my face, then escapes to open water.

"Things okay in Halifax?" I ask.

"I'm feeling like my feet are strong under me but I have a long journey back."

"Know why you and I are seahorse kin?"

"Why?"

"William Walrus says fathers give kids their legs, teaching them to stand, and mothers give them arms, teaching them to hold. Kids with shit parents start off as seahorses. To become men and women, we have to fashion arms and legs pieced together from make-do dads and mums tossed into our paths." I lift my skirt. "I've got Len and Iggy, Huey and Ellis here. Spectacular, eh?"

"Can hardly believe how hard I fell with what I had under me."

"More than once I've looked down to find I had a knee on backwards or a shin attached to my hip. You had to break yours so you could get them on straight."

"I'm half-blind, remember. Can hardly see straight, let alone find my arms for holding." His hands, one present, one absent, turn, palms up.

"Jewel can. Seahorses have extraordinary vision, they can look backwards, forward, and, at the same time, see tiny details right in front of them."

"I am seeing some things, Ari. I look ahead and last dance with you is what I see. I just have to know I can stand on my own before I get to the holding."

"Do what you need to do."

"What if it takes a hundred years?"

"Then you better have a fondness for shrivelled old raisins." I nudge his stumped arm with my ruined shoulder. "I've loved you to the moon since I was eight, but now being a wreck makes me like you, really like you in a way I never could like that perfect veneer. I'm here, Jake. However, whenever you want me."

He stands, pocketing his hand and his stump. "This piece of land has always been for you. Whatever happens, it's yours."

He walks away and I yell, "You mule-headed bugger, this land is our land."

*This land is Jewel's land. From the Cabot Trail to the Great Atlantic, this land was made for—*

*Oh, please, shut up.*

## SEVENTY-TWO

I return to Antigonish for my second year. Immerse myself in estrogen. All my professors are goddesses, perfectly flawed and flawed perfectly. I make friends, girlfriends. We swim, meet at the pub, explore Antigonish—its shore, inlets, and trails. I discover kayaking a gentle river works my shoulder with minimal agony. I buy a second-hand bike, moving through town in a way that exercises Sunday and me. The nest becomes both my creating space and a gathering place. I prepare Polish feasts, finding nothing connects fellow transplants like a home-cooked meal and few things connect girls like making jewellery. And weekends, I go home to M&N, to clay, to a wonder-full boy, known in the Cove as Mike Butters.

Psychology remains a splintery subject. Today, the lights are off and the guy beside me snores as sections of the brain are explored. A slide clicks and my professor says, "This area here is the hippocampus, so named for its resemblance to a seahorse." Hairs on my arm stand erect, moving across my back and up my neck. "The hippocampus plays a crucial role in consolidating short-term memories to long-term and is critical in spatial memory, which enables us to navigate in the world."

*What? I'm not crazy?*

*No. Just hyper-tuned to me, your navigator.*

I sit long after the lights have come on and students depart. My professor breaks my reverie. "Ari?" I look up. "Your paper."

I stand and collect my essay, "Clay Children: The Role of Significant Adults in Child Development."

"Please tell me you're considering psychology for your major. Art therapy is an exciting field."

"That I know. I'll send you 'Cracked Pots: The Potter's Tao' when I get it finished." Her briefcase snaps closed and Jasper pushes me to open up. "Can I ask you something?"

"If you're game for a walk."

"All that stuff on brain mapping. Can some brains have over-developed parts? Like, maybe a hyperactive hippocampus?"

"Absolutely."

"Is it a disease, like a disorder?"

"What it is, is a fascinating area of study. Overdevelopment or underdevelopment impacts functioning. I'm enthralled by those brain maps that stretch beyond borders."

"Like how?"

"My grandfather can tell you what day of the week any day in history landed. He's a living almanac. I have a client who sees numbers, music, and words as colours. How intriguing is that?"

"My hippocampus talks to me."

"Lucky you."

"Not crazy?"

"Does it help you navigate?"

"It does. Like, really."

"Cool."

"Um, if a kid got a whack on the head, could it damage their prefrontal cortex?"

"A severe blow certainly could. You?"

"No. Apparently, my dad got walloped with a bottle when he was little. If the story's true, he was unconscious for three days."

"That's awful."

"Or maybe awesome. He was smart and funny, gifted in many ways and he was completely, unredemptively depraved. A wacko zealot who had no impulse control."

"That's difficult."

"He's dead and I'm dealing, but I like the idea of the cause being a head-to-head with a bottle of Crown Royal instead of DNA."

"It's a valid hypothesis. I'd love to talk more. Schedule yourself into my office hours next week; bring coffee."

"How about lunch?"

She nods. "Love your skirt, by the by."

I scan myself: Mary's red boots; turquoise skirt, a Polish work of art from Sabina; yellow sweater knit by Mike; and underneath are snazzy bra and panties from Jacquie's boutique. *Huh, Jasper, a tribe may have dressed us, and messed with us, but we put these on.*

*You are clothed and in your right mind.*

*Right brain's the creative side. Let's make something.*

All the walk to my apartment, I step on cracks, sensing every absence and seeing Ari Joy Zajac got dressed all by herself. It's spring. A window-opening day. An unfortunate day for the Dick to show up. That he found my nest doesn't surprise me. Old cops have buddies who look things up. That the blue sedan still runs is the true shock. He manages now with one cane, moving like a wind-up toy when he spots me crossing the street. He lifts a fat envelope. "Just had to tell you myself, it's settled. Mikey's ours. I'm on my way to bring him back."

"Yeah. Tino keeps me informed. So, tell me, Dickie, how much do disability cheques increase with a kid?"

"That's not why. Laura misses him something fierce and he's my kid."

I've no doubt he longs for family and a life that doesn't feel so broken. "Sorry, but living with you is no place for Mike."

"Miss High and Mighty always thinking you're better."

"There's no high and mighty about it, Dickster. I've readjusted my thinking. Even if you start with the best maritime clay, if you mix in too much shit, you end up with a load of crap and there's not much you can create with it except maybe fertilizer. Give it up, or you'll regret where this lands you."

"What you gonna do, punch me out?"

"Tom Healy and Milt Fraser." Colour leaks out of the Dick's

face, except for his nose that stays spidery red. "We've sworn statements from them that you set up the robbery at the Zajac's store."

"Statue of limitations, girlie."

"*Statute*, dickhead. Not for murder. You'll go down for Iggy."

"Never in a million years would you have the balls to turn me in."

"You ever seen the gonads on a goddess? All the dominos are in place. You take one step near Mike and the goods go to the Crown attorney, metro police, RCMP, border crossings . . . Cops in Pleasant Cove are already on alert. They're real excited because they never get action much more than a dock fight."

"Don't do this to me. I—"

"What? You ever once show mercy to anyone? I hope you get as good as you gave."

He backs up. "You little bitch. You've never been anything but trouble."

"*You* forced *me* to live in your hell." A punch rises from my good arm, piss-loaded from the place deep inside where seahorses cheer, stopping when I see how small he is, how utterly insignificant.

My hand feels a live thing as I climb to my nest. *I need some clay, Jasper.*

*Let's get Sunday and go, go, go.*

SEVENTY-THREE

I wake, thinking something in Skyfish is calling me, a spirit wanting out of clay. I step into Wellies and don my holey sweater. Outside

400

the world is awash of silver. *Oh, it's moonlight on the ocean calling us.*

I'm pulled to the shore. The waves are singing, Creedence Clearwater Revival as it happens, and I dance, passing from my twentieth year to my twenty-first. Jasper belts out his version of "Bad Moon Rising": *There's a good moon rising. I see triumph on its way . . .* My arms won't lift to the sky, but they reach wide and my feet turn. *I see earthmakes and lightening. I see good times today . . .*

My head rises. I half expect to spot M&N or Huey, maybe even Jake on the ridge, but it's just me, me and Jasper. What I do see is the new path emerging from the rock slide, a path made by me over the past five years, gathering rocks for my hearth. *There're enough to build Turtle Cottage for Mina and Ellis.*

The cedar tree has found a roothold and grows like a broken finger from the rock face. *Dance 'round tonight. It's bound to bring you life. There's a good moon on the rise.* I collapse in a dizzy heap on the wet sand. On the very same shore where I was left as a babe, I know I'm both as solid and broken as these rocks. And from them, I'll piece together the hearth for my home.

Just past sunrise, Mike comes barrelling along the shore and into my arms. "Happy birthday." He hands me an envelope. "Don't open it until Huey catches up." A new sad little bit of a girl named Glory slows Huey down.

I scoop her up. I know from the Missus that her stepdaddy hurt her and I whisper the words that M&N heaped on me. "You're a good girl and nothing that happened was ever your fault." She points to the dogs and I set her down. "Smart girl. Go give Sunday a hug." She shuffles along like Granny Clease. "She talking yet, Huey?"

"Not a word. Go on, open the card."

"Who's it from?"

"Jake sent it with his last letter. Said to give it on your twenty-first."

On the card is an ink drawing of two seahorses face to face, tails twined into a heart. Inside: *Ari, The only place I know to begin is: I am sorry. Jake.*

"Will you help me work on Moondance this summer, Huey?"

"As long as you promise it won't sit empty."

"I've a sense little Glorys will be coming my way."

"This old world will never stop making them, eh."

## SEVENTY-FOUR

Summer's end, Jake comes home to see the Missus who has a gallstone situation. The distance he guards stresses up my hair. Mary tells me he's softened in the hard places and strengthened in the broken ones. "He asked if anyone was courting you. Huey told him that big fish circled like you were a teaming bait ball, but that you wouldn't be caught."

"What'd he say?"

"Just laid his head on the table like he was searching for a prayer. He's doing so good at school, just about got his second year under him."

Middle of the night, Mike near scares the gallbladder out of me. He loud-whispers through the screen, "Pssst, Ari, come quick. Magic's up."

The wind-whipped, dew-drenching run across Skyfish and Moondance is like when I was a hope-filled girl. Music, caught in the trees, rains down. Mike hushes me with his finger, then points to the window. Blue lamplight warms Huey's back. Sweet notes escaping through wavy glass land live on my skin. Jake stands, lining Huey in a way that makes them one body; in unison their faces lift to the music, then bow under its grace. The fiddle nestles into Jake's neck, fingers of his left hand touching each string. Right arm rests on his father's and Huey's hand is given, perfectly given, to the bow's dance over the fiddle's body.

The music that once passed through Jake has settled in his bones echoing through the lonely hollows, and I know at last he's hearing, "You're a good boy and nothing that happened, nothing that anyone did was ever your fault. Be free." I catch sight of Glory perched on the couch, moon washing her upturned face.

Mike whispers, and I smile at the east settling in his voice, "I'll see you home. Everyone'll sleep a good long while now."


Huey goes to his shed to fetch more nails. My heart bangs as Jake parts the long summer grass. He looks inside the open window. "That board's not level."

"What's a one-eyed man know about level?"

"I've got perfect vision in the other and I know level when I see it." He long-arms through the window, setting the level on the ridge. The little bubble veers to the right less than a hair. "Ha, see."

I nose up to him. "So, it's a dust mote off. What? You think my man's going to stand in here gasping, 'Bleedin' Jesus, that board's not level. How can I possibly piss straight?' Stupid friggin' boy."

"What man?"

"Who?"

"What man's pissing in here?"

I snag his collar with my hammer, delivering the words with an almost kiss. "You, Jake Butters. And if you don't hurry yourself up, I'll be going blind if I have to keep doing it to myself.

Then where will that leave us? You half-blind and me completely in the dark."

He stops a quarter-inch from my lips. "I still have bogs to wade through. If ever I was to hurt you again, I, I can't 'til I'm certain I'm on bedrock."

"Stupid man, not being with you hurts more than ocean salt on an open cut." I take just one taste from where the fiddle touched his neck last night.

He shakes off the spell and climbs through the window. "Gotta fix this."

Huey and Mike dance as Jake spends the rest of the day working on the house. The tie on my tool belt is knotted and hard to see over my boobs. "Little help here? I have to go to the gallery." Jake releases the knot with one hand and a finger lingers on my belly. "Quite the fiddle fingers you have there, b'y." I drop the belt. "Now, you better follow my plans for the studio porch. Make sure the gazebo circles the southeast corner."

"What? Let me see those plans. It looks like a bleedin' band-shell."


Moondance rises like only a potter and fiddler can spin wood and stone. Both our hearts have moved in, I can tell by the treasures filling the space: a table Huey made, Nia's heirloom rocker, Jake's first fiddle in the corner . . .

Jake turns his cap backwards, studying the outline of the upstairs hall window. "What're you on about woman? Windows have to be square."

"Mine will be rounded on top, like the moon. What would you like on top?"

He pushes away the remembrance of me, of us. "I'll swallow this foolishness, but no pine floors. Too soft."

"I'll go with oak plank if you agree to my totem pole in the curve of the steps."

"No way. That belongs at the entry. It wants a window looking out."

"Hey, you're right, it does."


It takes four men to install Moondance on my rock, two seahorses twined in a dance atop a crescent moon. Jake mops up his sweat as he looks up. "Christ, you make magic, woman."

*She makes love, too.*

Jake blushes, like he heard loud as church bells what Jasper just whispered.

Of all the places that have kept us, slept us, we are clearly the other's home. We spend shore weekends like when we were kids, where dying things are thrown back to the ocean and the washed-in treasures collected. Yet for every dance that moves us closer, Jake two-steps back.

Every Sunday he drives me down to Antigonish. I ask him up. He says, "Can't. Have an early class." He accepts my offer of the truck to take him back to Halifax, then Friday he returns, redwood bigger, stronger, rooted but branch-broken, still unable to take hold of me.

I wait on the sidewalk for our trek home. An eye-popping blonde has his head hanging out of the passenger window as the truck pulls alongside the curb. "Whoa, who's this?"

Jake reaches to move him over by the collar. "Second Chance." The Zodiac clone springs out the window after Sunday. "Looks like he thinks Sunday's one sweet bitch."

"Least one of us might get lucky." I whistle Sunday back and assess the long plastic-wrapped tube in the bed of the truck. "What's that?"

"A present for all the birthdays missed."

"Is it a whale penis?"

"Why the bejesus would I be gifting you with a whale wang?"

"Because I miss yours?" He squirms and I ease off as we journey home. "How was your week?"

"You should see the results coming in on the mirroring study we set up at the centre."

"I'd love to see it."

"Really?"

"Yeah, and I'm due for a session with Ryan."

He bypasses Skyfish, takes the driveway to Moondance, hoists the tube out of the truck, into our house, setting it in front of the hearth. "Turn on the lights." With a push of his boot, a hooked turquoise rug unfurls. It takes a moment for the rusty lines to form.

"Seahorses?"

"Couldn't believe when I saw it in a shop near the harbour."

"Can I kiss you? Please say I can." I read the wetting of his lips as a yes. It's soft and sweet, seductive and simply spectacular. "Thank you."

I'm helping myself to second kisses when—give me a friggin' break— Mike opens the door. "Sorry, I, um, have a situation. I promised not to tell, but think I should."

I ready for Dickaster. "What's wrong?"

"Alex."

"Koshkin? Please don't tell me—"

"He's in my nest."

"Here?"

"Yeah."

"Do his parents—?"

"They think he's on a class trip." Mike shrugs. "He just showed."

Jake cares little about the hows and whats; he just heads straight for a twelve-year-old that navigated his lone self more than a thousand miles. He sits on the bed, gathering Alex in a way that is exactly like Huey. "There's a good, lad." Alex collapses against Jake, trying to catch his breath between sobs. "Okay. There's nothin' so wrong that can't be made better."

It's a heavy tale: failing grades, bullies, a belief that his dad wishes he'd died instead of Natasha.

Mary calls before the Koshkins can be tortured over news that Alex isn't where he's supposed to be. The sorting is left to M&N and we take Alex to the shore. An ocean, dogs, a friend are good medicine. Jake watches them jumping rock to rock while my eyes drift to him. "What're you smiling at, Ari Joy Zajac?"

"You. You're so much like Huey."

"Right. I am."

He stretches his arms above his head, sun filling the space where his hand once was. He asks, "When you marry, will you be keeping your name?"

*Kick him. He said you, not we.*

"I won't ever let AJZ go, it's too hard won. What if I said I hope to add yours but want none of your father's?"

"I'd say Ari Joy Jacob Zajac would be as big a mouthful as J.J. Jingleheimer Schmidt."

"Good thing you're registered for summer semester. You need to learn some seahorse sense."

## SEVENTY-FIVE

The school year behind, clay days ahead, Jake and I bookend

the couch, spending drowsy hours before he heads back to Dal. The prototype on his right arm captures my interest more than *Watership Down*. With it, he can pinch hold of his book. "What if I told you that wonder you designed has the look of a seahorse about it."

He smiles easy. "I'd say if you don't stop interrupting my studying, I'll never get phase two completed."

The phone rings and I expect it's the Wests. "Well, at least someone on this planet wants to talk to me." I answer, "East here."

Our phone chats are kept as economical as possible. Libby asks for details on Alex.

"Some better. He unwound once Mary got him spinning at the wheel."

"He still there?"

"His dad came. They stayed a few days, then went back to check out a school associated with U of Guelph. It's small. Lots of outdoor and creative play."

I imagine Aaron's head cocked close to Libby's when he says, "Can't believe he got himself to the Cove."

"He said Mike and here were his only connections to a time when he felt okay."

"He in big trouble with his folks?"

"Mr. Koshkin was as loving as a Labrador. That he's like that after enduring the most terrible thing any human can feels the biggest treasure of any." I absorb their wonder-full chatter, then reluctantly say, "I should let you go. Send pictures of my goddaughter."

Jake stops reading his text and nabs the phone. "Aaron? This is Jake. I'm looking forward to getting to know you and Libby, and thanks for being there for Ari when I couldn't. Yeah, you're right about that."

He returns to studying and I say goodbye. I poke Jake's bum with my toe. "Right about what?"

"Nothin'. What is it they called the babe?"

"April. If she'd been a boy, he would've been saddled with Eagle, Aaron Peter Eagle West."

"Eagle? APEW?"

"Yeah, thank the god of our mothers it was a girl. Stop changing course. Right about what?"

"He said you were"—he half peeks over the book—"the kind of buggered-up wind that lands everything right where it belongs."

"Aaron said buggered?"

"Paraphrase."

"Do you forgive me and Aaron?"

"There's nothing to forgive."

"Then why this desert between us?" He re-enters the book. "You're driving me friggin' crazy, you know. I'm warning you, it won't be pretty when I start taking off my knickers in the forest, asking the trees if they have a naughty-knotty woody for me." He chews on his lip like the woods scare him. "Why, Jake? Did that cable snap off your pecker and you're just scared to tell me?"

He nervous laughs. "It's . . . I . . . Ari, I—"

Mary comes flying in, like a stressed doe. "Mike's mom's here."

"Laura? Here? Why?"

"Says she's taking Mike home."

*Oh, Ari. The last penny.*

*No. No. No.*

Laura is in the brown pant suit, showing years of hard wear. Her hair is slicked into a yellow-gray ponytail. She drove the blue sedan as far as Edmundston, where it broke down. Scrapped it for fifty bucks and bussed her way here. "It's time I'm bringing Mikey home where he belongs."

Mike is unreadable. Ecstasy? Misery? Resigned?

The hour passes when Jake should be heading back. He remains at my side as Mike shows Laura his world. "If your mum

409

came back after you'd been two years with the Butters, would you've left?"

Jake says, "Likely, yeah." From the ridge, we watch them walk, Laura leaning to Mike's ear to be heard over the ocean's fuss.


Laura sleeps in my room. Jake and I wait out the night paralyzed on the sofa. Dawn arrives, bright as a silver dollar. Mike comes in, heavy-eyed. "Ari, don't hate me, but I have to see her safe home."

"We'll get her a ticket. She can see her own way back."

"She's my mom and she needs me."

"Then she can stay here. You have to know the Dick sent her. He can't stand losing."

"Pop's in hospital. His leg went green and they had to cut it off. I need to see her back."

"No. You. Don't."

Jake says, "Least wait 'til school's out, Mike. It's just a month."

"Pops is being discharged."

"I'll hire a nurse, like Jennah did."

"Maybe. But she needs a ramp. I could make that."

"Why are you even thinking about leaving?"

"Kira told me to."

Jake says, "Kira?"

"His bloody dragonfly." Mike heads to his nest and I see Huey in the kitchen doorway. "Talk sense to him, Huey."

"I've never had a boat or a foster who didn't do better cleaning out some of the mess."

"Cleaning out? He'll be up to his neck in shit. What's all this hell been for?"

"Just because you helped him on his journey doesn't give you rights to navigate his course."

"You're his guardian. You've got rights."

"We've known since last spring that they got the papers. You just had his father too scared to act."

"Well, his nightmare is coming true. I'm making that call to Tino."

"It's an option. Maybe best one. You just make certain sure you're doing it for Mike and not yourself."

I go in search of Nia, confident she'll have sense to throw at Mike. She asks, "The Dick's in hospital, for sure?"

"Yeah. Tino checked it out."

"Would Ellis meet them?"

"You can't be serious, Nia." She shrugs uncertainly. "Oh, fuck this."

Smashing every pot in the studio feels necessary. I leave before I do. As I cross the yard, Laura touches me. "He's my boy."

I snap my arm away like her hand is acid. "Fuck off, you selfish fucking bitch!"


My truck is loaded for Jake's trek back to school. Mike asks for a lift to the train and takes Jake's silence as a yes. Chance, refusing complicity, hops out, stretching nose to tail in front of the vehicle.

*Get in, get in, get in.*

*I'm not having any part in this.*

*Get. In! On the drive we'll think of something to convince Mike to stay.*

No one says anything when I jam myself between Laura and the door. As we drive, she pecks at the silence. "You get to start summer holidays before all the other kids, ain't that a fun thing, Mikey?"

Mike says, "I love school."

Jake says, "Shame you'll miss the class trip to P.E.I."

"We'll take a trip there one day. I'd like to see where they wrote those Little House stories."

Mike sighs. "That's the Midwest. Green Gables is P.E.I."

Jake says, "I was looking forward to the awards night. Mrs. Brown says you could teach the science class better than her, Mike."

"Don't know where you got your smarts from, Mikey. Not from me, that's for sure." Laura's bony hip pushes against my thigh and I want to snap it in two. "Can't believe that house you built. It's really somethin'. Did I tell you that I got a real good job at Albert's Pro Hardware? Bert would give you weekend work in a snap, seeing you know so much about building. Wouldn't that be fun? You and me sortin' nails and stockin' shelves. You know, I haven't missed a single shift since starting in November, I swear. Not been late or left early, even with all the trouble with your dad." Laura can't let the silence sit. "And you know who else got a job? Your sister, that's who."

"Ronnie?"

"You got any other sisters?"

"Yes. Ari."

"Oh. O'course. Ronnie's at Molson's feeding bottles into the washer."

Jake bypasses the station in North Sydney. Mikey protests. Jake says, "Going right by Truro. That'll save you having to change trains."

Soul-murdering hours pass before we turn into the station drop-off. Laura's whisper fills the cab like toxic smoke. "If you had a son, wouldn't you fight for him?"

With that, Jake makes a manic U-turn, leaving a red Plymouth leaning on its horn. Mike squeaks, "Jake, I have to."

"Then I'll see you safe to where you need to be."

"What?"

"The miles are needed to sort this out."

When we stop for gas, Laura beetles to the washroom. Mike pukes over the fence. Jake, who has never been out of the Maritimes, never set a toenail past Moncton looks bordered between lost and found. I say, "I can take them. I'll drop you at school."

"No. Doing this together is what's right." I settle into the miles feeling the solidness of Jake's new legs.

Between Quebec City and Montreal, we take a motel, pairing into double beds, fully clothed. Jake snugs behind me in a comfort spoon. Laura is stretched, hands on chest, like a corpse at a viewing. *She's not jittering, Ari. She really is clean.*

*Shut up.*

Mike turns, his back to her, face to me, ocean-eyed. I lift the flowered spread. He scuttles over and under the musty sheets, snugging in, like all the nights we spent jammed in his tent.

Back on the highway, Laura tries to span the distance she likely felt when Mike moved away last night. He answers her questions in single syllables: "Yes." "No." "Some."

"Shame we couldn't bring your pup, but no dogs allowed. Maybe we could get a gerbil, or a rat. I hear they're real smart. Would you like that?"

"No."

Jake asks Laura straight out, "Why'd you go back with Mike's dad?"

"I was lonely." Laura touches Mike's knee. "And 'cause the best thing in my life came from him and me."

Mike exhales like a surfacing whale. "He's only ever been mean to you."

"He needs us."

"You're not a seagull going after garbage, or an oxpecker cleaning parasites off a hog. And you shouldn't let Pop's treat you like Cunt, living in a cage full of shit."

413

"Michael John Irwin, watch your tongue and what're you on about?"

"Your chickadee."

"My what?"

"Your chickadee spirit. You can have my nest, Mom."

"We're family. Family sticks together."

Jake snorts. "Now there's a load of pig shit. Family's pieced from the people who make us most whole, not the fuckers who break us."

*Well said, Jewel.*

At the rest stop west of Kingston, I take the keys. "I know the roads. They can be cluttery."

Two hours into silence and twenty miles from Toronto, Laura says, "Why a chickadee?"

Mike's shrug ripples through the shoulder-to-shoulder crush. "They're sweet. A group is called a banditry. Figure that's why you got mixed up with Pops. They don't run from winter. They're so brave they'll land on a hand for seeds. People say they're not as smart as some birds, but they adapt to change without much fuss."

"Where'd you learn all that?"

"Jake, Huey, books. Just watching them in the spirit trees."

"You're smart as they come, Mikey."

"Where to?" I ask.

"We'll go straight to the General. Dick'll be so surprised."


Jake stays by the door in the hall. I would, too, but Mike reaches for my hand like he did in all the uncertain walks to crapdom. There are six beds, all occupied by wasting old men. I'd say the Dick resembles an anorexic potato slug but that would be an insult to spineless creatures everywhere. "Well, well, well, there's my man." His rheumy eyes narrow at me. "Get that cunt outta here. All this trouble is your doing."

"You can count on big trouble from me, Dick." He pales whiter than the pillow at my iced stare. I return to Jake who is watching the reunion reflected in the mirror over the sink, ear bent to every word.

The Dick asks, "You playin' hockey?"

"No."

"We'll get you back in it. Won't we, Laura."

"He's been busy, I'll tell you that much. Top of his class. A scout with more badges than will fit on his sash. He even built a house." Laura repeats Jake's praises pretty much word for word.

"How old you now?"

"Turning thirteen."

"It'll be good to have another man around the house. You and me, eh, Mikey?"

I growl, "He's going straight to jail."

Jake hushes me with a finger and I hear Mike say, "No. Not you and me. I came back to help my mom."

"Now you show respect. You hear."

"Not to you. I won't dishonour Todd by respecting you."

"I ain't got nothing to do with that trouble with your brother."

"You never had much to do with any of us. And you never stopped O'Toole."

"I didn't know nothin' about what he was up to."

"Not true. I saw you be a detective." The Dick's pain mirrored in the reflection might be the saddest thing I've ever seen. "You could've been a really good one."

"B-b-bad luck is all."

"No, shit choices is all."

"You—"

"Know what? I hate hockey. And I knit better than Jacques Plante."

Laura bites back a smile. "Maybe you could make your dad a nice warm sock."

415

"Over my dead body."

Laura looks rosier, younger, as she rises from her chair, like a broken-winged bird discovering it still has feet and a beak. "You know, Mike, having a man around the house is more work than help, and I think you're owed a few more years of being a boy." Her head bobs like she's agreeing with the air.

"Laura, for fuck sake—"

"Shut up. Let me think."

"Think? You ain't got no brains for that."

"You said I didn't have the brains to keep a job. Find my way half across Canada. Bring Mikey back. I got brains for all that, and I got brains for making up my own mind." She walks out, marches really, straight to the nurses' station. We follow, us in body, the Dick in bellow. Laura speaks to the nurse at the desk, "You're right. I can't be managing him at home. Make the arrangements for Providence Villa."

"Mom?"

"I've things to sort, Mikey, but for now you're going back to school."

"I'll help you."

"Good. You and Jake can help by taking the piss-soaked couch to the dump."

"But—"

"I'll save up and maybe by Christmas I can bring you here for your holiday." Her small hand cups his man-child cheek. "I'm your mother. Don't argue with me."

I feel Jake's hand on my waist and lean into the ache of a boy whose mother never came back to claim him or tell him she wanted him to have his best life. "What made you drive here, Jake?"

"Maybe redemption for the all times I should've come for you and didn't. My whole life I've been this terrified kid stuck in 'what if.'"

"And now?"

416

"What if I said I'd take a rocket anywhere you needed me to?"

*Say, your moon is his to land on. Say it. Say it.* "Then I'd say we're ready for re-entry."

"Let's start by surprising Ellis and Mina."

A nurse skuttles by with a hypodermic aimed directly at the howling coming from the Dick's room. "Know what? Providence Villa is a universe worse than jail for him. Least in jail he'd have poker and scum buddies; instead he'll have a swarm of nuns, twenty-four seven."

I exit the changeroom at Jacquie's new boutique in embroidered jeans and a black angora sweater. "These are awesome."

"Wait 'til you see the bill. Arielle for a week this summer."

"Ten days, minimum." My hair settles into a party of serpentines. "Where'd everyone go?"

"You'll see." We go out the front, along Yorkville, down the stairs and into the Riverboat. It's loaded, port to stern, with my Toronto tribe. Jake is wearing Ellis's Pink Floyd *Dark Side of the Moon* T-shirt, not shy about the gear that holds his bionic limb in place. An hour in, Bernie takes the mic. "So, I don't know how long ago now, ten, twelve years maybe, this kid wanders in looking for a sister. Jabberiest mop I ever met, telling me about boats and fiddlers, seahorses and turning pots. Then she started bringing in tie-dye and love beads to sell. And, like she owned the place, she started taking orders to the tables, swabbing counters, drying dishes." Bernie looks smack at me. "Never actually hired you, ya know, kid." He raises a palm for the laughter to calm. "So, this afternoon, in walks Ellis and wonder of wonders, Jake. The guy I'd thought Ari made up to keep the boys 'round here zipped. No, really, I saw Salt Wild four summers ago, prettiest sound I ever heard, and I've heard my share. So, ladies and gentlemen, without further talk, I give you Jake Tupper of Salt Wind."

*Oh, Bernie. Oh, frig. Oh, no.* I ready to correct the mistake, but Jake rises without protest and perches at a keyboard. It really is a home crowd, not much different than a down-home kitchen party, and Jake is not self-full but self-found. "Evening. One of the young lads I work with plays the bodhrán with his toes, so I've no excuse." He one-handed skitters up and down the keys, testing rifts and chords. "So, Sabina, Mike tells me Simon and Garfunkel are your favourite. At his request, this is for you, all of you really, his bridge, Ari's bridge over troubled water." Somehow, he plays, plays perfectly imperfect. It's a melody suited to Jake's clear, pitch-perfect voice. His eyes catch mine when he changes lyrics to "Sail on Ari girl, all our dreams are on their way." It's sweet, sappy, sentimental; there are sniffles all around and all I can think is I want sex, really, really, *really* want sex.

Evening end, Mike asks, "Can we sleep in the nest like old times?"

I sigh. "Sure. That'd be loads of fun."


Predawn, Jake snugs behind me, boxers and PJs separating us. "We should make a start, so I can sort what I missed at school."

I turn, weaving fingers through his sleep-happy hair. "Thank you for this. For all of it."

"You ever see a new boat, when they cut away the rigging and release it for the first time?"

"Yeah. My dad took me to a launch once. It fell sideways into the water. Thought it was going to tip right over, but it righted itself."

"That's how I feel." Silver light sneaks into the nest. "Why do I feel in water here?"

"This nest is always just what you need it to be."

Mike sits up from the air mattress. "We going home?"

"Let's hit the road."

I pause at the door before locking up. Jake asks, "There anything you want to take to our house?"

"It all belongs here for now." I grab pillows and Sabina's care package for the journey. "Let me take first leg. I've a stop to make."

Mike says, "I can drive. I can. Huey showed me."

Jake says, "Same here."

"He taught me too."

*I taught you to drive, and you know it.*

*Right, Jasper, you did. You do.*

The sun opens like a paper fan, filling all the city cracks with light. I still don't understand physics but I'm oriented to space and time: I am here, right now.

*Oh, here's our haiku:*

> *Three gold veined cracked pots*
> *Destiny Not Absolute.*
> *We are here, right now.*


Somewhere on the map of my life, BS is in an unremembered box. Mum is dust in a pickle jar. Daddy occupies a dishonoured plot. O'Toole molders in a cage and the Dick is reduced to not much more than a fetal pig. *You notice the ones with the biggest meanness leave the smallest mark?*

I turn into Holy Cross. Natasha's grave is a party of flowers. By the dog treats and seeds around Todd's grave, I suspect Mina's been here. Mike lifts his face to the greening trees. "Can you sing the open window song, like on all the nights in our room?"

Jake asks. "Open window?"

"He means 'The Parting Glass.'" I say and start singing, "Of all the comrades that e'er I've had . . ."

By the time Jake joins in, all the windows in the sky are open.

" . . . but since it falls unto my lot that I should rise and you should not, I'll gently rise and softly call, good night and joy be with you all."

Mike says, "Your singing together is sugar wind."

My voice is bell-clear like my mum's. And mellow like my dad's. Blended, it is unlike either of them. It is singularly my own.


The boys wake when I gas up in Kingston. Mike asks, "Is this where O'Toole is?"

"Yep, Kingston Pen." We drive on, Jake at the wheel, me raiding the cooler.

"You think he was ever good?"

"I'm told back in the day he was a premium catch." I pass Mike his favourite: peanut butter and honey. "I gotta believe that everyone starts as good clay."

"He's an eel that got himself stuck in hot water. You think he could be good now?"

Jake says, "Huey told me the only way to stop being a shit is to stand up, square my shoulders, and stop being a shit." We all sit up a little. "And listen to that voice inside that tells us what's what." Jake has never really entered the seahorse crazy with me and I feel a little like dancing when he says, "Kira was right to tell you to come, Mike."

"She was," I admit.

Mike leans forward, peers out the windshield. "Look. The hood ornament." A chrome bird sculpture was the thing that sold me on this truck, more than the mechanics. "Remember William Walrus saying that I'd travel back home on a wing?"

"Geez, that was, like, five, six years ago?"

"Thanks for coming with me." He talks with his mouth full of sweetness. "Did I make you miss a lot at school, Jake?"

"I'll stay down and work through this weekend. That'll get me all caught up."

## SEVENTY-SIX

I sit under the tree where Jake told me to meet him. Dalhousie's campus buzzes. *They've won conference finals two years running.*

*You want me to stuff a volleyball down your snout?*

*Hey, I hear Jewel.*

*So do*—I spot Jake, moving across the quad playing, single-handedly. A tidy contraption fastening the bow to his stump. I lift my skirts in a little step-dance as he finishes with a toe-lifting flourish. "Well, what'd you think?"

I appraise the invention. "Black velvet band's a nice touch."

He snugs his arm around my waist and introduces me to the man with him. "Ari, this is Professor Zimmerman."

"So, this is Ari. That uncle of yours has opened up the most exciting research of my career."

"Pardon?"

Jake says, "The mirroring."

"Jake's been doing some remarkable work at the centre with the kids."

"I know. I met a few after my physio."

Jake smiles, soft, confident. "What if I said music's good as gold for fillin' cracks?"

"Then I'd say a potter and fiddler could turn broken pots into something pretty spectacular."

"Better get a move. Sadie gave me a list of things to pick up before heading home."

I wait while Jake zips into the printers. He drops the package on my lap and I open the box to the aqua programs, "The Marriage of Sadie Ellen O'Shaughnessy and Dr. David Patrick Macpherson."

"Whoops, they made a mistake; it says Jake *Butters*."

"That'd be me. What if I said for Huey's birthday gift, I've claimed the name I believe belongs to me?"

"I'd say nothing would make him prouder."

"You gave me the idea."

*Ari Butters. I like. I like.*

When he stops to pick up his suit, I reclaim the wheel and we drive up the coast. "Jake, what were you about to tell me before Laura crashed in?"

"It's hard for me to say." His head turns away.

"Have your feelings for me changed?"

"O'course." The passing miles near absorb his words. "Love you more now than I thought it possible to love."

"For pity sake. Talk to me."

"Ellis is the one who called me after your mum died. He got me to call you."

"I know. And didn't that moment of lifting your head out of the deep feel good?"

"It did. I stopped drinking—thinking maybe I could come help."

"Why didn't you go back to rehab?"

"When I heard you'd been near killed, I thought my wanting you back had caused it. I convinced myself you were better off."

"I get that thinking. It's easier knowing we're not that powerful, isn't it?"

I slow, coming to a stop to let a moose cross, and Jake watches its essence long after it has disappeared. "We aren't and we are. I never told you how your letters kept me afloat. There was one that felt like the times we'd just ramble and talk. I actually went to the library to find out what Ma Griffe was. What kind of name is that for a perfume?"

"It means 'my claw' and it smells like too much, a complicated everything when all you're longing for is the simple scent of your match. I'm a lonely seahorse, Jake. I keep spinning and spinning and you just close your heart."

"It's not you. It's . . . I suppose about too much stink, but it's not you." He talks to the padded roof. "I've sifted through a mountain of shit, found treasures, and pitched a ton. The standing feels right, but the holding . . ." He sponges his face with his T-shirt. Exhales, inhales, then exhales again. "I don't know how to get the stench of those lost years off me." He folds away. "There were women. Mismatches I crawled into. Anything breathing that had nothing of you in them."

"I made stupid mistakes, too."

"Not like me. I-I got Dulcie pregnant."

"We have a baby somewhere?"

"For Christ's sake, Ari, you're supposed to hate me for that."

"Oh."

"She ended it. Couldn't stomach the thought of havin' my kid."

"Oh, Jake, I can't know her reasons, but I do know you're the best man for me."

"I don't know how to touch you. It doesn't feel right. You should be with someone like the doc."

"Because he has clean hands?" He half shrugs. "Jake, I'm a potter." I stretch my scarred clay-etched hand in front of him. "You know what's on these hands. All of it. Horrors and joys." My fingers find the small wave of hair at the nape of his neck. "Mary always said you had to break to get at the hurt your father created, but what your mother did was the most terrible wounding. I know what it's like to be the invisible child, to be less than the pesky spray of a sneeze. Least my father noticing me felt a little like love."

He leans into my hand. "It's sweet, eh, that Mike was witness to his mum wanting the best for him?"

"It was. And just you know, Jake Butters, there's a woman on

423

this earth that wants the best for you." An hour along, I turn off on a road he's likely never travelled but where M&N have taken me several times.

"Where're you going?"

"I promised to get Sadie something."

"What's in Maitland?"

"The Shubenacadie. There are shiny stones on the bottom she wants."

I stop near a river curve that creates a shallow bowl of mud.

"There're no stones here."

My T-shirt peels over my head as my skirt hits the ground.

"Ari, get back here."

Icy mud eats up my toes, then feet, before oozing over my ankles.

"Ari!"

The muck consumes my arms as I search for gems.

"Sadie will skin us if we're late for the rehearsal."

"I'm stuck."

"You are not."

I pull and panic. "Really, my foot's caught. Ow, oh, ow. Jake, help."

He hops out of his shoes and jeans and tosses his shirt. "Bleedin' Jesus, why you doing such a stupid thing as this?" As he sets to rescuing my foot, I take him down in one clean swoop. "What the hell?"

I land on him. "Jake Butters, I love this stuff. I don't give a frig how stinkin' dirty you are, you dumb fool boy." My arms windmill launching dollop after dollop. "You're clay, not dirt."

He sits, looking as bewildered as an ostrich discovering two big arms have sprouted out of the ooze. He throws a blob which splats on my neck and the war is on with more whoops and fun than anybody deserves. With his last scrap of wind, he takes me down, flopping onto his back to catch his breath. Soon, he lets go, resting deep into the liquid earth. The sky above shimmers silver. Two hawks eye us before sailing up on a thermal.

"In my dreams, I had the baby in my arms. I'd take him home and stop messing up because he needed me to take care of him."

"Wherever that little spark landed, it's dancing because you're finally taking care of you." I rise like a vanilla wafer out of a chocolate fondue and extend my hand. "It's time we were getting home."

Auntie Mary pokes her head through the side window when we arrive at Skyfish. She asks, "Should I fire up the kiln?"

"No, we're done."


Salt Wind is reunited for the wedding. "Silver and Gold" fills the air as little girls in pretty dresses line up. Last count there were twenty-one. That's Sadie's way, anyone who wants to be her flower girl, put flowers in your hair and come. Before they are released, Mike ushers the Missus to her well-earned place of honour. For a month, students at Pleasant Cove have been cutting tiny tissue petals and they rain on the guests as fairies dance up the grassy aisle. David's best man moves like a pigeon-toed penguin, but he's a good sport as he twirls and cavorts the pair of us toward the alter. Laughter hangs like stars as Sadie appears and takes hold of Huey's arm, the man who has fathered her since she was five. Theirs is a sweet and graceful waltz with a twirl landing her at David's side.

Glory moves away from the fluttery girls. Her small hand tugs my dress and she says her first word since arriving in the Cove. "Up."

I scoop her up and she nestles under my hair like a duckling under a wing. I hear a voice, but it's not Jasper. *You want to see the rooms in Ari? Everything you need to feel safe is here.* Glory nods, like she's hearing each word. The Missus catches my eye, touches her nose. *Well, Glory be, aren't you light and isn't every stone in her set right.* As I turn back, I spot him beside Nia—William Walrus. He smiles, and in the wink of his eye, I'm eight years old and hearing, "See, little miss, the whole world can get turned upside down and still land right." Auntie Nia shrugs innocence.

After the I dos, I find William in the throng and sigh. "So, there's no magic? Just bean-spilling aunties?"

"No magic? Well, I've never heard such a thing. Your aunties have loved you for your whole life and have been watching over you." His great strawberry palm opens on my face. "And when they couldn't be at your side, they sent out word to all the clans to watch out for you. That's big magic."

"How do you know them?"

"Nia's daddy and me worked the railroad. I came for visits all the time. Huey and me became best of mates."

"How'd you know I'd need ten pennies to see me home?"

"See a lot of travellers in my line. Most have two cents' worth of trouble, a few a nickel's. Occasionally, I come across a sad sack with two bits, even a dollar of disaster. With what I knew of your mum at one end and your aunts at the other, a dime seemed a good bet."

"It helped seeing the load get lighter over the years."

"Never got lighter. You just got stronger. And that, little miss, is the biggest magic. You, *you*, didn't throw your pennies away on wishes, you kept riding the rails, earning that muscle."

"I have sturdy arms and legs now. I'm ready for that dance you promised."

"There are many ahead for us. Old William sees it. And that last penny is for keeping, a reminder that no matter what comes your way the world can always turn light side up."


Jake's spot is empty for the last set. A lift of Huey's chin points me to Moondance. I follow Jake's song to the front porch, wind

426

stirring the gossamer layers of my dress like ocean froth, lifting it as I climb the steps. "What's that melody?"

"'The Calling Home of Jewel.'" His gray eyes soak right into my centre. "You look like blue moonlight on the ocean."

I fan the skirt. "Just like Sadie to pick such a spectacular dress for her maid of honour."

"Snot on the shoulder's a nice touch."

"Had a cuddle with a duckling." The porch support holds my back. Through the big window, I see a candle flickering in Len's pot on the mantle. Jake sits, kilt handsome, collar loosened, on a twig chair, one bare foot perched on the rail. "You look so right sitting there."

"It's the home we dreamed."

"And built."

"So, I'm a little scared to pose this 'what if.'"

"Try me."

"What if I said I need to keep discovering what I'm discovering and I'll likely have a few years of school ahead?"

"I'd say if you leave me here, you needn't be afraid that distance will change my feelings. If you want me with you, then I'd say I'm well practised at being home wherever I land."

"What if U of T was doing research on what I'm studying and my professor thinks I should apply after graduation?"

"I'd say Mina and Ellis would piss themselves. I'd say the nest is waiting." The air holds the fragrance of a forest after a heavy rain. "Plus, and it's a big plus, if you run out of subjects, I know a guy who murders limbs."

He closes his good eye and scans the acreage between us and the drop to the ocean, the crescent where the ridge collapsed six summers ago. "Wish you could see what I'm seeing."

Fireflies wink in the greening wood. Fingers of mist search the grass for notes falling from a dreamy waltz sent from Skyfish, and beyond, sprits surface, all of them, devils and the divine,

427

white and black robes trailing as they ride the waves before rolling under. "I see them."

"Who do you see?"

"All the ones that shaped us into the unthinkable ones."

Jake rises, moving to the rail like a king before his people. "Thank you, you crushers and healers, pounders and lovers, foes, carers, teachers, tormentors, holders, releasers, sinners, and saviours, you have given us our life." He swallows tears, the ones that taste sweet. "Now, the lady and I can take it from here." The half turn of his body and tilt of his head sets our own universe into orbit. "What if I told you when I was small, a seahorse pair jumped out of my pocket and one wandered off when they heard a baby crying alone on the beach?"

"I'd say Jewel is the most unselfish of seahorses to have let Jasper stay with me until I was safely grown."

"What if I told you Jasper's in my pocket right now?"

"I thought things got switched around in that mud bath yesterday."

"Mouthy bugger, isn't he. Set me straight on a lot of things."

"That's Jasper."

"He says Jewel and he have been separated long enough, and if I don't do something about it, he's going to poke me in my good eye."

"Then you'd better let Jewel out of my bra and Jasper out of your pocket and get our seahorses into some water right quick."

"You ever going to put that imagination to bed?"

"Never."

"Right answer." He moves close, touching my face with both hands. Ocean breeze ripples the night around us like seagrass moving beneath the waves. "Last dance, Ari?"

In slow circles we turn. "What if our house burns down to the dirt?"

"We'll lie under the stars and I'll warm you in my arms." He pulls me close.

"What if all our babies die like Huey and the Missus's?"

He kisses the tiny scar on my cheek. "I'll mourn them forever and love a hundred in their memory."

"What if pirates think you're their Captain Hook?"

Neck, kissed. "I'll tell them all the treasure worth having is already mine."

"What if a great white helps himself to your other hand?"

"I'll teach and I'll dance and"—shoulder kissed—"I suppose you'll always have to be on top."

"And what if I die?"

He lifts my chin. "Please Ari, don't ever ask me to 'what if' that."

"Okay." Like dancing with light and water, earth and air, I hold on. "I won't die until I'm one hundred and you're a hundred and three, then we'll sail off the world together in our boat, *The Seahorse Dance*."

"Ouch!"

"What?"

"The bugger just bit my ear. Says our boat is *Jasper's Jewel*." On the ribbon of moonlight he twirls us 'round, lifting me through the door, and we are home.

## ACKNOWLEDGEMENTS

This book is about resilience, and resilience begins with family—the one we are born into and the one we piece together. Thank you to my sister, Susanne, who for my entire life has encouraged me to believe in myself. And to my brother-in-law, John: you inspire me.

Thank you to my spectacular children: Sarah, Ben, Mike, Mary, and Elisabeth. You have given me more stories of compassion and overcoming than any writer deserves. And, to my grandchildren, Jyn, Gemma, Desi, and Teddy, great-niece and nephew, Danica and JJ; extraordinary kids who give me hope for our planet's future and the promise of a library full of adventures.

And much gratitude to the special children I've worked with, who, like Ari, survive and thrive in the face of many challenges. And to the teachers, coaches, grandparents, step-parents, aunts, uncles . . . all who help them on their journey. All of you are the heroes woven throughout these pages. Most notably you, Cheryl Hermer.

This book celebrates creativity for its power to turn energy, both positive and negative, into something beautiful. Thank you to all who support the creative process. To my wonderful agent at Westwood Creative Artists, Hilary McMahon. Every encouragement from you is a gift. To the amazing team at ECW Press, especially Michael Homes, whose kindness and insight makes editing a pleasure. Thank you, Crissy Calhoun, Shannon

Parr, Jessica Albert, Susannah Ames, Claire Pokorchak, Jen Albert, and Michel Vrana, for believing in this book.

Some remarkable foster parents are found in *Cracked Pots*, and their wisdom and caring are a mirror to Ruth Walker. Thank you for fostering my writing, and that of so many others.

I am grateful to the Ontario Arts Council for supporting me and my imaginary friends. And to the Writer's Community of Durham Region and my talented WIP group: Sylvia Chiang, Sandra Clarke, Karen Cole, Patrick Meade, and Anne MacLachlin. You make me a better writer. *Cracked Pots* belongs to all of us.

Most of all this book is about community. If this pandemic has taught me anything, it's that we need one another and together we are stronger.

Without a doubt, the best part of this writing journey has been connecting with readers. Thank you to every reader I've met along the way, with special thanks to my beta readers, Cindy Guest Taylor and Jan Hawkins Patterson. The only things exceeding your love of reading are your generosity and crack editorial skills.

To Elyse Walters, reader and reviewer extraordinaire: you give countless writers the best gift they could ever receive— encouraging words. Thank you.

And to Linda Sherman-Nurick and every independent bookstore who give cracked pots, of all kinds, a home. You are the heart of our community.

During the writing of *Cracked Pots*, my real life became stranger than fiction, rendering me a spectacularly cracked pot. Thank you to my precious friends, Linda Lowery and Mary Sue O'Connor, for being the "Jasper" in my head and the gold filling my cracks. And to my "nurse mates": Janet Vendrig, Lori Martin, Lori Pinkerton, Lynne Hamilton-Rushak, and Pam Frisby—pandemic heroes. Without your support I would have lost the plot.

And finally, to you, Kathleen Boyle Hatcher. You were—and are—a treasure in this dark world. Your astonishing light will remain in every story I write.

PHOTO BY JOHN RAYNER

Throughout an eclectic career in community health, Heather Tucker gathered stories, now used as threads for spinning award-winning yarns. Her highly acclaimed debut novel, *The Clay Girl*, was a finalist for the Kobo Emerging Writer Prize and the Atlantic Book Award. Heather lives in Ajax, Ontario.

This book is also available as a Global Certified Accessible™ (GCA) ebook. ECW Press's ebooks are screen reader friendly and are built to meet the needs of those who are unable to read standard print due to blindness, low vision, dyslexia, or a physical disability.

Purchase the print edition and receive the eBook free!
Just send an email to ebook@ecwpress.com and include:

Get the
eBook free!*
*proof of purchase
required

- the book title
- the name of the store where you purchased it
- your receipt number
- your preference of file type: PDF or ePub

A real person will respond to your email with your eBook attached.
And thanks for supporting an independently owned Canadian
publisher with your purchase!